James
M. Bishley III

HEART OF THE ORDER

TONY ARDIZZONE

HEART
OF THE ORDER

HENRY HOLT AND COMPANY
NEW YORK

A portion of this novel previously appeared in *TriQuarterly*.

The author wishes to express gratitude for support received
from the National Endowment for the Arts.

Published by Henry Holt and Company, Inc.,
521 Fifth Avenue, New York, New York 10175.
Published simultaneously in Canada.

Library of Congress Cataloging in Publication Data
Ardizzone, Tony.
Heart of the order.
I. Title.
PS3551.R395H4   1986   813'.54   85–30513
ISBN: 0-03-008503-9

First Edition

Designer: Kate Nichols
Printed in the United States of America
10 9 8 7 6 5 4 3 2 1

ISBN 0-03-008503-9

FOR NICK

BATTING PRACTICE

In my day I was quite a ballplayer.

You should know that, Tip. The whole story, bottom to top. You should stand in the box and stare at every pitch I tried to drive. Feel the muscles in my arms and back each time I brought the stick around. See all the fences I swung for.

So take my hand, and I'll do my best to explain. Because one of the main things the game taught me is that you don't get much farther than the batter's box if all you examine is the surface. You have to see more than just the easy windup. The half-second hesitation at the chest. The leg kick, hitch, the arm whirling. You're no more in the game than a worm weaving its merrily stupid worm ass through the outfield if surfaces are all you understand. The box score by itself isn't worth a bench jockey's sixth-inning spit. You need to be there, in it, out on the field. So jump inside me, son. Play in my shadow. Make believe everything's just been created and is new, that the only world is the green one inside this ball park.

Right off the bat I'll tell you how this game turns out, so you can rock back on your heels and enjoy it. *We won.* In the only column that matters when all seasons have been played, your daddy won. I wouldn't take you to a heartbreak your first time out. Though don't get the wrong idea: you're not about to witness a laugher. No big lead in the early frames and then coast. No, this one is hard and tight all the way, ending with a nervous rookie third baseman coming in off the bench to make the game-saving play at the mound. The big left-handed clean-up hitter waving his lumber at the plate. The most peculiar instance of fan interference in the game's history. So get set for some smiles, some tears, some fingernail biting.

It's early now. Pregame. Time for us to go over the day's opponent. Time to stretch out, loosen up. Do our cals by the third-base foul line, play a little catch with the shortstop, rainbow the ball back and forth. Step out on the field and scoop grounders, fire the ball across the diamond to first, take our share of practice cuts in the cage. Give the fans a chance to find their seats, look at the sky, mustard their hot dogs.

Let's officially pencil yours truly into the lineup.

My name: Dan Bacigalupo. My position: the hot corner of third base. In my sweat socks and green stockings I'm an even six feet. Some who saw me play are surprised now when they meet me, remembering me as smaller, a little man in a big man's game. I smile and say it's because their mind's eye has me crouched over, on the balls of my feet, my fist pounding my glove's pocket. Oh yeah, they say, you were always bent over. Liked to mumble to yourself a lot too. Oh yeah, I say.

I played professional baseball for a total of fourteen years, twelve of which I can fully remember. I was on three championship teams, won a batting title, once was league MVP. In all I played for five different organizations, but at heart I still am and always will be a Denver Dyno, the club that signed me out of high school six days before my eighteenth birthday, taking me to their Class-A team in Pirate's Hook, Mississippi, from the North Side of Chicago, where I grew up in brashness and agony, oldest of five brothers (me, Gino, Dominic, Louie, Francis Junior) and two sisters (Rosaria, Tina). I'm thinner now than the day I signed. My face is more lined; my hair, a bit farther back on my forehead and now showing signs of gray. My voice is much softer than it used to be. My eyes, brown as an old Louisville slugger stained with pine tar, flash less but see more, I hope. Go through this game with me, son, and when the stands are empty again you decide.

I should say that our last name is one you learn to be patient with. It's a name nearly everyone misspells, that is nearly always mispronounced. Others' tongues aren't perfect; they need to be trained. Talk to enough sportswriters and you'll get the etymology down to a patter.

Bacigalupo (*baa-chi-ga-LOO-poh*). Italian. Literally, *kiss of the wolf*, from *bacio* (kiss) and *lupo* (wolf). Cousin to *bocca* (mouth, muzzle, opening, hole) and nearly brother to the expression *in bocca al lupo!* (in the mouth of the wolf!), which is a backhanded way of wishing someone good fortune. Thus, *wolf kiss* or *wolf kisser* (noun) or *wolf-kissed* (adjective), depending on how you feel that day.

Friends will shorten it to *'Galupo* (of the wolf), which always made me feel feisty, like a galloping colt on a Mediterranean hillside. Others will grin and make terrible puns. "Hey, Bocce," as in the Italian bowling game of the same name, "drag your balls over here!"

"*Baa, baa*," you'll bleat, "*baa*-chi-ga-loo-poh."

I'm extremely, perhaps overly, fond of my nose: thin, straight, never once broken. Not too many infielders can make that claim. I have a strong, even noble, nose. A nose a great bird, like an eagle or a hawk, wouldn't mind having. A nose, I imagine, that enabled centuries of our dirt-poor wolf-kissing ancestors to have something to hold up with dignity to the Sicilian sun. It's the mirror image of my father's nose (and yours, I think, too)—the main reason my mother married him, she has joked since I was a boy. Then the bevy of aunts in their rhinestone eyeglasses and identical curly black hairdos would laugh at her *double entendre* and hold their breastbones, shake their heads, and glance at one another like schoolgirls thinking of playing hooky. Family ritual, predictable as the box crumb cake and plate of *cucciddatis* next to the coffeepot on the table. Then one of the aunts always recited the old proverb that says from the nose and the thickness of a man's fingers a young girl could tell about the size of the part of the man that the bright light seldom sees. Of course, the men weren't in the room when the women discussed this. Your grandmother always blushed, then tried to change the subject by offering everyone more coffee. The part that comes to life each night, more full than the moon, the aunts would continue. Each night, *misca!*, everyone would say. You're terrible, my ma always told them. They'd agree. We're terrible, we're terrible, we'll all burn in Hell—everyone, including my ma, laughing and shaking her head until all eyes shone with tears and one of the aunts began to cough and choke ("It went down the wrong pipe!") on the fig cookies or the crumb cake.

In that regard (not checking noses and fingers, but rising like the full moon), I guess I've had my share of at-bats. During the two seasons I can't really remember, I went on a hitting streak that rivals DiMaggio and Rose. The part of me that comes to life each night was one of my recurring problems, as you, son, will soon see. You know I've never married. To the best of my knowledge you're the only ball I've ever landed in the bleachers.

You learn to keep your head down when you hit, and now I do so through my life. Habit. Also to hide the scars, thin as hairs. I wear long-sleeved shirts most of the time to hide the scars on my arms. We'll get to the play-by-play on them later. Few notice the scars even if I stretch my head all the way back. But I know they're there and I'm self-conscious. In my business, as a major-league scout out on the road searching for brilliance, for that inner power and light the potentially best young ballplayers have, I get to dress any way I want. So I opt for privacy and comfort here in the summer heat of America's Great Plains: cotton shirts and jeans or chinos, sandals, seldom socks (unless it looks like rain). I'm not one of those open-chested Italians whose unbuttoned Arrow or Van Heusen reveals a bathmat of dark hair and a gleaming jewelry-store window of gold crucifixes, chains, and *cornicelli*.

Though like most ethnics who came of age beneath city streetlights, when I was younger I was into flash and fashion. I'd stuff my legs into black pants everyone on Chicago's North Side called stovepipes, so tight a stranger with average eyesight could see each coin in your pocket and read the place of mint and year. Every sports jacket I owned had an iridescent sharkskin lining. I believed anyone who wore white socks or penny loafers was gay. Even in gym class, nothing but midcalf black nylon socks for me. I wore black shoes so pointed they could pop beachballs. Expensive buttonless Italian knits over a sleeveless cotton undershirt, which everyone called a dago-T. A palmful of Wildroot Original Cream Oil slicked back my pompadour. I always carried a comb. Then I'd ruin the effect by wearing my blue letter sweater, as I'd treat a string of always slender, always unsuspecting Immaculatas to a Frankie Avalon movie at the Uptown, the Riviera, or the Granada, where our feet always stuck to the sticky floor. The girl inside the crook of my arm would go gaga over the tanned muscled chests of the surfers on the screen, and I'd try to pull her back to oceanless Illinois, try to get her into a french kiss so deep that it would last forever, and all the smiling California extras would disappear into the waves, and I'd be able to forget about Mickey Meenan and my love for Grace Jankowski, and I'd never die. At night in bed with Louie and Francis Junior and sometimes Gino and Dominic, I'd imagine Immaculata girls at Chicago's Foster Beach drowning, and after I rescued them and carried them ashore they'd cling to me like an octopus in "Sea Hunt," and there'd be no breaking my hero's kiss. But high in the dim balconies their hands would stop me as surely as a good throw in front of the runner.

Why was Annette Funicello wearing a bathing suit and not her Mickey Mouse ears? Where was Jiminy Cricket? Any Disneyland of innocence? What happened to my guardian angel? Why did the beauties in my fantasies always behave? Always whisper so grammar-schoolishly with a breath hotter than a doubleheader in Mississippi in July that near the beach there was a cave, and it was dark and clean inside, and would I take her there? Inside the wet cave the girl would lie on her back, open her arms, smile. In bed with the darkness of my fantasy, I'd splash my Clorox gravy into a Kleenex.

That Danny Bacigalupo I need to pencil into the lineup too.

He seems like someone else now, a mixed-up kid on the side of the road I pull over for, offer a lift. He nods, then frowns outside my idling truck, so obsessed with Mickey Meenan's death and his ever-poorly-expressed love for Grace Jankowski that he's too guilty even to say thanks as he hops in.

Let's step out of the cage for a moment and talk about guilt.

Linguists bump chests and kick dirt when they discuss the word's origins. They can't tell where *guilt* came from. Theologians don't care; they're just real pleased to have guilt to throw around. But guilt isn't something you want to celebrate. The dime store doesn't sell greeting cards that say "Happy Guilt." Guilt is a foul-smelling cloud that stuffs your sinuses, then drips down into your throat and makes you want to gag. No postgame shower can wash guilt down the drain. You try to play hide-and-seek with guilt, but guilt always finds you. Then guilt says, "We're so close and I feel so good about you, why don't I start sleeping over?"

Take it from me, son. Me, the kid on the highway, and guilt were pretty tight.

Now that I look back, I can see that from kindergarten on I was primed to eventually come down with a good dose of it. Because just as the game has its men in black who call the balls and strikes, the fairs and fouls, the safes and outs, so my life had its crew of stern Irish women dressed in black hoods, floor-length black robes cinched by beads, and oversized white bow ties. The Sisters of Christian Charity, to whom I was delivered at age six by my well-meaning parents for instruction and the salvation of my eternal soul. Imagine the toughest Marlboro cowboy driving the naïve calf from its mother's shadow and then roping it, tying off its hooves, drawing out from the Pentecostal flames of the campfire the red-hot brand of Guilt and Fear, and then burning the calf's hide while it writhes and squeals like one of the Three Little Piggies being devoured by the Big Bad Wolf, and you have a fairly accurate picture of my life's early religious education.

I even believed them when they said that what they were doing was for our own good (universal excuse for a lot of evil, son). I believed them when they collected our monthly tuition envelopes and said it was our parents' highest duty, the very least they could do.

I believed that Protestants were misguided (led by a doubting lunatic, they refused to worship the Virgin or believe in Confession, the nuns would hiss), that Jews were worldly (they were looking for a material king, Heaven on earth), that all atheists and agnostics were damned (their downfall was their senseless egotism). Little ensures belief more than being told others are blind and stupid, that you are perceptive and wise. And after we were introduced to world geography I learned there were Muslims, Hindus, Buddhists, pagans, naked backward heathens—a myriad of wrong-minded religions and ways—popping off the inflated plastic globe with souls as starving for God's True Word as the broom-thin children with their hands out pictured in the ads for CARE.

I don't mean to be flip, but they were so insistent and I so

9

green and gullible that I took everything they said as gospel, which of course the good sisters claimed it was.

My parents only told me to do as I was told. To learn, to obey, not to waste all the advantages I had. After all, they continually reminded me, I was the first of their families to be born into this great country. I carried the weight of expectation of all the Bacigalupos, all the Paradisos. So I'd better not screw up.

My mother took me with her to Mass every Sunday. She was partial to rear, side-aisle pews, where she'd kneel and say several rosaries, ignoring everything else that went on except Holy Communion, which she'd receive with so much reverence and humility that I'd worry she'd levitate and never return to her normal self. After each Mass we'd light a candle beneath the statue of the sad-eyed Madonna. "For special intentions," my ma would always say, then pat her always pregnant stomach.

My father hit the pews with us on Christmas Eve and Easter Sunday, the only times other than weddings or funerals he ever wore a tie. He'd watch everyone and everything, turning like a top, now and then sucking his teeth, and didn't seem to know when to kneel or stand or cross himself. He never said any of the Latin responses. He never cracked a hymnbook and sang. He never stood and followed my mother in the line for Holy Communion. "I eat my own bread," he'd whisper calmly as she'd try to pull him after her into the aisle, then add, "Lucy, don't argue."

So I didn't argue either. And I concluded that I'd eat my own bread too when I was old enough. In the meantime I'd be a good kid and not waste the tuition money and learn and try to please my ma.

So I learned.

Not that the earth is flat or that the four humors govern physical size and personality, but misconceptions just as wrong. I'll lay out my ideas of truth with a capital *T* later, when I tell you what happened after the last game I played in Mile High Stadium.

10

I learned that in the sky is Heaven, a supposedly wonderful place full of clouds thick enough to stand on, saucers of light behind everyone's head, God's magnificent throne, and twenty-four-hours-a-day genuflecting. I could think of several places I'd rather spend eternity (any playground with monkey bars and unbroken swings, Wrigley Field, Lincoln Park Zoo, Riverview, in front of Aunt Lena's black-and-white TV), but the sisters told us our choices for dessert were Heaven, Hell, or Purgatory—no substitutions. Hell and Purgatory were made of fires so hot you got a headache just thinking about them. The heat was worse than a glowing waffle iron, the nuns reminded us every week, so intense that the flames boiled and bubbled the miserable marrow inside your bones. In Hell even the nails of your two little fingers screamed with agony. Eee-ouch! And you'd have to stay there with nothing to do but suffer for longer than any teacher was able to count. For more years than there are grains of sand on all the world's shores and beaches, and that wouldn't even be the first hundredth of the first second of time, which would never move because it was eternal.

During some of these "How Bad Is Hell?" lectures, my classmates peed their uniform skirts or regulation navy-blue parish pants, prompting the nun to put the gory details on hold and call for the janitor and his broom and pan and bucket of sawdust.

Thanks for cluing me in, I'd think as the janitor muttered to me how I should be ashamed, how I was a big second grader. "Daniel," the sister said, "try and sit still and perhaps your clothing will dry by lunchtime." I'd nod, then stare at my desk top. See, I was grateful. God punished bad people with Hell whether they knew about it or not, and Sister was giving me a lifetime of advance warning. I'll grow up and be a very good person, I promised God. I figured you had to be really evil to end up in Hell. Hell was for people like Adolf Hitler.

But then the good sisters pulled the old hidden-ball trick on us, and all of us smug little snotnoses were caught flat-footed, a mile off base. Because, the nuns informed us, even though we were barely able to cross Clark Street with the aid of a green light and two patrol boys, all of us had *already earned* Hell's hottest flames, all because of two people we hadn't even met.

Let's pencil in Adam and Eve, the moronic apple eaters. They had a fantastic thing going (the Garden of Eden, tons better than Heaven by the way the nuns described it), but then couldn't resist listening to the talking snake. They had to go and nibble the forbidden fruit, in the process blowing the game for the rest of us.

So God punished not only dumb Eve and Adam but everyone else who came from their apple seeds. Which meant *everybody*, from the Chinese with their chopsticks to the Eskimos with their igloos to the Australians with their crazy boomerangs. The sin boomeranged throughout the ages. Which meant we were all brothers and sisters (momentary confusion and panic: who can I marry, then, when I grow up?), damned to the never-ending broiler, furnace, blazing hibachi of Hell.

It didn't seem quite fair to me, son. I thought, Hey, hold your horses. *I* wasn't there to resist the temptation. *I* didn't get to choose. If only I'd have been there—man alive, that apple would've rotted on the tree! I might have *looked* at it once or twice. Maybe nodded to the snake, thrown him a dead alley rat so I could watch him eat. I might have touched the apple with my fingertips, given it a sniff. Maybe even put my lips, my tongue, my teeth . . .

I'd have eaten it too.

It made me realize I was one of the lucky souls. I knew the truth. Plus, I had a bona fide Catholic baptism stamped on my forehead. For at least a week I did my chores around the house without my ma having to tell me twice.

She was right, I concluded. You should eat God's bread. Kneeling next to her in church, I'd think of little pagans exactly my age all over the world who'd never even heard of priests or nuns. How, when they died, their tiny heathen hands and screaming fingernails would crackle in Hell like slices of bacon in my ma's big cast-iron frying pan. I'll travel all over when I grow up, I thought. I'll carry a hundred canteens of holy water and baptize every pagan I meet, even if I have to wrestle them down to the ground. "It's good for you, honest, no fooling," I'd tell them. They'd be grateful later on. They'd shake my hand and thank me when they saw me again up in Heaven.

The missionary life seemed extremely attractive to me, son. As long as you watched out for Communists and cannibals, and didn't step on or talk to snakes, going around sprinkling water on heathen foreheads seemed about the surest way to keep your buns out of the microwave.

The nuns cushioned the Fall of Humanity with another story, the Fall of the Angels. It seems that trillions of years before Paradise, some of God's finest archangels and seraphim got disobedient too. The Good Lord was on them in a microsecond. Also He had legions of good angels and archangels (my first lesson in the concept of a deep bench) waiting with drawn swords behind Him. The defeated lay at His ankles, gasping. God unplugged their halos, plucked their feathers, stripped them of their mighty wings. Then He stepped on a giant pedal that opened a yawning trapdoor in the clouds, and all of the militant angels tumbled down from the blue sky.

In that moment of eternity's early timelessness it rained angels—it rained devils—and they plummeted through space with a moan: falling meteors, comets, Skylabs, Cosmos 1402s, twisting in an everlasting sizzle as the eager tongues of Hell's waiting fires leapt at their cloven feet and their devil mouths and french-kissed them.

This was the creation of Hell. Wowee! we all thought.

Indirectly these stories also taught us a lot about this strange Being we called God. For one, He wasn't a father who took much sass. Also He didn't seem to give second chances (we didn't get to the New Testament until third grade). He was all-powerful and knew and saw everything, everywhere, always; and to top it off He was invisible. Ogres in the Brothers Grimm seemed more benign.

But what choice did we have? We couldn't raise our trembling hands and ask Sister to tell us another fairy tale. This, the stern women in black were teaching us, was for real.

Maybe I exaggerate. I don't mean to, son. But when I reflect on the pregame quality of my life I don't remember many lessons of kindness, love, reparation, forgiveness. Soft yellow light doesn't shine down through the windows of those childhood rooms. Those rooms are dark, wooden, full of coughing, dreamy, feet-shuffling children. Each year for eight years the well-meaning Sisters of Christian Charity trotted out these horror stories, and each year for eight years I listened with increasing fear.

We were told that, as Adam swallowed, the lump of apple caught in his throat and remained there, a constant reminder of our evil, sinful nature. We were told that the talking serpent still slithers through the world in the form of creeping communism. All we had to do was ask our fathers to read us the newspapers; President Ike was combating it every day. One of the statues in our classroom showed Mary stepping on the writhing serpent. "See?" the nun would say. It was all the proof we needed. Evil was in our throats, in our world, even under the foot of the Blessed Virgin. Evil was everywhere. After the flames kissed them, the evil angels escaped from Hell and worked their way up to the earth, where they walked our streets and alleys, always in disguise, always looking like normal people, always there behind a streetlight pole or the open door of a strange car, hoping to lead us into the darkness of despair, into temptation, occasions of sin, eternal everlasting damnation.

But the nuns had it all wrong, son. They were swinging the skinny end of the stick. They had us looking at the game backward. Our nature isn't to be evil. Our nature is to be better.

I see the stands are nearly full now; the turnstiles, just about clicked to capacity. Open a bag of peanuts and sit back. We're

14

loose, warmed up, ready to get the game of my life and death under way.

My parents, Mickey, Grace, Coach Grieves, Brother Gabriel, Book Johnson, Robert E. Lee Wingert, Lefty and Wanda Payne, your mother's daddy, Mr. Meenan. Adam Double, Free, and all the others who'll end up in the box score wait on the dugout steps.

I should tell you that my number is 13, so you'll recognize me down on the field. Every team from high school on gladly allowed me to wear it. No one else wanted 13 but me. Because, see, when baseball collided with Mickey's death and I was forced to abandon my dreams of becoming a missionary, I felt it was only right and proper that the rest of my playing days be spent in sheer defiance of misfortune.

Because the first of our line of Paradisos and Bacigalupos to be born into the nation of baseball earned his birthright and stepped right out of Paradise into the foul mouth of the wolf.

Because I believed the good sisters when they said that at seven you tag the age of reason, that from the moment the candles on your birthday cake go out everything you do from then on goes into the record book. Because at age eight I was involved in a very extraordinary, extremely tragic play. I wish I could say it was a bit part in a grammar-school production of make-believe *Macbeth* or *Hamlet*. It wasn't. It was purple-faced, bulging-eyes real. With one swing of my bat I became a murderer, one of those people Hell was created for, having killed my playmate Mickey Meenan with a very foul ball he should have caught or at least gotten out of the way of, and even though everyone told me it was an accident, I would have to blow out a lot more birthday candles to be able to shake off the error and learn to play my game.

I didn't want to be evil and reearn Hell, son. But if you've got the genes of a ballplayer it's not easy to pass up a fat pitch.

So I went with the pitch that began my life as a ballplayer.

THE GAME

1 2 3 4 5 6 7 8 9

TAKING THE FIELD

Let's give a big hand to the groundskeepers, son. Because four hundred million years ago, way back in the very early innings, your daddy's first field was a tropical sea. Dandy for frogs and fish and lily pads, but lousy for laying down straight foul lines. The sea knew it. So the sea laid down a bed of limestone and split for a sojourn in the oceans, and then the North Pole shivered and said, "Hey, let's get out of here, it's cold!" So a bunch of overgrown ice cubes slipped down through the Northwest Territories and Manitoba singing, "It's my kind of town, Chicago is." But since nobody had taught them not to overslide the base, when they hit State and Madison they just kept on going, inadvertently creating Denver and the Rockies, ending up in the Deep South, where they smelled the honeysuckle and whistled "Dixie" and promptly melted into the sea. Though they leaked enough water to make the Great Lakes, much to the pleasure of the natives who fished them, but who pinched their noses and called Chicago exactly what it was, *stinking onion creek*, and who were beginning to hear the ominous footsteps of Marquette and Joliet, a pale pair of Frenchies fond of sunsets on new horizons. Then Mad Anthony Wayne played a bloody series with the Indians at Fallen Timbers, and somebody built Fort Dearborn, and by the time the genocide was over the place had streets made of the limestone bed and cows that kicked over lanterns and hogs happy to be butchered and Carl Sandburg getting most of it down in his poems. Then thousands of hungry foreigners packed their rags into cardboard suitcases and shopping bags and floated over some of the same water that had once been a part of the tropical sea, and two of them, Lucia Maria Paradiso and Francesco Alfredo Bacigalupo, banged the box springs long and well enough to enter my name on the scorecard.

On the city's North Side, on a street named Olive, in the middle of a solid neighborhood of working-class Irish and Germans and Poles, with a few Italian families like ours sprinkled here and there, like basil, for flavor. Everyone lived in gray or red brick two-flats. Upstairs lived the tenants, preferably old people who didn't smell and who treaded their hallway quietly. The front of every house had a porch that faced a tree. Everybody except the old people and the Meenans and the Jankowskis had a new baby every year or so. At first we babies stumbled around our tiny backyards, eating grass and twigs and pebbles too large to stick in our nostrils and crunchy paint chips from the wooden garages that opened into the *stay away from there, do you hear me!* alley, touching fingers through the tilted square gaps in the chain-link fences that separated us, careful not to trample our fathers' tomato plants. Then we were promoted to the front yards, where we were yelled at by everyone. Because the new open space turned us into a herd of stampeding buffalo, and everyone had just planted marigolds or snapdragons or new grass seed. Perhaps because they were trained to be dainty, the girls at once obeyed. But we boys had no control over our shoes. So we fled and graduated ourselves to the alley.

The girls stayed in the front yards because they said the alley wasn't clean. Really they were afraid of the rats you would see sometimes munching on the day's garbage that spilled out of the big oil drums everyone kept to their back gate. Humorless men from the rodent-control section of the city's board of health marched through every spring stapling signs to the telephone poles: WARNING. THIS BLOCK HAS BEEN BAITED WITH RED SQUILL AND WARFARIN.

So we called ourselves the Rat Squill Warfarins and armed ourselves with fifth grader Joey Petrovich's baseball bat, and the alley became our kingdom, our playground, our limestone and asphalt Garden of Eden.

We explored every inch of it, naming every garbage can (Blue Streak, Rusty, Triple Dent), garage door (Big Ben, Lucky Green, Smasharoo), backyard gate (Squeaky, Busted Man, Fort Comanche). In the front yards our sisters stepped around the nodding petunias and drew squares on the ratless sidewalk with pieces of colored chalk. They began wearing dresses, barrettes and red rubber bands to hold back their long hair. From our knees in the alley we could hear them sing.

"I live on Ol-live!"

Over and over and over, until we thought we'd go mad.

"Ay lives on Ol-live!
Ee lives on Ol-live!
I live on Ol-live!
Oh lives on Ol-live!
Do you live on Ol-live?"

And they always sang *see wye see oh?* (can you come out?) when they called from the backyards to one another to come out to play. I'd hear my sisters Rosaria and Tina. I'd listen, tempted to open my mouth and sing *en wye* (not yet) or *eye ay ell double-*

21

you (in a little while). But we were Rat Squill Warfarins; our rules said we couldn't sing. Our voices might scare away the rats that we hunted with rocks and Joey's baseball bat.

Whenever it rained or when one of our fathers would unroll his green garden hose and soap down his car, the potholes in our alley would brim with delicious water and our playground would become the Chain of Great Lakes. We would play Dams and Beavers, on our hands and knees, using stones and sticks and pieces of broken glass. We'd see which one of us had the biggest beaver's buck teeth. Then Joey Petrovich's dark eyes would twinkle and he'd play Dive Bomber and smash our dams with his bat.

HOMES, Frankie Biermann taught us. Huron, Ontario, Michigan, Erie, Superior. Frankie had blond hair and polio and a brace on one leg. When you asked him if he had polio he said, "Yeah, that's how come my middle leg's so short." Skeeter Egan, who always wore his hair in a flattop and who could run faster than Old Lady Misiak's alley cat, and whose twin sister Deirdre was the most beautiful girl in the world, said Superior was the best.

Then for a while it didn't rain, and everyone's father's car was clean, and everything had a name, and the rats had made themselves so scarce that we forgot all about them. Then Lenny Sakowicz, whose arm muscles were as hard as cue balls, got a baseball and a genuine autographed mitt, and we all begged our parents for mitts. After my father told me no, "Don't be stupid, Danilo, I'll slap you, don't even ask," I got the scissors from the pantry and cut out all the pictures of baseball gloves in the Sears and Montgomery Ward catalogs my mother kept in a drawer in the china cabinet, and every night I'd stick one with my spit to the bathroom mirror, where he'd see it the next morning when he shaved. Each morning when I woke to go to school I'd find my mitt floating in the toilet bowl. Dive bomber, I'd think as I'd sink the bit of paper with my pee.

But enough of the other kids got gloves. Then Joey and Lenny created the Olive Street Alley League, and Frankie got a pencil and wrote all of the rules down.

Hitters gitters was the first commandment. That included even the backyards of childless old people who owned fierce dogs. *Ricochets are fair in play* was commandment number two. Off a garage roof was foul. Off telephone wires, fair. Pitcher's hands, you're out of there. Break somebody's window and everybody runs, with the hitter responsible for picking up the bat. Joey and the big guys foresaw most of the possibilities.

"This here's a league of line-drive sluggers," the big guys said. "Line-drive sluggos," echoed all of us little guys, even Frankie Biermann, whose leg brace made it awful hard for him to run.

Mickey Meenan was a very quiet kid, and most of the time he was around you didn't even notice he was there. He was tall for a third grader, gawky, spotted everywhere you could see with freckles, and he'd pick his earwax with his little finger or a stick and then stare at it for so long he made you ask him what he was going to do with it. "I dunno," he'd always say, and then he'd always eat it or wipe it on his pants leg and then start working on his other ear. All the kids thought he was spoiled because he was an only child. Really, we were jealous. Mickey had a hundred toys, none of them broken; a thousand comic books, not one page torn.

Other than Grace Jankowski, in our neighborhood of Catholic families Mickey was the only only child. Even though he was Catholic his parents sent him to the public school on Bryn Mawr. So he was doubly strange.

Mickey's father had a job with the city, sleeping in trucks parked along the street where they had big potholes or busted water pipes, and he'd let us gather inside his garage as he'd boast that his CAUTION MEN WORKING signs sweated more in summer than he did. He was a big man and always smoked a fat cigar, and he'd tell us how great it was to go up to Wisconsin to shoot birds, really blast them out of the sky, or blow little squirrels or bunny rabbits to smithereens, and then he'd take out his shotgun and put a finger to his lips and say, "Shhh, be vewy vewy quiet. I'm hunting wabbits." We'd clap our hands with glee. Then he'd tell us how he'd once been a professional boxer, though he quit before he got cauliflower ears. He'd let us look at his ears, and we'd beg him to do Elmer Fudd again, and he'd say he was pleased as punch we played with his kid, and then he'd grab Mickey and rub his head real hard with his knuckles. Mickey would say nothing, except his face got fire-truck red as he squirmed.

Sometimes we'd tease Mickey about eating earwax and being spoiled, until he invited all of us over to his house. Mrs. Meenan made a hundred oatmeal cookies and ten gallons of Wyler's lemonade, and Joey and Lenny swiped a bunch of comics, and Frankie fell on a couple of toys and broke them all to pieces, and Mr. Meenan laughed and laughed and stunk up the house with his cigar, and everybody but poor Mickey had a wonderful time.

It was an accident, and it happened before I could even drop the bat and run. Winky Winkler danced on second. Mickey was playing the garage door just behind first. It was a Saturday in early April and we had planned a triple-header, and we were getting good because several of us had our timing down.

Because it was a league of line-drive sluggos.

The ball cracked off the bat and I started to drop it as I ran toward first base, but I heard a hollow squish and Mickey stood there by Lucky Green staring right at me with no expression on his face. Then the world stopped as his bulbs went dim and he fell to his knees. For a half of a second I thought it was just a joke, that Mickey had suddenly been struck by a sense of humor, that he'd begin to pray in pig Latin or sing "I live on Ol-live!" or crawl like a turtle toward the ball. I wanted him to pick the ball up because I knew I could beat his throw. I wanted him to stand. I wanted him to say *something*.

Because suddenly I was terribly afraid.

By the time we got to him he had fallen to his face. Then Lenny and Joey and the rest of the guys rolled him over. His face and neck were turning blue. His throat was trying to pronounce the letter *K*. His eyes looked backward into his head.

"You're all right, Meenan," everybody said.

"Right off his Adam's apple! Didja see it?"

"Wake him up."

"Get the smelling salts."

"You shoulda seen it! It looked like he was trying to eat the ball!"

"You're OK, Meenan."

"Get up, sluggo."

"You killed him, 'Galupo. Honest to Jesus!"

"He ain't even breathing."

We got him under his armpits and tried to make him walk. "You're all right, Meenan." His feet dragged like a Raggedy Andy doll. "Honest, Danny, I bet you killed him." Some of the guys laughed, scared and nervous. Little Frankie Biermann looked like he was going to cry. Then somebody took off down the alley toward Mickey's house. "Take deep breaths, Meenan, you're OK, you're OK." He wasn't very heavy. His skin still felt warm. His head rolled on his chest like Mr. Sakowicz on Friday nights when the men from the foundry walked him home drunk.

Mrs. Meenan bawled over Mickey as she knelt on her front-yard grass. We were waiting for the ambulance. Much fuzzes out in my memory, son. I can remember feeling the earth beneath my feet begin to spin. Mrs. Meenan had a pink apron on over her housedress. Next to her on the grass was a yellow rubber glove. One of the ambulance drivers was black and smelled sweetly of after-shave, and the siren bearing Mickey and his mother away shook sunny Olive Street, and I thought I could hear the line of trees whisper their name. "Meenan," the leaves in the wind whispered. Somebody shouted, "Hey, Danny, better make yourself scarce."

There are times when events overload your circuits, son, and inside you blow a fuse. Your head suddenly goes dark. Dad says, "Lucy, where the hell did I put that goddamn flashlight?" You help him as he walks down into the basement, thinking maybe you'll get to see a rat, hearing the sudden roar of the furnace as it kicks in. The sound frightens you, but you're with your dad. Yet he says nothing as he shines his flashlight, the only light in the whole world, on the gray fuse box.

"Say something to him, Francis."

"Get me a clean shirt. I have to shave."

"Again?"

"I can't go over there wearing this filthy shirt."

Supper, some soup and noodles, and nobody talked until Louie started to sniffle, then cry. Mamma held Francis Junior and said, "Eat." Only the baby ate, one hand raised and wrapped in Ma's dark curly hair, the other holding her breast so she wouldn't pull it away. The rest of us sat around the table, not eating. Louie wiped his tears with the fist that held his spoon. Dominic poked his noodles with his fingertips. Gino stared up at the ceiling, making stupid sounds with his tongue, and Tina held her rubber doll just like Mamma held Francis Junior. Rosaria's hands hid her face. I looked at them, their dark heads, then down at my soup, then at the little piece of bloodstained toilet paper Dad had clinging to his chin, then at the dish towel he wore over his immaculate white shirt.

"Francis, there's somebody at the door."

"Rosaria, answer it."

"They want to talk to Danny."

"Don't just sit there like a dummy. Danilo, go."

Mamma thought I was asleep when they came back that night. Everybody was in bed. She kissed the others, then touched my forehead with her hand, pressing the coolness of her palm against me for several moments. Now I realize that she most likely said a prayer, that she meant the touch to be comforting, reassuring.

But it confused me then. I couldn't understand why she didn't bend down to kiss me, until the middle of the night, when sound-asleep Louie woke me by peeing out his misery against my leg.

She didn't kiss me, I thought, because my forehead now had the mark of Cain, and even in the darkness my own mother could see it.

I'll have to run away, I thought. With my deficient imagination I pictured myself as a hobo, no taller than I was then but having a burnt-cork Halloween beard, a stick over my shoulder, and all my belongings inside a red bandanna, riding the rails to the Wild West's unknown frontiers, my leg eternally wet with my brother's pee.

The next day I did run away, just before I could be taken to church. Ma was busy changing one of the kids' diapers, and Dad shaved in the bathroom. I scooted out the back door and ran to the Bryn Mawr El station, slipping under the turnstile and jumping on the first passing train, which happened to be going south. I can remember being terrified when the cars dipped into the dark tunnel just beyond Fullerton. I thought the El was always elevated and that God was sending me down to Hell. But then the ride leveled off. I rode that train until I was the only white on board, then got off, somewhere on the South Side. I took the next train that stopped at the platform, riding north to Howard Street, the end of the line.

Then I went back south, plunging deeper, no longer afraid of the tunnel or becoming the only white. People were even friendly to me. "Where you going, little boy?" "Say, you lost?" I pretended I couldn't speak, pointing to my mouth and shaking my head no. "Then you must be one of them deaf-mutes." I nodded yes and smiled. An old woman gave me a stick of gum.

I rode back and forth most of that unhappy Sunday. I don't know why I finally went home. Perhaps I realized the El had gotten me nowhere.

No one said a word to me about my absence. At my place

at the kitchen table there was an empty plate, a fork, a spoon. My ma looked like she wanted to ask me where I'd been all day, but my father's silence made the house too heavy for her or anyone to talk.

For everyone but me the murder was denied.

Or so I thought, completely forgetting Mr. Meenan, the man who hunted rabbits and was wise enough to escape cauliflower ears.

Son, I wanted them to shout at me, to grab my shoulders and shake me until my brains were scrambled and my spine clanked. I needed to hear that they were worried and angry. That would mean I still belonged and they still loved me. I realize now they were sad, ashamed, confused. But they couldn't have picked a harsher punishment if they had tried.

And then I became so sick that the doctor had to quarantine the house. Now, be careful with the causality here, son. I didn't fall sick with scarlet fever because I'd murdered Mickey Meenan, though at the time I was convinced that was why. I fell ill because I inhaled streptococci in one of those El cars, and a legion of homeless scarlet-fever bees built a hive inside my heart. Then the bees' bubbling honey leaked into my bloodstream and fried my cheeks, my legs, my bones. My guts flamed. Everywhere I was aching hot. Thrashing on the sweat-soaked sheets of my parents' double bed, I boiled like a lobster inside the steaming pot of my skin.

The Irish priest wouldn't come to bless me because of the quarantine. My mother rinsed my forehead and chest with holy water she'd pilfered from the vestibule. She filled the bedroom with a hundred red votive candles that flickered everywhere I could see, and then the room grew dozens of stand-by-themselves crucifixes, and three times each day my brothers and sisters knelt outside my closed door and recited the rosary and the Litany for the Dead. *Oh Lord, deliver them. We beseech Thee, hear us.* I ate ice cubes made of water and red wine. When I could I peed into a soup pot. My ma brought every vigil candle on the North Side into that room, and after each rosary and litany she cracked the door open and tiptoed in and had me kiss the feet, hands, side, and head of each of the crucifixes that stood behind the tiers of bouncing candles and hung on my sickroom's four walls.

You'd think I would have lain on my damp sheets praying for the eternal salvation of my wretched soul and for eternal rest for the dearly departed Mickey Meenan. You'd think the words *I'm sorry, dearest God* would have been starters in the lineup on my parched lips. They weren't even on the team. My mind and soul sang a different tango.

"My little sister Tina could've gotten out of the way of that liner, dear God. You know I ain't lying. So why couldn't You have let the spaz catch it? Or at least made him duck? A dog would've known enough to duck. You make the pigeons fly away when the ball goes near them. So how come it didn't work with Meenan? You can do *anything*, remember? You could've let it ricochet off his forehead. Given the kid a shiner. Busted his nose. Knocked out his two front teeth. Why'd You have to let me kill him? Our Father, Who art in Heaven. What You let happen, it couldn't have been worse! All right, so maybe You really needed him up there in Heaven for some strange and mysterious reason. Sister's all the time telling us that's the way You like to operate. But why pick on me? What did I ever do? You could've killed him a million other ways! You could've killed him with a garbage truck! You could've pushed his stack of comics down on him when he wasn't looking! So why me? You could've let him catch rabies from one of the alley rats. Why me? What did I do? *What did I ever do?*"

While my family knelt in the hallway outside my door, respectfully slurring *the Lord is with thee* and *blessed is the fruit of thy womb*.

If you think I thought a lot about Hell, you're right. How could I have avoided it? I'd let my fever work itself up until I felt I was made of fire, and then I'd squint at the endless rows of candles. The flames would shimmy in their little cups and I'd see a dancing sea of red. The image was really very lovely, son. But I'd pretend it was a glimpse of Hell, and I was just outside, in one of Hell's waiting rooms, about to receive my punishment. I'd try to imagine eternity and begin to multiply two times two times two until the numbers melted in my brain. Sometimes I'd pull myself to the bed's edge and reach out and stick my little finger into one of the flames. I'd try to hold my hand there forever, the multiplication tables hovering on my lips, but my arm always pulled my hand back. Then I'd feel my forehead for my mark of Cain, and lie back on my pillow, exhausted.

I'd play a game with the crucifixes. If I lay perfectly still there was always at least one whose hollow cheeks reflected the flames in a way that made His head move. I'd stare at that Jesus and ask Him questions.

"Are You happy on the Cross?"

No, His head would shake.

"Is Meenan still alive?"

Again, no.

"Will I be well in time to make my First Holy Communion?"

No.

"Does anybody love me?"

No.

"When I die, will I go to Heaven?"

Always no, no, no.

"Then stay on Your old Cross," I'd whisper, then feel terrible and cry until my tears made little puddles in my ears.

I'd think of baseballs, endlessly arcing in on me, my hands gripping the bat, my wrists snapping the sweet part against the lazy ball. They talk today about *baseball fever*? Son, I'd literally caught it. I played more games in my head than convents have black shoes and stockings. In every one I always hit safe line drives that were at least fifty feet over every fielder's head, that sailed like kite strings through the air, touching nothing, nothing, ever. Never old Adam's forbidden apple stuck in an innocent freckled kid's throat. No, my balls would always land with a magnificent splash in the middle of Lake Michigan.

Only when the fat doctor came to probe me with his instruments would the room fill with blinding light. I imagined him as Satan's chief inspector trying to decide which boiler room I'd be sentenced to and how high to set the thermostat. "His fever hasn't broken yet," he'd always say. "Let's give it some more time." Then he'd turn with a belch or a fart, and my ma would sigh and turn off the terrible light, then replace the spent candles, then call the little disciples to the hallway for the evening's rosary and litany, which was followed by another round of Sacred Wound kissing.

Meanwhile, my former classmates were shuffling through practice and then real Confession en route to their first-Sunday-in-May march up to the Eternal Bread Line. You can tell by my tone I was bitter, son. "So what if I miss making First Holy Spumoni?" I asked the flickering flames. I was sick of being sick and so jealous I wouldn't be with them that I wished none of them would have any fun. I prayed the monsignor would screw up and none of the Sacred Snacks would get consecrated. "No, no, no," Jesus said.

I pictured the church, glowing more greenly than kryptonite, as the priest topped each communicant's virgin tongue. Their sin-free souls gleaming like my feet in the X-ray machine at Maury's Bargain Shoe Store. I saw the ribboned pews and kneelers. All the kids filling their chipmunk cheeks with Christ. Everyone afterward posing on the church steps for adorable snapshots. Then they'd all tumble like socks in a dryer into a hundred just-washed Fords and Chevies, happily driving home to hamburgers on the grill, reheated roast beef, pineapple-covered ham, white First Communion cake. And all of them knowing why I, the little murderer nailed to the cross of scarlet fever, wasn't there.

By then I was able to sit up and not feel woozy, and that afternoon I held the wall and slid my feet to the window, pushed apart the dusty drapes, and pulled up one narrow yellow slat of the venetian blinds. I was able to gaze out on a sunny sliver of Olive Street, and I stayed there, dizzily holding on to the drapes, until Mr. Egan's pine-green Plymouth scraped its whitewalls against the curb and Skeeter bounded out of the backseat in his white suit and bow tie. Sanctifying grace was all over his face. He twirled his thick Communion candle like a baton. Then Deirdre slid from the car like an angel on Christmas morning. I guess I cried then, if my body had enough liquid in it to cry. I know that I began knocking down the rows of crucifixes and blowing out the thousand candles. It felt like a cruel birthday party I hadn't been invited to, and since I couldn't blow out all the candles with one breath, I realized I wouldn't get my wish.

Which wasn't that the liner had never left my bat, or if it had that it hadn't struck Mickey, or that Mickey could be resurrected. I was more selfish than that. My wish was that I could be normal again.

Because I'd seen what happened to the kids who weren't. The others ganged up on them like a school of pet-store piranhas. They took chunks out of you until you were barely alive. They tripped you whenever you tried to walk down their row. They stuck KICK ME I'M AN ASSHOLE signs on your back with chewing gum. They snotted out a gob of boogers on your seat, then hooted like hyenas when you sat in it. They hid Tootsie Rolls of dog shit in your desk. No one would sit with you in the lunchroom, mess around with you out on the playground, stand next to you when you waited in line.

So I blew out every one of the damn candles and kicked over the soup pot and then got up on a chair so I could take all the crucifixes down from the walls when my ma came in and screamed, "Francis, Gino, Dominic, Rosaria, Tina, Louie, Francis Junior! Thank God! Our prayers are answered! Danny's well!"

And I was.

Even late that summer when I watched the immense moving van flatten Mrs. Jankowski's petunia bed and the grunting workers carry all the Meenans' junk down their front-porch steps. Even when I smelled Mr. Meenan's cigar and then heard him behind me saying, "You just wait, you little son of a bitch." Even when I carried out the garbage and then went into the alley and found the precise spot where I'd murdered Mickey, and a lightning bolt didn't streak from the sky. Even when I returned to school that spring and sat at my trusty desk, inhaling the deliciously complex aroma of children and floor cleaner and chalk dust, each of my books in a new and foreign chapter.

Though you'd think I had become the world's scabbiest leper. Whenever I walked down the hallways, everyone—I mean *everyone*—gave me room. Even Mother Superior and the old janitor who played solitaire in the mop closet. When I sat in the cafeteria and opened my lunch bag, the entire table shut up more quickly than had the Pope himself come into the room. None of the girls would look into my eyes. Out on the playground I was able to join any game, even sixth graders' games, but nobody would try to tag me in tag, block my jump shots in basketball, call me over in red rover. The nuns gave me straight A's in conduct, B's and A's in everything else. Anything I offered in classroom discussion was nodded at and called a *very good point, Daniel.* Later that spring when the Olive Street Alley League got restarted, the guys said nothing when I stood by the garbage cans and watched, nothing still when I grabbed somebody's glove, fielded, shook my head no at the bat, became the league's Perpetual Fielder. And the next year when I finally made my First Communion, everything went as smoothly as a 6–4–3 double play, as easily as Spiderman scaling the world's highest building, as slickly as the thirty-weight motor oil my dad gurgled into our car. And every priest in every confessional forgave every one of my sins, even the murder, which I continually confessed.

"Bless me, Father, for I have sinned. I disobeyed my parents ten times. I made a crib sheet for my history test. I borrowed a dime from my brother Louie without telling him. I murdered Mickey Meenan. I am so sorry for these sins and for the sins of my whole life—"

They always took deep breaths then and fidgeted on their seats, and you could smell their after-shave or their sour breaths when they'd been smoking a cigarette. Then they all told me that God's Will was a strange and mysterious thing, as if that was news, and that *the Meenan incident,* as they came to call it, was indeed a great misfortune, a real tragedy, that he was a rose untimely plucked from life's glorious garden. But it was resolved, they said, absolved, forgiven, water over the dam, dust under the rug.

"You don't have to confess it anymore. Don't you understand, my child? It was an accident. Leave it in the grave. God loved the Meenan lad very much, you see, and He wanted to have him, to *embrace* him in His eternal arms right away, not in fifty or sixty or seventy years when the wee boy most likely would have died had his throat not interfered with the trajectory of your baseball. Simply put, you were God's agent. You were doing His bidding, acting in accordance with His Divine Plan, carrying out His most Sacred Will. Do you understand me, boy? Don't confess it anymore!"

Then they always composed themselves and gave me absolution and a penance of three Our Fathers and three Hail Marys, which always took me less than two minutes to complete. Then I'd work the church, making the sign of the Cross and beating my chest and genuflecting before each altar and statue and Station of the Cross, and I'd kiss the walls a lot, and then I'd slip the stolen dime from my pocket into the slot in the metal collection box beneath the sign that said FOR THE POOR, and as the coin echoed darkly and made the old people in the pews behind me turn around and stare, I'd light a red vigil candle.

"Make me normal again, dearest God embracing Mickey," I would pray.

I'd also worry that the cops would come back. Reopen the case, slap the cuffs on me. Put me in a delinquent home until I was old enough for prison. I knew what the kids meant when they whispered a guy was a JD. By then I'd been to the movies, and I'd seen plenty of Aunt Lena's TV. I knew the police always got the criminal, even if you were as tough as Edward G. Robinson in *Little Caesar*. I'd seen "Dragnet." The two detectives who came to the house that night were pretty much like them, factual and stiff, wiping their shoes in the front hall and taking off their hats, while my brothers and sisters ate soup and noodles in the kitchen, and my ma and dad worried about having to go over to Mickey's house, where they'd have nothing to say.

"Maybe we should bring them something, Lucy? A bottle of wine?"

"Francis, we'll bring them our pity and beg their forgiveness."

I sat in the front room and tried my best to explain. One kept looking at his watch. The other stared out the front window.

Finally they said, "Did you mean to kill him, son?"

The answer popped out without my thinking. "No."

They put on their hats. "That's all we came to hear."

Then they left, not saying anything more to me. And the shadow of my dad's thick shoulders stretched toward me down the hallway as he stood from the table, and my mother's tired silhouette eclipsed the light bulb hanging in the kitchen. Their whispers hissed down the long hall. But there was more to hear! When I swung the bat I did mean to murder something! I wanted to kill both the ball and what I was, to send both so far up the alley that all the kids would drop their gloves and cheer, and Ma would ignore the goddamn babies for half a minute and look at me, her oldest baby, and smile; and Dad's eyes would stop being so unhappy with me that he'd say what he never once in my life said, what I wanted awfully bad to hear, *I'm proud of you, Danilo, you did well, you please me.* But the pitch was low and away, and I went with it. Too eagerly, too hard. Too straight toward inattentive Mickey, who was more than likely dreaming about all his perfect toys, probably happy we let him play with us, even though he was a horrible batter who'd always squeeze his eyes shut and then swing on top of the ball, chopping it right back to the pitcher's waiting hands.

Guilty? Of course I was guilty. I was guilty of trying to be better than I was. Better than my tired and perfect father, who buried his life in a tomb of never-ending work. Better than my ma, whose life doomed her to nurture the endless line of babies babies babies that grew like tumors in her womb. Better than an alley full of rats and poison. Better than all the other guys on the block, whose tame, limited dreams had them growing up to be thirty-year-old gasoline pump attendants, or baggers at the Jewel or the A&P, with enough of a wad in their wallets for cigarettes, decent threads, somebody's used car. I wanted to drive a *new* car. I wanted the girls to sing songs about *me*. I wanted my brothers and sisters to be able to look up to me. I wanted to be better than my lousy neighborhood. I *had* to please my father, you see. And I had to please my own desires, to hit to my potential. I had to strive, excel. So I swung for the apple with every ounce of my might.

And the priests slid the confessional panel shut. The cops slipped out the front door, clicking their ball-points. My parents' shadows whispered in the hall. The air reeked of shame. So I hid, feeling then like the lowest of serpents.

Bless me, Father.

Because it was pride that made Adam and Eve reach for the apple, pride that made Icarus fly too close to the sun. Pride held the black Moor's pillow as he smothered fair Desdemona. Pride pushed peaceful Abel to the ground.

And God said, "You prideful shits, you're banished from the Garden." "You'll fall right into the sea." "You'll kill yourself once you realize how wrong you were about her." "You'll be a wanderer for all your days on earth."

The embarrassed shadows walked over to Mickey's house.

36

The unforgiving clock over the stove ticked and ticked. There'd be no stopping what I'd done, I realized. No chance to step out of the box or check my swing.

Grammar school raced past my guilty eyes.

Eighth grade, and now I made them all give me extra room as I swaggered down the halls. I was used to having no friends. I didn't need them anyway, I figured. Then hair sprouted from my groin and armpits. Every other Sunday my church pants were too short. Louie slept as peelessly as Dominic and Gino, but Francis Junior would dream he was a cocker spaniel and my leg was a fire hydrant, so I begged Ma to put the damn kids in the other damn bed. After all, I was the oldest, and respect should go to age. But really it was because now at night my boxer shorts bloomed with boners that throbbed and stretched toward the ceiling, making a pup tent of the blankets, and all my brothers noticed and laughed and caught colds.

Son, if I remember right, there's no ache as great as an eighth grader's ache. You've got all the equipment and it's desperate to be used, but inside you're still really a kid, a milk-drinking mother-loving innocent. Not only did my cock announce each dawn and want to doodle-do from the rooftops, it banged its horny beak against the clenched teeth of my zipper in the worst, absolutely most embarrassing of places.

Religion class.

The old nun would sit behind her desk, things like THE CALL and HOLY ORDERS, CANA and NUPTIALS on the blackboard behind her, when my peripheral vision would notice Deirdre Egan in the next row adjusting her ankle socks. My mind would start to drool. Her gams were so gorgeous that she made me want to crawl into my inkwell and die. Then I'd gape at her snow-white blouse as it stretched across a shoulder so lovely I'd tingle and grin like a cretin. For an instant I could see the actual strap of her brassiere. My blood would rush faster than mercury in a thermometer stuck in the mouth of an erupting volcano, as my mindless one-eyed mushroom slammed the bottom of my desk with so much force that it nearly ripped the desk's rivets from the floorboards, causing everyone to turn around.

"Do you have a problem you wish to share with us, Daniel?"

"No, Sister."

"Then wipe that smirk off your face."

Then Deirdre would stare at me as if I were an insect.

And though I knew it was a normal, red-blooded, all-American sort of thing, I figured my condition was somehow much more severe because I'd made Mickey Meenan maggot meat.

Because I could imagine the Bonerless Almighty chalking up still more sins on my slate. "Danilo, what do you think you're doing?" His voice sounded just like my father's. "She's meat on Fridays, understand? So are all the other good Catholic girls made in the Virgin's image and likeness. You'll never touch one, you're not good enough. They're out of your league, taboo. Can't you see it's part of my Divine Plan for them to sign lifetime no-trade contracts with good Catholic boys who've never murdered their playmates? Take my advice, Danilo, don't even look."

I understood completely. But my bocce balls had eyes and plans of their own. They led me like a bull with a ring in his nose through graduation party after graduation party toward Deirdre Egan and the girls of trouser-thumping conventional beauty.

Shyly I approached them, leper at the water of Lourdes. They'd staked out the six square feet surrounding the party's record player. When they weren't putting on fresh lipstick or dancing with a future Knight of Columbus, they were laughing behind their slender fingers, admiring one another's hair, or acting cool, teen-aged, nonchalant.

I cleared my throat. "Ahem. Will one of you please dance with me?"

They looked at me as if they wanted to throw up.

"What?" they said. "Not now," they said. "Not me," they

said. "I'm tired." "I'm sunburned " "I already promised Lance, Skeeter, Ned, Tyrone." "I split a fingernail." "I was just leaving to go home." Then they scattered like deer, quickly reassembling by the record player after I walked away.

I figured there were more fish in the sea. If the mermaids wouldn't twist or cha-cha with me, surely the dolphins would, the kind-of-pretty girls everyone said had personality. These were the girls who made the best grades, who weren't afraid of math, who knew folk songs by heart, who already wrote their own poetry. The girls who were marred by minor defects: moles, lisps, thick eyeglasses, vocations to the sisterhood, noses big as baking potatoes. Their territory was the six square feet near the party's front door, from which they greeted everyone but me with apt and affectionate nicknames, witty in-jokes, and waves of shrieking laughter.

"Hi!" I said with a life-insurance-salesman's grin. "How would you like to dance with me?"

"Distantly," they answered, then tittered. "Oh, that's *good*! You used an adverb! The first thing I thought of was I wouldn't like to at all!"

When they noticed I remained there, uncomprehending, they rebuffed me in aphorisms and foreign languages. "Art is long, and life is short." "Ours is not to reason why." "*Partez-vous, bête morbide, répulsif Quasimodo.*"

I walked away, a gaggle of giggles fluttering about my head.

Deepest sea diver, I told myself, you'll just have to descend into the brine's forbidden depths. where sunlight is a forgotten rumor, where the fish have the most peculiar names, habits, shapes. So I limped to the third and final outpost, the six square feet surrounding the inevitable folding table covered with junk food, where the shovelnose catfish and butterfly mudskippers swam, their gourami mouths dripping with chips and sour cream.

These were the girls only their cooties could love. The deformed, the acned, the fat. The ones who'd endured eight endless years of the gauntlet of insult and torment, who were told they resembled hippos, manatees, everything abhorrent in the zoo. Part of me felt revulsion, part of me pity for these creatures, so far away from the Code of Normal that the others hardly noticed they were even there.

Taking a gulp of air, I put on my most winning smile. "Please," I begged as I approached them, "would one of you dance with me?"

I don't overstate the ridicule these sideshow geeks heaped on me. They'd learned their tormentors' lessons well. The girl with the harelip snorted and raised one arm, then pointed to her damp armpit and said, "Dance with this!" Another, cursed with a double order of pepperoni on her cheeks and forehead, spat out a soggy mouthful of pretzel chewings at me. I was wiping the gunk off my shirt when I realized they might have thought my invitation was a joke, that I was teasing them, trying to set them up for yet another grammar-school cruelty.

"Honest," I said as the pizza-faced girl kicked me, "it's not a joke, I'm not pulling your leg, I've got nothing up my sleeve. It's just that here we are at this party, and nobody will dance with me."

Miss Dance With This flashed me her other armpit. Pepperoni Face then crouched behind me, and Miss Dance gave me a shove. As I tumbled to the floor the room shuddered with the sound of Miss Dance farting, and it was then as I lay flat on my back on the bottom of the barrel with everyone in the world laughing and pointing at me that I saw Olive Street's fattest siren, the very last pickle in the jar, Grace Marie Jankowski.

Who the kids called everything but her Christian name. Chunk, Chunky, Junk, Junky, Cow, sometimes Chunk Cow; and in sixth grade on Saint Valentine's some joker drew her portrait: the fattest Borden Holstein skiing down a slope of junk. Grace Jankowski slalomed past it all.

Through the third and fourth grades she greeted everyone, even the deaf monsignor, with a cheery *moo!* Each Halloween she waddled from house to house wearing a big bell around her neck and a ring of daisies in her hair. When she refueled at the fat girls' table in the cafeteria the kids would shout to her, "Hey Chunky, are you chewing your cud yet?" "Moo for us, Junky!" And the girl would stand, toss back her head, and moo. Everyone would laugh. And I'd think I never wanted to become like that, willing participant in the lousy game her name and overactive fat glands had played on her, even if I already was an actual murderer.

As our hormones tried to wrestle control over our minds, the jokes thrown into Grace's stall grew sharper. "Chewing your cud yet?" became "Chew on my pud." "Milk me off, fat girl." "Chunky, open wide for this!" Even the bored ladies who worked the cafeteria lunch line grinned at the riddle *What do you call it when the Chunk Cow tries to jump over the barbed-wire fence? An udder catastrophe.* For, by seventh grade, Grace had grown the school's biggest pair of udders.

"Thirty-eight D's," the boys shouted after her on the playground. "Fifty-two E's." "Sixty-four triple-F's." "Hey Junky, are you hiding a couple of basketballs in there? A pair of watermelons?"

She stopped mooing then. Her perfect blue eyes would darken, mist. With a flick of her hand she'd brush the laughing boys away like so many flies.

So I lay on the floor of the party looking up at her, the doughiest of dumplings. She had a longshoreman's meaty arms. Her hips were as wide as a whaling ship. Her hair, the color of straw strewn in an outdoor manger.

Son, I'd like to be able to tell you it was true love at first sight. It wasn't. But as Grace quivered curiously above me like a pink heap of Jell-O, I decided I'd show them all, that anyone, even this plump Polish *pierogi*, was better than loneliness. So like

Old Lady Misiak letting out her tomcat, I unleashed my libido, rising to my knees and unwinding a midnight serenade of growls, me-ours, and screeches. My hands flew into the air like a referee signaling a touchdown as I tugged at the tent of her blouse. "Please," I begged as politely as I could, "would you dance with me?"

Grace looked down on me then. I waited for her kicks, her spit. But she didn't move a muscle, and then I bounced to my toes and then stumbled into the really very pretty deep blue sea of her eyes. Without thinking I grabbed a paper napkin—on it was printed *Congratulations New Graduate!*—and wiped away several stray blobs of what looked like onion dip from the creases in her chins. Her skin was as soft as a baby's bottom. "You could finish your soda pop first," I said. All I could see were her blue eyes, more blue than the overly blue picture in our geography book of a tropical lagoon.

Gene Pitney's "Town Without Pity" spun on the record player behind us. The party had reached the point where Deirdre's band of future Miss Americas put on slow song after dreamy slow song, when the chaperones had slipped away to the kitchen to drink highballs and tell jokes, when the boys turned off one or two of the lights and everything was romantic, when everyone but me and the terrible trio were slow-dancing.

"You have beautiful eyes," I said. I dropped the napkin. I smiled.

Something worked, because Grace put down her paper cup of soda and placed a hand on my shoulder. Her other hand slashed the air, confused. I harpooned it with my own and then swung my other arm around what was most likely Grace's waist. I couldn't really tell. I felt as if I were trying to hug a building. But we danced then, me and Grace: the murderer nobody wanted a thing to do with, and the kindest, most gentle fat girl.

Looking back, I was the luckiest guy there.

All because the conventional beauties dead-bolted their doors when I tapped out my SOS on their bells, reserving their Toni permanents for the basketball players and the altar boys, the merry carolers who sang *milk me off*, the pimple- and blackhead-squeezing princes and jesters of snot, the ladies and lords of cruelty. In their smug sugarplum heads they dreamed of a world that was as glamorous as John F. Kennedy, as secure as bald old Ike, that would graduate them through high school into easy blue-collar jobs, crimeless white neighborhoods, grandchildren, retirement, happiness.

But I knew the world wasn't safe and secure.

So I clung to her, son, barnacle on the *Queen Elizabeth*.

And I courted her with every sweet song and lie the histories of music and flattery would ever know. I danced Grace beneath blue-and-white swirls of Scotch-taped crepe paper, whispering into her surprisingly unfat ear that I wished the ceiling would explode with bright sprigs of mistletoe so I could kiss the red Christmas of her lips. I danced her into the room's darkest corners and told her that just as old Wild Bill Shakespeare made Juliet for Romeo and Veronica for Archie and Mantle and Maris for the New York Yankees, so the Great Playwright in the Sky made Grace for Danny Bacigalupo. I danced her right next to the mermaids and dolphins—they sneered and gave us a wide berth—and said she should hold her head up high and waddle about the fatso-hating world proudly, because I was Zorro and Prince Charming and Vic Tanny rolled into one, and I would protect her always, for she was a most precious jewel. Between romantic slow songs I led her back to the folding table and held her napkin, and as she scarfed down each handful of Cheez-Its and Fig Newtons I said my love for her would be just as good, as sweet, as salty, as pleasing.

Outside, I walked her down the dark streets home.

"Look at the bejeweled sky!" I said, pointing to the stars, satellites, and twinkling airplanes.

My love looked where I pointed but said nothing.

"Hey now, look at that car," I said, trying to keep it light. "You figure it's a new Buick?"

My love was so taken by my banter that she remained dumb.

"Well, my fairest turtledove," I said, "looks like we're here."

Because there we stood, in front of her house on Olive Street, right next to where Mickey used to live, a few feet away from the front yard where his mother held him in her arms like Michelangelo's *Pietà*, waiting for the ambulance that would do nothing except cover his freckles with a sheet.

The wooden stairs of her porch groaned in anticipation beneath our steps. Once on the porch we shook hands like businessmen. Then the lamp inside the front room flickered behind the drawn blinds, and then Harold, Grace's father, a red-faced sumo-wrestler great Moby Dick of a man, came out and looked at us and shook his head and smiled.

"Well, what have we here? Oh me, oh my."

"Hello and good evening," I said as politely as I could. To our right a chorus of crickets was singing "Duke of Earl" in Mrs. Jankowski's petunia bed.

"Call me Harold," Harold said as he pumped my hand.

"I'm Danny," I said.

"I know who you are."

"I'm hungry," Grace said.

"Well, Princess," Harold said, "you've sure come to the right place!" He let go of my hand and laughed. "How about a little ten o'clock snack? We've got ham, roast beef, juicy turkey breast, swiss, muenster, Velveeta, and your mother just browned a fresh batch of home fries!"

My love's eyes beamed like a lighthouse on the high seas.

Harold grinned and cracked his knuckles. "We've got the horn of plenty, and there's room at the table for an extra plate. Care to join us, Scout?"

"No thank you." Then I made a little bow and ran away.

Knowledge is power, son. As I ran up the half-block to my house, I saw at once that the path to my true love's heart was via the vacuum cleaner of her stomach. So the next night, at the next party, I arrived prepared.

With pockets full of melts-in-your-mouth not-in-your-hand M&M's, jelly beans of every color in the rainbow, Bit-O-Honeys, palm-sized pound cakes, miniature marshmallows, Sugar Babies, and endless miles of red licorice whips that I cracked in the air like a lion tamer as Grace and I twisted and more or less partied down.

She was pleasant though still very quiet company. A natural dancer, once Grace planted her feet and bent her arms and cocked her torso and let go, the laws of physics took over and her body seemed to dance all by itself, rippling like a Slinky toy from feet to head, head to feet, with a tiny smile on her face. Miss Dance With This and Pepperoni Face threw insults and popcorn at us for a while, then reestablished dominion over the snack table, occasionally turning back toward me with a bark. The others ignored us, coldest shoulder.

I could think only of my Grace, my flesh-and-blood living girlfriend. So I danced, Timothy Mouse alongside Mrs. Jumbo. And she gobbled up all my treats, and the boys unscrewed a few of the light bulbs, and the girls put on a flapjack stack of romantic 45s. We walked home, now holding hands, to fat Harold and his private delicatessen. I ran away, wild.

I'd sit on my front porch, staring up at the dark bejeweled sky, and in place of romance all I'd be able to think of was eating. Even the sounds of the evening's insects changed from song to pigging out. Was that what life was all about? I wondered. I had no appetite, except for love. I wished on every falling star, satellite, and twinkling airplane that my love could change like Cinderella into a normal girl. Cinderella, ha! I thought. I was in love with Blubberella. Two-Ton Baker. Fatty Arbuckle, and God-Bless-America Kate Smith rolled in butter and cream cheese. I was unhappy, son. Don't let anyone ever tell you that first love is easy.

So I tried not going to the next stupid party, but I couldn't keep myself away. Then I asked all the other girls to dance again but no one, not even somebody's fifth-grade little sister wearing braces and pajamas, would have me.

It was clear to me. My fate was sealed.

Thus I launched my all-out attack on Grace Jankowski, who sometimes I absolutely ached for and other times, I'm grieved to say, I nearly hated, until I discovered the aphrodisiac that made her blue eyes wild.

It was chocolate, pure sweet chocolate, richer and darker than even the sin that stained my soul. Her Everest, her Matterhorn, her snowy Kilimanjaro could be ascended if you fed her chocolate. So I bought out entire drugstores with Louie's dimes and filled my arms with Fannie Mae Assorteds and Whitman Samplers, stuffing my love like a Thanksgiving turkey until a drool thicker than refrigerated Hershey's Syrup trickled from the sides of her mouth. I was intent on kissing that mouth, and after the last graduation party she let me.

She motioned for Harold to go back inside, then unwrapped a pound box of Brach Cream Centers. I lunged for her lips a few moments later, after she'd finished the top layer. As our mouths met I heard her swallow. She held the kiss, her lips moving ever so softly against mine. All over the universe, comets exploded and fell to the sea.

Imagine how a death-row murderer on his way down the corridor to the electric chair would feel if suddenly the warden burst through a side door waving a sheet of paper and shouted, "It's your pardon! Plus you've just won the New Jersey lottery!"

Kissing Grace Marie Jankowski for the first time felt like that, son. My silly metaphors don't do it justice. Kissing her felt *better* than that. It shamed any dime-store-romance virgin's swoon.

A very strange thing happened then, during the eternal moments of that first kiss. I completely forgot that Grace was bigger than the Goodyear blimp, larger than a six-flat, broader than the Field Museum. She actually felt small, timid, excited—like a frightened gazelle in my arms.

A cool breeze from the lakefront stirred us. "God gave you the right name," I whispered.

"What?" she whispered back.

We kissed a second time. I cannot describe the pleasure.

"Grace," I said. "You're full of grace."

"Oh," she said. Chocolate and kisses were loosening her tongue. "Oh, I thought you meant Jankowski."

1 **2** 3 4 5 6 7 8 9

BACK IN THE DUGOUT

See, I'd stand right next to the garbage cans, trying to blend in with the scenery, and I'd watch them until it hurt, until silly crocodile tears splashed from my eyes.

They'd say, "Hiya, Danny," or "Whatcha know, 'Galupo?," or "You ain't still contagious, are ya?" I'd nod, shrug, shake my head. They'd toss the ball to one another, skipping past me, slipping into the excitement and fun of that day's game. Forgetting me. Forgetting who they were. Becoming their favorite major leaguer. Some boys crammed wads of bubble gum into their cheek and pretended it was chewing tobacco and they were Nellie Fox. Some held the bat straight up in the air and tried to snap their wrists like Ernie Banks. "We're the Cubs!" "We're the White Sox!" "They're a bunch of bums!" "No, *they're* the bums!" Joey Petrovich shouting, "All right youse guys, let's hear a little chatter in the infield!" All the guys behind him punching their mitts, laughing. "Hey, no batter, no batter." I'd let my voice, a whisper growing louder, join and try to lead theirs. "C'mon, swing, batter, swing, no batter, swing, you strikeout king, you stupid chump, take a dump, camel's hump, measles and mumps, hey batter, no batter, no batter!"

Joey windmilling his pitching arm as if it were the Gay Nineties. The kid behind the cardboard plate making believe he was flashing real signs. One of the guys on the bench putting his fist to his mouth and saying in his deepest garble, "Now announcing, the first batter for the Olive Street Alley League, numbah seventeen, Lenny Sak-oh-wicz!" The fielders dancing forward on their toes. Lenny's cue-ball biceps bouncing as he waved the bat. Me, watching from down by the oil drums, shooing away the damn garbage flies, wiping the tears from my stupid leaking peepers.

I still can smell that moment, son. The sickly sweet aroma of fruit rotting in the cans heated by the sun. The sour scent of milk cartons. The harsher stink of meat scraps getting leathery on the bone. The boys' gentle sweat, the pungent fumes of fresh dog or cat shit, the dizzy exhaust from an automobile momentarily stopping the game as the car idles in the outfield while someone's father unlocks a garage. The tired peppery smell the alley got when the wind blew from the south, carrying all of the South Side's industry and even some of the sulfur from the smokestacks and flaming chimneys of East Chicago and Gary, Indiana.

Watch the ball closely and you'll see its laces spin. Frankie skies it, right at a cartoon cloud. Winky runs back, pounds his glove, waits. Pigeons flap away from a nearby garage roof. From someone's backyard a dog barks. We had no rules about balls that hit birds in flight, though *ricochets are fair in play* might make a convincing argument. Meanwhile, Frankie's black high-topped sneakers struggle to get around the bases. Leave the memory as it is. Let the ball go uncaught, the boy with the brace continue to dream he's hit a homer. Let these kids in my past play, oblivious to everything around them but the joyous mindlessness of the game.

I watch, so hungry to be with them, to be one of them again, that my mouth salivates a sixth Great Lake. Life cannot be all bad, I think, if there is this: spring's high unblinking sun and kids in caps, white T-shirts, pants so old that moms no longer care what happens to them. If there are floppy mitts, bases, an uncracked bat, and the most graceful object anybody could ever make. A baseball.

So when I picked up somebody's forgotten glove and put it on and punched its pocket and spat and stepped onto the playing field, concentrating with every burning calorie in my recently sick body, nobody said a thing. Then time began to move again. The clock grew arms and legs that whirled about the alley as I positioned myself for the next batted ball. Joey's arm circled the wonderful air. Skeeter grimaced and swung from his heels. My body reacted without my mind telling it to as my glove leapt to my left and intersected the sudden white blur of the liner, and the ball stuck, my palm buzzing with the sweetest pain a defensive player can know.

"Way to go!" they shouted.

"Whata catch!"

"Good move, 'Galupo, way to move!"

Then they ran from the field to take their turn at the plate. And I, unthinkingly, ran in a few steps too. But then I stopped, son. Because all at once the alley had the queerest, most bitter lemon-and-tomcat-spray smell. In a word: fear. It clouded my playmates' eyes like milk. It spread over the ground like hissing tear gas. It ricocheted from garbage can to garbage can, garage door to garage door, with nothing fair about it. No, this odor was as foul as February's thawing dead squirrels, as real as a bed of limestone, as paralyzing as Frankie's polio. Their cloudy dead fisheyes said it. I'd murdered Mickey Meenan. Suddenly everyone remembered. The guys stared at their hands, their shoes, the ground.

Because they didn't want to die.

So I turned, slower than Old Lady Misiak on her way to the

drugstore to refill her rheumatism pills prescription, then stared at the mitt I'd tossed to the asphalt. It was so quiet I could hear the leaves in the trees beside the alley breathing. I bent and picked up the glove, put it on, spat high in the air, pounded the mitt with my fist. Then I shouted with hope, "Come on, you Rat Squill fuckers, let's go!"

Maybe it was the profanity, maybe the shrill desperation in my voice. But everybody laughed. And then, like in a game of freeze, everyone unfroze. Lenny and Skeeter and the others ran out to the field. Winky swung the bat with vicious cuts. Joey wiped the sweat from his forehead. I stayed where I was, at deep short, my career as Perpetual Fielder having begun.

"Rat fuckers," everybody laughed.

"Rat Squill fuckers!" I corrected them. "You gotta add the squill for the rat kill. Fuck! Suck! Duck!"

"Whatdya say, team?" said Lenny, who was pitching.

"No batter, mad hatter, whatsa matter, let's play some base-ball here!" I shouted. "C'mon, you gutless wonders, hitless blun-ders, lightning thunders. Try and hit it past me, I dare you on your mother's eye! Apple pie, corned beef on rye, turkeys can't fly, try and make me die, let's go-o-o-o!"

They did. And everybody, even Frankie, swung for me from that day on, trying to hit hot liners that would slice the air with a deadly *shhhhh*, that would shut my mouth, bounce off me, off my chest, my head, my neck. I turned into a real ball hog, trying to get to everything. I dove like a torpedo to my left. I charged line drives. I goaded them to aim for me. "C'mon, smash it off me. I'm Puffed Wheat, shot from guns. Puffed Rice, don't be nice. I'll pay the price, you chumps, you donkey rumps." Son, they went for me and my nonstop mouth like I was the only duck in the shooting gallery. Because it was a league of line-drive sluggos. And because that was somehow fair, that they try to kill me the same way I'd killed the Meenan kid.

Sure, we talked about it. Because I wouldn't let them forget—

on the field sometimes forcing myself to stand as still as a tombstone, trying to dream about an Eiffel Tower of comic books, an F.A.O. Schwarz of unbroken toys. I'd let hard one-bouncers slap my cheeks. "Was he standing like this?" I'd yell, slumping over with the dopiest Maynard G. Krebs look I could put on my face. "Naw," they'd shout, "bend a little more." I'd bend, then stick my finger in my ear, drop my jaw open, drool. "Who wants to eat my earwax?" Whenever the ball cracked off my cap I got the loudest laughs.

"Great green gobs of greasy grimy gopher guts," I'd sing, "mutilated monkey meat, little birdies' dirty feet. Great green gobs of greasy grimy gopher guts, and I forgot my spoon, aw shucks!"

"You're sickening," they'd tell me after a game. They'd grin at me, shake their heads.

"You think *I'm* sickening?" I'd say. "What about *him*, what he did? You know, kicking the bucket like that?" I'd kick the nearest garbage can. "Man, he was dumber than a baboon's red butt."

"Remember the time he lugged that dead alley cat around in his little red wagon?" one of the guys would say.

"Hey, yeah, one of Misiak's. Rudolph. Got squashed by the CTA."

"It was stiffer than a board, remember? Musta been at least a week dead. We asked him what he was gonna do with it."

"Make Irish stew," I'd say. "Whatdya think?"

"Naw, he was on his way home to bury the thing."

"He was picking its earwax and eating its maggots," I'd say.

"He was crazy. He usedta bury everything. Birds, goldfish, worms."

"Maggots are real high in protein," I'd say.

"He even buried mosquitoes after he slapped 'em too hard."

"Naw," I'd say, "he ate 'em. If you eat earwax you'll eat anything."

"He had that little cemetery, remember? Way back in the corner of his yard. Remember all them little crosses he made out of toothpicks?"

"But his favorite meal of all," I'd say, "was Adam's apples. Breakfast, lunch, and dinner. Yum, yum!" Then I'd swallow, or try to, then roll my eyes back into my head and fall to my knees without a sound. I'd hold my breath so I could turn blue and say, "K-k-k-k," and everybody would forget about Mickey's cemetery and laugh.

They came to call it *doing a Mickey*, and some of them tried it too, but everyone agreed my impersonation was the best. Pretty soon whenever anybody did something stupid or uncoordinated or funny, it was *doing a Mickey*. "Hey 'Galupo, do a Mickey on this play!" So I'd roll back my eyes and pinch my pants like I had to pee, and they'd chuckle and the pitcher would put an easy arc on the ball, and the batter would cream me, absolutely wipe me out, knock the ball right off my chest, giving me so many bruises and welts that my ma took me to the fat doctor, who told me baseball wasn't supposed to be a contact sport.

And I was critical of Grace's mooing? How easy it is to see the faults of others, to be blind to those same faults in yourself.

Perhaps I exaggerate the amount of time I spent being ghoulish. I can't overstate the fear I felt, the guilty fluttering in my stomach and the depths of my bowels. I thought that joking would help drive the ghost away. So I renamed things: Lucky Green, the garage door Mickey played, became the Door to Heaven, then Heaven's Door, then Heaven's Whore. I called the spot on the ground where he slumped Mister Death.

"Tap it for luck," I'd shout when a guy really needed a hit. "Give old Mister Death a rub. Give Heaven's Whore a kiss."

No, I don't exaggerate.

"You're deader than Mickey," I shouted when I tagged a runner out.

"Worm food," I cried when I gobbled up a grounder. "Maggot

meal. Munch, munch, munch, oh yummy. Flies lay their eggs inside his eyes."

"Here's a fly for you," the guys would say, popping up or throwing the baseball high into the air.

"I got it, I got it." Running backward, my arms waving the others away. The ball would drop from the clouds and I'd pretend to be able to catch it, then at the last instant fake a trip and drop my hands. I'd let the ball hit off my back or the top of my head. Everyone always laughed.

I guess I'm losing points with you, son. Slipping from the story's hero to its fool. But errors are just as much part of the game as come-from-behind homers.

Some of the time—no, much of the time—I played as well as I was able. The grin fell from my face. I readied my hands. I waited on the balls of my feet. I concentrated with a desire so fierce that everyone else could feel it, could smell it, as I stared at the ball in the pitcher's hands and *willed* it, as absolutely as Mother Superior stopping a running first grader in the hall, to come to me. It would, and I'd make the play.

I'd dive to my left and snare the sinking line drive. I'd leap like a jack-in-the-box and stop the ball over my head. My throws were sure, on time. Going to my right was more difficult than any other play, so I practiced.

The trick was all in the footwork, I realized. Your instinct is to step toward the ball with your right foot, but that just throws your balance off. Your first move has to be with your left foot, a cross-step. So each night when I was supposed to be doing my homework down in the basement I took out Rosaria's old jump rope and skipped until I'd counted to one thousand, then worked on my footwork with an imaginary ball and mitt, going to my right and making the play, going to my right and making the play.

The thing is to work against your weaknesses, I told myself. Rather than hide them, make each weakness a strength. Then your new weaknesses would be your former strengths, and you could strengthen them even further. And then no one would ever own you, I figured, and you'd become all sorts of great things, whatever you dreamed you'd like to be, able to rise from little Olive Street like a Cape Canaveral rocket.

So I skipped rope in the basement, my feet whirling like Ma's Mixmaster. I went to my right and made every play. I believed with all my heart that I could make perfection a habit.

Let's skip ahead.

Past graduation and Grace's great kiss to my dad and his not-so-great graduation speech.

If anything ever was capable of crushing me, it was my father, the thick-shouldered Mount Etna who could reduce me to a sniveling bag of teat-hungry whimpers with a single nod, shake of his head, or gaze. I can't fully explain it, the power fathers have over sons. I know only that it's there, as surely as there are wolves and the *strega* in the forests of Italian folktales. Maybe it's that the boy constantly sees his reflection through his father's eyes. Maybe it's a feeling of always being measured, judged. At some crucial point the mother fades into the wallpaper. Her approval matters about as much as a kitchen chair. The only opinion in the world that counts then is the father's opinion. In the universe of childhood there's a shifting so vital it wrenches the stars.

I remember when I took my high-school placement tests and I came across this question: *Father* is to *son* as *blank* is to *blank*.

What I thought should be there: ticking croc to Captain Hook, glowing green kryptonite to Superman, silver-tipped bullet to Dracula.

My dad's grip held our family of nine together like Super Glue. When I think of him even today, I think of a closed fist. No bones about it, son, the man was strong. Though Ma was the sun whom we planets circled continuously, and who warmed us, and sometimes scorched us, with the steam iron of her love, Dad was gravity and the rest of Newton's physics. He was

J. Edgar Hoover and Rocky Marciano with tired blue eyes, gray hair, and a gun-metal-gray lunch pail. Our solar system had no choice but to obey his laws.

The story of his life makes Horatio Alger seem listless. Francis Alfred Bacigalupo appears first as a skinny boy leading his dirt-ignorant parents and six little brothers and sisters through the Babel of Ellis Island to Brooklyn, where he not only mastered the American language and became translator and arbiter for an entire neighborhood of pasta eaters but worked two jobs and went to school, juggling the flaming torches of time, work, and ambition like a center-ring act in Barnum and Bailey.

If he was anything then, he was good. He'd give you the shirt off his back, then figure out a way to get two more shirts so he'd be better prepared the next time.

Here the tale becomes metaphorical. At the standing-room-only weddings of third cousins, my father's closest friends, his *compari*, would pull me over and say that once upon a time my old man was the craftiest guy alive. Danilo, they'd say, if you only knew.

Knew what? I'm all ears, tell me.

They'd look at one another, raise their eyebrows. Well, let's just say that way back when, your old man tricked the fox into giving him its winter coat. They'd laugh. Then he talked the fox into thinking it wasn't naked. How? I'd ask. How do ya think? they'd answer. Brains! Then they'd give the back of my head a squeeze and say, Oh, if only you had half as much.

What I could glean at the time from this was that my father's ingenuity somehow brought him riches, which he shared eventually with just about every family at the wedding. It had made him a pretty popular guy.

Don't put bloody horse heads and Don Corleone into this story, son. My dad's expert ball handling had nothing to do with so-called godfathers. The wolf kisser tricked the fox, then tricked him into thinking he'd never been tricked. Grand slam? Unassisted triple play? Whatever, it wasn't easy.

Easy wasn't a word in his vocabulary. The first word in his dictionary was *work*. The second and third, *fair wages*. Let's turn the pages. *An injury to one is an injury to all. Workers of the world unite. Labor is entitled to all it produces. One big union, one big strike.*

Now you can begin to understand why the *compari* veiled his early years with metaphor. My father was a Socialist! Hush! The rat lurking in the corner with the tape recorder is Joe McCarthy!

See, he was busy pulling himself and his family up by their bootstraps when one day he met Lucy Paradiso, raven-haired beauty, sweatshop seamstress. Their union led to love and a clash with the sweatshop's management. Francis settled the walkout successfully. Then he became a factory-gate orator, then a labor organizer, then a contract negotiator and architect. Big Business was the fox; his wages from the union, the winter coat.

He could have gone as high in the union as he wanted. But his thinking was too red. He led a not-bloodless wildcat that brought in the company goons, whose guns shot real bullets, and he and my mother were chased across the map: through the swamps of New Jersey, over the hills of Pennsylvania, across the flatlands of Ohio and Indiana, to the gray smokestacks of Chicago, toddlin' town, but crowded and busy and ethnic enough to conceal them inside its big shoulders. There my father hid, ostrich with his head stuck in the sand of two menial jobs. He'd lost twice, see? Democratic socialism didn't take, and he'd sliced his own neck with the union, which was learning to fox-trot with fat-cat capitalism and like it.

Europe's face broke out again with the blackheads of war. He enlisted. Lucy worked in a munitions plant. My father's orders took him through the Pacific. Wild horses can't drag these stories out of him either, but Ma once hinted there were snapshots buried in drawers she no longer opened, a box of decorations she didn't have the time to find somewhere in the basement or the garage. I searched for them but found only an unreadable Catholic couple's manual of sex and a scrap of paper that had a picture of a laughing rat standing on the horrible word *SCAB*.

After God had finished the rattlesnake, the toad, and the vampire, He had some awful substance left with which He made a SCAB. A SCAB is a two-legged animal with a corkscrew soul, a water-logged brain, and a combination backbone made of jelly and glue. Where others have hearts he carries a tumor of rotten principles. A strikebreaker is a traitor to God, his country, his family, and his class.

> Jack London, author

Like the other survivors who returned to their countries in 1945, my dad married the future and buried the past. He paid the pot's fresh ante with the sweat of his back, hoping now to fill his hand with a straight flush of steady employment. But unlike the others, his dreams were dead. Life had no taste in his mouth. The events that took him from the Mediterranean to the States, then around the warring globe, made him grow weary and old.

Unless it was a weekend, we never ate with him. We sat at the kitchen table, ignoring his empty chair, trying not to be giddy with relief. Because as soon as he walked in the back door from his second job, the entire house changed. The air we breathed grew thicker. Each room he entered darkened. His exhaustion made us feel shame. He was our tired father, wanting only to wash and have his supper in peace and quiet. And we—we were noisy insects, grasshoppers full of useless play.

Nothing we did pleased him. So we ran away when we heard him coming, lest he see us and remember something we had done wrong or altogether forgot. Often he hit us when he remembered something, though he never hit us very hard. Worse, he gave us lectures, ridiculing us with an avalanche of words until our cheeks flamed with worthlessness. When the garage door slammed each evening, Ma stood automatically to warm his food, and we hushed one another and scurried from the kitchen like silly mice.

Why was it that he could have such compassion for the masses, and such difficulty in expressing his love for us? Was it because he felt as if he'd failed? Like we wouldn't love him if we knew? Or had something essential in him broken, like a good bat sawed off at your wrists by a blazing fastball?

It was my responsibility, as oldest child, to greet him. I dreaded it, son, for usually he met me with disappointment in his eyes. I knew he saw me as the lazy boy who frittered away his precious time playing baseball. As he'd bend to kiss me, dirt lining his face, sweetly smelling of sweat, his whiskers would scrape my cheek. The others would watch, waiting in a line that stretched behind me down the hall. "Your supper will be ready in five minutes," Ma would say. "How was your day?" He seldom answered. He'd kiss everyone, saying nothing, then wash and change into clean clothes in the bathroom.

Maybe I should have greeted him in the alley, pasted on a happy-go-lucky smile, taken his lunch pail, led him by the hand to the house, and filled his ear with warm anecdotes from my day's adventures.

"Guess what, Pop? I killed a neighbor boy today!"

But he was a stranger to me, and I was cowardly.

If fault is to be given, it was both our faults. Neither of us was wrong; *we* just weren't right. Because he was too busy providing us with shoes, blankets, daily loaves of Gonnella bread; and I was scared of him, understand, because I'd let him down when I hit the line drive that only Mister Death could catch.

"Danilo," he said to me the evening I graduated, the day after I'd kissed Grace. I stood in the boys' room, whistling "Zip-a-Dee-Doo-Dah" and staring at my sheepskin. "Danilo, on a day like today there are things a father must say to his son."

My heart pounded. Golly! I could tell from his syntax he'd give me a lecture. He turned and walked to the front room, his shoulders sagging. I followed him and sat down.

"Danilo, my son." He bit his lips. "On an occasion like this, well, a father should say something about the brightness of the future." He gestured toward the ceiling. "When life seems to open before you like a beautiful rare garden." His hand closed on the air. "You want to seize the roses in your hands, to fill your eyes with their colors, your nose with their sweet aromas. Your mouth waters at the sight of life's delicious fruits dangling from the bushes and the trees. All your senses are inflamed. That is youth, Danilo. Your belly rumbles. That's ambition. Fruit falls from the trees' highest branches, landing in the palm of your hand. Opportunity. So you fill your belly with the sweetness of this finest of orchards, and you leave some fruit on the trees for others, and you put some into your pockets for tomorrow, for rainy days. That's wisdom, Danilo. Do you understand? I'm saying four things." He made four fingers, then ticked each off as he spoke. "Youth, ambition, opportunity, wisdom."

I didn't understand, but I nodded anyway. He nodded too, then turned away. He didn't sit, so he had the whole room to pace. For a few moments he paced. Then he again faced me.

"Then all that's needed is to pull these four fingers together into a strong and powerful fist." He made a fist, waved it at me. "And what pulls them together? Make a fist of your hand, Danilo. You tell me."

I made a fist. I couldn't tell him.

"Watch me as I do it, then," he said. "See, I close my fingers, see, then hold them to my palm with my thumb." He pointed his thumb at me. "The thumb is what we used to call *figatu*. It means the strength you have inside, what some nowadays call guts." His fist touched his stomach, then rose in the air. "Your guts hold the hand of your life together and make you into a hard fist that can knock softly and politely on anyone's door or smash down any man who stands in your way. But if you've got no thumb, your fingers fly apart and you're left with nothing. Just an empty palm. See?" He made his fingers fly apart. "I knock on the door, but I have no *figatu* so my fingers fly apart." His hand touched his mouth. "You can see this even in newborn babies. Those that are sick hold their hands open, limp. There's nothing anyone can do. But the ones that live are born with fists, real tight ones. You stick your finger in and they hold on! Do you understand, Danilo?"

I nodded again, my hands opening and closing into fists.

He walked to the front windows. I thought the speech was over. I felt confused, but also good and proud, because I could tell that he'd worked a lot on it and maybe that meant he really did love me. I was happy at that moment, and I opened my mouth to tell him thanks. But then he turned, his blue eyes filled with ice, his thin lips turned down into a frown.

"I try to understand you, Danilo. I put myself into your place and try to think and feel." He shook his head. "Your mother tells me, 'Francis, have feelings. He's only a boy, give him time.' So I gave you time." He let out a breath. "How long has it been now? Five years? A little over five years? For what? You tell me. You don't even know! You don't have the least idea! 'Who is he?' I ask your mother. 'Are you really sure he's not the milkman's boy? The butcher's up on Clark Street? Maybe when he was a baby you took him outside and somebody stole my son from the buggy and left you this.' 'No,' your mother tells me. 'You're talking foolishness,' she tells me."

"What?" I said. "What did I do?"

"It's what you didn't do, Danilo. What you *didn't* do."

I held back my tears and stared at my hands.

"No one blames you," he was saying to the window. "Things happen. Life is often strange." He looked at the walls now, pacing, then he stood above me. "Sometimes children disappear. They fall into the well and drown. They sleep in the village stable and the donkey decides to sit on them. Accidents have their own way of taking place. No one is blaming you for the accident. But even someone from the most backward jungle who has never had the benefit of a family would know that if you play a part in one of these strange twists of fate, you must have the human decency to pay your own respects." He took a deep breath. "To pull your fingers together with your thumb and knock softly on their door and tell them that you grieve for them, that you can never repay them, that your head hangs before them in shame. A dog would know enough to do that! Do you think it was easy for your mother and me to do it for you? Do you think it was pleasant? I don't mean that first night—that night we went because we wanted to, because we had to, because we were your parents and a thing like that is done. But later, Danilo! After you were finished with your fever! Before they moved away in great sorrow, while the blood of their grief was still fresh."

My head hung to my knees. Tears dripped silently to the carpet.

"All you had to do was go out the door, walk down a few houses, go up their steps, say you were sorry. They weren't asking for the moon. They'd have cried a little, sure, like any parents. But they didn't blame you. They even wanted to give you some of his playthings, toys and books they wanted out of their house. And they wanted you to know that he was already very sick and wouldn't have lived too long anyway. Some kind of disease of the blood. They wanted to tell you he liked you, Danilo—why you, I don't know, you must have done something nice for him once, been kind, let him play, I don't know. But the fact is they waited for your visit. Even after they moved, they waited. And we could say nothing to you because, if it was to be, it would have to come from you."

I wiped my eyes, trying not to sniffle.

"Sure, you got sick," he continued. "They had me going over there every night to tell them what the doctor had to say. The mother was very worried it meant you were going to die too. The father said it would give you time to think. And then you got well and they rejoiced, and then you went back to school and out on the streets to play. And they waited, Danilo. I'd visit

62

them and they'd ask me what was the matter this time. Where was your decency, your respect? 'Is Danny with you tonight, Francis?' they'd ask me. 'Will he be coming over later?' 'You've promised not to say a word, it has to be from him.' 'Yes,' I'd answer, 'I know I promised. But please remember he's only a boy.' I could see how impatient they were growing. 'Only a boy?' they'd say. 'Has he no feelings? Did the fever make him forget our address?' From their windows they watched you talk to the kids out on the street. They saw you join their games in the alley. 'He's no good,' they told me the night before they moved. 'He's missing something in his heart, like our boy had something missing in his blood.' 'You better watch him like a hawk,' the father told me, man to man. 'He's a rotten apple. We heard him this afternoon playing. He feels nothing for what he did to our son. To him, it's just a big joke. You keep an eye on that one. This is just the start of your miseries.' "

My hands hung limp. I'd cried myself dry.

"So," my father said, "happy graduation day, Danilo. Now you're not a child anymore."

He towered above me, not blinking an eye.

"I can still find them," I said. "There's still time!"

"No," he said. He looked like he wanted to spit. "Don't fool yourself. You had your chance and it slipped through your fingers. Don't think you can shoe the horse after he's stumbled and broken his leg."

"But, Dad—"

"But nothing, Danilo. It's late. I have to work in the morning. Wash your face and go to bed."

That night I peed out my distress on Dominic and Gino. They woke up, angry as roused bears, and first blamed each other. Then both looked at me and pushed me from the bed. "Sleep with the babies," they said. Dad treated me as if nothing happened. Each night he kissed me, his whiskers barely scraping my cheek. Then I'd run to see Grace.

We'd walk around the neighborhood—I'd listen as she talked—sometimes ending up at the playground on Bryn Mawr, where she'd watch me run around the field house or do chin-ups on the monkey bars. After a few weeks I took her to a burger stand where she inhaled, like Popeye's friend Wimpy, all the two of us could afford. Then I hurried her past her front porch to the darkness of her gangway, where we stood beneath a dripping air-conditioner and gave each other improvisational lessons in the art of french kissing.

"Mmmm-mmm," I said, "that was nice. But maybe we're supposed to move our tongues around a little? You know? Not just squeeze them together?"

"If I had a friend," Grace said, "I'd tell her all about you. We could talk on the phone. I'd tell her everything!"

"Tell me," I said. "But this time, let's move tongues!"

"Don't be in such a hurry."

"Who, me? I ain't in a hurry."

"Don't you think it would be wonderful if you had a friend?"

I thought about it, dodging a drip from the humming A/C above me. "No. Not really. I mean, what good are they anyway? You don't need them."

"Sure you do, Danny. Everybody needs friends. I think they're the most important thing in the world. Like, if I had a friend I could tell her all the nice things you say, and we could *share*, you know what I mean?"

"I'm no dummy, little turtledove. I know what 'share' means. It means you divvy up. Like if we had a burger right here in front of us we'd split it, but it would be OK if you ate it all. C'mon, let's kiss."

"No, Danny. It means you give. And what you give is the greatest gift, the gift of self."

"Hey, that's nice, Grace. That's poetry."

"Don't be sarcastic. You need friends too."

"Sure, so I could yak on the phone with them."

"No, so you'd be happy." She looked away from me then, staring up at the glittering universe. "It's hard for a girl like me to have friends, you know what I mean? When you have a weight problem? Normal girls don't want to be my friend because then if we're on our way somewhere, like we're going shopping down-town maybe or just out on the street walking, and we see some boys, the boys won't want to talk to us. That's all that girls think about. Boys."

"Why wouldn't they want to talk to you? I'd talk to you."

"Because all boys think about is girls. Skinny girls, girls like Deirdre Egan. Not fat pigs."

"You're not a pig. You're just a girl blessed with a very abun-dant and beautiful body. C'mon, kiss me."

"But you didn't talk to me until all the other girls laughed at you."

"Grace, I was saving best for last."

"Danny, last Sunday in church when my father and mother and I sat down we cracked the pew."

"Faulty carpentry, Grace. I know exactly the one you mean. I nearly cracked it the other week with my mother and Tina and Rosaria."

"Don't make up lies for me, Danny. Don't talk down to me. Don't deny me." She was getting mad. Her molars were grinding away, and she was starting to breathe like a chugging train. I knew even back then that anger wasn't very conducive foreplay to french kissing. "Don't pretend I'm any less or anything more than I am. I can read a bathroom scale, you know. I can stand in front of the mirror. I know what it's like trying to find a decent-looking dress in my size. I've got eyes. I've got feelings. I'm human."

"Beautiful eyes," I said.

They were the right words, son. They made Grace's anger and frustration flicker off for a moment, then disappear like sum-mer fireflies. "The most beautiful eyes a girl could have," I said.

"Eyes that artists paint real lovely pictures of. Eyes so full of beauty and lovely feelings that they make you look as pretty as tiny little Tinkerbell."

She melted like butter on the Sahara, rolling her head to one shoulder and opening her arms. Whispering, "Kiss me, my fair foolish prince."

Our kiss was so French that for a minute or two we wore berets and sipped champagne in a sidewalk café on Rue de la Rapture.

Then I drifted through new-student orientation at Saint Paul's High, an all-boys outfit run by the Christian Brothers. They were a well-meaning bunch of guys who wore black dresses and little white bibs beneath their necks.

Like nuns they vowed poverty, chastity, and obedience. Unlike priests they couldn't bless or consecrate a thing. They talked a whole lot about the Jesuits, so much they made you wonder why they didn't sign up with them. They believed that boys turned rotten as Lampwick if they spared the rod. So they swung fat fraternity paddles (*boards of education*, they called them) with which they warmed our brainpans. Licks always came in doses divisible by six. They never let us forget we were poor boys, because their founder, Saint John Baptist de la Salle, started them up centuries ago specifically to teach the shoeless and starving, and anyway, they said, all the rich kids went to the Jesuits.

Even though they were a teaching order, hundreds of them in California made brandy and wine. They'd get angry and reach for their paddles when you asked them if they got free samples. They were either very old or very young, nearly bald and fat or skinny and still pimpled. The exception was Brother Gabriel, my first real baseball coach, who we'll meet a little later on.

They said sports came second to education; but to look at the school even a dope would conclude it was the other way around. Because in all three first-floor hallways there were shining trophy cases overflowing with bounty, with silver and gold statuettes, loving cups, plaques, bowls, footballs, nets cut down after championship games, dusty photos of team after team, All-City this, First-Place that. They gave you six licks if they found your greasy fingerprints smudging the glass. Near the ladies' john (the principal's gray secretary and the bursar had to pee somewhere) was the Honor Society board, growing lichen.

So after orientation I found myself on the football field.

Where giants laughed insanely and knocked their helmeted heads against the goalposts, and where sprinters far swifter than Skeeter flung back dark clods of dirt with their cleats as they zigzagged like berserk sewing-machine needles across the grass. I didn't know what to do or where to go until one of the giants noticed me and spat.

"New meat?"

I nodded.

"Da uddah end of da field!"

Then he threw himself on the ground and rolled on his neck like a lunatic having a fit. And though I knew very little about the game, I looked where he had pointed, at a dozen or so rows of fat and skinny boys dressed just like me in old sneakers, blue Saint Paul shorts, white school T-shirts.

They were listening to a man in an orange TetraMin cap, purple Hawaiian shirt, white tennis shorts. You could tell by his arms and chest he'd once been fit, only now he'd let himself get a bit flabby. Around his neck hung a whistle. His legs were hairy and tanned. His name, Coach Charlie Grieves.

"—not looking for any pussy willows. Just the best, gentlemen. I want boys who are all the way with Santa Fe. My name may not be Standard Oil, but I expect more and I'll get it! Are we on the same wavelength? We'll get along fine if you're hungry for the game, but if you're just looking for a letter so you can impress your little Kewpie doll at Immaculata, I suggest you hightail it over to the cross-country team. I want survivors, not the ones who belly-up to the top of the tank and die." He turned to me. "Excuse me, son, but I can't help but notice that you're late. I'll tolerate it once, OK? Take a place in line. So where was I? Yeah, I don't want any cream puffs. No cake eaters. This is a tough game, be-lieve me, and I'll be real sad watching you cough up your Twinkies every time we play a halfway decent team. I want meat eaters! Do you hear me? Carnivores! Kids with ketchup, mustard, relish, a taste for the game!"

Then he told us to hit the dirt. "I said *hit it*, gentlemen. Now hit it again. Harder! Harder! Let's go! Get up, only losers love the dirt! Hit it! Hate it! Harder! Good, now let's begin with some calisthenics."

Around me they dropped—sore, winded, vomiting—in a slow-motion Mickey Meenan death ballet. Grieves earned his name that first week of practice, son. He gave each of us enough grief to last a century of widows. He ran us, stretched us, threw us into the air and down to the ground. "Conditioning!" he screamed in our ear. "The very first ingredient in a winner or a good steak is conditioning!"

And as we conditioned he told us stories: how he used to own Grieves's Friendly Four-Wheel City, a used-car lot out on Cicero Avenue, but he sold it because it made his heart hurt to see all the suckers spend their nest eggs on lemons. Now he owned Grieves's Friendly Underwater World, a pet shop on Kedzie that specialized in rare and exotic tropical fish. *Hit it, that's it, once again, gentlemen!* He told us what to really look for in a convertible, why snails in a tank are never any good, how isometric exercise is better for the contemporary athlete than lifting weights, and who discovered the recipes for ketchup, mustard, and relish—all of which had something to do with winning football games. But I may have missed the point because all I could think of was how badly I wanted to belly-up and quit.

To stop. Just to stay on the burning August earth, like the other cake-eating pussy willows. Thinking about quitting enabled me to get through. My brain made little deals with my body: do one more push-up and we'll quit. So I'd do the push-up. *Faster, gentlemen!* Then my brain would renege. Another. Until practice would mercifully end and we'd limp to the mildewed locker room, where the varsity players threw their jocks at us and snapped wet towels at our bare asses and tried to catch us so they could rub Ben-Gay on our balls.

But I hung in. Because I had something to prove. That I could take it, endure, swallow all Grieves could dish out. My father was on my mind all the time. Making the team would mean something, I thought. Plus, it hurt, and hurting seemed somehow right, like that was what I was supposed to be doing.

Grieves didn't give me time to analyze the situation further. One day out of the blue he broke out the helmets and pads, proud as a new father to announce that the last pussy willow had been mowed down at the knees. We'd made it. We were too sore to cheer. Now all that remained, he told us, was filling the positions.

An upperclassman taught us how to suit up. He told us to wear our T-shirts inside out until we'd made the varsity. Never to lend someone your mouthpiece. That a single short-hair of an Immaculata senior taped inside your jock cup would make you fearless.

Then Grieves lined us up beneath a goalpost. Like Patton inspecting his troops, he walked up to each of us and looked us up and down.

"You're big and fat," he said. "You're a tackle.

"You're short and fat. Play guard.

"You." He'd hand the kid the ball. If the kid didn't drop it he'd say, "Running back."

He put the guys who were ugly or scarred on the defense. The first three kids who held the ball by its laces he made quarterbacks. The guard with the widest ass became our center. A guy with big feet and new shoes, our kicker. Finally he walked up to me.

"You're awfully skinny and none too tall."

I puffed out my chest and inched up on my tiptoes.

"I guess I'll try you out at end, son."

So I followed the other ends and began to learn patterns, drawn in the dust by a sidelined senior's crutch. Coach Grieves was busy watching his three quarterbacks drop back and try to throw. Behind him the linemen slammed their bulk into one another. The backs tried to run and hold the ball at the same time. The defense threw their scarred, ugly bodies at oversized punching bags. Bringing the defense with him, Grieves worked his way over to the ends.

"I'll throw. You catch. They try to tackle. Got it?"

When my turn came I raced up the field, made my cut, kept my eye on the ball. Grieves threw me a bullet right between my numbers. The ball brushed my fingertips, then stuck. Then I turned up the field and ran directly toward the nearest defender, dropped my shoulders, and knocked him down.

Coach Grieves blew his whistle.

"No, no, no. Let's try it again."

This time he passed just before I made my cut. The ball seemed beyond me, but I dove, fielding a strangely shaped liner with no glove, with only my bare hands. I got it on the fly. The guy defending me was nowhere near. But then I saw him and without thinking ran straight for him, again lowering my helmet and shoulders, again knocking the kid right down.

Grieves's whistle blew.

"Cheese and rice, *avoid* the tackle! One more time."

I ran, cut. He pumped his arm, didn't throw. I looked for the defender and smashed him to a heap on the ground, then got up and tackled another guy, cleanly at his knees, then went for the biggest scar-faced meatloaf charging down upon me like a demented cement truck and threw my body at his shins, causing him to fall over me with an *ooof!* and a thud so mighty it rattled every rice bowl in China.

Coach Grieves was standing over me as I got up.

"What do you think you're doing?" he shouted.

70

"I'm getting a taste for the game!" I screamed back without blinking an eye.

He smiled, then stared at the ball in his hands, then at me again, then at the three guys I had tackled.

"What's your name, son?"

"Bacigalupo, Coach."

He motioned to the manager for his clipboard.

"I eat nails and raw chicken heads for breakfast, Coach. I drink cake eaters' blood. In the third grade I murdered a kid and then got scarlet fever, and my girlfriend Grace is the fattest blimp in the world!"

"You're full of garbanzo beans, Batchagoopa."

"I'm an animal, Coach. My ma has to keep me on a leash. Bacigalupo knows no fear!" Then I beat on my chest like Tarzan and threw back my head and shrieked.

"OK, animal. Follow me."

I followed him, son, to the ring of running backs who suddenly seemed taller, stronger than me. Grieves tossed the shortest one the ball and told him to run through me like I was water. The others snarled behind their face masks and snapped their teeth. I cut down the first two at their knees, but the third went right over me until I managed to whirl, grab his jersey, and leap upon his back. Then I clung to him, sparrow on a rhino, feebly trying to trip him. He ground out another ten yards before I figured I should slip down his back like a fireman on a pole and grab his ankles. He fell to the grass and fumbled. I stepped on his helmet on my way to the ball.

My heart pounded. Grieves's whistle pierced the air. Everyone on the team had been watching.

"Gentlemen," Grieves said with a smile, "you've just witnessed instinct! No other word for it. And you're looking at our new middle linebacker and team captain of the defense!"

I beat my chest, screeched like a cage of mynas, did six steps of the cha-cha, then shouted, "Defense! defense! defense!"

We lost more games than we won.

But Coach Grieves assured us we had guts and all the other condiments of real winners as he and the yawning assistant principal handed us our letters, a woolly *P* with a yellow football sewn into its bottom loop, during the gala postseason celebration in the school cafeteria.

Olive Street wasn't impressed. Grace spooned Bosco into her mouth and asked me to open the refrigerator and see if there was any ice cream. My ma said, "That's very nice, Danny, you're late, sit down and eat." Dad stared, then closed the bathroom door. Dominic and Gino laughed and whispered, then told me my letter stood for what I slept in every night in Louie and Francis Junior's bed.

Winter iced the windows, glazed the streets, sprinkled the houses with powdered sugar. I hibernated in underheated classrooms full of sneezing boys. Grace grew a size or two fatter, and since the gangway was always too cold for even a closed-mouth kiss, we'd end up in the hothouse of her kitchen, watching Harold construct sandwiches longer than the Golden Gate Bridge.

Then I saw the notice for baseball tryouts.

Baseball! my heart sang. On a real field with genuine bases, brand-new balls, umpires who bellowed like tubas. Baseball! With fans in the stands, an actual dugout, a scoreboard of victory or defeat. Lazy flies. Screaming line drives. Sun-brushing pop-ups. Grounders I'd eat up. I was the first freshman in the drafty gym, my T-shirt inside out.

Two varsity players sauntered in, rippling their muscles and complaining about winter fat. I watched them stretch out the nets. Then a hundred other freshmen joined me in the bleachers, all of them pounding their mitts. I sat and pounded my bare hand, then got up and stretched out and was running a few laps when a big-eared Christian Brother came in wearing a St. Louis Cardinals T-shirt over his robe, and blowing his bugle of a nose.

"On your knees, boys," he said in a whisper as he folded his hankie.

We prayed an Our Father and a Hail Mary, then sat in the bleachers.

"You'll have to listen closely," he said, "because I've got a bad cold. I caught it last night when I was out walking. I was out walking because I wanted to reflect on what we'd do here today. So I decided I'd start out just by talking." He blew his nose again. You could hear him trying to work up the congestion.

"You know, when I was your age I played a lot of ball down in St. Louis, where I grew up. I played every chance I got. Little League. Pony League. I lived baseball, ate baseball, dreamed baseball. I didn't know it then, but I was standing at a fork in the path of my life. Some of you may know that the Cards drafted me in the second round. It was like the script from a Hollywood movie. Promising hometown boy, his favorite team since he was old enough to see a big-league game. Dream come true. Well, what more could you ask for?"

He raised his arms and shrugged, then began coughing. "But something was holding me back. God had other plans. I had one of those vocations the good nuns probably told you about back in grade school. Can you picture it? Here the St. Louis Cardinals were doing everything they possibly could to get me to play a game I loved and would've died for, and an inner voice was telling me to do something else! Don't think for one second I was stupid not to have signed. I did the smart thing, boys. I did what I felt was more right. I even joked to the Cardinals that they'd picked me second but God had me tagged as a first-rounder. Now, what does all of this mean to you?"

He looked up at us, real serious, then loudly sneezed all over.

"I'll answer my own question. You get used to that if you're a teacher. It means I did right by me, so maybe I'll know enough to do right by you. I pray to God I'll know who to cut, who to bench, who to play. I pray I'll know what to say whenever you come to me with your problems. I'll take an active interest in your lives and in your game, because for all I know maybe the

Cardinals, or maybe God, will want to sign one of you. And that's my job, to teach and help you. Are there any questions? No, don't call me Coach. Call me Brother Gabriel. That's been my name for nearly twenty years. No more questions? Then what do you say? Let's play ball!"

You know I made the team, but let me tell you about two difficulties.

The first was my lack of a mitt.

Evidently the tryout posters spelled out the requirement clearly, for the hundred other would-be ballplayers brought one and kept it close at hand, even when the varsity assistants beckoned them to bat. So when the assistants called my group to display its skills in the field, I took my spot glovelessly, and the first ball hit to us was to me, a few steps to my left. A sharp two-bouncer testing the octopus from Olive Street. My bare left hand flew out and stabbed it. I threw a chest-high rope to first. Then the assistant hit the next ball, a vicious line drive, directly over my head.

You do things long enough and they turn into habits. I spread my feet and leapt, expecting to spear the liner with the webbing of a glove. When the ball deflected off my fingertips, I groaned. Partly from fear it would smash my face (it didn't), partly from pain (my poor betrayed hand suddenly throbbed), and partly from embarrassment (look at the gloveless hot dog out there committing an obvious error). Meanwhile, the ball spun high into the lights behind me. I turned and saw I still had a chance to catch it before it fell. So I ran and dove. The gym's hardwood floor rushed up and kissed me. The tips of my fingers touched the sinking squib a moment before I hit the floor and bounced, blacking out into an absence of entity.

They were crouching over me when I came to. Brother Gabriel was waving a Medusa's head of fingers in my face.

"How many, how many?" he kept saying.

"Did I catch it?" It hurt to speak.

"Do you know where you are, son?"

"Third base or shortstop. Perpetual Fielder. Brother, I've really got a taste for the game!"

One of the assistants helped me to stand. Gabriel peeled my fingers from the ball. "Get him downstairs and keep an eye on him."

"No," I said, so close to crying that everything blurred again. "No, see, I've got a thick head. I'm all right. Nobody has to watch me."

"Playing without a glove like that is like trying to get through life without the sacraments."

"Bless me, Brother, for I have sinned."

Gabriel's eyes smiled and appeared to brim with tears. His hand reached out, waved the assistant away, then touched my shoulder. The gymnasium lights behind him gave his head a glowing halo, and then one of the lights twisted itself down from the ceiling and appeared to glow between us, illuminating one of the redbirds on his T-shirt. Then the little cardinal flew off its perch and did a neat somersault and smiled at me and made a fist of its wing to signal that I'd made the catch. Hemorrhaging brain cells or the presence of something else, I still don't know. But I fell to my knees.

"Hail, Gabriel! You're full of grace! The Lord is with thee!"

He took my head and cradled it against his chest, drawing my face into the still-visible glowing aura. I felt something then. A tingling. The game was filling me. It was my Annunciation of Baseball. I realized from that moment on the game would be my life.

Moved by my catch or my prayer or my tears on his T-shirt, Gabriel held my shoulder and walked me downstairs. In his office he opened a desk drawer, unlocked a metal box, and said, "Here, I played third too when I was your age." Then he brought out into the now normal light a nearly black but beautifully broken-in infielder's mitt. "You may borrow this, Daniel, though promise me you'll try to do it honor."

As he handed me the glove, I promised with all my heart. Putting it on made me feel like a newly anointed priest.

But the next afternoon he handed me my second obstacle.

"Hey, Daniel," he said with a big smile, "it's your turn to bat."

What could I do, son? What could I tell him? *No, see, the last time I touched one of these things I killed the first baseman? Sorry, Brother, but I only field?* To bat, or not to bat.

"Sure, Brother," I said, praying a speedy novena for four consecutive and absolutely unhittable balls.

But the varsity assistant who was pitching had only down-the-middle-of-the-plate strikes for me on his dance card.

"What's the matter?" Gabriel said with so much honest concern that I could feel myself blushing. "Still fuzzy from yesterday's knock on the head?"

How can you lie to a guy who unlocks his secret junk box, lends you his old mitt, talks to you more kindly than anyone ever has?

"I don't want to kill anybody," I said.

He laughed. Son, he thought it was a grand joke. He tilted his head back so far I could see that even his tonsils were laughing. Though his cold was much better, he then sniffed. "Dan, I love your moxie."

"I'm serious, Brother. A hardball's a deadly weapon."

"There aren't any blind boys out there." He pointed. "Do you see any white canes? Any seeing-eye dogs? Hey, if they can't make the play, they can always duck."

I looked and saw no blind boys. "But sometimes," I began, "sometimes you can hit the ball so hard you don't give them enough time."

It erased the smile from his face.

"Take your cuts, son," was all he said. Then he turned away.

I felt lost. I could hear the low hum of the dormant scarlet-fever bees inside my bloodstream beginning to wake up and buzz, or could it have been the sound of the gym's fluorescent lights? Anyway, the sound reminded me of all the balls I'd splashed into Lake Michigan. Then, before I realized what I was doing, my eyes were following the ball from the smirking pitcher's hand toward me and the plate. I watched the ball blur the distance between us, and I felt my shoulders and arms *swing batter, hey batter!* crease the air with my bat—my arms extending, my wrists snapping, my torso uncoiling, powered by the push from my thighs and calves strengthened by jump rope and football. Then I felt in my hands the sweet sting of an honest hit. The ball sliced the afternoon and exploded into the highest net, then fell harmlessly into the hands of an open-mouthed freshman outfielder.

"Good wood!" the angel behind me exclaimed.

Good? Son, it felt as dark and sweet as mortal sin.

Then, with the keenest edge of my Catholic logic, I figured that since one damns you to Hell for all of eternity, another can't make it that much worse. So I stayed at the plate and sprayed the gym with a dozen furious liners. None of the fielders tried to catch them with their necks. Some of my drives were caught by their mitts, but most went over the infielders' heads, crisp singles, or into the nets above the outfielders for extra bases and praise from Gabriel, who said I had as natural a swing as any he'd ever seen.

He didn't make it easy for me, son. If anything, he drove me harder than the rest. He pushed me to discover my many weaknesses.

Balls hit to my right still handcuffed me a good third of the time. I didn't have excellent or even very good foot speed on the base paths. I was a born sucker for the offspeed curve, nearly always swinging way out in front of it. I slid into the bag with too much of my body and not enough of my foot. And I didn't like to go with the pitch and hit to right, toward the first baseman, whose face (I saw) was always freckled, always innocent, whose eyes I always thought were dreaming of tidy rooms full of Lionel trains and perfectly glued battleships and stacks of comics so virginal they seemed like they'd never been read. No, I wouldn't hit the ball toward first. I pulled nearly everything. But I made the team, playing a surprising errorless season at third and leading everyone in base hits, and I took home my first two trophies, one for Best Defensive Player and the other for Most Valuable, voted on by the team.

Gabriel was named the new varsity coach at the ceremonies, so my future looked pretty bright. Coach Grieves was also moved up to the varsity, put in charge of the defense. Shaking my hand in his office that day before I left to take the bus home, he told me to stay in condition and then offered me a summer job at Grieves's Friendly Underwater World after I assured him I'd go out for football next season.

Ma kissed my cheek when I told her the news, then told me to wash and eat before it got cold. Dad listened, nodded, told me I should have argued for a dollar an hour instead of the seventy-five cents Grieves offered. Then he shut the john door. Grace squeezed my hand and rushed me into the kitchen, where Harold toasted me with a banana milkshake and then insisted I sit down and join them for a second supper with no saying no to at least third helpings of Mom Jankowski's miracle pork roast, corn, muffins, peas, bread, and two kinds of potatoes smothered in gravy and oceans of butter, melted cheese, and pint-sized globs of egg-white–enriched sour cream.

That night, once again, locked in the prison of the dreams or nightmares I could never remember the next morning when the light from the window was hazy and gray and I didn't know if I was Mickey or Danny, dead or alive, I peed out my anguish on Louie and Francis Junior.

There was so much clutter on our dresser already, so much mess, so much to clean, that Ma put my two trophies in the hallway closet, along with the mothballs and our winter clothes.

THE ON-DECK CIRCLE

Sure, my world was far from perfect, but I could deal with it.

The teams I belonged to had both finished just under .500, which seemed about right. Mediocrity felt safe, assuring. But then overnight we began to do something peculiar. We played way over our heads and started to win.

Two in a row. All right! Three in a row. Hey, get a load of us! Five in a row. You know, I never doubted it for a minute.

Suddenly there was a crowd around me, and they were cheering. I lapped up the limelight and asked for more. They gave me enough to gargle with, son. All at once I was what I'd wanted to be. I'd slipped into first place. *I was a winner.*

Standing on the forty yardline with my hands on my hips, or on the edge of the infield grass, pounding my glove, I felt my head swell so much that no helmet or cap fit me. *Me*, the starting varsity middle linebacker and captain of Coach Grieves's defense that outscored the offense and won! *Me*, the starting varsity third baseman for Brother Gabriel's disciplined squad that streaked to the top! The school bought a new trophy case and grinned. Everybody suddenly loved me. Even when I needed a little help bringing down a charging fullback, or when I barreled into second with too much head and shoulder, not enough hooking hand, and they picked up the first down or slapped the tag on me and the outcome no longer looked like a sure thing, the fans forgot and shouted themselves hoarse just as long as I got my hands in the quarterback's face on the next play and forced him to throw an interception, as long as I fouled off the junk during my next at-bat and drove in the leading run.

Everybody adores and coddles a winner, son. You can tattoo that inside your forehead, deposit it in the savings and loan.

Before I show you how winning caused me to fall from Grace, let me tell you how I learned to win from my two coaches.

Though a Marquis de Sade on the practice field, in life Charlie Grieves was every bit as kind and zany as Captain Kangaroo. After I told him what my dad said about my wages, he laughed and said sure, a buck an hour it is. He gave me my very own TetraMin cap and put me in charge of the shop's hundred or so aquariums. Then he tossed me a net and told me to go scoop dead goldfish. I told him the only things I knew about fish were that they swam and when you ate them they had bones. "Then learn," he laughed and threw a big book at me, Axelrod's *Exotic Tropical Fishes.* "The names and prices are on all the tanks. When you don't know something, ask."

He talked to everybody who came into the store, each day in a different Hawaiian shirt and constantly munching on seeds and nuts. Even though we were a fish store, that summer he took in the neighborhood's sick and neurotic bird population. Sparrows with broken wings. Parakeets who plucked their chest feathers. Canaries who refused to sing. He bandaged the sparrows, sprayed the parakeets with lice killer, played the Beach Boys and Jan & Dean for the canaries. Then he filled the front of the store with parrots and finches and cockatoos. "You've got to go with what's flowing," he'd shout to me over the surfing music. "In business you adapt or shut the cash register."

That fortune would find his address sooner or later he had no doubt. His basic philosophy was that you needed to be ready for the windfall that would eventually come your way. He didn't waste his energies trying to bring the luck about. He just set the table, worked, and waited.

So he bought and sold his string of Grieves's Friendly enterprises, in the mid-fifties beginning with a grocery store on Halsted, Grieves's Friendly Foods. People had to eat, he figured. When the neighborhood went Hispanic, he changed the store's name to Grieves's Friendly Comidas. His gringo bread grew moldy on the shelf. What wouldn't spoil? he asked himself. What would keep and keep? A hardware store on Lawrence Avenue, Grieves's Friendly Nuts Bolts and Screws.

Ace undersold and killed him. So he opened Grieves's Friendly Toy Town, a hobby shop on Damen, but it did well only in December. Then he purchased the Four-Wheel City, grew sick of rolling back odometers, and then abandoned the earth altogether and tried the fish store, which during the time I knew him was just keeping his head above water.

Fortune did strike, in the guise of a timely heart attack. A week before our first game, our head coach, Hank O'Malley, sat down in the faculty lounge and sank his teeth into his life's last cheese danish. That afternoon on the field newly appointed Head Coach Grieves told us that what had happened was tragic and sad, but we should note that the man had been eating cake.

He emphasized physical conditioning above all else. We'd be a strong team, able to play a doubleheader if we had to. Strong defensive hits would cause fumbles, and some would bounce our way. Strong linemen would punch out holes, and maybe the backs would find them and at the same time hold on to the football. Swift ends would slip their coverage, and if the quarterback wasn't being gang-tackled maybe he'd get on the ball.

Our offense consisted of four basic plays. First down: Run up the middle, usually off guard, or, if the hole isn't there, off tackle. Second down: Bunch the backs and try a sweep around the end. Third down: Throw the long pass while the line tries to hold and mumbles a Hail Mary. Fourth down: Get the kid with the big feet out there and kick. Our offense executed 25 percent of its plays perfectly. We were a superb punting team.

You can fault the man for lack of imagination and predictability. But believe it or not, his drowsy consistency lulled most of our opponents to sleep. They'd figure he couldn't possibly run off guard on first down again. They'd convince themselves clever Grieves was setting them up for a big play. So they'd defense the end sweep or jam the secondary against the pass and be sucked right out of their shoelaces. And our offense would pick up yardage.

Our defense would tackle hard, administer the serious licks. We played what we called Anarchy Ball. Which meant no one chewed your ass if you played a guess. I'd study the linemen, find one who'd telegraph the play by setting up differently or looking or not looking in a certain direction. I'd shout my hunch to the team. More times than not I'd be correct. And on every play we hit them, hit them, hit them. By the second half we'd have eroded them into error. Then we'd scamper upfield with the ball. Score. Win.

You set the table and waited for it to happen in the game according to Grieves. You got yourself in the best possible physical shape and didn't try anything fancy. No halfback option passes, no fleaflicker Statue of Liberty plays. We played simple hit, grunt, punishing high-school football. We made our opponents beat themselves. And after they played us, they knew they'd played a football game.

If Grieves emphasized strength and the body, Gabriel put the accent mark on discipline and the mind. His philosophy stressed rules and fundamentals. No Anarchy Ball on his diamond. Gabriel's approach was pedagogic; his game, based on the moral idea that there are right and wrong ways to play. He spent the fall and winter running off dark mimeographed sheets of *thou shalts* and *thou shalt nots*, which he gave us to commit to memory.

Under his wing we couldn't just be good ballplayers. We had to be *smart* ballplayers. Smart ballplayers never and always did certain things. They never tried to steal a base unless they had their coach's approval. They always ran out every batted ball. They never swung on 3-and-0 unless they were specifically told they could. They always knew the situation (inning, outs, men on base, count), even when on the bench. In the middle of a game he'd turn and ask you. If you didn't want to run laps till dawn, you knew. He made us know the defense when our side was up at the plate. "Ball to you, Dan, where do you go with it?" It made us be in every inning of every game.

Smart ballplayers never swung at a bad pitch, which was *any* pitch out of the strike zone. Smart ballplayers always took the ball. If the batter in front of you was given a walk, you always made the pitcher throw you a strike. Gabriel would bench a hitter for swinging on the first pitch after a walk, even if he got on safely. You could hit it over the center-field fence and he'd still sit you down.

Why? Because walks were absolutely the worst thing a pitcher could do, since one led to another, which led to a pitcher's complete unraveling. Home runs too often took the steam out of rallies and sobered the other team. Home runs were for fans, he said. Walks and singles were for smart ballplayers.

Throw strikes! was his indisputable command to our pitchers. Spot the ball, vary your speed, keep it down, nibble on the corners, sure, if you've got the arm that day, but *put the ball over the plate*. He'd tell pitchers it was better that they give up the gopher ball than issue a walk. Huh? they'd say. I should give up a homer? You bet, Gabriel would answer, because that way you make them beat you. You don't beat yourself.

Smart ballplayers didn't beat themselves. Smart ballplayers

played to the best of their God-given abilities. They even made occasional errors (we were pretty surprised to hear that!), but they were the right kind of error, the genuine boot. "You're not fielding machines," he told us. "I won't get on you if you misplay a ball. The next day in practice I'll teach you how to play it." But mental errors—*Kyrie eleison!* Forgetting the situation, throwing to the wrong base, getting picked off, missing the cut-off man. Unless someone shot you maybe five times between the eyes, there was no excuse for a mental error. Though they didn't show up in the box score, and though half the fans didn't even notice them, smart ballplayers realized that mental errors were worse than trying to catch a pop-up with your elbow.

For a while we griped and chafed. When Gabriel's big ears weren't around, we called him Commander Gabriel. But after half a dozen games we began to see that his way of doing things was the way the game was meant to be played. We didn't feel nearly as bad after we dropped a game if we played it as smart as we were able. "They sure beat us," we'd say in the locker room, then shrug. "Beat us? We got adulterated!" We started laughing off the losses, which came less frequently. Because we weren't beating ourselves, see?

Son, those games you think are in your pocket, those two-run leads going into the ninth, and your pitcher walks the lead-off hitter and the next man singles and your outfielder panics, trying for the meaningless runner going to third, and the batter takes second on the throw, and one dumb thing leads to another and you lose. . . . Those games are real hard to shake. You feel like a sea gull who's been through a major oil spill. When you had it in your hands. When you could already start to taste it.

We'd watch other teams make our old mistakes. It gave us confidence. We'd look at one another, wink. Then we'd walk up to the plate with a little more spring in our step, more snap in our bats. Out on the field we'd be faster. We'd make the games laughers, then salt them away.

Soon everyone on the team loved him. Angel Gabriel. In our minds he not only could have started for the Cards, he could've been as great as Ron Santo, as strong in the field as Brooks Robinson. A cinch All-Star. First-ballot Hall of Famer. What he gave away because of his vocation was what we all wanted to become.

Then I let my love go overboard. After practice, the bus home, supper, the whiskers on my cheek, and the thousand slaps of Rosaria's jump rope, I sat down and wrote crazy prayers that praised him and baseball.

THE BALLPLAYER'S CREED

I believe in God, the Original Leadoff Hitter, Creator of Baseball and earth, and in Jesus Christ, His only Son, our All-Star, Who was conceived by the Holy Ghost, born with a Gold Glove on His Hand, suffered under the boos of fans, was crucified in the early innings, died, and was sent to the bullpen, buried. He descended into the minors; the third season He arose again to the Big Leagues. He ascended to the Hall of Fame, sitteth at the right hand of God, the Commissioner of Baseball, from thence He shall come to call the balls and strikes on the living and the dead.

I believe in Abner Doubleday, the Holy Major Leagues, the communion of double plays, the forgiveness of errors, the resurrection of the team when we're behind in the eighth and ninth innings, and life after we hang up our spikes. Amen.

Danilo Bacigalupo, author

HAIL GABRIEL

Hail Gabriel, full of my fat girlfriend Grace! The Ball is with thee. Blessed are you among high school coaches, and blessed is the fruit of your sweat and brains, Our Team! Holy Gabriel, Coach of the Varsity, pray for us when we kick an easy grounder or miss the tag or strike out with runners in scoring position, now and at the hour of when you make us sit down on the bench. Amen.

Danilo Bacigalupo, author

"What are these drawings on the side supposed to be?" he asked the day after I'd slipped my prayers beneath his office door. We sat in his office, after practice.

"Smiling rats." I smiled. He didn't say anything. "See?" I pointed them out to him. "And I put little crosses here on their caps."

"These are rats wearing baseball caps?"

I nodded.

He took an exasperated breath. "Whatever motivated you"— he hesitated—"to write these?"

I shrugged. I thought the answer was obvious. Prayers give praise. I thought they might please him, him being a brother, a ballplayer who'd listened to his inner voice. I wanted to thank him somehow for teaching me the game's fundamentals. I hoped he'd get a laugh out of *the communion of double plays.* I said nothing. He swiveled back and forth in his chair, folding and unfolding his arms over his Benildus Club T-shirt. Then he sat still and crossed his legs. A chunk of mud fell from the rim of his heel on his left shoe.

"Dan, I really don't know what to say. I don't want to come down too hard on you, but— But these are desecrations. I'm not amused."

Then he gave me a lecture on heresy. The nuns had covered most of it in grade school but I listened anyway, then started to grow angry. For Christ's sake, I thought, can't a guy even have a little sense of humor? He was going on about how the last thing Holy Mother Church needed was to be ridiculed by her own

86

children. I reached across his desk, picked up the scraps of paper that had taken me a week to write, then deposited them into his wastebasket.

That put the lid on his oration. He stared at me. We were both standing. It was one of those extremely uncomfortable silences where you and the other guy both realize the next words will spell friendship or doom.

"Maybe I'm blowing this all out of proportion," he said.

"I thought you'd get a kick out of them," I said, "because you were once a ballplayer."

His eyes looked past me for a moment, as if he remembered something. "Sure." He nodded. "Sit back down, Dan. Maybe God doesn't mind this kind of clubhouse prank." He gestured toward the wastebasket. "You know, I've always thought of Him as gentle and loving, not so stern and stuffy that He can't take a little humor."

"I've always thought of Him as a great big fist"—I made one and showed it to him—"just waiting to come down and smash my head."

He smiled. "I should listen to myself, Dan. I'm the one being stern and stuffy. OK, so we'll chalk this up to an error of enthusiasm."

"Gee, thanks." I still felt like a dog.

Then he told me we should shake it off, forget it ever happened, that God more than likely got a laugh out of it too. How his idea of God had a Supreme sense of humor, and now that he thought about it, wasn't parting the Red Sea a pretty good joke on the Egyptians? Just imagine the look on their faces when the waters began to rush back. Then he said everything was square between us, and he had me kneel by his desk and we bowed our heads and prayed, this time using the real words.

I worked off-season weekends and all that next summer at the pet store, making good money that I'd get each Friday in a stack of singles. I'd leave the stack next to my dad's empty plate.

Here, it said to him as he walked in the back door, *here's a fat pile of moolah earned by your worthless son, the kid you never talk to, the low-life scum who was too dumb to know to apologize after he made Mickey Meenan croak.* I played park district ball and we won the championship. *Here*, the trophy said to my ma, *here's another hunk of junk from the worthless punk who still wears an Ash Wednesday of guilt on his forehead.* I had bigger, woollier letters to sew on my school sweater, which I also wore everywhere and always, even when it was warm enough outside for short sleeves. And, when I could, I spent time with Grace.

She was changing. Something wonderful and weird was happening to her at Immaculata's. She was expanding her mind, reading books she didn't have to, talking about strange stuff that made me scared. That made me pause, think. But I didn't want to think. Then I hurt, still haunted by Mickey. I was like a bleeding heart tetra with swim-bladder disease, swimming at the most screwy angles, sometimes unable to rise from the bottom of my tank, sometimes bobbing sideways near the surface. I had no equilibrium. Everything was an extreme to me. The slightest change in my water would set me off.

"You know, we're very lucky," she announced one night. We sat studying at her dining-room table, the fall of our junior year. Me in a dark shirt and my letter sweater, trying to make sense of geometry. She in a pink checked dress as wide as a picnic blanket, her blond curls tumbling to her shoulders.

"Oh yeah?"

"Yeah, Danny. I've been thinking. And I think we're both really kind of fortunate, if you just look at it the right way."

I had nearly all the equations I'd need for the next day's test scribbled on my ruler. "How's that, Grace?"

"Well." She folded her hands and smiled. "Sister Mary Regina and I were talking this afternoon after study period about happiness and sadness, pure joy and real pain. And we—"

"Martyr stuff. I know all about it. Saint Filet Mignon."

"I'm serious, Danny. Sister Regina said that each person's capacity to experience happiness is balanced by her experience of pain and injury. It's like this." She tossed back her hair and then drew a long line on a sheet of paper, then shook her head and grabbed my ruler. "Let's say the center of your emotional capacity is here, at the six, and you experience something terrible, like your parents die in an airplane crash."

"Break out the parachutes, Grace."

"Listen! So they die and it's just terrible." Her finger moved from the six to the three. "See, that's your pain. And it's great, but you're promised an equally great pleasure sometime later in your life that will balance it all out!" Her finger slid across the ruler to the nine. She was smudging all my equations. "Do you understand, Danny?"

I nodded. "Yeah. If your mom and pop are out at the plate you get a nine on Sister Mary Holy Smoke's ruler scale."

"Be serious, Danny. Pain deepens your soul. People with deep souls have more capacity to experience joy and ecstasy. An idiot would feel nothing." Her finger moved an eighth of an inch. "And therefore an idiot has very little capacity to feel joy and to love." Her finger moved two-eighths of an inch the other way. "We're very lucky because we've both experienced great pain in our lives." Her finger worked its way down the ruler, past the three, the two, the one, then pointed off the table and beyond, all the way toward her mother's china cabinet.

"But our folks are still alive," I said, even though I knew it was a dumb thing to say.

"Of course they are, Danny. But we've both been through our own little hells. Don't you understand?"

I nodded and hid behind glibness. "You mean the big Saint Mel's game when the center head-butted me so hard he splintered my jock cup?"

"I mean the Tragedy Behind Mrs. Misiak's Garage." Her eyes froze me. "I mean the fear and guilt you must have felt, watching your friend die, and later having Mr. Meenan scream at you like he did the day they moved away, and you just standing there, taking in all his insults like you were made of stone. I mean the years I played the court jester, the fat lady in the circus, mooing like the school's pet cow, when inside I was secretly screaming with pain. I mean the guys who'd push me up against the school lockers and pull on the back of my bra strap—"

"Don't talk about bras," I said.

"—who'd pull on it, Danny, trying to hurt me, whispering the dirtiest ugly filth in my ear and trying to feel me up, like animals, Danny, like they were animals! I mean the girls who'd refuse to be even my acquaintances, who wouldn't even talk to me in the bathroom, all because of my weight problem, all because—"

"Weight problem?" I said. "Grace, you don't have a weight problem. You're just a little overly healthy."

"Yeah, Danny." She looked like she wanted to cry. Her nostrils flared like bellows. Her chest heaved massively as she sighed. "Yeah, go ahead and tell me I'm not the fattest pig on Old MacDonald's farm, and you're not the kid who accidentally killed Mickey Meenan."

I said nothing, staring into her beautiful blue eyes.

"We're a pair of freaks in the circus, Danny. The kind people pay a dime to see. The kind people make fun of. Nobody else loves us, even if at school you're a star. Nobody *really* cares if we live or die. But that makes us very very special, you see, because we have a great capacity inside our souls to love. We're deep, you jerk! Can't you see that we're deep?"

Of course she was right, son, at least about herself. I sat there and held her hand while she wept so loudly that Harold came in from the front room and asked if it was time yet for a Dagwood sandwich. Grace swallowed a giant sob and said, "Not yet, Pops, go back and watch TV." Then she cried some more onto my sweater, then looked up and tried to smile.

"Can't you see it, Danny?" she said in the littlest voice in the whole world.

I leaned forward and kissed her. Our lips nibbled each other like gerbils eating lettuce. Our tongues entwined like mating slugs. Then she stood and took me by the hand to her bedroom, her finger shushing at her lips, and there we kissed in the pure forgiving darkness. Then she took my hand and put it on her dress over her breasts.

"I love you, Danny," she whispered. "I'm yours. All of me, as long as you stay nice, and it's late and dark, and you promise never to hurt me, I'm yours. You can have me, Danny. You can have this"—her hand brushed mine across her breasts—"and this"—her hand led mine down her waist to her knees and then just below the hem of her dress to her bare skin—"and even this, Danny, one day soon, after you promise to love me eternally and never hurt me and be mine for always, and I'll always be yours because we're twin souls destined to share the flesh's limit of pain and pleasure." Her hand led mine over the outside of her dress and up the insides of her thighs as she parted her legs for an instant and then squeezed my hand between her legs, causing me to explode and explode and explode.

Sixteen, in the suddenly bright bathroom of the Jankowskis of unknowing Olive Street, wiping the inside of my boxers with squares of toilet paper, a smile on my face so broad it nearly cracked the mirror.

You'd think I would have been wise, son. You'd think I'd have floated out of her house and later returned bearing a Switzerland of dark chocolates, a South America of exotic flowers, a moon of perfumes and vinaigrettes and rare ointments with which she could scent her body in preparation for the day of my eternal promise to love her. But you forget that I was a big varsity two-letter man (*P P*, Dominic and Gino chided me, *look, even your sweater says peepee*), and I was beginning to realize that fewer and fewer of the girls I met knew of my past, my murder, my secret.

Taking out the garbage the next evening, I stared up at the sky. There above me hung the usual dull lineup of stars. Beneath my nose hovered the old olio of odors. I dropped the lid on the can and walked over to Heaven's Whore, then looked down at Mister Death. I touched Mister Death to see if I could feel the hot fires of Hell. The ground wasn't even warm.

"Damn it!" I screamed at the sky as loudly as I could. "I don't want to be deep! I want to be as shallow as an eighth-of-an-inch idiot!"

Somebody up there must have heard me, son.

Because I realized that Grace's being as fat as a float in a homecoming-game parade meant she was doomed to wear her sign of deepness on the outside, where everyone could see it, like Hester Prynne's scarlet letter. But my two varsity letters meant I was a big man. My curse of deepness was hidden. Only the kids I grew up with knew I had blood on my bat.

"You think you own me?" I shouted at Mister Death. "Ha ha ha. Rise up from the bowels of Hell if you do, I goddamn triple dare you!"

Nothing happened except down the block a dog barked.

"You're just a dumb garage door," I said to Heaven's Whore. "You're just a stupid hunk of wood." Then I spat on it. Nothing happened.

I felt pretty good. I looked again at the sky. "You hear that, God? Hey, the heretic is talking to You! Quit picking the cheese from between Your toes and listen to me, will Ya? I'm Danny the Wolf Kisser! And I believe in *Me*, the Third Baseman Almighty, Creator of a hundred million double plays!"

I gazed around the squalid alley and smiled.

"Lone wolf," I whispered with sudden romantic sadness. "The solitary wolf who prowls the deep forests all alone. Banished by his family. Insulted by his brothers, who are dogs. Who nobody in the world loves except his pals the vultures, because they feast on the stinking carrion of death."

I clapped my hands. A cup of self-pity mixed with a heaping tablespoon of melodrama and a dash of complete nonsense warmed over the smoking fires of bullshit does wonders for your spirits, feeling better than any priest's hurried *ego te absolvo*.

The prior evening's orgasm had released more than my sperm. It also let loose the idea that if Grace was willing to tantalize me in her boudoir, what would all the other girls on the North Side be willing to do if only I gave them the opportunity?

Opportunity? I thought. I'd be giving them an honor, a rare privilege. Like ladies at the butcher's, they'd take numbers and stand in line.

Maybe what Grace had said about promises and tomorrows scared me, son. Maybe I felt she was upping the ante beyond my paltry stack of chips. Maybe—this is difficult and embarrassing to admit—because I'd gotten my rocks off I hungered for her less. Looking back now I can see she was the best thing that ever happened to me. I can't explain. I can only tell you what I did next. I followed the methods of science and put my theories into practice.

Scientific Observation Number 1: The Lone Wolf doesn't take his fat girlfriend with him to sock hops.

Up until the fall of our junior year she went where I went, Lassie and Jeff, Trigger and Roy Rogers, Sancho Panza and Don Quixote. Everybody who was anybody knew us as an inseparable pair. At first the guys at school stung me with jabs like, "Woof woof, what a dog!" and "Hey, Danny, tie her to a parking meter!" I'd answer them with a wild-eyed stare. "Show some respect," I'd say. "You're talking about my girlfriend, understand?"

Then they'd retreat, because they were sensible, and they had me pegged as looney tunes, out to lunch, an elevator that didn't stop on all the floors. Because they'd seen me play, particularly against Saint Patricia's Prep.

Saint Patsy's was a genteel little school located out in the suburbs. Their mascot was a bookworm covered with dollar signs.

Their school color was bleeding madras. They joined our conference after JFK formed the Peace Corps, figuring they should visit disadvantaged foreign places too. We hated them because we knew if we were lucky, someday we'd end up working for them.

Happily we were slaughtering them, pounding their perfectly orthodontured teeth into the dust. Near the game's end their marching band, which was more a symphony, thought they heard the final gun, so they pranced onto the field. But the ball was still in play. Some vanilla wafer was running backward with it, and I was mad with pursuit. It was then that the tuba player saw me and let out a note that sounded like a terrified elephant. The back saw him too and started downfield. The rest of the defense was trotting to their locker room. The kid in the band held on to his tuba like a *Lusitania* passenger gripping a life preserver. He made little scared sounds and tried to hop away. Then the back made his cut, figuring the Music Man would screen him. I knew enough not to leave my feet. Counting the tuba, all four of us tried to occupy the same square yard of space. There was a loud *oom-pah-pah*, a barbershop quartet of *oofs!*, then a sickening *ca-runch!* Behind us, the opening notes of "Exodus" announced that the game was over.

By the next Monday morning at school, word had it I'd tackled the tuba player with one arm and the running back with the other. By lunch I'd thrown the tuba player ten yards in the air. By seventh period I'd jammed the back's helmet into the horn, then carried both into the end zone. On Tuesday everyone including the blind albino president of the school's photography club claimed they saw the play. I'd tackled half the band, hit the first trumpet so hard his instrument flew through the uprights, broken six of the back's ribs, and peeked up the skirts of all their cheerleaders.

"Tell us about it," everyone begged that Tuesday at lunch.

I smiled. "It was a cornet that split the uprights."

So the Big Man told Grace, "Hey, these stupid sock hops

only make your feet hurt anyway, and besides I've got a ton of things to do. So let me give you a rain check. I'll call you Monday, little Boston cream pie. Bye."

Scientific Observation Number 2: Set loose in society, the Lone Wolf proves he knows no etiquette.

At my first solo sock hop I grabbed the first skinny thing I saw.

No introductions. No pleasantries. I simply, literally, grabbed her around the waist. She had everything I wanted in a girl: two legs, a head of hair, no eyepatch, a nose, a mouth that I immediately assaulted with a kiss, and two hands that slapped me immediately afterward, *pop! pop!*, sending me skidding backward across the slick gymnasium floor.

After I was smart enough to lie, "Oh, a thousand pardons, I thought you were someone else!" she retreated to a neutral corner, surrounding herself with girlfriends who tittered and all spoke at once.

Son, I didn't so much want their kisses as what I thought their kisses meant. Acceptance. Approval. The stamp of U.S. Grade-A Normalcy.

So I picked myself up from the dance floor, then went back to the attack, every bit as crude and unimaginative as Coach Grieves's offense. I should have thought in baseball, not football, terms. I should have waited for my pitch, then gone with it.

Instead I plunged ahead like an offensive lineman, remembering that I should adapt or shut the cash register. Now I grabbed only the wrists of unsuspecting Immaculatas, pulling them gracelessly (yes, I pun) to an open spot on the dance floor. Midway through the song I'd send my kamikaze lips toward their Pearl Harbors. *Pop!* went each slap on my cheek.

Try talking to them, dummy, an inner voice told me.

"Hi." Go for the kiss. *Pop! Pop!*

Third down. New play. Say hi, dance with them, *then* kiss them.

Pop! Pop! Pop!

Punt.

Muttering to myself, I roamed the suddenly chilly gym. I couldn't figure these skinny girls out. Didn't they know who I was? Would I have to fill my pockets with licorice whips and chocolates? Then the Great DJ in the Sky announced a ladies' choice. A hand reached out and touched my arm.

"Dance?" a pretty voice asked.

Scientific Observation Number 3: The Lone Wolf deserves to be lonely if he lets the cat get his tongue.

The girl was nearly as gorgeous as Deirdre Egan, with big eyes, dark lashes, a smile that made my kneecaps melt. She seemed as normal as Tuesday, then as dreamy as a starry Saturday night. Her hand on my shoulder felt warm, weightless. The faint scent of her perfume made my mind reel. She'd picked me out of all the wolves in sheep's clothing? First and ten!

For a while we danced wordlessly, until she raised the subject of the *P*'s on my sweater.

"You lettered in baseball *and* football?"

I nodded.

She said, "Gee." Then, "You know, I never went out with a guy who had *two* letters."

I tried to swallow, but my mouth was a clot.

"You're not here with somebody else, are you?" she said.

I shook my head, then finally worked out a sound. "No."

She said gee again. By this time I was in love. Inside my boxers I grew a Louisville slugger. She was doing all the talking, telling me her name, her address, who she knew at Immaculata's, at Saint Paul's. When she asked if I'd ever met someone she named, I nodded or shook my head. She must have figured I was socially autistic. The song was ending. I realized she might walk away. I squeezed her hand, held her tight.

Then Heaven spun another slow song and she stayed.

"You're not real talkative." Her hand touched the back of my neck. "Are you, Mister Two-Letter Jock?"

"No," I said. "I'm talkative."

My reply made her laugh. "Then why aren't you talking to me?"

I felt her breath on my neck, her hair against my cheek, the front of her blouse now starting to get neighborly with my letter sweater. For an instant she let my hard-on brush her hip.

There were ten thousand things I could have said. Even *I don't know, I guess I'm shy* would have been better than the silence with which I answered her. Her question, *Then why aren't you talking to me?*, echoed in my ears, the sound rising at the end like a shriek, a siren. All at once I felt absolutely miserable. The unknowing girl sensed it. I could feel something in her sag; then she snapped into utter pretty-girl nonchalance, dancing less closely with me and turning her head to say hello to a friend or someone passing by. The song was the sock hop's last. It drifted to its end with a flutter of violins, and then the lights overhead broke the darkness and bleached everyone's face and made everyone look down. Then the couples laughed and grabbed each other's hands, and everyone scrambled to the bleachers to find their shoes. The girl walked away then, disappearing into the brightness.

Son, I'd like to be able to go back to that moment, say *I don't know, I guess I'm shy*. She would have said *Shy?*, and I would have nodded. *Why be shy?* she'd have said then. *I just broke up with my girlfriend*, I'd have answered.

SHE: *Why'd you do that?*
ME: *Because she made me think too much.*
SHE: *What about, Mister Two-Letter Jock?*
ME: *Death.*

No. I'd like to go back and be light, casual.

SHE: *Then why aren't you talking to me?*
ME: *Because, babycakes, I'm in love!*

We'd have laughed at that. She'd have said *Oh yeah, with who?* I'd have answered *Who do you think? Gina Lollobrigida?* We'd have laughed at that too, and then I'd have said *Well maybe if you play your cards right, someday I'll let you know.* Her line: *You'll do me the big favor, huh?* And we'd have gone back and forth like that, walking outside hand in hand, cuter than two hamsters running the wheel, maybe getting a Coke in some neighborhood hangout, walking home, until we kissed our first kiss on her front-porch steps, so perfectly, so sweet-sixteen, that the moon would have looked down on us and winked.

As I found my lonely pointed greaser shoes in the place where they always rested alongside Grace's wide rubber-soled flats, I felt a twinge of sorrow, then sucked in my gut and told myself I'd stumbled onto a valuable strategy: walk around muttering to yourself and keep an ear cocked for ladies' choices.

Time hullabalooed and did the Freddie. On weekends the Lone Wolf cruised the outskirts of dance floors and talked to his clothes. On week nights I skipped rope and practiced going to my right in the basement, then walked over to the Jankowskis' and studied with Grace. No dunce, she wanted to know exactly what was what.

"What?" I said. "You want to know what?"

"What's going on between us?" Her blue eyes shimmered like a windblown sea of flowers. "I mean, I'm delighted to study with you, Danny, and now and then we do go outside for a walk around the block, but that's not really what most people have in mind when they say that a boy and a girl are going steady."

"We're going steady?"

Her fat blond curls nodded.

"Then maybe we should take longer walks." I smiled. "But I thought you told me they gave you puffy ankles."

"Danny"—she shook her head, looked down, then back at me—"sometimes you make me feel like I'm your dog."

"Ha ha ha," I laughed. I could tell we weren't going to get

much studying done. I shut the book I was trying to read and stared at the china cabinet.

"Why don't we go out anymore on weekends?" she asked.

"Because Lindbergh and the Lone Wolf fly solo." Mrs. Jankowski had lots of junk and doilies in there I'd never noticed before.

"That's no answer." She touched my arm. "Tell me why. It's because you're ashamed to be seen out in public with me, isn't that right?"

I turned to her and made a face like I smelled something rotten. "Grace, my darling little pint of buttermilk, that's so off-the-wall I could barf."

"Then answer my question."

"I just did."

She squeezed her lips together and shook her head. "Sister Regina told me I need to be more forthright about my personal feelings. She says just because I have a weight problem it doesn't mean I should let people push me around."

"Hey, let me write that down!" Mocking her, I reached for a pencil. I could see what was coming. It made me feel mean. "Wisdom like that and fifty cents can get you into the bleachers, Grace."

"Don't make fun of her, Danny."

"I'm not making fun of her, but Christ—everybody knows you shouldn't let other people push you around."

"She said I shouldn't be one of life's spectators. And she lent me a book."

Grace reached for a big envelope and then handed me a huge fancy book.

"A nun gave you this?" I thumbed through a few pages. "These are all pictures of fat ladies. Look, this one's hardly wearing any clothes."

"That's Art, Danny. That's culture and refinement. Stuff you don't know anything about." She shook her thick curls and stuck her nose up in the air. "Sister Regina told me that corpulence used to be very fashionable in some societies. She said some of the world's most beautiful women used to have weight problems."

The book was full of paintings of brown-eyed, raspberry-lipped chubbettes leaning against marble pillars or lounging on antique furniture. Most of them flashed you their rosy nipples but covered their ace of spades with their hand or a sheet. Now and then you could see a little cockpit hair.

"Beauty's only skin deep, Danny."

I smiled, finding one with her hands behind her head and no drapery. "Then some of these ladies are awful beautiful. Their skins run pretty deep."

"Beauty's in the eye of the beholder, Danny." Her fingers began to rub my hand.

I shut the book. "These are really nice pictures."

"You're not listening to what I'm saying."

"Then spit it out, Grace. You get only fifteen seconds in the huddle. Call your play."

Grace swallowed. "Sister Regina's helping me develop a positive self-image. She says there are people in the world who are their own worst enemy. They think little of themselves, so that's what others give them. Little. Crumbs from the table. Scraps for the dog."

"I thought you liked to eat *after* we studied, Grace."

"You leave me only your scraps, Danny."

"Tonight you can eat my whole plate, OK?"

"Damn it!" Her fist rattled the table. "You know what I'm talking about!"

"Yeah, more of this Regina novena holy deep crap."

"It's not crap, Danny."

"It's not crap?" Something inside me snapped. My voice soared higher than the Prudential Building. "It's not crap? It's not Sister Mary Genuflect buffalo turds? Who do you think you're kidding,

Grace? Come on! This is the real world! Look out the window. Open your damn eyes. If Sister Regina is so smart, you think all she'd be doing is teaching high school? If fat tubs of Crisco are so beautiful, how come Miss Universe isn't Porky Pig?" I slammed my hand on the book. "All of these naked buckets of suet are *dead*, Grace. By now the teeming maggots have eaten through their bones. That's what the deep crap gets your culture and refinement. A lousy coffin they stick six feet under. And you want to know why they bury it, Grace? Because otherwise they have to smell its stink. Yeah. Death stinks, Grace! And deepness sucks dead donkey dongs. You want to know why we don't go out on weekends? That's why. Because I earned two varsity letters, and nobody knows about *me*. Because I'm making scientific observations. Because otherwise I smell the stink all the way up my nose! And if you want to be beautiful like everyone else, I've got the answer in three little words. *Shut your mouth. Eat only air. Diet, diet, diet.* Feed your damn two kinds of potatoes every night to your old lady's petunias or to the garbage can, or leave them drowning on your plate in all the butter your ma uses, or else you'd better get one of those H. G. Wells time machines and go back a couple centuries so you can pose for one of these pictures in the *Book of Dead Fatsoes*"—I took a breath —"because that's where we all end up anyway, Grace. Right next to the old garbage can without making a sound. With our eyeballs rolled up backward. Our faces turning purple. Ready to say *pleased to meet ya* to good old Saint Rigor Mortis. And you never know when or why or who's going to do it to you."

I shook my head. Grace's face and neck were splotched with ugly splashes of red. "Or how it feels the next morning, when you open your eyes expecting to feel normal and happy, and then it hits you in the forehead like a fist. Or the next year, or for the rest of your life, until you're so sick and tired of it that you want to crawl on your hands and knees and make a pilgrimage to Saint

Amnesia." I laughed. "Except Saint Amnesia ain't there." I realized I was standing, that my body was trembling.

"Let's face it, Grace. You're as fat as the full moon and I'm a murderer, and I don't know which is worse. So give me a break with all of this deepness bullshit, OK? I'm deep up to my fucking ears."

"You don't have to be vulgar," was all she said.

She sat as still as a statue in a museum. I gathered my books with hands that shook like they had Saint Vitus dance, then walked from the room, telling Harold on my way out to take it easy for once on the mayonnaise. Why did I say *that*? I thought when I was outside. The air was wet and heavy, full of the smell of coming spring. I walked home, unlocked the front door.

He was sitting in the front room, the night's newspaper spread across his lap, his mouth open, his eyes closed as if he were dead.

"You won't have no more trouble with me," I said.

He opened his eyes, his brows leaping.

"Did you hear me? I said you won't have any more trouble. Whatever you want me to do for as long as I keep on living here, I'll do. Just give me the decency of telling me before you turn it into a federal case, OK?"

"What?" he said.

I stood over him. "You know what I'm talking about. And I don't mean any disrespect, so don't look at me like you want to spit. I'm not a scab, you know. I'm your son. And I know that doesn't mean a whole lot to you, but that's the way it is and we'll just have to live with it."

He looked at me, his eyes blinking.

"Maybe you're not the greatest father in the world, or I'm too dumb to see it, too ungrateful, too unworthy. But I'm tired of all your secret plays, you know what I mean? They drive me crazy sometimes. I ain't a mind reader, and I don't have ESP, so you'll just have to lower yourself and open your mouth like the rest of us and put what you want me to do into words, or write me a letter, or tap it out in Morse code on the wall."

He shook his head. "Danilo."

"I'll be out of your house by the day I turn eighteen."

"Danilo, nobody said—"

"That's right, Dad. Nobody said. That's just the point. Nobody says nothing around here."

He squeezed his eyes with one hand, pulled on his mouth, then folded his newspaper slowly, neatly. I looked at his broken nails.

"Danilo, *figlio*—"

"I want a truce. You understand? I want you to get off my back. I want peace. I want—"

"Do you know what you'll do?" His eyes were calm. They stared at me. "How will you make a living after you move out?"

"I don't know," I said. "Did you know when you were sixteen?"

He nodded. "Yes."

"Well you're you, and I'm me."

"What brought this on, Danilo?"

"I don't want to talk about it."

"You criticize me for not talking and then you don't want to talk."

"I didn't say I was perfect."

"Sleep on it, Danilo. Don't be so rash. Things have a way of looking different in the morning light."

"It's decided," I said. "The only thing I'll sleep on will be my bed."

Then I turned and walked to the bathroom. I splashed cold water on my face. I drank some of the water. Then I walked back up the hallway. He was still sitting in the front room beneath the yellow light, looking down at his hands and neatly folded newspaper.

"Good night," I told him.

He told me good night.

I walked into the boys' room. Then I pulled Gino and Dominic out of bed. "*You* sleep with the babies." I showed them both my fist. They stared at me, their jaws slack, then nodded.

That night I slept, for the first night I can remember, alone, dry, without dream or nightmare.

1 2 3 **4** 5 6 7 8 9

SWINGING AWAY

Things didn't look very different in the morning light.

I lay on my back in the big bed. The gray glow of dawn was just starting to sneak around the drawn bedroom shade. My eyes rose from the window to the ceiling, where I saw the same cracks seeming to make the same round face, Mickey's, whose sad countenance still literally hung over me.

The house was silent. Then in the other bed my four brothers shifted and sighed. I sat up. Dominic hugged the wall, one arm crooked up over his face. Gino lay sideways, knees drawn to his chest, beneath his slack mouth a pancake-sized puddle of drool. Louie dangled a hand from the bed, his legs making a V beneath the blanket. At his side lay Francis Junior, curled like a piece of elbow macaroni. I looked at Mickey's face in the ceiling, then back at my brothers. Their breath hovered in the air.

I quietly turned the dead bolt and eased the two chains off the front door, then stood out on the porch and looked at sleepy

Olive Street. The air was chilly and smelled like wet dirt. Across the street a dozen pigeons slept on a slanted roof. A robin lit on the lawn next door, flicked its head—once, twice—squinting with one eye at something in the grass. Ah, I thought, the early bird and the worm. In a year I'd be packing my suitcase. I whistled the beginning of "Good Bye Cruel World" and watched the robin. The bird looked up at me for a moment, as if to say shut up, then all at once shot its bill into the lawn and came up with a beak full of dead grass. So much for old sayings. The robin shook its head, flapped its tail, then flew off into the sun.

Time took wing, followed. I spent that spring making further scientific observations and thinking of, but not seeing, Grace.

Images of her would pop into my mind everywhere: on the bus to school, in the middle of class, even out on the diamond. I'd think of her crying at a movie, shattering the theater's darkness with row-shaking sobs. "Aww, it's OK, Grace," I'd tell her in a soothing whisper. "Life's *so* tragic," she'd say, her eyes never leaving the screen, the flickering images reflecting off the tears pooled beneath her eyes. I'd remember her happy whenever we'd go bowling, hefting a red ball that in front of her looked small as a tomato, the big smile she'd get when she knocked down all the pins. "That was beautiful, Grace!" I'd yell. "You're beating the pants off me!" She'd beam, breaking sweat, then prance back to the line, tilt her head, and fire another strike. I'd think of her quiet sometimes when we'd sit together on her sofa watching TV, with Mom Jankowski and Harold in the kitchen making buttered popcorn or fudge or chocolate-chip cookies, and she'd turn to me when I didn't expect it and squeeze my hand and kiss my cheek, then rest her head on my shoulder and sigh so softly it'd seem the world was made of velvet.

Anyone with an ounce of sense would have rung her doorbell, said, "Hey, what in the world are we doing? We've got to talk."

Scientific Observation Number 4: The Lone Wolf doesn't have even an ounce of sense.

106

Because instead of trying to regain Grace, I refined and polished my fool's act, pursuing the slender Immaculatas with a renewed vigor. Now I cruised the weekend dance floors with the boyish bashfulness of a Tom Sawyer who always listened to Aunt Polly. I smiled, asked the girl to dance, held her a puritan arm's distance away. She talked and I responded, Chatty Cathy. After a while she thought me an Eagle Scout. She'd dance more closely. I'd be gallant, touch the small of her back, brush imaginary lint from her blouse or sweater, then impulsively stroke the soft line of flesh from her shoulder to her ear. I'd offer to take her home, since I was concerned for her safety, since at night the city was a jungle. Then when we hit her front steps I'd be on her like King Kong.

It would get me a kiss, sometimes of cheek or hair or collar, then usually a surprised *pop* that sent me sprawling to the sidewalk.

"I don't know what came over me!" I'd exclaim. "Honest, hey, usually I'm not this rude, this crude, such a beast. But you're so beautiful, so sweet—"

It'd appease her. "Calm down, will ya? I was just getting my keys. You could give a girl a little advance warning, you know?"

"No, I don't know. I need to be taught. I've never met a girl like you before."

Reassured to hear the oldest line, she'd relax and smile.

"Teach me?" I'd say, taking her once again into my arms.

Son, let me add that these girls, though always thin, were no bathing beauties on the cover of *Sports Illustrated*. These sock hops, no antiseptic scenes from "Happy Days." There was no Richie Cunningham grinning a grown-up Opie's retardation at his unreal friend, the unflappable Fonzie. No ponytails bouncing like the latest shampoo commercial. We were greasers, son, full of human imperfections. Pink acne medicine spotted our cheeks. Gold nicotine stained our fingers. Our chins and foreheads leaked more oil than '61 Fords. There was little that was happy about our days, our nights, our future. Most of us were sad and much too smart to dream. Because we knew we were the sons and daughters of Chicago's white working class, that if we were lucky we too could marry the factory, and end up like our folks—a fate worse than death.

So, like midnight diesels at a highway diner, we idled in the parking lot. We rumbled, belched smoke, numbed our minds with bennies, booze, beer. Guys with green crescents of crud beneath their fingernails talked carburetors or mag wheels, occasionally glancing at the girls with a "Get a load of that dog" or "I'd fuck her, oh yeah, I'd plank that broad till she turned blue." Charming? The girls, always in groups, like nuns, ignored them or whirled with a raised finger.

Their sweaters more times than not reeked of sweat. You could see where their blouses had lost a button and they'd used a safety pin. Most sprayed their hair so heavily with gunk that it was stickier than cotton candy. Our DA's and pompadours were so liberally greased that whenever it rained, droplets the color of skimmed milk splashed on our shoulders, trickled down our necks. After a few weeks you knew everyone by their clothes. Few if any of us third-stringers had money for costume changes, though the week after Christmas you'd notice a department store of threads so new that some sleeves still waved a price tag.

I don't mean to darken the field with these details, son, but I want to show you how I didn't fit in. How, over my obligatory black stovepipes and red greaser knit, I insisted on wearing my unbuttoned letter sweater, the sight of which made any respectable male greaser want to hold his nose and groan. And to the girls, well, I was a breath of fresh, crazy air.

Believe me, I wanted to be cool. But now that I'd told my father I'd be leaving I knew my jock had to be my way out of Olive Street, that I'd have to overcome my fears, excel, impress.

Scientific Observation Number 5: The Lone Wolf knows no fear.

Fear is often sensible. Don't confuse it with cowardice. Fear can lead to a kind of respect; respect, to one kind of wisdom. Hold that thought and let me present one of the game's more interesting tensions. Smart batters try to get out of the way of high, tight fastballs. Smart pitchers learn to throw the fastball high and tight.

They're a separate breed, pitchers. As a rule they're tall, moody, even more prone to superstition than are other ballplayers, friendly more to one another and the catchers on the squad, obsessed with their hands and fingers and whether they've got their "stuff." Their eyes frown each spring, not thawing into smiles until they can make the ball pop so loudly it rattles the school windows. Then they try to turn their faces into stone, though you can see them smirk up at the clouds when their pitches hop, hum, drop, curve, do whatever their long and immaculately clean fingertips tell the ball's laces.

But since they were young—only high-school arms—the ball often got away and rode in. Being hit, especially on the noggin, is what all batters feared. You could tell when it dawned on a pitcher that this sensible fear could be used to his advantage. His eyes would shrink to the size of pinheads. His cleats would rip the earth. His arm would reach back and brush the sky's blue belly for that extra 15 percent Gabriel was always goading us to find.

"That's it!" Gabriel would shout. "Pitch 'em tight! Fire that ball! Good heat!" The batter would touch his eggshell of a head, then stare at his bat as if it were a toothpick.

Sure you have a helmet, but your helmet is a toy. Sure you can try to get out of the ball's way, but sometimes it comes in on you as invisibly as an odor. You think you hear its laces slicing the air and then it explodes behind you as big as a grapefruit in the catcher's mitt. "Stee-rike!" the ump roars.

"And that was his change-up," the catcher whispers.

Watching others take their cuts at the plate makes batting

appear to be the easiest thing in the world. Ask any fan. He'll tell you what's wrong with every player. But standing there beneath a plastic helmet not knowing if the next pitch has a rendezvous with your temple makes batting awful hard to do.

So some batters give in and take a half step back from the plate. Some entirely surrender the outside corner. Then the pitcher has won this battle of nerves. Sure, stepping back gives the batter more time to duck and makes him less of a target, but stepping back also gets him fewer base hits.

Mr. Koufax said it: "Pitching is the art of instilling fear." Batters cede the half step if they're sensible. If they're wise enough to realize that dead hitters have extremely poor batting averages.

But not the Lone Wolf, number 13, Danilo Francis Bacigalupo.

No, I hogged plate. Watched the ball all the way to the bat. Allowed my body to do the rest, practicing until hitting became reflex. I decided every inch of the plate was mine, by God, and if a fastball had my name on its laces? Well, I'd killed Mickey with one, hadn't I? So maybe getting beaned would be justice. "Will this be the time?" I'd mutter to myself in the on-deck circle. "Is it time to cash in my cookies?" If it is, so be it. But if it isn't, as long as I'm alive I'll kill the ball. Hit it anywhere I want, as far as I am able, for as many at-bats as I have left.

I'd pray that when I was beaned it would happen with the bases loaded, the score tied, two outs, bottom of the ninth. I prayed my weeping teammates would have to drag my slumped body up the first-base line, touch my lifeless foot to the bag. Then it would be in all the newspapers, and I'd be a hero. And then the curse would transfer to the pitcher, and *he'd* have to live with knowing *he* was a murderer.

I also gave the ball a lot of thought. I swore that when I hit it, it changed shape. I knew it grew larger as it came in on me— anyone with eyes could see that—but when I really drilled one I could see it sometimes flatten against my bat like a squashed balloon, and sometimes I'd hear the little guy squeak. *Crack!* *Eeek!* At the same time. In practice I'd retrieve balls I'd absolutely hammered, certain one side would be flat. They'd be as round as Grace. The stamp of the company below the laces. Made in Haiti.

I figured Haiti had something to do with it, so I went to the library, and I concluded that the thousands of wonderful underpaid Haitian women who worked in baseball factories told their little friends stories before they stitched them closed about how horrible it was for Little Baseball to meet mean old Mister Bat. How Mister Bat would sting the daylight out of him if he could, so Little Baseball had better learn to stay out of Mister Bat's way. That was why some balls were so lively, curving down and away from your swing at the last instant. The way the pitchers threw them had nothing to do with it, I figured. The pitchers used the same grip and motion each time out, but their results varied greatly from outing to outing. No, having or not having their "stuff" was all smokescreen. The life was in the ball. The little guys were definitely alive. All Little Baseball really wanted was to be taken home as a souvenir by some gorgeous girl who'd put him up on her bureau, where he could watch her undress for bed. Pitchers knew all of this; it was why they were so superstitious. Sometimes they'd have conversations with the ball—you'd see a guy sitting by his locker holding a ball, just muttering away—and sometimes you'd see a guy out on the mound look at a ball, listen to it for a moment, then ask the ump to throw it out of the game. The pitcher heard the ball say something he didn't like, you can bet on it.

Then I understood that all batters were taught the same philosophy. Our mothers stitched us together in the wet Haitis of their wombs, then sent us out onto the dangerous sidewalks, alleys, streets, and expressways, telling us to avoid speeding trucks, bullies' fists, rabid rats, Communists, the candy of strangers, and baseballs that wanted to make sauce of our Adam's apples.

Scientific Observation Number 6: The Lone Wolf sees that there is always something dying, and whatever isn't dying wants to eat.

Grieves gave me a dollar-an-hour raise and my own key to the Underwater World that summer, and it was my responsibility each morning to open up. You'd think I was Elvis or the Beatles on "Ed Sullivan" by the way the animals would greet me. The birds in the front grabbed their cages' sides and squawked. The parrots cried out phrases from the music we played, "Little deuce coupe!" and "Dead man's curve, awk!" The rabbits thumped in their hutches. The rodents ran furious circles in their boxes, then stood on their hind legs and smiled. "Hello, scabs," I'd tell them. "How ya doing, feathered friends?" I'd turn on the overhead lights. "Have no fear, the food man's here."

Then I'd put on *Surfing's Greatest Hits* or the latest Jan & Dean or Beach Boys—Grieves's orders, for the ambience, but I'd keep the volume low so I could hear myself think—and then I'd check everyone's water and dish out the grub. Then the shop grew quiet, settling into the sounds of munching, flapping wings, cracking seeds, rustling newspaper strips in the rodent cages. Then I'd do what I liked and did best. I tended to the fish.

If churches had huge aquariums instead of altars, there'd be a lot more religious people in the world, believe me. It's no accident the Man from Galilee was known by the sign of a fish. I'd slowly walk up to the tanks, a serene smile on my face, hearing the soft hum of the air pumps, the bubbling gurgles of hundreds of undergravel filters and air stones. Tank by tank the fish would rush to the front, nosing the glass, schooling, then try to break surface. I'd press the light switches on, then stand back. There are few things prettier than a tank of neon tetras, blue- and red-striped, awakening from their slumber. The dizzy speed of a swarm of zebra danios. The rounded flash of a dozen tiger barbs. The floating elegance of angelfish. "Good morning," I'd whisper to each row of tanks. It would take me forty-five minutes to feed them.

As I fed them, I made my inspections, looking for closed fins, signs of shimmy, spots of ich. Healthy fish have movement, erect dorsal fins, good appetites. The dying lose color and withdraw, hovering in the rear of tanks like timid ghosts. I was always treating some disease or another. I hung boards that announced NOT FOR SALE over the faces of sick tanks. "Nip it in the budarooney," Grieves would tell me. I had a good success rate, even with shipments that came in with fungus. But what always surprised me was when a fish died for no reason. It would lie, colors chalked, curled like a toenail clipping, upon the gravel. "Oh," I'd always say, more a sudden breath than a word. I'd take my net from my back pocket and scoop it into an old Maxwell House coffee can, which I used only to transport the dead.

Maybe the only bad thing about a ballplayer's life is that he's never in one place long enough to set up an aquarium. Tending the tanks taught me to see, to really see, and to do so quickly—to scan the entire field and then focus on the particular, the different.

I always cared for the goldfish last. Not because I was a tropicals snob, but because their tanks depressed me. We had several eye-level tanks full of beautiful Japanese imports—veiltails, chocolates, calicoes, blues, red caps, black moors—and they were splendid to see, swimming with their silken, flowing fins. But just beneath them were three long uncovered tanks full of the common variety, the type of goldfish kids won by tossing a Ping-Pong ball into a bowl at the parish fair. We put no gravel in these tanks, no filters, no plants; just air stones. Though the sign on them said COMET GOLDFISH 10¢/EA 12/50¢, everyone called them feeders. See, they weren't *fish*, potential pets that would be loved and cared for. They were swimming, breathing food.

They moved in and out fast. I scooped them by the dozen. "Lemme have the fat ones," the customers would always say, and I'd nod and say, "Sure, the fat ones." Then they'd take the feeders home to their oscars or piranhas, and the goldfish would bunch in a back corner, stream out one last shit, wonder who'd be gobbled up first. I knew how they acted, what they felt. I had to feed our tanks of live eaters. Little kids would tug on the leg of my stovepipes, ask, "Mister, when are they gonna eat one?" and point. "Get outa here," I'd say. But they'd fingerprint the tanks, Romans in the Colosseum. Now and then I'd hear a roar from the witless eight-year-olds. Then a big cichlid would circle the aquarium, a pair of orange tailfins protruding from its mouth. "Mister, hey, you shoulda seen it! Man alive, was it neat!"

How could I tell them I'd not only seen it but lived it?

See, Mickey was a feeder. Grace was a feeder too, the meatiest in the tank. Things eat or are eaten. You're either carnivore or food. Life wasn't a balanced community tank, resplendent with gentle blue discus, rosy tetras, dwarf gouramis, algae-eating suckermouths. Life was a piranha tank. The sharpest and quickest jaws survived. And I was one of the survivors, merrily circling, Mickey in my stomach, Grace's tailfins drooping from my mouth.

Spit her out? Ring her doorbell, offering chocolate and apologies?

No way, José.

Because by then this piranha had press. We're talking big-time Chicago newspaper articles here, which I cut out and stuck with spit to the bathroom mirror, never to see again. Son, allow me to strut some stats.

My first year of varsity baseball: .623 batting average. Second year: .801 and city record for most times hit by pitch. *Black-and-blue high-school phenom Dan Bashilippo leads the nation in bases-per-at-bat ratio*, one newspaper article claimed. Another nicknamed me Danny Bee. *Sweet Danny Bee stung the ball again, going 6-for-6 with four singles, a double, and a round-tripper to lead St. Paul to another convincing victory over* . . . One of the suburban papers took a musical approach. *No relation to Johann Sebastian, but every bit as much a maestro on the bases, young Dan Bach, as his teammates affectionately call him, orchestrated another symphony of batting and fielding mastery.* . . .

Read the headlines.

BACH'S BACK BOOMS A BOUNTY!
Bee's Errorless String Creates Hive of Interest
BLEACHERS SET ON FIRE AFTER GAME
Arson Suspected—No One Injured
Fires Strike School for 2nd Time
PREP GRIDDER BLITZES WAY INTO RECORD BOOK
DAN DEFENSE DRUMS DE LA SALLE TO DEFEAT
Colleges Say St. Paul Linebacker is 'Sure Thing'

Senior year, and the honey had run from the diamond to the gridiron. I was visiting universities, smiling and shaking a lot of hands. The Big Ten wanted me to sign a letter of intent. Notre Dame and a school in Kentucky were pressing me hard. I was flying high. I had no strings to hold me down. I was sure I'd be out of the whale's belly by the day I turned eighteen. But then Charlie Grieves, bless his soul, let the air out of my beachball.

"Danny, Danny, Danny," he said after our third game. We stood in his office. "What the hell has gotten into you?"

"What's gotten into *you?*" I said. I stood in my sweaty T-shirt and filthy uniform pants. "We won again, didn't we?"

"Danny, we had that game won the day I scheduled it." He took off his cap and ran his fingers through his hair. "But you made it close, blitzing on every play." He shook his head. "What the hell kind of football is that?"

"That's Anarchy Ball, Coach."

"Bullshit. You looked liked a Sara Lee cheesecake out there, and *I* don't like Sara Lee. They sliced you and diced you—"

"But Coach, I—"

"But nothing, Dan. Now shut up and listen. You're as good a little man as I've seen play. Don't misunderstand me. You're inspired. You've shared a sundae with the Devil. That's why I like you, why I've always liked you. But *I* pull your strings, do you hear me? I told you at the half to lay back and play the zone. Do you have wax in your ears or what? I nearly took you out in the third quarter."

"Took me out?" I shook my head. "Coach, are we talking about the same game? I caught them *four times* behind their line of scrimmage. What did we pick up, thirty yards?"

"We were ahead by seventeen, Danny. We had it won. You tried to rub their noses in it. We're winners now, so we should play like winners."

"I was playing like a winner."

"You were playing like a Ball Park Frank." He turned and spat into his wastebasket. "The main reason I kept you in the fourth quarter was because of these crank calls the office has been getting. Look, I bench you once and every nut in the world'll think he's coach. Besides, by then you'd shot your wad. They were wise to you. They knew you'd blitz. Everybody in the stands knew you'd blitz. So they took you out of every play." He laughed. "They dusted your tonsils but good. Dan, they *embarrassed* you, and that embarrassed me and the school. Understand? Now get out of here. I'm tired of looking at your stupid face."

That night my stupid face had a date with a slender Immaculata. We got to the Riviera early, so we killed some time at a drugstore fountain. When she got her soda, she smiled and asked if I wanted her cherry. I grinned at that and said sure. Then she looked at me, still smiling, as she bent her head and put her lips around the straw and sucked. She sat up straight, licking a stray drop from her lips, then poked the scoop of ice cream on top with her spoon. It made soda spurt out of the straw.

"I guess I made it excited," she said and smiled again.

Oh yeah, she made it excited. We made out in the dim balcony for most of the movie, and I tried to feel good, to forget about what Grieves had said. But his words echoed in my ears. *They embarrassed you. Everybody in the stands knew.* I worried I'd blown my chances with the Big Ten, Notre Dame, the school in Kentucky, which made me blow my chance with the Immaculata.

"What's the matter with you, Danny?" she whispered in my ear. "Don't you like the way I kiss?"

I looked at her and realized I couldn't even remember her name. What was I doing? I thought. Where was Grace? But then I kissed the girl with all the passion I could muster. As our tongues embraced in the deepest french kiss in my life, I wondered if she could taste the dirt on my tonsils.

"Did you see me play today?" I asked, expecting her to tell me how awful I'd looked. I hoped she'd say I looked awful. Then maybe I could talk about it with her, discover what was wrong.

"Oh yeah," she said. We stood out on Broadway Avenue. "You were really great, making all those tackles." Cars going everywhere and nowhere rattled past us. "Especially after those crazy threats that if you played, you'd die." She giggled and locked her arm around me as she led me to the El. "You were just fantastic. Everybody knows all about you at Immaculata." We waited on the platform for a southbound train that would take us to a party where everybody knew me. "And, you know, everybody's talking about you, which college you'll pick, how wonderful a football player you are." At the party we danced. Somebody had a bottle of Southern Comfort, which everyone drank, which to me was no comfort. Then, under the guise of showing me a clipping in her purse that called me the Mad Dog of Defense, she led me to a bedroom, telling me again I was brave and wonderful. She found her purse, smiled, then pulled me down on the bed.

But my fire was out, doused and trampled by Coach Smokey.

"Help me," she whispered after she locked the door, as she unbuttoned her blouse and unzipped her skirt.

"Touch me," she told me as her bra floated like a double parachute to the floor.

"You're no fun at all," she complained as my dead fingers tried to help and touch her, as we lay like two lumps on the bed.

"Internal injuries," I lied, slapping my abdomen. "The price of victory on the gridiron. Near-total cellular breakdown. See, the old gut bag has only so much juice."

"But you guys are usually such animals the night after a game."

"Hey," I said, "not the *real* athletes. Not big stars like me. Grieves was telling me after the game how impressed he was with me today. Do you have any idea how much pain and cellular breakdown my body's been through?"

"You poor thing," she said.

The escape was little solace. I closed my eyes and fell asleep. When I woke an hour later, everyone grinned at me and cheered.

"Way to pick cherries, 'Galupo!" the goons on the party's sidelines said. The thick juice of envy dripped from their lips.

I said nothing, then left with the girl whose name I still couldn't remember.

The next Monday morning I stood before Charlie Grieves.

"I've still got a taste for the game," I said, "but if you want me to, I'll clean out my locker, turn in my equipment."

"You're spitting pablum," Grieves said.

"Coach, I'm talking to you straight."

"Danny, you disappoint the blazes out of me."

"Well maybe that's the reason why I'm quitting."

He brought his face so close to mine that I could count his nose hairs. Then his arms wrapped themselves around me in a big hug. For a moment I felt like letting go, bursting out with the biggest sob this side of Toledo, confessing my hunch that the death threats were connected to the bleacher fires, and the fires were connected to the murder, and to me. But I forced my hands to stay at my sides. I took deep breaths and turned back to stone, until he stepped back, checking his wristwatch and looking past me at the door and fidgeting with the knot on his tie.

"You're making me late for health," he said. "Shouldn't you be in class?"

"I got study hall. If you want, report me."

He shook his head. "I don't want to report you, Danny." Then he turned and slammed his fist against the wall. "For the love of Christ," he shouted between clenched teeth, "you've got everything a kid could ever want, and you blow up over a little criticism? I'm trying to help you, Dan! Why the hell do you think I'm in this job? For the money they pay me? Ha!" He shook his head again. "You've got some really top-notch schools taking a close look at you, and you could trade four years of football for a first-class education, and here you are telling me you want to quit."

"Maybe I'm a pussy willow. Maybe you should mow me down at the knees."

He stared at me with the look he reserved for kids who'd come in asking why their parakeets were sick after the kids had put them, just to see what would happen, for an hour in the refrigerator.

"If that's what you want, Danny boy, that's what I'll do." His voice was calm now. "If you want to try for a college scholarship, I'll help you. If you want to play like a can of Chef Boy-Ar-Dee meatballs, I'll yank you off the field. You're not the only one on the team. The fires and threats make everyone uneasy, including me. Our games mean a lot to all our players. Now excuse me, son." He walked past me to the door. "I'm late for a lecture on nutrition."

I slunk into study hall, then went through the motions during that week's practice, but my heart was no longer in it. That Saturday, in front of scouts from seven Big Ten schools, Notre Dame, and the college in Kentucky, I played an embarrassingly poor four quarters, falling back on my ass every time a back or lineman challenged me. For the first time I can remember, I heard boos.

Though we won the game, I felt no joy. Something—some edge—had slipped through my fingers. Maybe I felt my father was right after all, that I was no good. Or maybe I wanted to prove to the world that I couldn't succeed. If so, son, I was very successful.

Grieves took me aside, trying to fire me up, get my ketchup, mustard, and relish flowing. But I was as meek as the inheritors of the earth, which I inherited the next seven Saturdays, my arms tackling so much dirt you could grow tomatoes and marigolds in my shoulder pads.

The Big Ten, Notre Dame, and the school in Kentucky said sure, come if you want, we'll probably have room for a walk-on. But no scholarship for you, Timid Puppy of Defense.

Then winter descended in miserable ice storms. I slid to weekend dances at Immaculata's, at Saint Paul's. I had no buddies to talk carburetors with. There no longer seemed to be any point in trying to paw slender girls. Each night in the basement I skipped a million miles of rope and went to my right, to my right, to my right, fielding a million imaginary one-hoppers. Upstairs Ma washed dishes in the sink. Dad worked, peed, ate, slept with the newspaper on his lap, his open mouth forming the first syllable of the word *exhaustion*. Whenever I got restless I went outside into the frozen antarctic wilderness, pretending I was walking my dog, an imaginary Saint Bernard I called Bernie.

"Bernie!" I'd shout at the crisply iced air. "Hurry up already and take your shit!"

"Let's go, Bernie, mush, goddamn it, it's freezing out!"

"Bernie, get away from that dead petunia bed, for the love of Christ, heel, fetch, come here you fat mutt, you embarrass me!"

And I'd look up at the warm yellow light behind the drawn blinds, and I'd think of the big kitchen and Harold with his head in the refrigerator searching for the sweet gherkins or saying he'd brought home a surprise, two gallons of ice cream, and Grace fastidiously arranging the napkins and plates for the sandwiches and reheated mashed potatoes and the Nile river of gravy, butter, melted cheese, sour cream that would make my stomach turn—

"Damn it, you worthless dog, you're the milkman's son, Bernie!"

Mushroom gravy. Letter of intent. The *Book of Dead Fatsoes*.
Failure. Bernie peed on everybody's lawn. Then he stopped and
howled like a coyote on the spot where Mickey lay in his mother's
arms waiting for the siren that was too late, and one of the drivers
smelled of after-shave, toilet water, baseball mitts floating in a
Great Lake of piss. Why didn't they want to dance with me,
Bernie? I asked them all as politely as I could. And why didn't
he ever say one fucking word about the pile of singles I'd leave
each Friday next to his plate? Oh, the hell with it. "Bernie!
Bernie, you evil dog! *I* pull your strings, do you hear me?" The
wind blew tiny knives of snow against my neck. In the still sky
above, the moon glowed like an idiot child holding a flashlight
up to its face in an eternity of darkness.

Then Bernie snapped his leash and raced past the dead petunia
bed and up the porch steps, and I followed him, my heart pounding, then rang the bell.

"Danny!" Harold said. Then, turning into the house, "Hey,
it's Danny!"

"I was just outside walking my dog."

Harold nodded, smiled. "Sure, Danny." Turned again. "Hey,
Princess?"

She walked up the hallway, the most beautiful girl in the
whole world.

"Cabin fever," she told her father, pointing at me. Then she
nodded. "Why don't you bring Wormy inside with you? He must
be cold."

"Bernie," I said. "See, he's a Saint Bernard."

"Right," she said, "Bernie. Here, you close the door. I wouldn't
want to catch his tail."

She looked thinner. Not exactly skinny, or even average, or
plump, but less than amazingly obese, a degree shy of elephan-
tine.

I couldn't believe I was there. I unbuttoned my jacket. "Long
time, no see, huh Grace?"

"Oh, I've seen *you*. It's you who haven't seen *me*." She smiled. "Does Bernie want a bowl of water or something?"

I turned to ask him. He wasn't there. "I think he already went to the kitchen to help himself." We walked together down the hallway.

"He's trained, Danny? He won't make puddles on the carpet?"

"Bernie? Sure. Best dog in the world." I smiled.

"But I hear you outside screaming at him every night. It doesn't sound to me like he's trained."

"Ahh," I said, "that's just the two of us having a little conversation. I have to shout because he's a bit deaf."

"He talks back, Danny?"

"He barks, Grace." I shot her a look. "Dogs bark. Something to do with their vocal cords."

"People bark too, Danny."

I didn't know what to say to that, so I shut my mouth. We sat at our usual places at the dining-room table. Nothing much had changed. Mrs. Jankowski's china cabinet was still full of doilies, junk, and Mrs. Jankowski's china. The old tablecloth was still the old tablecloth. Grace's pile of books was still her pile of books. I took off my jacket, sighed.

"So . . ." I said.

"Sew buttons," Grace said. "What do you want?"

I looked at her and shrugged. Her hair was still the color of straw. Her eyes, still deep, magnificent. She was wearing a blue blouse that brought out their color. "Grace, you have absolutely beautiful eyes."

"Windows to the soul," she said slowly, almost sadly.

"Then you must have an absolutely beautiful soul."

"I've been told that. I've also been told a lot of other things."

I didn't want to step into that, so I tried to make pleasant chitchat. "How's school?" "How was your summer?" "How's good old Sister Regina?" *Fine, fine, oh very fine.* Between questions and answers we could hear the clock on the china cabinet ticking.

Finally Grace said, "You're an awful person, Danny, you really are. First you try to destroy me, and then you disappear for a year, and then for two months every night you shout to an invisible dog outside my windows. Then you decide to ring the bell and tell me I have beautiful eyes. Well, just what do you think I am? Your servant? A doormat? Do you think I sit inside this house pining away with love for you? Do you think my life revolves around you and your stupid whims? Well, you're wrong, Danny! You're a terrible terrible person and you're wrong!" She shook her head. "There was a time when I would have given you all you wanted. *Anything*, Danny. I would have starved myself to death for you and let you take me anywhere you wanted, do anything with me that you desired. More than you were capable of dreaming, because then I was starving for love, and you were the only one who was giving it to me. And I thought you were sensitive and tender, but I was wrong. You're wrong! We're wrong! I was willing to give it *all* to you, and you treated it like it was nothing! Like I was some kind of dog. You're the ugliest person I've ever met, and, believe me, I've met some ugly people. I opened up my feelings to you, and you treated me like I was a pile of shit. Excuse my French, Danny. Pardon me for living. But I can get along just fine without you, and don't you think different for a minute! I may not be perfect and I may not be half as pretty as Loretta Shea, but I'm a human being with a—"

"Wait," I said. "Whoa. Who's Loretta Shea?"

"Who's Loretta Shea? Who's Loretta Shea?" Saying this, she looked up, addressing the ceiling. "I absolutely cannot believe you have the gall to ask me who's Loretta Shea!"

"Honest," I said. "I don't know her from Adam."

"How soon the swine forget. Loretta Shea is only the girl you slept with four months ago, Danny. Only the girl who's told everyone north of Kankakee each and every erotic detail. Of course, back then you were a big man, a real somebody. You were going places. Now she only talks about what's-his-name, the guy who was your fullback."

"Hey, I never—"

"Don't add lie to insult unless you want me to spit in your face."

"But, Grace."

"But nothing. She took away the last shred." She laughed, again at the ceiling. "See, a year ago I didn't know what to think, about you, about me, so of course I blamed myself and stupidly thought I'd scared you away, that I was too forward with you that night in my bedroom, and you just got cold feet since everybody knows that girls are much more advanced in these areas than boys, and boys can be so dense and childish. But when I heard that you'd slept with Loretta Shea!"

"Honest, please, on Abe Lincoln's grave."

"Shove his top hat up your ass. Hell hath no fury like a woman scorned! And you realize you are talking to a *woman*, Danny boy, a flesh-and-blood woman of experience and passion so deep it would undoubtedly make you pee."

"You mean you—"

"Several dozen times, you bestial oaf, you insensitive donzel, you rogue, immature—"

Leaping across the table, I tried to kiss her.

"That Stanley Kowalski crap doesn't cut the mustard with me, you ninny Neanderthal! I've waited for this moment for a long time! Boy, you're in the presence of a woman of the world! So why don't you take Wormy the invisible dog and go back into the cold and yank your yo-yo!"

As I stood and grabbed my jacket she once again addressed the ceiling.

"Sweet Virgin Mary and Patroness of Womanhood, ain't revenge sweet!"

Bernie followed me out into the night's cold cruel air, his

bushy tail tucked sadly between his legs. Together we stood on the sidewalk in front of Grace's house. Many great tears slid down Bernie's cheeks and smashed on the ground like light bulbs.

"Don't cry, Bernie," I whispered. "You're a Saint Bernard. Remember your purpose, to help travelers like me lost in winter storms."

But Bernie only stood there by the snowbanks and went on weeping.

"Bernie!" I called, slapping my thigh.

"Bernie!" I shouted, as I walked backward up the street.

"Ber-nie!" I screamed at the top of my lungs.

But he wouldn't budge, and the cold wind roared. And my legs and hands were trembling. Even though I felt like crying, I knew *I* didn't shed a single tear. "I'm leaving, boy," I called out.

He woofed then. It meant he had to go on another mission of mercy.

"So long, Bernie."

I buried the Lone Wolf in the melting mud of spring. He lost the will to go on the same morning I hung my letter sweater in the closet of mothballs. Then my bones rubbed the sleep from their eyes and stretched. Overnight I grew two inches. "I'm six feet tall," I said several thousand times to the flabbergasted bathroom mirror. All my clothing, particularly my faithful stovepipes, recited the Litany for the Dead.

Then I too turned to prayer. It was baseball season.

"Dearest God," I prayed, "this is Danilo Francis Bacigalupo, killer of Mickey Meenan. Please fill the marvelously broken-in mitt of Brother Gabriel, Your faithful servant, with a sure pocket of error-free sanctifying grace. Help my eyes see the ball and hit it far and well. Protect me from runners sliding in high with the evil intent of spiking me. Make baseball my path from my father's house. And thanks for the extra inches. Amen."

In my dreams I stretched like an acrobat and caught every batted ball. I played bunts flawlessly. I ran back from third and snared all the soft tricky flies. Each morning I woke up feeling exhausted, but I was pure, nearly as clean as a couple of kids tumbling from their dad's green Plymouth on First Holy Communion Sunday. See, I was trying to feel good about my life.

But something I didn't understand was still terribly wrong.

Because on the practice field under Gabriel's nose I started to stink to high heaven. Grounders I could've fielded when I was in sixth grade trickled between my legs. Liners Tina could've caught with her eyes closed bounced off the heel of my mitt. My throws to first played hopscotch in the dirt or sailed beyond the first baseman. I swung through balls a year ago I would've creamed. My teammates teased me then, saying I had ground-out-itis, a terminal disease whose only treatment was perpetual exile on the bench.

"Sit down," Brother Gabriel told me after practice the Saturday before my senior-year season was to begin.

Where a Cardinals pennant had hung on his office wall now he had a blue banner that said CELEBRATE THE RISEN CHRIST! His desk was covered with papers. Rosters, I imagined, even though he'd already made the final cut. At once I was convinced I'd be the exception. He was giving me my walking papers. As I sat down I blurted out my darkest fear. "You're giving me the ax."

"No." He sat behind his desk and smiled. "I just want to talk."

There was a hole in the eye of one of the cardinals on his T-shirt. I stared at it.

"What's the matter, Dan? Lately you haven't been yourself."

I shrugged. "I'd better be, Brother. Nobody else would want to be me."

"Well, maybe that's the root of our problem."

Then he told me he'd been watching me, and it seemed to him I was playing without joy. Could I be pressing too hard to try to duplicate last season's .801 batting average? Was the pressure of my errorless string at third taking all the fun out of the game? Baseball was, after all, only a game, and I used to have so much zest and enthusiasm. He told me how much I'd impressed him the day we met when I went after the ball barehanded and knocked myself out. How he thought here was a boy too poor to even have his own mitt, yet he played with such eagerness, without regard for his safety. He said the world was full of kids who had no mitts, kids born without toes or fingers, arms or legs, working ears or eyes—and how did I think they felt when they smelled the bright air of a spring day and wished they too could play baseball?

I told him I honestly didn't know. Then he asked me to close my eyes and imagine I was one of those kids. I did as he instructed.

"Relax, Dan. Pray. Fill your heart with love and joy."

When tears began to run down my cheeks, he told me to open my eyes.

"You're crying for them, aren't you? Your soul is overflowing with thanks that you're you and you're alive! You can feel God's eternal love—"

"No," I was saying. "That's not it at all."

"Nonsense. Don't be deceived. God loves you!"

"No! He hates me! I'm a foul ball in His eyes!"

"He loves you, Daniel! I know it! He—"

"No! *Because I killed Mickey Meenan!*"

The confession wiped the elation from his face.

After I told him the whole story he sat back, spread his fingers, slowly touched opposite tips to each other, then closed his hands and lifted them to his lips as if in prayer. The afternoon sun from the windows behind him gave his big ears a glowing aura.

"Well," he said, "that gives you your life's vocation, doesn't it?"

"What?" I said. "I don't follow."

"Your vocation, Dan. Your purpose. The reason the Lord made you. Your true path in life. It's obvious enough to me."

"Then how about cluing me in on it?"

He sucked his lips into his mouth and then smacked them with a loudness that startled me. "Facts," he said, standing. "Let's examine the facts."

I nodded.

"Fact: God created you in His image and likeness. Fact: He works in strange and mysterious ways. Fact: Ever since this bizarre catastrophe you've been miserable, searching for the event's true meaning. Fact: You're about as gifted a seventeen-year-old ballplayer as I've ever seen. And, fact: The Good Lord doesn't give us talents so we'll bury them."

"Yeah, yeah, yeah," I said.

"Yes, yes, yes, Daniel. Yes, yes, yes. Your purpose in life might be to play the game for this dead kid."

That stopped me cold.

Gabriel smiled. "The ball you hit nine years ago connects you to this boy more strongly than the physical act of love binds the union between a husband and a wife." He meshed his fingers, then shook the tangle in my face. "You're not walking the earth alone, Dan. Mickey's spirit lives within you. Up until now you've struggled against it, against the fact of his death, what you've done. God intended that, didn't He? And now He intends for you to quit wrestling with your guilt, for you to accept it. How? By playing ball for the love of this boy Mickey! His spirit certainly lives in the tabernacle of your soul. In a way, you and he are wed eternally, merged by a commingling of event, by God's strange and mysterious Divine Will." He smiled, then walked behind my chair. "None of this is news to you. You know you're not as alone as you think. And now you've recently grown a few inches and aren't really comfortable with your body. Isn't that right? Tell me you've been relaxed out there. That's the physical reason why you're slumping, why you chop down on the ball, why line drives skip off your mitt. You're *taller* now. You're bigger. But your mind hasn't yet made the adjustment." He stood before me again and folded his arms. "Now try to get your mind, body, and soul in tune. Fill the emptiness inside you with for-

giveness and love. Invite this boy's spirit into your house. Go
ahead. You've got the room now. Close your eyes again. Welcome
him! I'll pray with you."

I closed my eyes and heard Gabriel whispering his prayers,
then let my mind wander from his office to the streets, to the
alley of my childhood, where I pictured Joey Petrovich. My mind
didn't want to stay there; it leapt a fence and ran toward Grace's
house, imagining the two of us in her bedroom. *Go back*, I told
it. *Dearest God. Though this is just a lousy psych job, so much religious
hocus-pocus—* Then another voice shouted, *No, Danny, don't say
that, don't desecrate.* Then I heard Mr. Meenan behind me *you just
wait, kiddo* and I smelled the smoke from his cigar. Grieves chewing me out. *They sliced you and diced you.* The afternoon I quit,
and he turned to the canaries. *Suit yourself, Danny, Danny boy
you're in the presence of a woman of the world! So why don't you take
Wormy the invisible Mickey, honest, we'll only look at 'em, we won't
rip 'em,* though you have more than we're able to dream of, why,
how can that be fair? *Eat, Danny. Care to join us, Scout? We've got
the horn of plenty, dance with this! Don't just sit there like a dummy,
Danilo, wake him up, make a fist of your hand, do you have a problem
you wish to share with us? No, Sister. Then why aren't you talking to
me, to me, to me? Because I borrowed a dime from my brother Louie
and I murdered the Tragedy Behind Mrs. Misiak's Garage,* don't confess
it anymore, *look, you killed him, he ain't even breathing!*

I live on Ol-live!

Divebomber. Mickey. Dearest *Mickey, come mingle in my soul!*

I opened my eyes I was blinded. The windows. My T-shirt
dark. Drenched with sweat.

"Are you all right?" a voice whispered.

I nodded. I could hear the silence in the room.

"You were talking to yourself, Dan. Here, drink this."

It was a paper cup of water. It was in my hand. I put it to
my lips. He stood over me. His hands on my shoulders.

"Good. Breathe. That's it, real deep. You're fine now."

Son, I believe in grace and the flow of grace. I believe that the mind has unexplained powers. I believe that batters can psych themselves out of or into slumps, that pitchers can know, even before the ball leaves their hand, they're throwing a double in the gap or an unhittable strike on the outside corner. There are moments down on the field when you can actually feel the shift in the flow. Heads turn. The umpires try to ignore it. The bullpen pauses between chews. Inside the dugout the bats rattle a little in the racks, sensing it. A play later the announcers call it a swing of momentum, and physicists call it something else, but it's grace, son, sweet proton-popping grace, 100% pure Holy Ghost juice. I sat in Gabriel's office, swimming in it. The right eyes would have seen me glowing. Imagine your *culu* being given a triple enema with Lourdes water. That's how clean and new I felt.

"You're fine now, Dan. You've made a clean breast of it. Continue to pray, and understand that God loves you more than you'll ever know."

More than I'll ever know? I thought. Then my little finger rose to pick my earwax, and I heard the eight-year-old voice inside me. *I dunno.*

He slept for a couple days, or maybe he was just shy. Then during our season opener he made his first appearance.

Sixth inning, and I was happier than a new uniform because I'd hogged plate like my old self and drummed out a dandy pair of hits. I pounded my glove at third. Then a sharp but very playable three-hopper tried to sneak past me to my left. Though I stretched for the ball, it was Mickey who came up with it, and the dumb kid was so amazed he bugged out our eyes and in all his excitement to make the throw lost the handle. The ball squirted up over our head. I caught it and made a damn fine throw to first, but the runner was safe. The loudspeakers squawked, "Error."

Gabriel ran from the dugout, calling time, because by then I was sitting on the bag, holding my knees to my forehead. Some of the fans were applauding the end of my errorless string. I didn't care about the end of the string; I cared about Mickey.

For as sure as the opposing team's runner stood on first, surprised and pleased to be there, *Mickey Meenan dwelled within me.*

Call it schizophrenia, overactive imagination, miracle that brought back the dead. Son, the label is less important than the fact.

"Did you hurt yourself?" Gabriel shouted. "Danny, what did you pull?"

He meant what muscle or tendon, thinking my posture on the bag meant I was injured. I looked up at him and grinned.

"Brother, I pulled a Mickey! I did a Mickey!"

You can read about the season in my clippings, son. The gist was I had outstanding potential but was mortal after all. Mickey tagged me with seventeen more E-5s that season. ST. PAUL PHENOM SLIPS is an example of how the fourth estate put it, stashing their fancy metaphors in a bottom drawer.

My .801 average dipped to .615, but toward the end of the year I somehow began to display long-ball power. In all I popped twenty-seven, most of them coming with runners on and us even or down. The pitchers began smiling at me in the locker room, lending me clean towels, new socks, their lucky fingernail clippers. They said they always thought of me as a real close friend. The opposing pitchers played target practice with my batting helmet, then grooved one or gave me the walk. True to Gabriel's philosophy, they then unraveled, and we rallied, held, won.

COACH HOLDS HOPE FOR SENIOR, announced the *Daily News.*

COLLEGES EYE PREP SLUGGER, said the *American.*

Mickey loved the attention, lapping it up faster than Bernie sucked down Gravy Train. I told Mickey to cool out, take it in stride, that I'd been through it before and wouldn't believe a thing existed until I held it in my hand. Besides, I reminded him, we had a season to finish. We couldn't decide anything until then.

We skipped rope and practiced going to our right in the basement, and he would ask me the dumbest questions in the world.

What did Gabriel mean the other day when he talked about the infield fly rule? How come the batter in yesterday's game ran to first on a dropped third strike? With a bunt, once you pick it up, where do you go with it? So I took him to the library, where we checked out a book on the game's fundamentals, and together in the basement we pored over every diagram and page.

"See, Mickey, third base, where we play, is traditionally called the *hot corner* because most batters are right-handed and most of them pull the ball, so we see some hot action. It's got nothing to do with temperature, OK?"

"But it's real hot out there!"

"It's hot everywhere on the field, Mickey."

"It's not hot at first! I'm the first baseman! You said, Danny, all the guys said!"

"Hey, sure, but that was years ago."

"I wanna know about first!"

"There's nothing much to know, except sometimes you flip to the pitcher covering. There's no nickname. Most of the time all you do is run over, put a foot on the bag, and catch the throw."

"Uh-uh! I know! Pitcher's hands you're out of there!"

"No, Mickey, that was in the Alley League."

"But I wanna play first!"

Then the basement door would open. "Who're you talking to down there?"

I'd stand and walk to the bottom of the stairs. "Ma-aa, I'm trying to study. Can't a guy even do his homework?"

Three weeks before the season's end Gabriel called us into his office.

"Dan, I don't know how much longer I'll be able to hold them back."

"Who?" I said. "More college coaches?"

"I want to go to Notre Dame!" Mickey said. "Win one for the Dipper!"

"Gipper!" I said. "We don't want to go to Notre Dame."

"Save the infield chatter for the field, Dan." Gabriel's face was all business. "I'm telling you, it's a real zoo around here. I've been trying to keep them away from you so you can play out your season, but some of these scouts won't take no for an answer."

"Scouts?" I said.

"I know!" Mickey said. "He was Tonto's horse! The Lone Ranger rode on Silver!"

"Major-league scouts?" I said.

"Roy Rogers' was Trigger. The Cisco Kid—"

"Sure," Gabriel said. "Major-league scouts. I've done exactly what you asked me to, told them absolutely not to contact you at your home and to bring all questions and offers to me."

"Jesus!" I said, sitting down and slapping a hand over Mickey's mouth.

"Now listen to me, Dan. They're going to be coming at you with offers." He smiled. My jaw dropped. "Yeah, you're the area's brightest prospect, and a few have you pegged as best in the Midwest. Be polite and hear what they have to say. Don't sign anything until you're sure. I'm in your corner—"

"Hot corner!" Mickey peeped.

"—and I'll do whatever you want me to. The Lord knows, I went through it all myself. These will be exciting times. But first ask yourself this. Do you want a college scholarship and four years of education that nobody can ever take away from you, or do you want a crack at the majors?"

"A crack at the majors!" Mickey and I said at once.

Gabriel smiled again and put his hands to his lips. As he turned to face his windows, I could see that tears shone in his eyes.

"Dan, I look at you sometimes and I see myself twenty-seven years ago." He turned back around, dry-eyed. "I envy you in a way because you'll go where I couldn't, but in another way I'm very happy for myself because now I can more fully understand my vocation. It's helping kids like you."

"Thanks, Brother. I won't let you down. I'll make the game my life."

"The game was my death!" Mickey whispered.

"My life," I repeated. "Baseball is my life."

Then the three of us knelt by his desk and thanked God for His bounty and prayed for the wisdom to choose the best offer and for the strength to play the way God intended the game to be played. Three weeks later we again prayed, this time with the Denver Dynos scout, who Mickey twice asked how come if he worked for dinosaurs he wore shirts with alligators and penguins. Both times the man laughed and said, "I can see you're a kidder. That's good, you'll need a sense of humor in the bushes." Later, of course, I had to explain the expression. "No, Mickey, he meant the minor leagues." But the four of us prayed. Then I made sure I grabbed the scout's fountain pen before Mickey did. At the bottom of the contract I signed my name.

Danilo Francis MICKEY Bacigalupo

Then everyone shook hands and Brother Gabriel winked and shut his office door and took out a bottle of Christian Brothers brandy, and we toasted one another, Denver, and the minor leagues.

Then Mickey said, "Didja bring the check?"

The scout laughed and said sure, then, "He's a bright one."

"Money talks, nobody walks, unnatural interruptions of deliveries are balks, hey batter, hey batter!" Mickey said, and everybody laughed.

We had a week to report to the Dynos' Class-A farm team in Pirate's Hook, Mississippi. My high-school graduation was two days away. I knew I couldn't stand another speech from my father. After we cashed the check in a currency exchange and went downtown to buy a new glove, Mickey begged that we celebrate with cheeseburgers and ice cream. "No," I told him, "we've got to go home."

"Home?" Mickey said. "We got no home! We're orphans!"

"Not yet," I said as we rode a crowded northbound El.

"I wanna wear the new mitt! Please? I wanna spit in it!"

"Sure, Mickey, but keep it down. People are starting to stare."

He was feeling awful melancholy. On the walk home from the Bryn Mawr El station he sang "Auld Lang Syne." I pocketed some of our bonus for expenses, then dropped the rest and the copy of my contract next to my father's plate. Mickey wanted to cry but I wouldn't let him.

"Mamma!" he shouted when she walked into the kitchen. He fell to his knees and kissed the hem of her housedress. "Mamma, Mamma, I been a lousy son!" He kissed her shoes. "Mamma, I love you!" He kissed the kitchen floor. She said she loved him too, then patted his head like a dog.

I stood, composing myself. "I signed, Ma. I'm a professional ballplayer. I blow this popstand in a week."

Then I let Mickey hold her and kiss her cheek. Then he kissed Rosaria and Tina. He kissed Gino and Dominic and Louie and Francis Junior. He ran to my parents' bedroom and kissed the crucifix over their bed. He kissed the wall, the floor, the bed. Then he ran out the front door.

I went with him, of course. As soon as we got out on the front porch, he started to cry.

"Mickey," I said, disgusted, "don't be such a wimp. It's what you always wanted."

"Not me! I was a good kid! I had a secret blood disease!"

"Sure you did."

"I always put *everything* away!"

He quivered so sadly that he made me sad too. I wondered

what I could do to cheer him up. "Hey, you want to go see our girlfriend?"

He sniffled, rubbed his eyes with his fists, then nodded.

The sky was growing dark. We walked past his old front lawn and house, which I distracted him from seeing by making him count all the cracks in the sidewalk. Then we reached the Jankowskis'. A thousand petunias in a thousand different colors looked up at us and nodded their little heads.

"Do you remember Grace?" I said.

"Yeah! She's the little fat girl! The one who likes to moo!"

"Not any more, Mickey. And now she's not so little either. But she's the girl we love."

"Wow!" Mickey said, and when Grace answered the door he shouted, "Wowee, wow wow wow!" and grabbed her hand and kissed it like a Frenchman. She stared at us funny and asked us to come in.

We sat on her front-room sofa. Mickey turned into Mister Conversation, telling her all about the scouts and the offers and how we bought a new mitt. I let him do the talking. She hung on his every word. When he told her we had to report in a week, a red ink washed up across her neck and face like a cartoon character who'd just swallowed a chili pepper. Mickey didn't notice. He took her hand and told her she was his sweetheart, the girl he truly loved and adored, and would she write to him, would she keep a candle burning for him in her window, and when he made it to the big leagues would she come to see him play?

"Danny," she said, "damn it, you're breaking my heart."

That shut Mickey up.

I dropped her hand to the sofa. "I'm sorry, Grace. I guess I shouldn't have come by."

"No," she said. "Danny—"

Putting my arms around her, I kissed her lips and learned that lovers' hearts don't break, they bleed salty tears that sear

136

more keenly than acid. The pain was like a slap to my face. She kissed my neck, my cheeks, the tears burning in my eyes. I wanted to never let go of her. I didn't care if she'd been a woman of the world several dozen times. She was Grace, dearest Grace, fattest most beautiful Grace.

At the door I kissed her again and whispered, "I love you. I always will, I swear, on my heart and soul."

"I wanna go back!" Mickey screamed as soon as we hit the sidewalk. The night was warm and suddenly eerie. "I wanna marry her! I wanna take her with us to Mississippi!"

"You're such a naïve child," I whispered sadly. "Mickey, you're a real no-mind. She knew that meant good-bye."

"Good-bye? Whatdya mean, good-bye? We still got a week!"

"For what? We've done everything we can here." I laughed. "We've put everything away, get my meaning? We're leaving in the morning, first thing."

"No!" he shouted. "I don't wanna go! Turn around! Please! Pretty please! Look, she's waving to us from her window!"

"You turn another fraction of an inch and I'll murder you again, you little maggot." I was running then, fighting the tears in my eyes.

"I wanna go back! I don't understand!"

"Understand?" I shouted. "I'll show you what you can understand!"

I jerked him by the hair through Old Lady Misiak's backyard and took him to Heaven's Whore and the spot called Mister Death.

"The murderer always returns to the scene of the crime," I told him, "but this time he brings back his victim!"

Mickey stared at the green garage door, then down at the ground.

"You understand now, little dummy? Little inner voice inside my head? Remember being such a dumb fucking garbage-can turd that you didn't even think enough of your own ass to duck?

Huh, Mickey boy? Remember eating the liner with your Adam's apple? Where's all your *wannas* now? Huh? I can't hear you, wee lad. And I know why. It's because you're *dead*, because I *killed* you." I took a deep breath. "You stupid fart from the asshole of existence! What the hell were you thinking about that day anyway? You ruined my life, you ignorant toad. You slimy hand kisser. Let's get one thing straight. I'm getting tired of baby-sitting you, and—"

He was slipping away from me, stepping back into the darkness, toward the spot called Mister Death. His hands were raised. I saw him clearly. Son, that could have been the end of it right there. Maybe I would've seen nothing more, or maybe I'd have watched his shadow melt into the door or the ground. But he dropped his arms then and softly spoke.

"I was thinking—" he began. "I was thinking— Um, how nice it would've been if, if I wasn't me! How neat I'd feel if I was a guy—" His eyes leaked awe and admiration. "A guy more kind of—like you, Danny."

Lightning creased the sky behind us then. I turned and counted. One thousand one, one thousand two, then BOOM! the rolling clap of thunder roared down the alley, and the sky tore itself open and poured down a monsoon of rain. He was back within me then, terrified of the thunder. Inside me there was a trembling. Son, you'll just have to take my word. About this and all the rest of it. What he said had moved me, and he was real scared then—just a kid, at first, in the beginning. I put my arms around myself and told him to be cool, that the lightning was far away.

"It won't hurt us," I whispered. "Nothing will. Ever again."

"Yeah?" he said. "Really really? You'll be nice from now on? You'll be my buddy?"

"Yeah, I'll be your buddy. I give you my word."

As we walked together back to the house, the rain drenched us.

He said nothing when I entered the front room, dripping like wash on the line. Then he looked up from his newspaper, cleared his throat, and told me, "Congratulations."

"Thank you," I said. I puffed out my chest and stood on my tiptoes. "And see, I did it just like I said, by the time I turned eighteen." I moved closer to him so I'd drip on his shoes. "I'm leaving in the morning."

He stared at me. "But your mother said you'd be here another week. I wanted to—"

"I changed my mind, Dad."

He looked down, then turned and stood and left the room. He came back a minute later, handing me a towel. "Danilo, I know we've never been very close."

I put the towel around my neck. "That's an understatement."

"If there's anything I can do—"

"I'll let you know if there is." I stared him in the eye. "I know your address and phone number."

"Your mother will miss you," he said.

"The other kids will keep her busy."

"Danilo, there are things a man finds very hard to say."

"Then don't say them." I shook my head. "Or save them for your other sons. Or your daughters, for Christ's sake. But don't start now. Don't you dare change on me now that I've finally learned how to get along without you. I don't need you anymore, you understand? I'm grown up. I'm not your kid anymore. First thing tomorrow morning I'm leaving."

"I know I've made mistakes—"

"Everybody makes mistakes. It's what you do *after* you foul up that's important, remember?"

"Danilo, allow me to say that you've made me very proud."

"Proud?" I wanted to laugh in his face. "Why are you proud all of a sudden? Because I can make my own way now? Or because you think maybe you had something to do with it?" I looked right into his eyes. "Well, don't flatter yourself. Whatever I accomplished wasn't because of you, Dad. You've been in my way my whole life. Whatever I've done or become, it was despite you."

He looked down at his hands.

I walked away.

Later Mickey asked me how my heart could be so hard.

"Because," was all I could say. We lay in bed. In the darkness above us the cracks in the ceiling now formed a baseball. Mickey pointed out to me the laces. "Go to sleep," I told him. "Tomorrow's a new day."

1 2 3 4 **5** 6 7 8 9

SAFE AT FIRST

I thought the storm that poured down on Chicago that night was the world's way of letting me know I'd be missed. By midnight it had stopped thundering. The rain, hard and steady, filled the streets and alleyways with dark puddles of sadness and regret. I roamed about the sleeping house, imagining the city was weeping for my departure.

"Begorra," the priests and the Sisters of Christian Charity said to themselves that evening, "the reason I can't sleep is because I'm as unhappy as this noisy rain pounding me windows, because come morning the parish loses its finest son, the murderous-good ballplayer Dan Bacigalupo!"

"I should've danced with him when I had the chance," moaned Deirdre Egan in her beauty sleep. "Held his hand, kissed his lips, run my beautiful slender fingers through his greasy hair. Alas, heavy sigh, now Danny's leaving to become a magnificent major-league ballplayer!"

"Don't cry, Pops," Grace told Harold. "Here, console yourself by eating Idaho and this herd of cattle Mom just took out of the oven. I'll unload the bread truck and get the sour cream. Even though I've slept with several dozen stupid jerks who probably wouldn't recognize deepness if they fell into it, I'll love Danny for all eternity and then some!"

"He had more ketchup and mustard than Del Monte and French's," Charlie Grieves told his closet of Hawaiian shirts. "Not once in his life did he eat cake! Now in the morning, sniff, he'll leave the driving to Greyhound!"

"Thanks, Almighty God!" prayed Brother Gabriel, kneeling beside his bed. "I see now that my life's sole purpose was to coach Dan Bacigalupo!"

Deep in the darkness of the Underwater World the exotics and tropicals gurgled, "No one tended us better." The feeders shoaled and whispered, "Even though he scooped us to our deaths, no one loved us more." Somewhere on the planet Mr. Meenan put down his cigar and told his wife, "He's taking good care of our Mickey, I can feel it! Danny's as good as a Delicious apple! I sure as hell forgive him. You do too? Great!"

The editor-in-chief of the *Trib* was shouting, "Stop the presses! Look what just came in over the wire! I want it on the front page!"

PREP SLUGGER DEPARTS FOR MINORS
Fans Throng Downtown Bus Station—Thousands Weep
Mayor Declares Day of Mourning

I imagined the five Great Lakes pounding their shorelines, trying to wave good-bye. Men from the Department of Streets and Signs putting up a plaque in the alley. *Here's Da Place Dan "The Man" Bacigalupo Got His Start*. Denver rolling out the red carpet, giving me the city's key, a ticker-tape parade to Mile High Stadium, home of the Dynos. The mayor's speech: "Dan, on behalf of Denver, the state of Colorado, and the Rocky Mountains, let me thank you for bringing us our first World Series championship!" Deafening roar heard as far away as Honolulu. Thousands then chanting, "Dan the Man! Dan the Man! Dan the Man!"

In the dark front room I raised one hand for silence. "When you signed me out of high school, maybe the best in the Midwest, I had no idea at all that this would happen." (Roar.) "Who would've thought the Dynos, once they played me at third, would've gone on to win ten, no, make it fifteen World Series in a row!" (Another roar.) "Who would've thought I'd bat over .400 in each of those fifteen seasons!" (Roar again.) "You're a great city! I love you!" (Earthshaking roar and pandemonium.)

Well, at least that's what I thought.

The reality was I'd left things pretty much in a mess. The fabric of my life dangled several untied threads, to Charlie Grieves, to Grace, my family. My mother made it loud and clear early that morning as I stood with my duffel bag and mitt by the back door.

"You refuse even his offer of a ride to the bus station. Well go ahead, take the El. Why should today be any different? You've been running out that door away from us all your life."

"Ma," I said, "it's not a big deal."

"It is to him." She turned back to the table. "Why would he have even brought it up? He knew he'd be late for work." She turned from the table and stared at me. "So maybe we're not perfect. We both made mistakes with you, who ever said we wouldn't? But we gave you a roof over your head. You never went hungry. That's more than he had when he was a boy. This is your family, Danny! Sometimes you act around here like we're a hotel."

She stacked our three plates, walked to the sink, then ran water on a dishrag. "If you knew how much I pray," she continued. "How much he thinks about you and worries." She turned off the water, wiped the table, caught the crumbs in her cupped hand. "You try working two jobs and feeding nine for all these years. You try caring for children, one at your feet, one at your knees, one in your arms you got to feed." She dropped the crumbs in the garbage bag, rinsed the dishrag in the sink. "I hate to talk to you like this, today of all days. But I don't know how to get through to you." She turned the water off again. "We love you, and we'll miss you. So go before I cry or he gets angry again."

I nodded, then left her in the room with her mix of love and rage.

The bus bounced out of the downtown terminal in a gray puff of sewer gas. Its air brakes squealed a moment later at a red light. I let Mickey work the neat's-foot oil into our mitt. "Do a good job," I whispered. "Do it slowly. Do it right." In the other seats lonely old women gazed out the rain-streaked windows, a man in a green shirt slept, a woman with her hair in curlers hushed two cranky kids with doughnut halves and plastic toys, two uniformed sailors leaned forward and chain-smoked a pack of Pall Malls, a kid in a stocking cap blasted a transistor radio. B. B. King. Bo Diddley. "I'm a Man." The bus hit the Outer Drive and rolled.

When we passed the Museum of Science and Industry, I remembered a field trip my fourth-grade class went on. How I descended into the cold bowels of a coal mine, banged my knees inside a captured Nazi sub, walked through an immense beating heart. Stepped inside a room that was really a telephone of the future—the ceiling and dotted plastic walls concealed the receiver and mouthpiece—and I dropped the last of the five dimes my ma had given me that morning into the slot, then dialed home. I sat on the little bench waiting. The number rang. Once, twice. Then the walls and ceiling bellowed, "Hello?" My ma's voice, from everywhere around me.

I said nothing. "Hello, who is this?" my mother said. I put my hands over my ears. "Say who you are!" the room shouted.

In the background I could hear Francis Junior crying. "Don't play this joke! I don't like this joke!" Then the room buzzed with the tone that meant she'd hung up. The room grew quiet as a tomb. My back broke out in sweat. I yelled, "Ma! Ma, it's me! Ma? Ma!"

We headed south. Other mothers with children replaced the one with the doughnuts and toys. Other buses replaced the one washed by the Chicago rain. We followed the path made four hundred million years ago by the glaciers. Farms, fields, and towns flew past the window. The wheels beneath me hummed. Mickey rubbed the glove. Now and then I slept. The sun fell and rose and fell and rose again, until we screeched to a dusty stop deep in the heart of Dixie.

Actually it was Pirate's Hook, Mississippi, a hot, humid, sleepy little place, barely as big as a North Side neighborhood. It lay just north of the Louisiana border and a healthy fly ball from Bogalusa, on the banks of a river named Pearl.

We hopped off the bus and looked around. It seemed they had a lot of room down there. Nothing was crowded. Across the street stood a hotel. Two or three shops. A tractor. Some old houses. The sky was big and as hot as a match. The earth had an orange tint. Nothing moved except the Greyhound bus raising the dust in the distance.

"Well," I told Mickey, "we're here."

"I died and came back so I'd come here?"

"You bet, Mickey. Pound that mitt."

Then we saw a man on a horse galloping like there was no tomorrow. The man was as black as Gabriel's old mitt. "What's chasing him?" I asked.

Mickey giggled. "Ride 'em, cowboy!"

While I didn't expect a brass band, I did think more than just the ticket man snoozing behind the counter would be awaiting the Dynos' new first-round draft pick. The ticket man blinked, then squinted at me—I stood with my back to the blazing sun—

nodded when he saw our mitt, sort of smiled, and said, "If you're lookin' for the ball field, it's on a little ways up the road."

Indeed it was. Past the diner—a pair of bleached signs in the window, COFFEE 10¢ and HOMEMADE PIE FRESH DAILY. The Texaco filling station—inside the dark cavern of the shop, a white man watched a black man work; outside, two hounds slept in the shade of the idle pumps. Across a road—no lights, signs, or even a yellow stripe. A tavern—parked pickup trucks, muted music, and COLD BEER in the blackened window, painted blue icicles dripping from the COLD. A couple of frame houses—patched screen doors, cane chairs out on the porches, boats leaning against trees out in back. A '53 Chevy up on cinder blocks—Mickey recognized the year. Another sleeping dog. Underwear hanging on a clothesline. A blue bicycle on its side, baseball card clothes-pinned to the frame so the card would flap against the spokes. A real big tree Mickey thought might be a magnolia. I told him I didn't know beans about trees. A phone booth just like up north. More boats. Trees. Shade. A green statue of a man with a sword on a horse. Mickey wanted to climb the statue. I made him walk on. It was too hot and humid to play on statues.

To our left there was something set back in a field of weeds. "Can't be," I said. "But let's check it out anyway."

Mickey started to whistle "Take Me Out to the Ball Game."

"My God!" I said. "No, come on, dearest God—"

Inside a nearly collapsed chain-link fence there were bleachers where no more than a couple hundred people could sit, a rusted backstop, several warped rows of boards advertising headache powder and chewing tobacco that marked the outfields and sep-arated the grass from the pussy willows lining the river beyond right field, and the most pitted, miserable, sorry-looking infield we had ever laid our eyeballs on.

"This has got to be the grammar-school park," I told Mickey.

"I like it!" he said. "Look at those neat craters around second base!"

"The dugouts aren't even dug out."

"But look at all those holes in the tin roof! Boy, if we have night games, we could sit on the bench and watch the stars!"

"Watch the stars, hell," I said. "Where's the clubhouse? The players' lounge? The box seats? The press box? I don't even see a bullpen."

Mickey pointed down the lines at two rows of folding chairs. "It's neat! Major-league! Batter up! Play ball!"

"Major-league my left nut, Mickey. It's nursery-school. Hobbyhorse. We've got to be in the wrong place! Hey, we're a professional ballplayer! We need to find a stadium. When the team finds out we came here instead, man, they'll laugh and laugh."

Our conversation must have been louder than we thought because someone waved and shouted hey and moseyed over toward us. He was old, a good seventy or eighty, with bright golden eyes and a faded green cap on his head.

"You one of the new bloods we been waitin' on?" the old man said.

I introduced myself.

The man's cap bore the greener outline of a torn-off *D*. He gave us a wide smile. "I'm Homer. Trainer, statistician, groundskeeper, equipment manager. Shoot, you name it, I do it. On behalf of the Pirate's Hook Dynos Professional Baseball Organization Incorporated, kindly allow me to welcome you to the minor leagues!"

It wasn't as bad as I'd first thought, son. Mickey kept reminding me that the park was prettier than our alley back on Olive Street, and Homer was cordial and kind. He took us down under the bleachers ("Watch that you don't put your foot in a rattrap now!") and showed us the locker room ("You think this one's bad, you oughta see what we give the visitors!") and the showers ("Yeah, I know, we been meaning to get the hot water fixed."). He told us that most of the players used the public toilets just a ways up the road from the stadium. He was real pleased to see we'd brought our own shoes and mitt. "Equipment's scarcer than humility in an Episcopalian." His fingers poked our duffel bag. "You didn't happen to bring along a bag of balls?" I told him no. "Yeah, we lose a whole lot to that river. Other teams like to poke them out real good." Then he unlocked a dingy office, startling a couple of sleeping rats, and gave us our uniform. "You sure you want thirteen? You real sure now? Well, looky here, right at the bottom of the pile!"

Game time was about five hours away. Homer told me to see the manager, Bob Wingert, as soon as he arrived. I stashed the duffel bag in a locker and headed outside for the public toilets.

Even though the shirt was old, and the pants were patched and stitched together mainly with fishing line, my first professional uniform sent a ripple of pure pleasure down my spine. The shirt was white with green pinstripes. A big Palmer script *Dynos* stretched across its chest. On the left shoulder there was the team emblem, a beautiful three-inch-long green dinosaur; most likely a baby brontosaur, Mickey told me. I gave the mirror a screech. My fingertips traced the word *Dynos* and the thick swirl that ran down under the name from the *s* like a lizard's tucked-back tail. Though the room smelled of feces and urine, I felt as blessed as a newly named pope dressing for his first Mass in an incense-filled sacristy in Saint Peter's Basilica.

"Glory be to God on High!" Mickey sang, soprano.

"And on earth," a bass voice responded from the door, "a juicy piece of ass to men of good will."

I turned and saw the darkest face I'd ever seen, made even blacker by the dazzling white of his smile. This face went beyond dark chocolate, fountain-pen-black India ink, a minute past starless midnight. The man I was looking at was so black he was nearly blue.

"Booker," he said and shook my hand. "Booker T. Johnson. And some call me Book or Booker T. or T.J., and those are my friends. And some call me names that are a lot worse."

I smiled, letting go of his hand. "I'm Danny, Daniel, Danilo Francis Mickey Bacigalupo. From the Italian, meaning—"

"Baa-chi-ga-*loo*-poh," he rolled off his pink tongue. "Wolf, wolf. Wolf balls?"

I laughed. "Close. Kiss, kisser, or kissed. *Bacio* means 'kiss.' "

"Kiss," he said and laughed. "Wolf-kissed. Hey, I like that!"

"You're the blackest man I've ever seen!" Mickey said.

Book looked at me and nodded. "Yeah, I'll bet I am."

"I didn't mean—" I said.

"What?" Book said. "To notice my skin color? The Dynos may sign some piss-poor ballplayers on occasion, but to my knowledge they haven't signed any blind ones. You got eyes." He was beginning to undress. His utter blackness filled the room. "Hey, I don't mind people who speak their thoughts. It's the ones who're silent you got to watch out for."

"Can I touch you?" Mickey said. "Just your arm."

"I'm loose," Book said. He stuck out an arm to Mickey. "But Danny, you just aren't pretty enough for more than this."

"You're like a panther!" Mickey said.

"Hey, don't lay that rap on me!" He laughed. "Not a Black Panther in Mississippi!" I didn't know then what he meant. He smiled. "It's just skin, man, pretty much the same as yours. But you won't mind if I don't reciprocate, since I've touched a great number of white arms in my time. By the way, do you know you're changing in the colored john?"

"The colored john?" I said.

"Uh-huh. They took the sign down, but habits die hard."

"You want me to get out?"

"I don't mind if you don't mind."

I didn't mind, so I said nothing. Then I said, "What do you play?"

"Meanest short in the league. How about you?"

"Third."

That made Book smile again. "Then you're—*you're* the first-round draft pick! The answer to our prayers!" I nodded. "I read about you in the paper, but I didn't connect the name. Say, I *am* glad to meet you, Danny Lupo. You're supposed to be able to hit for power, average, have a rifle arm and a pretty fair glove."

"That's me," I said.

He'd finished changing. "You know what they say about hands. It takes two to clap. One washes the other." He stared at me until I nodded. "Now, I don't mean to lay a line of sandlot rah-rah on you, man, but I can help you and you can help me and we both can become better."

"You bet." I smiled. We shook hands again.

Some of the other blacks were coming in now, surprised at first to see me. Book introduced me around. We tossed our stuff in the lockers beneath the stands, then took our time walking to the field.

"My strength's defense," Book was telling me. "I'm a fielding whiz. I'm the barracuda of the left side of the diamond. Call me off or I'll run up your back. I'm pure speed. I get on first one hundred times, I'll steal eighty-five bases. That's gospel."

"Money in the bank," I said.

"You got it, third baseman! We're talking now! We're talking one-way airfare up to Mile High in Denver! Big-league ball, here we come! Now you, the best thing about you is that you'll get older. Trust me, Lupo, I've done the research. I've been studying this organization up, down, and sideways ever since I signed. We made all those trades the middle of last year, remember, and they put the club in the race. But Denver still hasn't won a pennant. So *Sporting News* has them saying they're a little tired now of trading. They know their future's getting ripe down here on the farm. Believe it. Two, three years from now, they're gonna pull us all on up! And I plan to be on that flight when they make the final boarding call."

"Buckle your seat belts!" Mickey said.

"Oh yeah," Book said. "They'll need my speed. You're talking

150

to their future shortstop. And they'll need your bat, third base-man. They made a real big deal about your stats when they signed you. Of course, you'll need to play a decent bag, and you've got to protect that line. I mean, if you learn one thing down here, that's it. These boys are all pull hitters. They just love to sneak it down the line past you." He shook his head. "It gives Wings fits watching extra bases rattling in the left-field corner."

"Wings?" I said.

"Wingert. Bob Wingert. Good Ole Boy Robert E. Lee Wing-ert. Hey, you remember Boston back maybe twelve, thirteen years ago? Wings was the king of the K–Y Jelly ball. Dirtiest damn pitcher you'd ever want to see. Lived on his greaseball and pure junk. Hit more batters than anybody who ever played the game. Ended a whole lot of good careers. Then some uppity blood from Detroit clipped Wings' wings"—Book laughed—"with a line drive right off his pitching elbow. The man was never the same after that."

"I got hit once with a liner right off my Adam's apple!" Mickey said.

"And you lived to talk about it?" Book laughed again. Mickey chuckled and threw an arm around Book's shoulders. Then Homer ran up to us, nearly out of breath.

"Where you been?" Homer said. Ten feet behind him stood Wingert.

The man's face was as cracked and tanned as a dried-up riverbed baked under a broiling Mississippi sun. A line of juice from his chaw of Red Man stained his chin. The whites of his eyes were yellow. He wasn't big. His handshake was firm and dry.

"I don't like to say things twice," he said, "so you pay close attention to me, boy, whenever you hear me speak."

"Yes, sir," I said.

"I don't warm to ass lickers, but you shoulda been waiting for me in the parking lot the moment I drove up. What's done is done. By tomorrow you'll know our signs. Talk to Homer in the morning. Bed check's at eleven-thirty, not eleven thirty-one. Get a watch if you ain't got one. Homer'll teach you how to read the hands if you don't know already. Launder your uniform before each and every game, and I expect to see it ironed. This is a professional ball club. Don't pull no high-school grandstand-play bullshit. Keep your damn pecker out of the local pussy, not that any of it would have you. Don't ever appear in public drunk. We got Louisiana just down the road for that, but up here we got community relations to maintain, you hear me boy? You'll bunk with Purvis at the hotel. You'll be on time for the bus." He paused, stared into my eyes. "And you'll recreate, on and off the field, with boys of your own color."

I looked at him.

"But Book's my buddy!" Mickey said.

Wings looked away, chewing real slow, then turned his head and spat.

"I don't like you." He shook his head. "No, I don't like you at all. There's few men I meet and in less than two minutes decide I can't stomach, but you're one of them. I won't even try to pronounce your last name. I won't remind you that you're a visitor here, and guests are obliged to show their hosts some manners. Now, I'm gonna try to forget I ever met you, boy. But you'd better be either real good so I can kick you on up, or you be as poor as old Aunt Jemima's piss so I can have the pleasure of cutting your balls off this team, you hear me?"

"We'll be real good," Mickey said.

That evening in the dugout I stayed as far away from him as I could. I watched the Pirate's Hook Dynos try to play professional baseball.

If we were the future of Denver, the Mile High City was in for a Death Valley low. Most of my teammates stood at the plate and hacked, swinging for the river. They didn't try to advance runners. They didn't run out their outs. The outfield played with dangerous indecision, nearly colliding twice, then letting routine flies drop between them. They seldom threw to the right base. Their third baseman had a strong arm but let the ball play him. At bat, the catcher stood at the plate like he was posing for his portrait, or else the wood was glued to his shoulder. The second baseman walked and singled but both times was picked off. The only exception was Book.

He didn't belong on the team. He was so good he made shortstop look easy. He played hitters perfectly, then confidently charged the ball. His throws to first were letter-high. His fluid pivot at second turned the double play. He popped up his first time at bat but legged it out, racing all the way to second by the time the ball was caught. That's heads-up baseball, son. Some batters don't even make the effort to run the first ninety feet. Later he beat out an infield single, stole second standing, then danced off base so well he forced the pitcher to balk. At third he swung down his arms, faked a steal of home, became so distracting that the pitcher forgot where the plate was. He fired a fastball a batter on stilts would've thought high. Booker waltzed in with the run. Wings said nothing as Book ran into the dugout.

Two outs in the fifth. Runner on second. The Dynos down by six. Wings nodded at me and mumbled, "Get out there."

Son, imagine a country mile of golden flowers that suddenly explodes, the flowers rising all at once from the earth, becoming a crazy swarm of fluttering butterflies. That's how your daddy felt just before his first professional at-bat. Oh, I tried to act cool. I made an O of my mouth and took in a deep breath. Then I pulled a bat from the rack and stretched on deck, hearing the announcer mispronounce my name for the sixty or so sleepy fans. No more than ten clapped. I did half a dozen knee bends and took thirteen practice swings, and the umpire said, "Let's go, kid, it's hot as hell." The catcher undammed a foot-long stream of spit.

"Our first at-bat, wow!" Mickey kept saying.

"Dearest God," I said to the sky as I dug in, looked at my feet, checked where the fielders were playing me, then stared at the pitcher and watched his snappy fastball dissect a corner off the plate.

"Stee-rike!"

Pretty good stuff, I thought, watching the pitcher's hands and eyes. I picked nothing up. No relaxation to suggest something offspeed, no grimace to hint at a slider. He nodded at the first sign. Fastball again. So he wanted to finish the inning quickly, I thought. Of course, what did he have to lose, with a six-run lead? I watched the ball to the bat, which Mickey grabbed from my hands and swung.

Not well or wisely, since the pitch was low and away. Mickey had fouled ball one into strike two. I raised a hand, got time, stepped out of the box.

"Do that again and I'll kill you," I whispered.

"Again?" Mickey mumbled. "You'll kill me again?"

"I'll kill you so many times you won't know if you're living or dying."

"Well, maybe I don't know the difference now."

"What's that supposed to mean?"

"When will I get *my* turn to hit?"

"Batting practice, Mickey."

He said, "Aww," and rubbed our eyes.

"I'll teach you everything I know. Break you in slowly. Come on, give a guy a break. This is pro ball, Mick. Everything I do counts up here. Don't you think I'm scared too?"

"You're scared?"

"Damn straight."

"You'll let me bat later? Promise?"

"I promise, Mickey. Cross our heart."

"For Chrissakes, let's go!" said the umpire, and I nodded, dug in again, checked my feet, the fielders, watched the pitcher bring in his arms, then throw them out as he began his delivery.

I picked up the third fastball just as it left his hand. It flew so splendidly that I could see its laces bite the summer air, and at that moment I realized where I was, standing at bat in a miserable ball park in the bottom of the country, while everything I knew and loved was back up north, in Chicago, about seven hundred and fifty miles over the left-field fence. I sipped the humid Mississippi air. An insect buzzed near my ear. From the bench someone shouted a long "Go-oooo!" I watched the ball and swung for it, with all that my life then knew. The ball cracked with glee off the fat part of the bat.

Then Mickey was screaming, "Run, Danny, run!," and we were running, and as I rounded first I saw the ball bounding between the two fielders toward the left-center-field wall. I ran, rounded second, and looked for the third-base coach to tell me whether to hold up or continue. His arms were windmilling, so I ran, not breaking stride, watching him as he raised his palms and then flung them down past his knees, and I dove and slid headfirst into the bag, hearing the ball skip above me, the infielder grunt, the crowd going, "Oh, yeah!" Then the ump flattened his palms and cried, "Safe!"

Triple. Sweet Mary, a Holy Ghost hit!

"First thing in the morning," Mickey screamed as we stood and dusted off our shirt and pants, "we'll have to find a Laundromat!"

"Right after breakfast," I shouted. Then I heard the scattered applause from the stands. While it wasn't very loud or even enthusiastic, it was the sweetest music I'd heard in my life.

Though I died on third and Wings sat me wordlessly again on the bench and we dropped the game, I was happy.

Then Book and the other black ballplayers disappeared, and Homer reminded me I was rooming with Purvis. After I found him I asked, "What's the matter, I thought we were a team, where'd they go?"

Squat and neckless as a mailbox, uglier than a bulldog, Purvis shook his head and said, "Just where the hell do you think? Their hotel." Purvis was our catcher and had been up to the Double-A team in Razor Bluff, Arkansas, but had just been sent down to work on his hitting.

"But don't we all stay at the same hotel?" I said.

"What planet were you born on?" Purvis said. "Those pinstripes on your belly ain't the only thing around here that's green."

Then he shook his head again and told me to tag along. We followed the other white ballplayers to one of the town's white taverns for something to eat. Purvis pushed me into a booth and raised two fingers at a waitress. A minute later she came over with two glasses and a pitcher of beer.

"Too bad about tonight," she said, pouring the beer. "You boys know what you want?"

There were no menus. Purvis said, "Honey, you know what I want."

The waitress laughed. "Keep dreaming, Luther." Then she turned to me and said, "What about you?"

On the evening of your first professional base hit you like to go all out, celebrate. I told her I wanted prosciutto and provolone.

She smiled and leaned closer. "Say it again, honey."

I pronounced the words slowly. Purvis was laughing.

"You're real cute." She turned to Purvis. "Should I slap his face?"

"Provolone's a cheese," I said. "Prosciutto's Italian ham."

"You're an Eyetalian ham," Purvis said. "Charlene, see what I have to put up with coming back? My new roomie can't even goddamn speak English."

"Ham and cheese," the waitress said. "And, Luther, you want yours rare?" She raised a hand. "I know, you like it with the blood dripping." She leaned down again and patted my hand. "Next time just say it simple and anything I got is yours, honey."

Purvis drank his beer in two swallows. "You're a case," he said. "Drink up, time's a-wasting." We talked for a while. Then

Charlene brought Purvis his steak sandwich and me my Mississippi ham and cheese.

"So it won't be for no longer than a month," Purvis was saying. "Maybe fourteen days if I can get on a streak. I just got to iron out some kinks." He picked a piece of meat out from between his front teeth. "Yeah, so after my first strikeout I knew he'd pitch me tight." He sucked his front teeth, then ate the piece he'd picked out. "Because if I was calling the game that's where I'd go. Jam it right in on my fists." He made like he was holding a bat and showed me his fists. "So the second time up I was waiting on him, see. Then I figured he knew that I knew, so I thought, Hey, get smart for a change. He'll go outside on me with his hard slider. Then I figured he knew I knew that too, so he'd try to stay a step ahead and come in on me." He scratched his forehead with rough flicks of his fingernails like there was something up there bothering him that wouldn't go away. "So I knew he knew I knew—are you following this?—and the damn catcher knew it too, so I got all confused and when I get confused I guess I get paralyzed, and the son of a bitch got me with three fastballs down the middle of the damn plate."

"That's about all he threw tonight," I said, nodding. "Fastballs."

"How do you know?" Purvis said.

"I watched."

He shook his head.

"How come you think so much?" I said.

He looked at me as if I had asked him why he went up there with a bat. "So I can hit the damn ball, you fool."

"But you don't hit it with thinking."

"Bullshit."

"I never think about anything!" Mickey said. "I just get up there and swing!"

"Sure," Purvis said, unbelieving. He poured and drank another beer.

"Really," I said. "I just try to watch the ball to the bat."

"No way in hell." Purvis shook his head. "I know a hitter with a system when I see one. I wish I had one of them computer brains like you."

"Honest," I said. "Like everybody I'll try to pick up a certain pitch, but I don't stand up there analyzing and reanalyzing. Every pitch is new. I just watch the ball and swing."

"Hitting's all up here," Purvis said, tapping his forehead with his beer glass. "It's mental, damn it. Ain't I right?"

Mickey spoke for us. "Hitting's in your arms and wrists, your eye and your body! The brain just gets in the way. Trust the bat! Swing, batter, swing! Unplug the thinking machine, what do you got to lose?"

Purvis bit his bottom lip real hard, then flicked his forehead again about fifteen times.

"Sorry," I said. "I'm nobody to talk. I've been down here less than a day and I'm talking like I'm Ted Williams."

He shook his head again, like a spastic metronome. "Mister, don't sell yourself short. You may be dumb enough not to have grabbed Charlene's hand and said what you wanted real simple, but you got an RBI, three bases, and a one-point-triple-zero batting average. Whatdya think I'm sitting here talking to you for? I'm in a slump! They sent me back down to goddamn Single-A! Man, I'm trying to pick your brain!"

It was past eleven, so we walked down the road to the hotel. No Holiday Inn, the place could have been called Cockroach Hideaway. It was full of the fastest, scurrying little brown cigar butts Mickey or I had ever seen. "Look at those suckers run!" Mickey cried when we turned on the bathroom light.

Purvis sat on his bed in his Jockey shorts and snipped his toenails, then used a long piece of clipping to pick his back teeth. I stood in the bathroom and stared at myself in the mirror, feeling sad and suddenly lonely. Homesick, I ached for familiarity, particularly for Grace, who I pictured out on the town with one of her several dozen dashing young studs. I thought about calling her, then thought no. I'd call or write no one. They were all in my past.

"Why do I wanna cry?" Mickey whispered to me.

"You don't want to cry," I said.

"I do! I feel real bad! Like I could just die!"

"Not again, Mickey. Let's not pick up bad habits. Never again, you understand? You're with me now, so I'll take care of you. Just don't pull the bat away from me, like tonight."

"I couldn't breathe, Danny! It didn't hurt, but I couldn't—" He held his throat and made little K sounds until I got dizzy.

"You're OK, Meenan. Get up, sluggo."

"Then everything was black, and I walked up the dark alley!"

"We dragged you, Mickey. Me and Winky Winkler."

"No! I walked! Then I went up to Heaven!"

"Alleluia, Mickey. *Adoramus.*"

"No, it wasn't like *that*."

"Then what was it like?"

"I dunno."

"He was a big guy with a white beard and a halo, right?"

"No. He was like Tinkerbell! Then He was Felix the Cat! Then He was Mr. Wilson from 'Dennis the Menace.' Then the Green Lantern!"

"What'd He say?"

" 'Dominoes Nabisco! Get some Tootsie Rolls!' "

"Oh yeah?"

"You betcha! And then He sprinkled my forehead with holy water! Then I kissed His wounds! Then everybody played baseball!"

I was throwing water up on my face. "That sure sounds like Heaven."

"Naw. I'd rather be alive!"

"But you are. You're as alive as I am. Right, Mickey? You never died. I never hit the ball that killed you. The ambulance never—"

"Liar, liar! Pants on fire! Nose as long as a telephone wire!"

"You done yet?" Purvis said then from the doorway. I didn't know how long he'd been standing there. He shook his head as he walked past me to take a leak. "Man, I've roomed with *allllll* kinds of ballplayers in my time, but you're a real tin can full of cocktail nuts, I swear to Jesus."

Heat. Humidity. Roaches. Hotels. Bus rides so long your bones ached. *Welcome to the minor leagues.* Most of the food you could afford was fried or boiled tasteless. Most of the people you saw out the bus windows were bad-teeth, gut-hungry poor. Any Olive Street garage would have been a mansion in parts of southern Mississippi. The worn clothes my ma gave to Goodwill, a prince's robes. I came to love and hate the place, son.

What I hated was the unfairness, that some born there were condemned to live and die in such poverty. What I loved were some of the people and the land. The women and men bent over sweating in the rolling fields, and then you'd see a shack, and beyond the broken front door, inside an old tire painted white, were blossoming geraniums. Honeysuckle tumbling down a leaning fence. White cattle egrets atop the backs and at the feet of a grazing herd of cattle. Kids with ashy knees and elbows pulling fat catfish from a river, and they look at the bus and grin, hold up their wriggling string. The world seemed bigger to me down in Mississippi. Even though the air was always hot and thick, it seemed as if there were more of it to breathe.

Wings used me as a pinch-hitter for a few weeks. I produced until he had no choice but to let me start. Once I started there was no getting me out of the lineup. Book and I joked that we covered the left side of the infield better than the tarpaulin. I still didn't like to go with the pitch and hit toward first, but I drilled liners everywhere else. My average soared. Book continued to stroke effortless-looking singles to all three outfields and to run the base paths as if he owned them. The Jackson paper called him Mister Speed. We became pretty tight.

He and the other blacks on the team sat in the back of the

bus, and soon I became the guy who'd get them burgers or bottles of soda pop when we stopped on the road somewhere for lunch. I guess they could have gone in themselves then, but not going in made things easier. We were ballplayers, remember. We had towns to get to, games to play. We didn't have time for making points, even if the point was a right one.

If the places didn't have a toilet marked COLORED, they'd pee out back in some field. I'd stand lookout. I'd talk to the whites who'd come over, wanting to know what was what. No valiance here, son. Don't conclude that I was some noble right-thinking Freedom Rider willing to spill his blood so the cause of Civil Rights could be advanced. Of course, there were hassles now and then. But Book was my friend, and all the others didn't mind me.

Mickey absolutely loved Book and would bore him for hours with the story of his life, death, and reincarnation. Book listened to it all and appeared to believe every word. Then he'd change the subject and we'd talk about the game, how to play different situations, how not to repeat the mistakes of games past, how to communicate with our chatter so as not to tip off the opposing third-base coach, how to put good wood on the old horsehide, to foul off the potential pop-ups and weak grounders and trash pitches and hang in there, wait for our pitch, the ball we could drive, for his lovely singles to all three fields, for my singles and extra bases.

We taught Mickey everything we knew, and Book taught me what he knew, and Mickey kept the three of us entertained, reciting the story lines of vintage comic books. Sometimes we just sat on the bus looking out the dusty windows, feeling the miles pass beneath our feet. And sometimes we planned and dreamed about Denver—everything we did and hoped to be was geared toward Denver—where we'd anchor the infield and win the pennant and World Series with our gloves, our bats, his pure unstoppable speed.

So really it was selfishness, not right thinking or doing the moral thing. My life had no room for morals then. I was a minor-league ballplayer trying to rise. There was only baseball.

But Purvis, who was thinking less and hitting more, disagreed.

"You got me on the damn fence, Dan," he complained. "Look, I'm real grateful to you for the new outlook and all, and I've hiked my average sixty-three points. But you're turning into a goddamn nigger lover on me and that makes it hard on your old roomie. Because if I had a neck it sure as shit would be red. You understand?"

"Screw it," I said. "We're ballplayers."

"No we're not, you fucking goose. We're *white* ballplayers."

"Luther, I don't care if a man's got purple polka dots."

"Look, all I'm saying is that I'm starting to catch shit. The guys got you pegged as either a nigger lover or a homo, and I had to convince them not to think the worse. But either way I'm catching it! I don't like it! Not one bit. Now, I can put up with your mumbling to yourself half the damn time and I'm thankful for the batting tips, but life's leaning on me."

"Lean back, Luther."

He shook his head, then flicked away at his forehead. "No-ooo," he moaned like Marley's ghost. "I ain't strong enough for it! Can't you see the writing on the wall? I've been up to Arkansas, man! They sent me down to Single-A! They're gonna flush me down the tubes! And now every time I step on the field I feel Wings looking at me, his eyes burning into me, judging me, watching how I handle his fucking pitchers, timing my throw to second, computing my piddling batting average every time I don't come up with a hit. Then my brain starts a-whirring and evaluating and second-guessing till I just don't know what to do. Then I hear you telling me just to play the game, let my body do what comes natural. Eating, fucking, and sleeping is what comes natural, Dan. Man, I'm tied in knots! I ain't lucky like you or Booker Johnson, playing like it ain't no big thing, like you two actually enjoy it."

"You're worried about Wings?" I said.

"Who the hell you think I been talking about? Princess Grace?"

"He's just an old fart, Luther."

"He sends up the reports, don't he? How the hell do you think you move up in this game?"

"You take off your cap when they play the national anthem, play the ball—not let it play you—and never swing on three-and-oh."

"I wish that was all there was to it," Purvis said. "But something tells me the world don't work quite that way."

Though he was probably right, neither Mickey nor I wanted to admit it.

Because we'd seen who stayed in Pirate's Hook, who moved up to Razor Bluff. Book saw it too. This was his third year at Class-A, and before that he'd played two years of college ball. The starting Double-A shortstop had trouble putting on his glove, let alone getting the ball out of it. Book's being here all this time wasn't fair. I told Mickey we needed at least a year of A ball, that we'd rise with time and seasoning.

He'd nod, take his cuts in the cage. He was improving, though he was overly fond of the long ball. He'd tell me his secret desire was to be a real sluggo, a home-run king, clean-up hitter on a pennant contender. I'd explain we just weren't born with the strength or size. "Let's play the cards we were dealt," I'd tell him. "There's no other option, Mickey."

"Mantle," he'd say. "That's who I want to be. Mickey Mantle."

"Meenan," I'd say. "Be Mickey Meenan. That's who you are."

Purvis's enemy wasn't Wings, I realized. His enemy was Luther Purvis. I knew if he let himself alone for a while he'd make it up to Denver, where he'd play a solid backup, be a fine man to have on the bench. He was dependable and durable as a fireplug. He'd squat for nine full, day after day. He'd hurt so much each morning it'd take him ten minutes to lift the sheet. About pain he never complained. There were moments at night on the bus when I'd look at him nodding in the seat across the aisle from me and I'd see in him my father, the same exhaustion, drive. The same absence of joy and pleasure, the same unhappiness with anything less than the ideal. Even on days when he went 4-for-4, he'd say that if he'd been smarter and if I didn't love Negroes and if Wings had or hadn't said something to him in the dugout he'd have been able to stretch a single to a double, a double to a triple, a triple to an inside-the-park home run. I told him catchers didn't have to hit inside-the-park homers, that catchers had to do what he was already very good at, which was catching balls, calling a smart game, soothing the temperamental pitchers, making the sure throw to second on attempted steals, giving the bottom of the order a little punch. But that wasn't good enough for Luther Purvis.

"Book," I said one night after a game outside of Natchez, "just how good do we have to be to move up?"

"How far up?" Book said.

"All the way. The Bigs. Mile High."

"You've got to be good, Lupo. Like you are, but for a lot longer. Like a lover, you've got to prove to them you can last." He nodded. "And me, I've got to be even better. Understand?"

"Yeah," I said. We walked down the dark hot streets of Natchez.

"No you don't," he said. A mist of sweat glistened on his forehead. "I just asked you if you understood something you can't possibly understand."

"What do you mean?"

"Well, to begin with you're you. I mean, you and crazy Mickey."

"I'm not crazy!" Mickey said.

"I don't mean to insult your schizophrenia. But hear what I'm saying. I've got to be better because I'm black."

"Well, don't I have to be better because I'm schizophrenic?"

"I'm not schizophrenic!" Mickey said.

"No." Book smiled. "You're white. Both of you. You just have to be very very good."

It sank in on me later that night after I knocked on the back door of a house that Purvis had told me about and went inside, leaving Book and Mickey by a tree, to buy a Mason jar of moonshine that the three of us later shared in the shadows of a park not too far from the hotel where Book and the other blacks were staying. Maybe it was seeing that Book couldn't have knocked on the door for the whiskey. Maybe it was watching the old black man inside the kitchen snap to like a dog when the fat cracker moonshiner barked his name. Maybe it was sipping the sweet whiskey. I realized Book was right. To rise, he had to be far better than a white ballplayer. He had to get past all the obstacles facing any minor-league ballplayer plus the even worse hotels, the fans who'd ride him and not quit, even the players who slurred his race, and the bigotry of Wings, who buried Book's speed and potential in the seventh spot of the batting order. The larger injustice eclipsed my picayune passel of problems. We drank ourselves drunk and then some. There was nothing I could say.

"Hey Mick," Book said, "why don't you run down another of your Casper the Friendly Ghost stories for us?"

"He passed out half an hour ago," I said as sober as I could. "Couldn't hold his liquor." My voice felt like a pallbearer at a funeral, dipped and coated in darkest grief.

"Why the sad sack? This is supposed to be party time."

"Wanna know something, Book? Life's unfair."

He laughed. "You're dumber than you're ugly. Where'd you ever get that life was supposed to be fair?"

"But I used to feel so close to you," I said. "And now it's like you're on the other side of the moon."

"I'm not that far away." He touched my shoulder. "I'm just behind you, deep in the hole, playing short."

"But I thought we were good friends."

"We are, fool." He smiled. I could see his teeth in the moon-light.

The whiskey in the jar seemed to glow. I held it just right so I could see the moon in it. Then I was on my feet walking, though my legs felt as if they didn't stretch all the way to the ground. Book was lighting a cigarette, even though I'd never seen him smoke. He handed it to me and said to inhale. I did and coughed so loudly I thought I'd wake up all of Natchez.

Book laughed. I tried it again. Then again.

Something relaxed my arms, shoulders, all the muscles in my body. A big grin plastered itself to my face. Man oh man, I felt good! Our legs sliced the summer night. I started to notice what before I'd ignored. Suddenly I could hear and smell and see. We slowed and shared another of his cigarettes. It snapped, crackled, and popped like a bowl of Rice Krispies.

"Seeds," Book said, then, "keep a secret." I said, "Secret," nodding, amazed at the idea of unknown things. Book put a finger to my lips. My head stopped nodding. "I was born in Minnesota, town called Saint Cloud, whitest damn little place a white man'd ever want to see." He laughed, so I laughed, since that was funny. "Were you ever an altar boy? No? Well, I was an altar boy!" That was even funnier, so we laughed. "Everybody I meet figures me from some grimy inner-city slum or some backroad coal-mining town, you know, because of my color? But color's just that. It's just *color*, just skin, just the pigmentation of human flesh." I said, "Human flesh."

He stopped laughing. "Listen to me. When I was coming up, there were days the kids would beat on me so bad I'd have given the Devil my soul to be white for just five minutes, just long enough to get away. But I don't want to be white, and I don't hate whites." Then he told me that his mother was a music teacher and he'd played piano all his life. Ragtime to classical, and in high school he even composed. Then Juilliard offered him a schol-arship, but he went to Norfolk State, athletic free ride, starred in football, basketball, baseball. "I spent half my life sitting on a piano bench. That's why I'm so fast! Now I've got to move!" He told me he played piano in every black bar and brothel in every town we went to. He told me he was trying to integrate his life, be musician and ballplayer, Northern and Southern. Be Booker T. Johnson, no more and nothing less.

"Come on with me," he said, putting an arm around my shoulder.

This time I waited beneath a tree with Mickey, who was still passed out. On a high branch above us a mockingbird sang a medley of bird tunes. Book knocked on the back door of a house. A light came on. He went inside. Then the screen door opened and Book motioned for me to come.

I thought all brothels had pink furniture, fancy chandeliers, rosy-lipped women in lace corsets, fishnet stockings, garter belts. This brothel had very old brown furniture, four women in bathrobes who'd been watching TV, and an old scratched piano in front of which Book sat and began to play "Rose Leaf Rag." I offered the women what was left in the quart Mason jar. One ran to get some ice.

"It's a two-step," the fat one said as I danced with her. Her skin was the color of cured tobacco leaf. "Lord!" the others said behind us. "Look at that boy tryin' to dance! Liff your feet! Don't shimmy-shammy! Booker T., where you say he's from?"

Later, in the light of the kerosene lamp in her room, I told her she was lovely, that I hadn't done it before and really didn't know how, that it was fine with me if we sat up and talked. She took my hand, then washed me gently in a deep blue bowl. "Nothin' to keep to yourself here, child. You was born well equipped. Just learn to use it nice." She patted my back when it was finished.

"What's it like," I said, "being you?"

"Don't talk," she said. "When I feel good, take."

Then Mississippi felt a lot more like home. Then the next

afternoon, after I found out there hadn't been a bed check, with a head full of needles and fuzz, I started the hitting streak.

I walked to the plate in the top of the first. Runners on second and third, two outs. The game scoreless. My mind was still in the brothel. What did she mean, I thought, *take*? The first pitch came in high. Ball one. The second nipped the outside corner. Strike. I felt loose, empty. I stepped out of the box and tapped my bat against my cleats.

Don't talk, take, go with it. Something dawned on me then. Like if I wanted to, I could just live. I didn't have to feel bad. I didn't have to be plagued by the past, unless I wanted to be plagued. Then Mickey, who I'd nearly forgotten, got very upset and yelled at me.

"You're growing up! Stop! I don't like it!"

"Tough shit," I whispered and stepped back in, knowing that I'd hit the next pitch solidly, drive the ball all the way to the wall. The ball strained for the outside corner again. As easily as flicking a sleeping cockroach off my pillowcase, I doubled off the wall in right.

Then I stood on the bag, brushing the dirt from my uniform, and realized I'd gone with the pitch to right. Fantastic, I thought. I put my hands on my hips. I led off the bag. I decided on the next pitch I'd steal third.

The pitcher didn't even look back. The shortstop's mind was still in the locker room. I broke with the motion, ran, slid headfirst into the sack.

"Safe!"

Son, there are games when it's all over in the top of the first inning. Greek tragedies, their outcomes are inevitable and clear from the start. That game was your daddy's game. I knew it. The other team was about to know it too. I borrowed a page from Book's book and faked a steal of home. It rattled the pitcher so much that he walked the next batter, then tried to pick me off and threw the ball away. I scored. The runner on first took second. The opposing manager trudged to the mound. Book, our seventh batter, stood near the plate.

"Hit it to Saint Cloud," I said and winked.

He nodded and smiled. The reliever took his warm-ups.

Book homered on the first pitch. Three kids scrambled for the ball in the parking lot as Book loped around the bases.

That afternoon I went 5-for-5. Book hit three homers. Even Purvis got a pair of two-baggers.

Then we rode into the next town and I went 4-for-4, 3-for-4, 5-for-5. We returned to Pirate's Hook. 3-for-4, 4-for-4, 3-for-3, 6-for-6. My lumber was humming a storm. I had the booming bat. 4-for-4, 4-for-5, 3-for-5, 5-for-5.

It was a .907 clip. My .386 average led the league.

Mickey threw a tantrum. I never let him hit anymore, not even in batting practice. He'd be silent for days, then kick and scream and keep Purvis and me awake all night. Little did I know that the little freckled earwax-eater was planning a *coup d'état*.

Son, you know your baseball. Two men cannot simultaneously occupy the same base. At least one of them has to sit back on the bench. Maggot Meal was planning it would be me.

Meanwhile, Book was setting the league record for most home runs hit by a shortstop, though he wasn't at all happy with it, saying that power didn't get him this far and wouldn't carry him to the Bigs. Several times a week now we drank and smoked in fields or parks near where Book stayed.

"I'm snakebit!" Book groaned. "I've got to stop hitting these homers! I'm cursed! I'm a damn shortstop! I'm Mister Speed!" His voice seemed close to tears. I was so drunk I could hardly see him in the night's darkness.

"It's no big thing," I said. "Don't hog the smoke."

He hissed at me. "Yeah, that's easy enough for you to say. You're the man hogging all the singles." I could hear him taking another toke. "There's only so many in each game, you know." He toked again. "There're times when I get up there, and I just know a homer's in my bat. Man, I feel like I should just take the pitches, like I should just strike out!"

"Not to worry!" Mickey said. "Go with the pitches! Drink up, Danny! Pass the smoke!"

"Yeah," Book said, "so put this in your progress report. Book Johnson, shortstop. Excellent defense, superb speed, home-run power and potential." He passed the joint, then took a pull off our bottle of Jack Daniel's. "So they bring me up and they look for the long ball, and if I don't come through with it, I wash out. So I have to go for it, and my average takes a nosedive into the shithouse. Then I never get on first and can't display my speed. My speed on the bases is my long suit, man! Then what'll they do, try to convert me into an outfielder?" He shuddered. "So I can't hit and can't steal and they'll be teaching me a new position, and that'll throw the rest of me out of sync, and before long they'll call me Mister Has-Been and wonder what the hell is a shortstop doing trying to play the outfield and make it up on power when that ain't his natural trump, and then they'll flush me down, you understand? Hey, I'm telling you I'm a finely tuned instrument made to do certain things, and these home runs have got to go! No room in the inn. Call a priest, I need exorcism."

"I'll take your home runs!" Mickey Iscariot announced.

Book stared at him. "Kid, I wish like anything you could. I'd put 'em on a silver platter. Give me your singles and the green light to steal."

"Just touch my hands," Mickey said, "and say the words 'Home runs, be gone!' "

Book laughed and touched my hands. "Home runs, be gone!"

"I left you a couple," Mickey said, "because we don't want to go overboard on this and the fans really like it when a shortstop hits a homer!"

"Hey," I said, "wait a minute. How's this deal affect me?"

"I believe he just gave me a whole bunch of your singles," Book said as he lit the roach. The match illuminated the happy grin on his face.

"A whole bunch of my singles?" I said. "What about my average?"

Mickey laughed. "Nosedive! Shithouse!"

"No," I said. "Absolutely not. No way in Heaven, Hell, or Mississippi! I'm leading the damn league! I'm a finely tuned instrument too! This deal's null and void."

"Don't do that to me," Book said.

"He can't trade away what's mine," I said. "Possession's nine-tenths of the law."

"You're absolutely right," Mickey said. "But who said all those hits are yours in the first place? Huh, Danny? Huh, big man? Whatdya think, I'm still a dreamy first baseman? That I haven't been busting my tail out on the field? Give me a break! *You're* the custard-sucking éclair who's been getting us ripped every night, breaking curfew, drinking, smoking dope, spending our valuable juices when you think I'm passed out or asleep. Hey, I don't mind a little party every now and then, but seven nights a week, Danny? I've been carrying you for an awful long time! If those hits aren't mine to trade, then where does that put me? Whatsa matter, Lone Wolf, cat got your tongue? Like either I'm living inside you, or I'm dead! So which is it, Danny? Is Mickey dead or alive?"

Book was enjoying it all, thinking I was screwing around, having fun. I said nothing. I realized it wasn't fun, son.

"Possession *is* nine-tenths of the law," Mickey said. "And I hate to clue you in on this, Watson, but I only swapped what was mine!"

Then they began to talk excitedly about Razor Bluff, the Triple-A club in Deadwater, Kansas. Then how they'd take Denver and the Rockies by storm.

"Book and Mickey!" they said, slapping hands. "Dynamic duo! Short and first!" Then Mickey predicted that Book would win Rookie of the Year. He described Mile High Stadium decked out in World Series bunting. He whispered the scores of all seven games. He said they'd share Series MVP honors, be on the covers of *Sporting News* and the following season's Street and Smith's. I sat back and listened, son. They didn't miss me. They'd forgotten I was even there.

"We'll be roomies!" Mickey was telling Book. "We'll make commercials for Gillette! Every shortstop in the sandlots will want a Booker T. Johnson model glove, and all the first basemen will want one signed by me! We'll be All-Stars! We'll be inducted into the Hall of Fame! Mister Speed and Mister Bat! They'll retire our uniforms! Your lifetime batting average will top .320, and you'll steal more bases than Scrooge McDuck has millions! We'll have long, wonderful big-league careers—I'm talking twenty-plus years—and the fans will want to carve our faces in the Rockies! They'll make a movie about us too, and the guy who plays you will win the Oscar!"

Book's smile was brighter than a full moon.

"And what about Galloping Lupo?" he said. "Danny's gonna go along with this switch to first base? He'll get out of the hot corner?"

Mickey's finger rose to our lips. "Shhhhh. Book, I hate to say it, but he's got nothing to do with our plans!"

"Wolf Balls," Book said, "I believe you're undergoing a major personality breakdown! Your schizo's on the skids!"

"Naw," Mickey said, "don't worry about Danny. He'll get what he wants."

I reached for my voice to break in then, so I could tell the dreaming little corpse that what I wanted was for him to sit on a broken bat, but my voice was no longer there. Never before had I been unable to silence him when I wanted. I felt a flush of undeniably horrible panic. Then a voice behind me whispered *let him be, don't pop his bubble, what you hear is just the booze and the dope*. Yeah, I thought, what I heard was the dope all right. Though I realized then he'd seized the upper hand.

And when I reached for control on the field, it wasn't there.

The final six weeks of the season proved it.

Nosedive, did he say? Did he predict my average would end up in the shithouse?

I went 21-for-147, an anemic .143 pace.

Oh, of course I had plenty of homers in my bat. Twelve of my twenty-one hits splashed in the Pearl River. But none were clutch hits. None timely, coming when we trailed, with men on base in front of me. Worse, there were games when the score was tied and the bases would be full of Dynos. Wings would stare at me and spit. I'd try to remind Mickey that since the previous batter got on with a walk we should make the pitcher throw a strike. Mickey would chuckle, get the swing-away sign from the third-base coach, then hack at curves in the dirt, fastballs up around our eyes. He gave pitchers more K's than he tried to pronounce in the alley the afternoon he was dying. Gabriel would have sat him down on the pines till Judgment Day. Meanwhile, Book hit a hailstorm of singles, stealing second, third, even home, with the regularity of a prune eater chewing Ex-Lax. And Purvis kept his mind off keeping his mind on the predictability of pitches and continued to slug out a stream of doubles. The bench nicknamed him Two-Bag. With a couple of weeks left in the season, Wings informed him that he'd been reassigned, to pack his two bags for Arkansas, for Double-A.

"You know, I couldn't a done it without you," Purvis told me as he packed his straw suitcases. His elation made me green.

"Yeah," Mickey said, "when it comes to hitting, I wrote the book! Did I ever tell you you remind me of Fred Flintstone? A yabba dabba doo!"

"Let me give you a tip," he said. "Quit swinging from your damn heels! You're a joke out there, I'm serious, I swear to Jesus."

Then the season ended.

With a home game and a big crowd of nearly a hundred, who came mainly for the fifteen-cent hot dogs and for the fireworks display that was promised after the last out. I finished my first year of professional baseball with three strikeouts and a towering home run that slapped the drooping flag out in center. We were already ahead by four runs. As I rounded the bases I felt as if the fans were unhappy with me for prolonging the game. The night was sauna-hot. I felt cheaper than a fifteen-cent hot dog.

Mickey clapped his hands as we ran, skipped, raised his arms as if he just kicked a winning field goal. Then he did two cart-wheels and several somersaults on our way to the plate.

Mickey, I whispered. *What are you doing to me, Mickey?*

Book won the league's batting crown. The announcement came over the PA just before the park's lights went black and the fireworks sizzled and creased the late summer sky.

I can't realistically explain what I did then, son. I mean, I can recall bits and pieces, but nothing that would stand up in court. I remember how I felt, which was real real bad. I ached and wanted my mamma. I held myself to myself and curled into a ball. I knew perfectly well what I was doing. I was making myself scarce. Crawling into my inkwell to die. Running out the back door, heading for the El. Charging down the hallway screaming something about too much mayonnaise.

I could feel myself shrinking, hiding in some dark corner of my brain. Synapses sparked wildly around me, like cracks of lightning or trailers of fireworks shot off too close to the ground. Dugout. BOOM! BOOM! KA-BOOM! I smelled gunpowder, or was it the smell of the juices boiling in my brain? If he wanted control over us so bad, *he could have it*, I thought. Let the ignoramus try living without me for a while. I heard Book say something about winter ball and the Dominican Republic. I kept on shrinking, then kicked the floor of my brain with my spikes, until Mickey got two Extra-Strength Tylenols from the trainer. They flattened me out, let me tell you. I stumbled around, half dead, then unfolded a Murphy bed from a wall in my mind and covered my head with a blanket, closed my eyes, prayed *dearest God, oh dearest God, oh dearest God* until everything I knew and was and ever hoped to be fell away.

Then time didn't pass; it flew by, speed-frame.

The blanket over my head turned to stone. I crouched inside a tiny cave. There were moments of peaceful darkness and soothing relaxation, moments when I was forced to endure brilliant flashes of blinding light. Now and then I'd try to reach out, but I could never quite touch anything. My cavern filled with a cottony haze. Wafer-thin flakes, like goldfish food, drifted dreamily past me. Occasionally I could hear voices, but they were light-years away and played on 78.

I don't know what the first astronauts felt as they were hurled in their capsules through outer space. Perhaps it was something like what I felt. A cringing, tight-jawed, cheek-shaking bracing. A sense that time and velocity had gone amuck. So I was hurled through inner space.

Then, splashdown, and I could open my eyes.

And taste spring, spring somewhere on the solid earth, and I was fully back inside the skin of my body, fielding a lovely white baseball, and the motionless sun was warm on the small of my back, and a blue-eyed coach in a Dynos uniform was smiling and clapping his hands and yelling something to me about good stuff.

1 2 3 4 5 **6** 7 8 9

FIELDER'S CHOICE

They said I'd pulled a Rip Van Winkle.

Took a powder, played Sleeping Beauty. That for over two years I didn't shout *here!* when the good sister took the morning roll.

We were walking down the third-base line from the field. The sky was big-screen wide and so blue the color was painful. The air, hot but extremely dry for Mississippi. The coach's praise still echoed in my ears. "Good stuff, Bacigalupo! That's it! Great stuff! *Now* you're finally playing like a third baseman!"

Then Mickey tumbled me to the ground, horsing around, wrestling. The kid was as glad as an old dog to see me after so long, I guess. Then all at once it felt like he was fighting me for real. The stinking Judas wrapped his arms around me and was squeezing the pressure points inside my shoulder blades. I pushed his hands away. He flipped me back in the air, bouncing my ass on the outfield grass. "Hey," I shouted, "what gives?"

He let me know by gouging my eyes with his thumbs. So he wanted to play for keeps, did he? I bent his hands back at the wrists, pinned his shoulders to the ground. He kicked like a sissy, then roared, "No!" Then he twisted me into a pretzel, trying to make me eat my kneecaps, until I was able to grab his dumb hair, then spin back on top. I shoved his stupid face into the grass. "Give up!" I yelled. I pushed his right arm up his back until I nearly popped it from its socket. He thrashed like a netted Siamese fighting fish. Someone was trying to roll me over, force open my mouth, shove in some kind of stick. I slugged whoever it was, then elbowed the escaping Mickey back down to the grass. "Quit or die!" I screamed.

He was losing now and knew it. I slapped his face twice, laughed, then shot my fist right into his solar plexus. That winded the freckled coffin stuffing good. Then I made him eat dirt until he cried uncle.

Then I brushed the grass from my face and calmly stood. Around me there was a gawking circle of ballplayers. They grinned and broke into applause. Some old guy, a coach or trainer, held a towel packed with ice to his eye.

Then Book, sweat and panic popping from his face, ran up to me. "Are you OK? Payne's on the phone with a doctor right now. The trainer says it was near a grand mal."

He looked fantastic. His arms and shoulders had thickened with rippling muscles. "Book," I said, "long time no see."

He stared at me, put his hands on my shoulders, then grinned. "The Wolf is back?"

"Like the U.S. Cavalry."

"More like Muhammad Ali," Mickey said, rubbing our chest, then our neck. "It's all right if I talk? You won't punch me again?"

"I'll settle with you later." I looked at Book. "Who's Payne?"

"He's the skipper, and a damn nice— Look, here he comes."

A tall man with sparkling blue eyes and a dark shadow of beard on his face and upper neck jogged up to us. Immediately

I liked him. He told the group of ballplayers to get back to work. Then he put his arm around me. "You're feeling better now, aren't you, son?"

"Yeah," I said, "I feel just swell."

"I've got to admit, you had me real worried there for a minute." He had a tanned, handsome face. He was one of those guys you wouldn't mind growing up and looking like. On his left hand a thick gold band glistened in the sunlight. He was the coach who'd praised my play at third. He smiled with genuine concern.

Which made it even harder to lie, but what choice did I have? I knew I couldn't tell him I'd just come back from a two-year snooze and me and Mickey had to duke it out to see who'd be ruler of my body.

"Yeah," I said, shaking my head, trying to be real sincere, "you know, last night we ate Chinese. And I forgot how the next day I get these violent reactions to that glutamate stuff they sprinkle on the chop suey, you know what I mean? I've had the problem since I was a kid."

"That's true," Mickey said. "MSG really does give some people—"

"Hey," Payne said, smiling and raising his hands. "I don't deny it. You don't have to convince me. I just hope that's all there is to it. But I want Leroy and the doctor to look you over. Right now."

"Sure," I said. "No sweat."

"You looked real good at third," he said. "You think over what we talked about yesterday." Then he nodded and jogged back to the infield.

Mickey licked his wounds. "Tell me everything I need to know," I said as we walked toward the clubhouse.

"Yes, Dorothy, you're in Kansas." He nodded our head. "Triple-A. And that was Lefty Payne, our manager. The old guy you walloped was the trainer, Leroy. Last night we really ate ribs. Welcome to charming Deadwater, Kansas. Population, ninety-one thousand—"

Our spikes clicked on the locker-room floor. I looked around. Wire stalls for our street clothes, fluorescent lighting, what looked like a weight room to the left. Everything smelled clean. What a step up from Single-A!

Leroy was holding a frozen hamburger patty to his eye. "You settled down yet? Or am I gonna have to defend myself and put the likes of you to shame?"

I told him I was sorry. He said never mind.

By the size of his knuckles and the crookedness of his fingers, I figured he'd once been a catcher. He had us strip down and sit on a table. I was amazed when I locked in the mirror across the room. Mickey had chowed down a lot more than ribs! He must have swallowed a good ten pounds of protein and then told it exactly where to go, because our upper body pulsed with muscle and definition. I stared at my reflection with envy. Man, I looked strong! Not overdone, no baby-oiled beefcake. Leroy was thumping me here and there, told me to stop flexing, squeezed this and that.

"Never seen nothin' like it in my en-tire life," he said. "One minute you was playing the bag like a third-string washout with diarrhea, then the next you looked like you was born for the base. Slick and smooth? Hoo-eeeee! Somebody up there done gave you the moves, son! Now shut your mouth or you'll look stupid."

"I'm just fine," I said. "It was something I ate."

"Yeah," Leroy said. He was taking my blood pressure. "Food's a strange thing, ain't it? Like one day it's living and it don't think it's food, and the next it's dead and there on your plate staring up at you, and you ask for the ketchup. Makes you stop every now and then and think, don't it?"

"Sure does," I said.

"Yeah," Leroy said. "Sometimes it just don't agree with the proposition. You already got it inside you, so there's nothing that can be done. But you feel it when it starts a-complaining, don't you?"

"You sure do," I said.

"Yeah," Leroy said. "But I got my own little theory."

"I'm all ears."

Leroy smiled. "Food didn't have a damn thing to do with that fit you threw. Don't jump off the table, hear me out. You had that fit sure enough because you done finally realized deep down in the recesses of your psychology that Lefty's right and you should make the switch back to third."

"I should switch *back* to third?"

"Sure, dummy. Quit squeezing your hand, I'm done now. Last two seasons down at Razor Bluff you been playing—"

"First," Mickey said, "about as well as I could under the circumstances, but maybe this year now that I'm, uh, a little more myself, maybe I'll switch back to third."

Leroy slapped his thigh. "That's the thinking! I know it every time when a man gets hit with sense! I knew it soon as you slugged me. Yeah! Lefty's never wrong. And third's where you started out, wasn't it?"

"Yes," I said, "it was," icicles of hatred for Mickey Meenan dripping from my voice.

"You ask me," Leroy said, "first's a position for the old boys when their legs get too slow to play the outfield but they still got some crack in their bats. Either that or you get some real big young buck who hits a tornado from the south side of the plate. A batting order needs balance between righties and lefties, way I figure. The heart of the order best have both. Now you got *some* size, but you're not that big, and you're a righty. You ask me, you're a natural-born third baseman."

"Gee," I said, "how come I never thought of that?"

"Sit down," Lefty Payne said after the doctor had given me a clean bill and I'd showered and dressed and Leroy had told me the skipper wanted to see me pronto in his office. Lefty smiled, motioning to a chair. The walls were covered with old black-and-white photographs of him back in his playing days, and smaller color pictures of Lefty shaking hands with men in business suits. The brass, I figured. His desk was piled with books and charts. To one side there was a snapshot of a pretty, thin-faced woman goofing around wearing a man's hat. The place was clean and bright. He offered me a square of bubble gum. His jaw muscles knotted as he chewed.

"Leroy tells me you check out fine."

"I feel great," I said. "I can't tell you how glad I am to be here."

He studied me for a moment. Then he blew a pink bubble until it popped.

"Dan, I'll level with you. You've been around me now long enough to have heard me discuss my philosophy of managing this ball club. You know I believe in cooperation and respect. The press has me campaigning for the job up in Denver, and that's true, I want it when there's an opening. I've earned it. Because it will be my players down here in Deadwater that will carry that team someday. They know it, I know it, so it'll be just a matter of time." Lefty nodded. "Now despite all your eloquent arguments in the past, I continue to think that your future in this organization is at third base. I'll listen to it all again, but I'll warn you that my patience isn't as long as you're winded, and—"

"Coach, I agree with you."

He stopped chewing. "Don't tell me it's because last night you ate Chinese."

"No," I said, "actually it's because I've sort of woken up." I took a breath, trying to figure what he'd done in my absence. "I guess a part of me had hopes of becoming a power hitter and playing first, but—"

"But you *are* a power hitter, Dan. You know your stats as well as anyone. Twenty-three homers at Pirate's Hook, thirty-two your first year at Razor Bluff, then last year, what was it, thirty-six?"

"Thirty-seven," Mickey said.

"Thirty-seven home runs," Lefty said and blew another bubble. "You know you're part of this organization's cream. You, Booker Johnson, Comet Haley, maybe Bagman Jones once he gets straightened out. Barring injuries, all of you have an excellent chance of making the big club."

"Forget the past," I said. My hand erased it in the air. "I'm a third baseman. That's where I started and where I hope to stay."

"Well, that's what I've been thinking all along, Dan, but your antics down at Razor Bluff didn't help matters any, and the way you've played— You know as well as I do you were making far too many mental errors." He started to blow another bubble but then stopped. "I'd have brought you up for a while last year if I knew I could work with you, that you'd be this reasonable. But your reports. Hell, Dan, last year I could have used you."

"My average was good enough?"

".241's nothing to write home about, but we'd have worked with you."

".241?" I could have punched Mickey from here to Saskatchewan. "Coach, I can hit .300. Better than that, I'll hit .333."

He smiled. "Well, you can try."

"I can do more than try," I said. "I can do it."

He shook his head and laughed. "That's what we've been trying to tell you, Dan. Relax out there, drive the ball, go with the pitch to right. The home runs will come, believe me. Every time you step up to the plate, you don't have to kill the ball. There're eight other batters in the lineup to knock you in once you get on base. If you're not on base, nothing can knock you in. That's the way I play this game." He stood.

"Now, you work hard, I mean *real* hard, on your defense. Show me some of the stuff you had down in Pirate's Hook. .241 hitters are a dime a dozen, you know that as well as I do. Defensive gems are rare. You'll make it up on your glove, Dan. The bat will take care of itself."

"I won't disappoint you," I said.

Then he said he wanted to rest me a day or two because of my fit, that if I felt anything funny he'd take me into Wichita for a brain scan. I told him I hadn't felt this fine in years.

"You ungrateful little vermin!" I said to Mickey when we were outside. "What the hell were you trying to do? Ruin my career? He said he might have brought us up last year if we'd have played third!"

"Don't slug me again," Mickey said. He made a V of his fingers. "Peace. Love. Nonviolence."

Book's big smile greeted us as we walked through the door of our room. "Schizo man, all right! Great to see you! Welcome back from Neverland!"

"Thanks," I said, "and I didn't return a moment too soon. Bozo the Clown here had our career floating in the toilet." I walked over to the bed that I guessed was ours and sat down.

"Oh yeah?" Mickey said. "I did my best."

"Your best." I laughed. "You hit .241."

"You didn't even take batting practice." He paused and folded our arms. "So what was I supposed to do after you nodded out on me? Gone into a coma too? Let us become *completely* catatonic? I'm a first baseman! You forget there's a life to live between us, hibernation brain."

"I love it!" Book said, slapping his hands.

Mickey shook our head at Book. "See what I have to put up with? He comes down with sleeping sickness and then he blames me for bringing his ass up to Triple-A."

"The dead man's got a point," Book said. "Lupo, you flew the coop. You played hide-and-seek but hid where nobody could find you. We would've called in the FBI, but we didn't exactly believe they'd buy the story." He shook his head, then stretched. I couldn't get over how muscular he'd become.

"We've been working out some, I see," I said.

Book grinned. "Pumping i-ron. And now we're roomies." He

waved his hand around the room. "Look, a real shower. Towels. Clean sheets. Carpet that don't give you fungus if you walk barefoot. And best of all, A/C!"

Mickey laughed. "Though we've had some pretty hot times even with it cranked all the way up to Super Cool, haven't we?"

"Amen. We've been super cool!"

"What's all this supposed to mean?" I said.

"Payne told him my reports from Boring Bluff mentioned something about antics," Mickey said.

"Antics!" Book said. "Hey, now that's choice!"

"Let me hear it," I said. "Come on. Tell me everything."

Fasten your seat belt if you ever hear your mouth say those words, son. Because Book and Mickey then commenced to tell me more than I wanted to hear. Talk about rampant libido! Mickey unleashed every howling wolf in the history of the Bacigalupos, then set them on the trail of each earthly delight ever discovered by man. Their stories about me made ancient Rome seem about as lively as a Mormon church supper. Not only was I known to every moonshiner between Lake Pontchartrain and the hills of West Virginia, I had become such a marijuana fiend that my habit alone supported several South American villages, and my appetite for clubhouse-door groupies was greater than all of Lipton's tea, Contadina's tomatoes, Wrigley's sticks of chewing gum. I'd doubled my pleasure and doubled my fun, all right. I'd burned my candle at both ends with a blowtorch. My Flying Dutchman had deflowered more corpulent virgins than Holland had tulips, windmills, and wooden shoes.

"Talk about big women!" Book was saying. "Danny, these perfectly luscious skinny little southern belles in halter tops and skin-tight pastel short-shorts would just about be drooling your zipper to rust and you'd smile and push them aside, then head for the fattest sow rooting around the chili-dog wrappers in the parking lot."

"I—I slept with these women?"

184

Mickey smiled. "Only size eighteen and up need apply."

"I don't believe any of this."

"You want to read our fan mail? Book, where'd we stash that box?"

"Out in the truck."

"We've got a truck?"

"It was your idea," Book said. "The day after we came back from the Dominican Republic. You remember winter ball? You said let's get ourselves some wheels and see the world and fly our flags at full mast, or some nonsense like that. I wanted the red T-bird but you insisted on the pickup."

"We needed transportation to Chicago," I said. "And the pickup was the better buy." It was beginning to come back.

"We didn't go to Chi-town then," Book said. "That was the next winter."

"All I remember is that we went to Chicago."

"We did," Mickey said. "But that was the second winter. Remember, you wanted to say hi to Grace?"

I held my head in my hands. "All right. Tell me what happened."

"Nothing happened," Book said. "Except that fat man made us those horrible sandwiches."

"Harold," I said.

"You know, I never had a pot-roast, turkey-breast, cream-cheese, lox, and potato sandwich before. I was kind of getting into it until he ruined it with the *mole* sauce."

"It made me throw up in the snow," Mickey said.

"That's right," Book said. "That was when we saw your father."

"My father! We saw my father?"

"Only for a minute," Mickey said. "Book was taking a leak against the tree out in front of your old house."

"I had to whiz mighty bad. Then a whole swarm of Italian kids ran out and wanted to touch my arm."

"He came out and said hello to us," I said.

"He came out and you dropped your pants and shot him the old red-eye." Book nodded as he spoke. "Then he just kind of stood there on the porch. You told him that in ancient times when a man gets old and stupid his eldest son would throw him down a well. Then you shouted something like, 'Figs on you!' and showed him both your fists. Then you puked in the snow, then threw all our money at him. Your brother Louie picked it all up. Lucky for us we had a full tank of gas. After he shook his head and went back inside, you ran down the block shouting for some dude name of Bernie."

"Dear God!" I said. "You guys have ruined my life!"

"You made applesauce out of mine," Mickey said. "Don't forget that."

Tears filled my eyes. "Where was Grace?"

Book tossed me a T-shirt so I wouldn't slobber all over. "You mean the fat man's daughter? She wasn't home."

"She went to a convent," Mickey said. "We sent her to a nunnery!"

"No she didn't," Book said. "He's lying to you, Danny. She just went away. Split for parts unknown. The sad fat lady told you."

I wiped my eyes with the T-shirt. "Anything else? Just how low did I sink? Do I lick toilet seats? Jerk off in the dugout? Do we rob churches or orphanages? Tell me—am I wanted by the police?"

"None of that," Book said, "though what you do after you shut the john door is your own business. In fact, your country doesn't even want you. Do you remember the night of the lottery?"

I remembered a short story of the same name from high-school English. "Don't tell me we crushed some poor old woman with rocks."

"No, fool," Book said. "This is America, remember? We're

a civilized land. Rich, poor. White, black. Red, yellow, brown—everybody gets along. Our president had himself a real democratic lottery so everybody could know exactly who has first crack of getting his ass shot off in Vietnam."

"Vietnam?" I said. "What's Vietnam?"

"Har-dee-har-har," Mickey said. "But we lucked out, thanks to your birth date. We landed in the three hundreds! My old birth date made the top ten! You know, if you hadn't killed me thirteen years ago, I could be dying in the jungle right now!" Mickey patted our shoulder. "You saved my life, Danny."

"Any time," I said. "What else do I need to know?"

Book looked at me, then lowered his eyes. "You wouldn't happen to recall spring training camp in Triple Springs, Arizona, would you?"

"That's not important," Mickey said. "I'm starved. Whatdya say we go get some chow and a glass of suds?"

My hand went to our stomach. "I'm kind of hungry too, but what's this about spring training in Arizona?"

"We didn't do too hot," Mickey said.

"Speak for yourself," Book said. "The Denver coaching staff told me I'll be up there this year. But Mickey stunk the joint up."

"Well, I'm a first baseman! What do you expect?"

"Just how bad did we do?"

"Let me put it this way," Book said, "you knew enough to stand in fair territory. After that—" Book laughed. "No, serious, Mick handled first all right, but when they put you out at third you looked like oyster shit. So I guess he tried to make up for it at the plate, but—"

"We fanned a lot, Danny."

"A lot?" Book said.

"All right," Mickey said, "we struck out every time. But hey, believe me, they've got some fast arms up in the majors!"

Surprisingly I laughed at the news. Because it was Mickey's

failure, not mine. Lefty Payne said I was part of the organization's cream, and if all I needed to make it up was a strong glove—Well, I knew I had a strong glove. I took a deep breath, then went for a long walk with myself and Mickey.

Deadwater wasn't a town that sold many souvenir picture postcards. It was as bland as cottage cheese and built around a rather unspectacular, aptly named lake. Though parts of me craved an ice-cold beer, I felt calm and on top of things. I told Mickey the fits had to stop at once or else the men in white coats would discover he wasn't dead and put him in a rubber room. He told me not to talk to him like he was a baby. I'm as grown up as you, he said. Then why did you attack me? I said. He said because he was afraid.

Afraid of what? *Everything, Danny.* You're spitting pablum, Mickey, talk sense. *I'm afraid of you, you're like a pillow on my head. You do everything better and it's like sometimes I can't breathe, and I try and try but the pillow on top of me gets bigger and heavier and I'm afraid I won't be able to push it off.* That's just a nightmare, Mickey. I'm your friend, I won't hurt you, you're not alone. *I'm not?* You're not. We'll push together, OK? He said *OK.*

We walked along the water's edge. But now you know I'll have to ground you for a while. Believe me it hurts to do it. No more drinking, no more smoking dope, no spurting our juice with the groupies. And for a while you're going to have to cool your heels on the bench. No hitting and no fielding, Mickey. We're too close to the majors to screw around. You let me take care of things a while. Cross me and I'll jump in Lake Deadwater with lead bat doughnuts in our pockets. Glub, glub—catfish will eat our eyes.

You'll let me hit when we get to the majors? You'll give me the green light to swing away?

I said as long as the third-base coach doesn't tell us to lay down a bunt. He said *promise.* I said promise, then crossed our heart.

Then pieces of the past fell more clearly in my mind, like thick snow on a windless winter evening. I remembered, then reexperienced and felt. Son, what they omitted from my Chicago visit was that I was crying the whole time. Because Grace had disappeared and I realized I'd probably lost her forever, and then my father wouldn't come down the front-porch steps. I said, "Dad?" He just stood there, above me, not moving, staring at me as if I were an alien from outer space. So I'd have to walk up to him? No way! So I bared my ass, because that's what he made me feel like. Standing there below him in the snow with Grace gone. And because I hadn't yet learned how to tell him I loved him.

And the women? Well, the slender beauties let me know they were willing and more than able. But they didn't need me, I thought. I'd be no more than makeup to them, something they'd put on for a while, later wash off. And I was afraid of them. I didn't understand them then.

No, the ones who needed me, the ones I could be myself with, were the shy two-hundred-pounders. I was beginning to remember. Mickey and I walked to the pickup. "You really think I'm pretty?" she'd say. I'd say yeah, take her hand, smile. We forced nothing from anyone. Mickey said we loved them with all our heart.

The letters were in a shoebox behind the front seat. There were sixteen in all. I read them and remembered.

His razor was sharp!
And he didn't bluff!
He loved me two times!
It wasn't enough!

Now he is gone away!
A-playing his sport!

I'll remember him always!
Pleasure liner in my port!

> Guess who?
> (Peaches!) xoxoxo

Dear Danny,

Though you likely don't remember me thanks and good luck
on the road trip. Talking to you Sat. night meant the world
to me. I was depressed but now I am cheerful.

That famous philosopher you told me about was her name
Sister Regina? I looked all over the library but they don't
have her books. The librarian Lila says maybe if county rev-
enues go up they can order them in the fall. In the meantime
I will memorize her advice and not be a spectator in life's ball
game. Even if you're born like me, heavy and short and most
of the time sad, but maybe not any longer.

> Dolores

D is for the dear dear things you told me.
A is for the azaleas in bloom.
N is for the nice nice way you kissed me.
I is for the insects that night loomed.
E is for the exciting way you touched me.
L is for the love in your hotel room.

Put them all TOGETHER they spell DANNY!
P.S. You sure hit the long ball with me!

> Love Always,
> Sharon Ann

We walked back to our hotel room. Book was listening to
some gospel music on the record player we'd bought in Tennes-
see. I recognized the tune, remembered when he first played me

the album. Suddenly the past fell into place. There, I realized, letting out a sigh. *There.*

Then I remembered striking out each time in spring training, even in the B games. I understood I might be a step away, but I wasn't ready for the big leagues yet. In a year, maybe less, I'd be ready.

I sat on my bed. The thought scared me.

Because the most frightening thing you can do to a dream is to dare to make it real. I don't mean that in your mind you act it out, don it like a costume in a play. I mean make it happen. I mean take it in your hand and put it in your mouth, rip it with your teeth. Can the reality ever be as sweet as what you dreamed?

This is why some people lock their lives in losing. They don't want to risk giving up the sweet comfort of their dreams. Failure can be as snug and warm as a wool blanket, and you can hold it to your chin for the rest of your life and say if only that, if only this. *If only, if only:* the response in the Litany of the Blessed Losers. Losing locks the dream for all time in a golden tabernacle, and losers get to kneel at the altar of their failure and continue worshiping. Losers keep their god. Winners bring it down to the earth, where it walks and eats and stinks like all the rest of us.

When you think of me as I was, son, I want you to think of me inside this moment. Don't picture me in Mile High Stadium, in the major leagues, standing over first base, my hands squeezing the bat. Don't remember me in Pirate's Hook with rain on my cheeks when I discovered you. Don't paste the moment of me making the play out on the mound in Denver in the scrapbook of your mind. Think of me in a hotel room in Deadwater, Kansas, on the evening of the day that I woke up, in a T-shirt and jeans, sitting silently on my bed, staring at the darkness of my shoes, listening to Mother Smith and then to Muddy Waters while Book lay back and stared at the ceiling, the two of us then young and magnificent and filled with all the hopes of hungry ballplayers in the minor leagues. Think of me as clear-eyed and calm. Think

191

of me as hungry. Hear me clap my hands and then tell Book, "We'll win."

"Whatever you say, Lupo, you crazy can of pork and beans."

Then we got our mojos workin' and went out to that ribs joint Mickey had mentioned. I was back in control. Though Mickey pleaded with me for a beer, I sipped iced tea. Book had smoked a number in the pickup on our way out. It felt great to be alive again! Barbecue sauce dripping from our chins, we did what idle ballplayers do well. We sat and shot the shit.

"It all comes down to this," Book said, waving a rib.

"I agree," I said. "The first rib, Eve, Adam, the Garden of Eden."

"No, Bible man, I mean protein. Meat." His teeth tore off a chunk. "You want meat, and who doesn't, you got to get yourself a herd. You got a herd of animals, you need fields for them to graze. So you're looking for a stretch of property, see, and so is everybody else who's into spare ribs, and things get kind of tight, so you battle—"

"Good and evil," I said.

"Protein," Book said, tossing a bone at me. "The bottom line's protein. We're talking food chain here. You're looking for real estate for your herds, which are growing all the time, so you need explorers." He pointed and changed voices. " 'Hey, go check out what's over that horizon.' 'Go cross that ocean and tell me what's there.' " He nodded. "Then when you get the new turf, you need armies to protect it and hold the trespassers back."

"And that's right?" I said.

"I'm not talking wrong or right." He ripped into another rib. "I'm just trying to figure things out. See, I think that's why you whities wiped out the Indians. You wanted their land for your spare ribs. And that's why you slipped down to Mother Africa and stole the slaves. To pick the cotton for your shirts and napkins so you'd have something to wear and wipe your mouth with when you ate your spare ribs. And that's why our country's in

Vietnam. Because we don't want them godless Commies horning in on our spare ribs."

"I'm thirsty," Mickey said. "Can't we have just one beer?"

"Nope," I said. "Nope to both of you. And kindly include me out in the slaughter of the Indians and the stealing of the slaves. The Bacigalupos were innocent *contadini* then. We didn't have a thing to do with it."

"If you did," Book said, "you'd have to do something about it, right?"

"Sure."

Book smiled. "I got you leaning, Lupo."

I tore off a fresh rib. "Nope."

"*Cerveza*," Mickey mumbled. "*Por favor!*"

"Say the world *is* based on good and evil, like you say. Then how come the old apple stain is on your head? You weren't in the Garden of Eden. You say you didn't have a thing to do with it."

I leapt with both feet into my contradiction. "Book, you know as well as I do. Because in a way we were all there too. Because the sins of the father and mother get handed down."

"*All* the sins," Book said, "or just the ones they talk about in church?"

He had me. If I was in the Garden, I also stood with Columbus as he lopped off the hands of Arawaks who didn't bring him enough gold. Later I was more subtle and gave the natives diseased blankets. I shackled Africans, then marched them aboard the *Desire*, the first American slave ship, chaining them in spaces not much bigger than coffins. I was my country 'tis of thee. Then, today, through time.

What did the earth do with all the death? I wondered. Where did all the blood go? When would the planet gag, when would the blood stop soaking in, when would it start to puddle and darken on the streets and in the fields?

"It's on my head, too," Book said. "On it and in it."

We were finished eating for the night. I didn't want to look at the plates of bones and smeared barbecue sauce. "So what do we do?"

Book's face sagged. His eyes locked with mine. "What we're meant to do, I guess. Be what we are. Ballplayers. But hold on to what we know, learn some more, and always try to do right by everybody."

So you can see there was a lot up in the air. I was juggling a lot of balls, or at least I was trying to. I figured I'd better take them on one at a time.

Beginning with baseball, and it wasn't easy because now I had Mickey's pull-everything-to-the-warning-track timing and all the new muscles to contend with. I went back to the basics, back to pitcher versus batter, letting my body do the swinging, shutting off my mind, which wanted to think and guess too much. If my theory worked for Purvis, who'd made it up to Denver, it would work for me. I hung in and realized that Mickey was known for backing away from pitches that came in tight. So I hugged the plate and played stop-the-inside-fastball with my rib cage. I let the league know the plate and box were mine and I was willing to be bruised. It didn't matter that Mickey had traded away our singles; I had more, I told myself, where they came from. By the season's third week my hits were dropping like doo from a flock of pigeons, and now and then a roaring homer boomed off my bat.

God, the game was sweet. I had it! Power and percentage. Guts and a good eye. After I was getting a hit a game, I closed my stance some and reached inside myself for more. Going with the pitch, I punched balls I shouldn't have been able to hit to the opposite field. I always took extra batting practice. Then my hits came in bunches, with extra bases in the gap or down the line, and lots of ribbies. My average climbed to .332. And when they offered me the walk, I took the walk; and when the third-base coach signed for me to hit toward first to advance the runner,

I hit to advance the runner. From the dugout steps Lefty Payne saw it all.

From the dugout he watched me as I played the hot corner, knowing Book, the league's best shortstop, was behind me. I protected the line, playing it tight. My glove had the good touch. I charged balls, and what I didn't catch I knocked down, and what I couldn't knock down I let bounce off me. Then I pounced on the ball like Sylvester on Tweety and took my time to set my feet before I made the throw. My arm was as strong as any right fielder's. Even with a high sky I swallowed every pop-up. Even when we played in I knocked the ball down and fired it home. I started to take charge, going to the mound to settle our pitcher when he was starting to unravel. I'd make some funny wisecrack about the fans, the batter, or the ump. There were stretches when I felt as loose and crazy as when I'd been the Perpetual Fielder in the Olive Street Alley League. I completely ignored Mickey. The hot corner was mine! The dirt around third was peppered by my spikes, the base was wettened by my spit, the air was filled with the love song of my intrepid chatter. "Hey, no batter, mad hatter, whatsa matter. . . ." Only the most deserving balls got by me. Payne's blue eyes saw it all.

He managed a fine game, maybe the best I've seen in all my years. He was every bit as smart and disciplined as Brother Gabriel, but he also played on intuition, hunch. He put on a lot of run-and-hit. The runner broke with the pitch, and the batter slapped the ball, ideally into the hole vacated by the shortstop, who broke with the runner toward second. If the batter missed, you risked the man being thrown out. But if the batter connected, it took away the double play; and if he singled, the runner more times than not made it all the way to third. His philosophy was one of controlled aggression. Know when to push, when to force the edge between defense and offense to swing in your favor. Know when to play the percentage, when to play it safe. He stressed above all else the fact that there were nine hitters in the lineup, and each inning they got to make three outs. Your duty wasn't to try to win the game by yourself; your duty was to get on, to advance runners who were on, to drive the runners in scoring position in. He praised the scratch single as much as the home run. Make contact, drive the ball, the hits will fall. Pick each other up. Everyone will have his turn being hero. Nobody is special on the team; what's special is the team. You don't win if you don't score, and you don't score if you don't get on. Get on, get on, get on, any way you can. Payne's game was grit, scrap, hustle. Hey, look alive out there, and if you had to make errors it was better they be errors of aggression. He told the pitchers to challenge each batter and to work on their control. But not to become fancy. Fancy pitchers led the staff in walks and died in Double-A. You're up here because you've got good stuff, so throw it, whatdya think you're getting paid for. Put on the heat. Smoke it. He taught all the pitchers better leg kicks so they'd have more on their fastballs. Then he taught them his change-up. Your fastball is only as good as your change-up. Pitch, get it over, mix it up. It's all right if they hit it. That's why there are men behind you wearing gloves. There's no defense against the manager's nightmare, headache, ulcer, the sin of sins: the base on balls.

They were glorious days, son. My sweet, pure days of Triple-A. I came to understand something else about the game then, as I dressed in a clubhouse that was actually decent, as I showered beneath a head that held enough hot water for the whole team, as I didn't have to worry if in practice I cracked a bat or fouled a ball into the stands, as I ate better meals because my meal money was better, as I played before knowing, healthy crowds. The Dynos could have made their facilities down in Pirate's Hook as good as those in Deadwater, but they didn't for a good purpose. Lousy conditions motivated you to want to move up, and once you moved up you never wanted to go back down again. Son, I never wanted to see Pirate's Hook again! Not after having my own clean stall with my nonmisspelled name in magic marker stenciled across it. Not after playing on a home infield that wasn't made of pothole and concrete. So I kept my edge sharp and looked alive. And, much to Mickey's displeasure, I kept both my whistle and my dipstick dry.

"You really bum me out," Mickey would tell me on nights when we sat in a bar with a dozen other ballplayers and I drank iced tea or 7-Up. "You're worse than a prohibitionist! Can't we even sip one lousy draft beer?"

"Nope." Then I'd drown him with tea or carbonation until he belched.

"Just look at all these women!" he'd moan. "Look at that big fat one! Oh, she's dripping for us, Danny! She's oozing, willing, and twenty-one! Look at her tongue circling her lips! She wants to take us 'round the world!"

"She's eating salty pretzels, Mickey. That's sweat you see dripping, nothing else. For your penance say three Our Fathers and Hail Marys."

"Help!" Mickey screamed. "I'm locked in a Trappist monastery! Help!"

I knew I was right, son, at least about not drinking and not smoking dope. Every trade has its occupational hazards. Butchers get fat and chop off their fingers. Bakers get diabetes and burn their arms. Ballplayers are prone to drug and alcohol abuse. Why? Because what are you supposed to do after a game—go back to your hotel room and watch your roomie pick his molars with his toenail clippings? You're too wired for TV, cards, or sleep. You want something to eat, somebody to talk to. It's night, and all the public places that are open have gallons to sell.

No bartender in the land pours Just One Drink. He pours The First Drink, then Hit You Again or Get You Another? You've just spent ten days on the road, endless hours on the bus, you went 0-for three games in a row, and you're ready to drink

Ireland or die trying. You look in the mirror behind the bar and all you can see are the shining bottles standing in such lovely, perfectly tiered rows. All the pretty colors, flavors, promises. What else can you do with your hands? Ice tinkles so nicely in a half-full glass. Why not get stinko? Everybody else is tanked. The joint in the parking lot feels so smooth between your fingers, and you know how softly it kicks after you sip its sweet smoke in. Why not get wrecked? You're married, and you know your wife won't mind you going to bed with Madam Grass or Miss Bottle. You're single and Miss Bottle or Madam Grass are all you can pick up. The night is long. You're trying to rise in the organization. You got a key hit or made the game-saving play or kicked the ball the one time it really counted or went 0-for. You're young. It's night. You need to celebrate, forget. Bad habits are the easiest. Everybody else is, and the bartender, the bottle, the joint, the first sip. . . .

Thanks, but no thanks. Iced tea, 7-Up, sometimes ginger ale.

My favorite answer to why I wasn't drinking or smoking: *What, after the way I've been hitting?* Always good for a smile, it worked both when I was in a slump or on a tear.

And even though gorgeous groupies sidled up to me and blew the warm sexy winds of temptation into my ear, I resisted, grinned, kept the conversation down to gab and chat, ball and bat, believing it would somehow make me a better ballplayer.

"Talk about Deadwater!" Mickey grumbled one night in June as we walked to our hotel. "Danny, *you're* dead water! You're violating nature! You've got so much love juice backed up in our balls they're turning into kidney stones! You've got our baby-blue scrotum thinking it's the Hoover Dam!"

"I've got a .348 average, Mickey. I've got my *culu* an inch away from the Bigs. Quit drooling at the waitress every morning and read the sports page. The Dynos' third baseman is hitting .239 and last week made two errors. Their shortstop's popping all of .206. These guys sip Geritol between innings, Mickey.

Their backups are veterans of the Spanish-American War. Their gloves are so old—"

"Yeah, but I bet they get a lot more hair pie than we do!"

"So what if they do? I hope they get so much they swim in it. *I'm talking baseball here, Mickey!*"

He was still complaining as I unlocked our hotel room. There on Book's bed were his packed suitcases. Book turned from the desk beneath the light by the window, pencil in hand.

"I didn't know how long you'd be out, man. I was writing you a note."

"Denver or a trade?" I said, hoping he wouldn't say trade.

Book smiled. "I'm still in green pinstripes."

Then I smiled, though already I was missing him. "Fantastic!"

When they move up, you wish them the best and tell them never to come back down again. They say they know you'll join them soon. You say sure you will. You don't offer to drive them to the airport. They go on their own because for a while, at least, that's how they'll be. If it's Book Johnson, you shake his hand, then hug him so hard that Mickey remembers what his ma always told him before she sent him to the store: "Don't squeeze the bread, squeeze me instead!" And all three of you laugh.

"I'm gonna miss you, Fruit Loops. But the way you've been playing—I'll be seeing so much of you in Mile High you'll make me sick."

"Yeah," I said, "I'm real tired right now of having to look at you every day. You taking the truck?"

He shook his head. "When they send you down, you drive. But when they call you up, you fly. man! I may not even need the airplane!"

So Book flew.

A very capable but much weaker hitting shortstop named Gonzalo Rodriguez replaced him. He didn't speak much English, so I tried to learn to *yo hablo español.* On the road I roomed with a right-handed pitcher named Tommy Chance. Every night that he didn't pitch, Tommy ate a bag of Oreos and drank a quart of milk, watching TV until the screen turned to bouncing fuzz. On nights that he pitched, he made long-distance phone calls to his girl, then took her picture with him into the bathroom, shut the door, ran water in the sink. I warned him about the sweets, how they were a one-way road to lard. "Next thing you know you'll get fat and they'll call you Fat Chance." The dummy liked the idea. Every morning he'd stand naked before the mirror with his belly stuck out, then watch himself go into his motion.

Book hit the ground running and didn't look back. You can't tell much from the next day's box score, but he was batting eighth, getting a single or two a game, and within two weeks had ten stolen bases. Patrick Hennessey, the Dynos' veteran third baseman, dropped to .221, then went 8-for-11 over three games. Rodriguez nodded even when he didn't understand me, which could drive a guy nuts. Fat Chance got hit bad and talked longer on the phone. Mickey begged for ice cubes made of water and red wine. My average soared to .352. Eleven homers, sixty-one RBIs. Not a single error notched my mitt.

"Have a seat," Lefty Payne said as I entered his office. There were less than six weeks left in our season. We were in the middle of a pennant drive. I figured he was going to send me and Rodriguez to Berlitz.

"You're real young," he said, "and in the best of worlds you'd be able to stay here with us for the maturity and experience you need." I noticed that he wasn't chewing gum. His eyes, in fact, looked sad.

"But this isn't the best of worlds, Dan. They're hurting at the gate up in Denver, and you're young and flashy, and you've got can't-miss written all over you. So"—he took a breath—"against my better advice—"

Dearest God, I prayed, oh dearest God!

"—I have to tell you that your contract's been purchased by Denver."

I whooped. Lefty's eyes fell back to his desk.

"I say that," he said, "because I'm just not sure you're ready. Call it a gut feeling. Pennant race aside, I think you're still too young. *Develop* the young players, I tell them. Don't bring them up until you're absolutely sure. Maybe I'm not being fair by telling you all this. I don't believe in rushing ballplayers. The majors have eaten up a lot of promising prospects who've gone up before they were ready."

"Well, I'll do whatever the club wants."

He shook his head. "I saw this move coming three days ago. Hennessey nearly went fourteen-day DL. Sore ankle, and Pellegrino can't play third every day, not at his age." He shook his head. "Last night I was talking about you with Wanda." He gestured toward her photo on his desk. "And she knows my hunches are usually right. Frankly, I was hoping they'd trade for someone to get them through the year." He shrugged. "Well, that's what I told them when they called. I couldn't be more pleased with you, Dan, don't get me wrong. But pressures can be intense up there. You know, you've got nearly all the tools. I wish I could put my finger on it. But something about your game still isn't right." He shrugged again. "Well, I'm a man who speaks his mind. I've seen a lot of players come and I've watched a lot of players go. I apologize if I'm wearing black at your wedding."

I was too excited to say anything, so I just sat there. Payne stared at me, then nodded. "You'll do fine, Dan. Just go slow. Take your time. The Dynos are high on you. They'll give you time to find yourself, make mistakes, grow into the position. That's really what I want to say. Be patient with yourself. Learn from Hennessey and Pellegrino."

"You're afraid I'll look like shit and they'll send me back down."

"No. I'm afraid going up will throw you off. You're just now hitting your stride. You need to play every day. You're much too good a ballplayer to ruin."

I stood. Then he stood and we shook hands.

"Prove me wrong," he said. "Make it all work out."

So help me, son, I tried.

I flew to Denver, arriving at Mile High in time for the seventh-inning stretch. Believe me, I stretched. In my street clothes I stood in an actual major-league dugout and stretched. Mickey had bought a green Dynos souvenir pennant on our way into the park and waved it with all the glee of a little idiot. I tried to maintain a cool façade appropriate to a rookie infielder. I frenetically chewed my bubble gum, kept myself from trembling, and acted as if nothing fazed me. Shaking the hands of my major-league teammates, I kept Mickey from asking them for their autographs. I was in the major leagues! I promised God I'd pray thirteen million novenas.

Though later I'd think I should've prayed the Litany for the Dead.

But I didn't know that then, that night, as I met the coaching staff, the manager; as Book got me a cot so I could stay with him and Leon Puma in their room; the next day as I put on my uniform prior to the twilight game. I knew nothing as I took batting practice. Nothing as I sat on the bench and watched the Denver Dynos take the field. I was as happy as a third grader just to be there. Then, in the sixth, the manager told me to pick up my glove.

"Go in for Pellegrino. Play your game, kid. Nothing fancy."

I made sure I didn't trip on the dugout steps. The third-base umpire smiled and wished me a long career. I said thanks, took the throw from the catcher, fired it to Booker T., paced the dirt, spat for luck on the bag, then pounded my glove's soft pocket as the announcer told the fans my name. They gave me a smatter of applause.

"Hey, no batter, mad hatter, whatsa matter . . ."

The night sky hung like a black sheet over the stadium. Immense bowl brimming with light, sides pulsing with people, a thousand muted sounds. My heart went rat-a-tat-tat. Slow down, Danny boy. The first pitch snapped the catcher's glove. Strike. Be ready. Be in the game. Pound that mitt, that's it. Ball. Get in the game, forget, focus. Strike two. Breathe, hey, relax. Pound that mitt. The batter started his swing. Try me, try me, see if I'm major-league! Stee-rike! Take the throw, send it around the horn. Way to go! I was in the game. There was one out.

The next batter flew to shallow right.

The third—

The ball slapped the sleepy grass and sped toward me in a blur to my right. Directly down the line, a sure double or triple. Third's a reflex position, son. Without thinking I cross-stepped, my glove stretching past my chest, reaching for the ball as I'd reached for it a hundred thousand times in my basement. My glove stabbed it as it flew over the bag. Then I spun, now in the air in foul territory, and cocked my arm and threw. There was no time to set my feet or check if first was where I thought it should be. The batter sprinted for the bag. The first baseman thrust his glove hand above his head. The ball kissed his mitt and then the batter's foot spiked the base and then the ump punched his fist up into the belly of Heaven.

"Out!"

The roar of the crowd enclosed me.

"What a play!"

Book, face brilliant in a smile. He rubbed the top of my cap with his open glove as we ran together to the dugout. Like it had been before, Booker T. and me, playing the diamond's left side together. The crowd was screaming still. The manager was the first to slap my hand. Teammates around me. "Way to be!" I tingled with pride, tossed my glove to the bench. Then the manager said, "Look alive, son, you're up, grab a bat, nothing fancy."

They cheered even louder when they saw me walk from the dugout. Then the stands buzzed with talk, and I could feel them relax and sit back. Well, we've seen what he can do with his glove, they were saying to each other. Let's see what this rookie can do with his stick. Mickey's eyes stared up proudly at the stands. I took a deep breath and had us look at the ground as we walked beneath the piercing lights to the on-deck circle.

"My turn to hit!" Mickey said at once.

"No," I said, "Mickey, please, no."

"Hey, you promised!"

"Not now." I began my thirteen lucky practice swings.

"Let me bat!" Mickey shouted.

"No," I said. I made the sign of the Cross. The loudspeakers boomed my name. The third-base coach signaled swing away. I pushed Mickey deep inside myself and stepped up to the plate and dug in.

The first pitch, red-laced and gently twirling, came in on the outside corner, low and away. I went with it. Swinging for it as hard as I could from my heels, driving it with all the strength in my wrists, arms, shoulders, uncoiling torso. The ball cracked off my bat and screamed down the first-base line toward the dreamy, again dreamy, first baseman, who must have been figuring out his batting average or balancing his checkbook or deciding whether or not after the game he'd eat Greek or Mexican or Italian *dear Jesus Christ, dear Virgin Mary, I didn't know* but the big left-handed first baseman didn't have his eyes on the ball.

It hit him full in the throat. Face-first he fell. I ran up the line, my hand squeezing my bat, shouting, "No! Not again! Dearest God! No!"

Wake him up.

You're all right, Meenan.

Get the smelling salts.

Right off his Adam's apple! Didja see it?

He ain't even breathing.

The first baseman's eyes looked backward into his head. For a moment in the stadium there was absolute silence. Then I could hear the flag in center flap in a sudden breeze. The first-base umpire, who'd rolled the guy on his back, looked up at me and stared. A woman in the box seats behind the other team's dugout covered her eyes. Everyone could see the guy was dead.

I opened my mouth to say something—to say anything—and then the soul of Mickey Meenan poured from my mouth and spilled into the empty body lying on the ground. Then the big first baseman blinked his eyes. The trainer got there with his bag and knelt, and Mickey twitched a finger. The crowd saw it, turned to one another, smiling, and then everyone at once began to cheer. The guy brought his knees up to his chest, and the crowd saw that and cheered even louder. They'd sure seen something. The big guy stood and put one hand to his throat and swallowed, then cleared his throat and swallowed again. For a second he looked at me. I wanted to say *Mickey, Mickey* but his eyes stared past me, and then he bent and picked up his fallen cap and stood and waved it at the fans. They cheered like he'd just won the pennant for them, like he was one of their own, their star, their hope, their pride and joy, their big left-handed first baseman.

Someone shouted to me to step on first, but I had no stepping left in my body. I had no taste for the game. I dropped my bat and walked across the infield, down the dugout steps, through the long dark runway to the locker room, where I sat by my locker and held a towel to my face.

Then I wept.

He was standing in fair territory when the ball hit him. I guess he must have finally realized the ball was still in play and picked it up and stepped on first because as I bawled like a baby near my locker I could hear the crowd's sudden terrible dark cheering, and the next morning's box score gave me an official at-bat and a goose egg in the column labeled hits.

Major-league batting average: triple Cheerios.

MIRACLE AT MILE HIGH!
DOUBLE DEFIES DEATH!
Breathtaking Tragedy Averted in 6th Inning

The articles quoted the team physician as saying he'd been sure that Double was a goner. The big first baseman's name was Adam Double. His fair face and contented grin filled a square on the bottom of the front page. Every morning news show ran tapes of the play. Going through it once was bad enough, but watching myself swing and hit him again and again in slow motion on national TV— Bring up the lights, I thought, the sock hop's over.

Though I'd hardly had time to take off my shoes. I hadn't even unpacked my duffel bag. I was up, as they say, for a cup of coffee. I sat on the edge of my cot in Book and Leon's hotel room, then put down the newspapers and shut off the TV.

Book stepped out of the bathroom, a white towel around his waist. Puma had already gone down for breakfast. "Hey, Lupo, hustle up. Leon's not gonna wait on us all day. Let's go, man. Eggs and bacon time."

"I'm not hungry," I said.

"Come on, Danny, change your clothes. Shave, take a shower. You'll feel like a new man."

I didn't think I could tell him that I already *was* a new man, or at least one man less than I used to be.

"So where'd you disappear to last night? You and Mickey do the town?" He smiled, trying to be light and cheerful, then turned back to the mirror and picked his hair.

I said nothing. After I'd thrown my uniform to the floor, I dressed and went for a walk, walking till dawn, feeling as empty as the deserted streets.

"Let's go, Molasses! Come on! Beautiful morning. Brand-new day. Hey, Loop, we've got a whole lot to do before tonight's game. Now that you're here, I want to check out of here and find us an apartment."

"Count me out." I stood and picked up my duffel bag.

"Run that by me again?"

"I said, count me out. I'm going down."

Then I shook Book's hand, though there was no strength in my handshake. My other hand waved his words away. I didn't know if you could go AWOL from baseball, but that was what I'd decided to do. And once outside, my feet on the streets of Denver, that was what I did.

You take care of a dead kid long enough and he grows as familiar to you as your shadow. You teach him baseball, let him kiss your girlfriend, even trust him with your body when you take a two-year sleep. And then he leaves, saying nothing? Leaving you worse off than before because now you know your bat has to be registered as a deadly weapon with the police, because accidents as horrible as that don't happen twice.

So I stuck out my thumb into the breezy morning traffic and hopped inside the first open door. I hitchhiked south and east, zigzagging my way over the next few days across Colorado, Kansas, Oklahoma, Texas, Arkansas, Louisiana, until I found myself riding into Jackson, Mississippi, and then I knew where I stood.

I was returning my life to Pirate's Hook. Because I could hardly go back to Deadwater, and Denver wasn't my home, and the thought of going back to Chicago in such disgrace— No, I'd reached the peaks and failed, so it was only right that I fall as far down as I could. Slip from the majors to Single-A.

Perhaps I knew in some subconscious way that you'd be there waiting for me. Maybe I was hoping Wings's arms would catch me, set me straight. Though I was certain that I was finished with baseball. To hell with it, I thought. It just led to death.

I tried to hitch a ride south from Jackson, but nobody would stop for me in the rain. So I gave up and walked, alongside rainsoaked fields. When I was tired, I slept beneath trees. The downpour was appropriate, I figured. I began my professional career in the rain, and that's how I'd end it.

The reddish earth gulped water until it gagged. At least the storm had no ambition of being minor-league. It graduated into a flood and in places swallowed fence posts and stop signs. The Pearl River rushed and roared.

At last I sloshed into Pirate's Hook. I waded toward the statue near the ball park and climbed the statue's base. I swung myself up onto the horse, then straddled the statue's hard shoulders so I could talk to God.

The field had disappeared beneath the water. The Pearl had grown so wide it now lapped the rotting benches in both dugouts.

"Well," I said, "I guess You're happy now. Once again You got what You wanted. Hey! Are You up there? Are You any-where?" I looked up at the gray sky. "I can't hear You, You'll have to talk louder. Whisper right into the grid, me lad, there's a long line of sinners waiting. You lousy son of a bitch! You stinking excuse for a Father! I don't give a flying fuck for Your strange and mysterious ways, howdya like that! Or are You too busy up there laughing at me to hear me? You wouldn't know mercy if it bit You in the face! Go back to sleep on the couch with Your holy newspaper! Extra, extra, read all about it! DANNY BACIGALUPO DOES IT AGAIN! He kills people with base-balls! Well, fuck You! Damn me to a million eternities in Hell for all I care! Didn't You think I *wanted* it? *I had it, God! I was there, playing in the majors! It was in my fucking hands! You had me tasting it! Then You took it right away!* Whatdya think I worked for all those years, so I could sell peanuts in the bleachers? Oh God, Oh Jesus Christ, Oh Holy Ghost! I earned it, didn't I? You can't say I didn't work for it. Why did You have to take it away? Sweet Virgin Mary, please make Him talk to me. So forget it. I don't need to play anymore, really. I just want to know why. What did I do? Huh? What did I ever do? Oh, Father, my Father, Who art in Heaven. Hallowed be Thy Name. Thy Kingdom come. Thy Will be done. Even if it means I can't play baseball. Give us this day, our daily bread, and forgive us our—"

In the distance, bolts of lightning cracked the sky. I held on to the statue's raised sword, crying, a wet tired mess, trying to cover my head with my arms, praying for all I was worth. Then I heard a voice.

"Dan?"

I thought it was the Lord's. I looked at the sky eagerly. "Yes?"

"Dan Bacigalupo? Is that you up there, preachin' to the rain?"

Then I realized the voice belonged to Homer, who was splashing his way toward me in the waters below.

"Well, I'll be!" Homer said. He was wearing dark rubber hip boots and a Dynos cap covered with dangling fishing lures. "Well, shut my eyes! Speak of the devil, I was thinkin' about you, trying to figure how we was gonna get in touch with you!"

"You're in touch with me now," I said.

"Damn tootin'! I'm so pleased. You just saved me a trip in my nephew Edgar's bass boat to the county orphanage!"

Take a deep breath, son. You're about to be penciled into the lineup.

I shifted my weight on the statue's shoulders. Lightning again sparked on the horizon. The silver and gold lures on his cap glistened like a treasure chest. Old Homer raised his arms to help me down. Soft thunder rolled over me as I descended. His grin was the brightest thing I'd seen in days.

1 2 3 4 5 6 **7** 8 9

MAN ON BASE

Together we spashed across the infield to the higher ground of the pitcher's mound, where we stood in shin-deep water and from which Homer pointed to the right-field wall.

"He floated through right there, I suspect," he said, pointing to an opening in the boards just beneath the second *o* in the Goody's Headache Powder sign. "You know, we always meant to fix that hole. A ball gets out there and bounces on through into them pussy willows on the bank of the river and it's a ground-rule double."

I nodded, only partially understanding.

"Yep," Homer said, "way we figure, them pussy willows done saved his life. He was caught in them real good. I even found three balls! He couldn't a been out there no more than a couple hours. He was real warm. Had a whole lot of rain on his face and he was sittin' in a puddle of river water inside his little basket, but he was bundled up real nice. No worse for the wear." He shook his head and smiled at me. "See, me and Wings was out here with a yardstick measurin', you know, how deep it was at home, at first, at third, keepin' charts, so as we could figure when the flood'd be cresting, and then Wings says to me he says, 'Homer, you quit sloshing, I think I hear something!' So the both of us listened real good. Then we heard him again, sure enough. Wings would a gone out there himself and made the rescue except you know what this infield's like with all them sudden holes. A man can be walking knee-deep in water and then he hits a hole and he's in up to his elbows! You remember. Conditions can be downright treacherous."

"Where is he now?" I said.

"With Wings, at Claudette's diner. Getting dry."

"What made you come back here?"

Homer tapped his cap. "Old fisherman's intuition, I'd say. You catch a good one in the morning somewhere, you just got to go back later that day to see what kind of creature takes its place." He grinned. "Works too, don't it? Sure enough, I found you!"

"Sure enough," I said, staring at the dark water. Lightning once again split the sky.

You and Wings were in the back of the diner by the grill with the two waitresses and the cook. They shushed us as soon as we stomped in. You were sound asleep in the cook's fat arms.

"There's the damn Yankee slime!" Wings said in a raspy whisper as soon as he saw me. His face was as cracked as ever; his eyes, yellow as oleo.

"He's come back to do right," Homer said. He shook his raincoat on the floor. "Oh yes, I seen it! He was up there on top of the general's shoulders screaming out sorrowful prayers like a revivalist preacher! He's been born again too, I bet!"

One of the waitresses said, "Amen!" Wings stared at me, then spat a line of tobacco juice into a paper cup.

"My, my, how the mighty have fallen. You know, I never

had anything but distaste for ballplayers like you. You're a disgrace to the game, you hear me, boy? You'll never play for me again! If I had my way, any batter who hurt another player would be jerked out of baseball so fast—"

"I wouldn't play for you again if you got down on your knees."

Wings smiled. "That's just what I wanted to hear, you lowest breed of scum. You're a violation to nature, you know that? Mixing colors that'd be better off separate and injuring innocent men out on the field"—his hand squeezed his old pitching arm and I remembered Book's story about the liner off his elbow that ended his career—"and fathering little bastards."

I wanted to hit him, but I realized my life had seen enough violence. There was no use even arguing with him, I thought. At his feet in a splash of mud and water sat your wicker basket. On the table next to his cup of spit lay the folded note.

To the Finder,

With fearful trepidation but High Christian hopes I hereby leave this week old child in accord with my now departed daughter's dying wishes. Though I fear the Wrath of God I am too old and poor as the hills to raise him right. Still I pleaded with my daughter who done wrong but I forgive. No Daddy she said No Daddy No Daddy. The boy should be raised up by his own daddy. He is the 1st baseman DANIEL BLOTCHAMANGOOP of the Razor Bluff baseball team she said at the end. They live the lives of Gypsies she said. Daddy take him down to Mississippi to void the scandal. Leave him on 1st base where his daddy plays. Write Dearest God on the baby clothes. He will Know what That Means! before she died in my arms in a pool of blood. He is a fine child and doesn't much cry already Baptised by my hand. So to the Finder take this boy and letter of proof to his daddy. I pray to God he is a Christian. May God Forgive us All.

212

"Ain't it poetry?" Homer said.

"You won't be able to deny it," Wings said. He snatched the letter from my hand. "I'll see to it myself. I'll hire a lawyer—"

"I don't want to deny it. I just want my baby."

The cook turned with a fat red smile and handed you to me.

You were awfully small. More red than any other color. All over your little shirt and pants were *dearest Gods* and crosses and lines that I guessed stood for rays of grace. Your lips were pink and perfect, like glazed ceramic. Your tiny eyelids were shut tight. Breath rushed back and forth through your little nose. Quickly I remembered to check your hands, and I smiled when I saw that both were tightly clenched into fists. Yes, I thought, my son has *figatu*. I could hold you easily in one arm.

My son. This is my son. You moved your tiny fist then to your mouth. Inside me something shifted, swung. I moved from the rank of sons to the universe of fathers. I thought of Chicago, my parents. Your mother, whose face I couldn't picture, dying in a pool—

I bent and kissed your cheek. Oh son, who at that moment may have saved me. Suddenly I knew where we had to go, what I had to do.

"We named him," one of the waitresses said.

"What?" I said.

The other waitress covered her mouth with her hand and laughed. Homer giggled. The cook grinned. Wings scowled.

"Sure," Homer said. "There wasn't but one name after all the little fella had been through."

"No," I said, "it's not your right." I realized they'd been kind and I was spoiling their fun, but naming you myself seemed to be my right; more, it seemed to be my responsibility. You were now my responsibility. I looked at the hurt in their faces, then around the diner, my eyes settling on a nickel and a dime left on one of the tables beside a plate.

"You don't draw too many babies out of the bulrushes," Homer was saying, "and then not have the common sense—"

"His name is Tip," I said. "And thank you, really, thank you all for what you've done, but my son's name is Tip."

Son, allow me to present your etymology.

Tip (Am.), precise origin unknown. 1. (noun) a piece of change, a gratuity, a small present of value left behind, as in a restaurant, in return for a service of kindness. 2. (noun) the slightest action a baseball may make in contact with a still or swinging bat, as in *foul tip*, though you were the fairest in all the land. 3. (verb) to overturn, to upset, to incline or tilt, as in what your pure and simple existence was about to do to my life.

We didn't stay in Pirate's Hook for very long. Long enough for me to wash and shave and eat and then to realize that you needed to eat too, and that after you ate you needed a good belch or two to be happy, and then after you belched you needed to void yourself of waste. So I gave Homer a few of my T-shirts and filled the space in my bag with cans of formula and diapers. The cook taught me how to test the formula's temperature on my arm. The waitresses showed me how to fold the diapers. "When will I know he's hungry?" I asked, and everyone laughed and said, "Oh, he'll let you know." Homer wished me the best of luck. The cook stuck a cigar in my mouth. Both waitresses gave me a kiss. Then they held you for the last time, and everyone kissed you. I thanked them all, then walked up to Robert E. Lee Wingert.

"I'm leaving," I said.

"That's your business," he said. "It's got nothing to do with me."

"You know," I said, "at least you had a career. What did you play for, thirteen seasons?" He nodded. "That's something you can always look back on, be proud of. I played the last thirteen seasons with death on my back. But you don't give a damn.

That's just your problem. You don't give a damn about anybody but yourself."

"Watch your mouth, boy."

"When you got injured, you were a veteran. I had one at-bat, one pitch."

"One more than you deserved." His face cracked deeper into a frown.

"Maybe you're right," I said. "But you don't do young ball-players much of a service." I looked down at you in my arms. "Anyway, thanks for helping to save my baby."

I started to leave. He followed me.

"After he hit that ball, he laughed! You hear me, boy? It splintered my damn elbow into more pieces than you can get in one of them dime-store jigsaw puzzles, and that rookie coon stood there on first and laughed! He was real proud of what he done!"

"Then take it out on him. Not everyone else."

His eyes studied me, then fell on you in my arms.

"You take care of that little boy, now."

I nodded.

On our way out of town I told you that Wings was meant to be a sign, a walking example of what can happen to a man when he lets bitterness fill his heart. You understood the lesson so well that you bawled like a little baby. "Wa-wa-wa-waah! Wah-wah! Waaaaah!"

"Weep for humanity, Tip," I said, then got wise and slipped you a bottle and changed your pissy diaper.

By the time we got to Natchez I realized I needed a better system. So I bought an aluminum-frame backpack and a sling like a home-plate umpire's chest protector, into which I could comfortably slip you, both of which freed my arms. I bought paper diapers I could throw away. I traded my duffel bag for two big all-metal thermos bottles to keep your formula warm in. I warmed your formula whenever we stopped to eat. Waitresses all over the South are just as sweet as pralines and pecan pie to

AWOL ballplayers traveling with babies. A pretty redhead in a Natchez café suggested that if I wanted quicker rides I should get my hair cut real short and make a sign. MAN AND NEWBORN INFANT. So I got my ears lowered and made the sign. People who picked us up asked right away how they could be of help. "Just keep on driving north," I told them. "Where you headed?" they asked. You slept in the sling. "Where're we headed? Where are any two men on base headed? Home."

Which wasn't anywhere yet, Tip. Because then all I knew was what I had realized in Claudette's diner, that my next play, the play I had to make, was to find your mother's grave and your grandfather and somehow make amends.

Because even someone from the most backward jungle would know that if you play a part in one of these strange twists of fate you must then have the human decency to pay your respects.

"Tip," I said as we climbed down from the back of a truck hauling crates of protesting chickens to the slaughterhouse, "hey, you've got to help me." I brushed tiny feathers from your brown hair. We were on the outskirts of Razor Bluff, starting the walk into town.

"We're a team now, understand? It's you and me. I get on, you knock me in. You get on, I do the same for you. Now, I've been here before, but then again it's like I haven't, because my dead friend Mickey Meenan, who's now really Adam Double, had control over my body and mind then." You twisted your face and started to cry. "I know these substitutions are confusing, and you're coming into the game pretty late. Someday I'll tell you the whole story from the very beginning, I promise." Inside the sling you opened your blue eyes and smiled. Gas, more than likely, but your smile warmed me all the same.

"Lead me, Tip. You've been here before too."

You had little choice in the matter, since you rocked in the sling on my chest. I talked a steady stream, not nonsense infield rhyme but a new father's attempts to piece things together. I wondered if your granddaddy really left you on first base like his note said. I didn't doubt Homer found you in the basket in the pussy willows. But how could you have floated *toward* a cresting river? No, you'd have floated from first base toward the visitors' dugout or toward home plate.

I tried to imagine myself in the old man's place. No man who would go through all the trouble of driving from Arkansas all the way down to southern Mississippi would abandon a week-old baby in a flood. He'd make sure you were found. Sure, I told myself and you, he waited by the field until he saw Wings and Homer measuring the flood with the yardstick. Then he stuck you in the willows, then hid where he couldn't be seen. Then you cried or maybe he gave you a pinch, so they'd hear you. He watched Homer draw your basket from the water, assured you'd get to me since Homer was wearing a Dynos cap. Then he drove home, content he'd done the right thing.

"Isn't that how it happened, Tip?"

You didn't disagree. The conversation linked us, and I whistled "Tea for Two" until we reached the county cemetery.

When you've feared and mocked death as long as I have, you don't enter a cemetery doing the watusi. Even though a full sun shone on the grass, I was knee-knocking scared. My heart drummed more loudly than a New Orleans funeral march. It seemed I was like Midas: Everything I touched ended up in the Friendly Underwater World's rusty Maxwell House coffee can. Mickey. Adam Double. Now this woman I hardly knew. We searched for fresh graves, newly broken ground, a bouquet of wilted flowers.

"It'd be easier if they put the corpse's weight on the headstones," I told you. "Here's a new one. Nope, she was seventy-two. Let's look for a real big hole, because you know she was a big woman. Probably beautiful and wonderful—" I started to cry. You were whimpering too. For a minute we both howled, trying to top each other's volume.

Then, still sobbing, I put you on the ground and changed

your diaper. The sun hid behind a cloud. "Cooperate with me, son. The note said they were poor, so she *has* to be here in the public cemetery. That's it, lift your legs so I can wipe. You want your bottle now? Sure. Here it is, Tip. Yum yum. Wait, son. I think— Look!"

An old man stood, hat in hand, over a new grave.

"Lamb of God," I whispered, "who takest away the sins of the world, grant unto her rest. Lamb of God . . ."

Though the old man gave us no sign, and years later I'd learn I was wrong, as I stood there I was sure he was your granddaddy. You didn't help; you squinted your eyes and sucked up your lunch. We crouched four or five graves away from him. Should I confess who I was? I wondered. Or was it better to leave things as they were? You made the decision for me, son. At that moment you spat the bottle's nipple from your mouth and let loose a shrill, bald cry loud enough to wake the dead.

The old man turned and stared at us. I stood. A blackbird flew behind him in the distance.

"May dearest God forgive us all!" I cried.

He nodded at us, pulled one sleeve of his tattered shirt, then knelt.

"Don't worry whether I'm a Christian," I shouted. "I'll do the right thing, take my word!"

The old man rubbed his mouth, then stood, staring at the dark earth. You belched damply, then started to fuss. I gave you back your bottle. Around us, weathered tombstones cast their long shadows on the earth. Lambs. Urns. Crosses. Winged angels. The old man squeezed his eyes, then began to walk away.

"Wait!" I screamed. "Mister, wait!"

And I ran toward him with you in my arms, the damn weepies again bringing stinging tears to my eyes.

"Mister," I said, "mister, I'm sorry, I didn't know! I would have been there with you when she died if I did, but I didn't know! I'm terribly sorry! The baby's just fine, as you can see.

I'll love him more than I could ever love any person or thing on this earth. I never meant to hurt you or your daughter. I'm sorry, please, I accept all blame. You have every right to hate me, but won't you forgive me, please?"

I had fallen to my knees with you in my arms. The man's hand rose above us, then hesitated. Then he patted my head as if I were an old hound.

"Grief's a mighty weight," he said. "I know it addles the mind. You think your poor shoulders can't carry no more of it and then the Good Lord says, 'Here, tote this!' and you ain't got no other choice, 'cept to remember that Jesus hauled a righteous heavy cross. Say amen, son."

"Amen!" I said.

"You feel real pained, don't you?"

I nodded. You drank your bottle and stared at us, wide-eyed.

"The living hang together," he said, entwining his fingers, "sort of like a web. Every time someone passes on"—he ripped apart his hands—"a piece of you gets tore away too. You gotta bleed for a while before it heals. I know how you're feeling, son. You and your baby been yowling the past quarter of an hour. But the pain'll skin over. See, the Lord's always sending new life back down to take the dead's place."

His finger pointed at you. I nodded.

"Watch your child, now," the old man said. "He's your obligation. And don't be a fool, put something on his head. There's quite a breeze blowing through the world, and it's real easy at that age to catch a bad cold."

Again I nodded. "Then you forgive me, mister?"

"Sure, I forgive you. I forgive every man I meet! But I suspect you got your plow in the wrong field." His hand shot toward the sky. "Ask Him!"

"I will," I said. Then I stood.

He nodded to me, cupped his hand over your head and smiled, then limped away. I watched him grow smaller and smaller. Then

I looked down at the grave. The wind rippled the summer grass. There was no marker on the earth.

"Forgive me," I said to the dark dirt. "Please."

I looked up at the sky. "You too, please, forgive me."

I stared again at the earth. "You know, I'm probably not even talking to the right grave, but whoever you are, you're dead. And she's dead, whoever she is, so that puts you a lot closer to her than it does to me. So, if you could, would you pass my words on? Please ask her to forgive me. And while I'm at it, may you rest in peace." I looked around the cemetery. There were graves as far as I could see.

"All of you. Here, and in every place of burial on earth. Forgive me. And may all of you rest in eternal peace."

Walking away with my pack on my back and you sleeping on my chest, I felt pretty good, as if I'd done something.

Then once again we hit the road.

Everybody has an idea about something, son. On the road I learned to listen to the crazies. I listened to people who claimed they'd met and shaken the tentacles of visitors from outer space. I learned who really killed JFK. One man told me he had a cure for everything from arthritis to zits, based on FM radio waves transmitted through pyramid-shaped blocks of sea salt suspended in cod-liver oil. I met a woman who said she communicated with vegetables. To prove her point, for nearly ten miles she sang to you in Green Bean.

Those without extravagant stories sometimes talked to me about the war, protest, communism, black power, the proper length for a man's hair, and what should happen to women who burned their bras and believed in sexual equality and liberation. These drivers, who often wore suits and ties, would become so absorbed in their insecurities and hatreds that they'd weave in and out of their lane. I got us out of those cars fast.

"Die on the road, you goddamn pinko nigger-loving faggot!" they'd tell me as they crunched to a stop on the highway's shoulder. "And you'd best teach that baby of yours to speak Russian and Red Chinese!"

Then they'd spit gravel at us as their V-8s roared away, their AMERICA: LOVE IT OR LEAVE IT bumper stickers getting tiny as they raced off into the red, white, and blue star-spangled horizon.

Give me a ride with the crazies anytime.

The pickup truck was exactly where I'd left it, parked in the lot behind Deadwater Municipal Park. I was glad to see it. The engine coughed and rattled but then turned over and sounded fine. I didn't know where we'd go, but I knew we'd go somewhere. I was pleased nobody was around. Then I looked at you lying next to me on the slippery seat and imagined your intelligent baby brains dripping down the dashboard. "No," I told you, "this won't do."

So we left our stuff in the truck and walked to the ball park. The day was made for lazy fly balls. I wanted to sit in the stands with you and talk, but we had work to do. I knew where Leroy kept his tools. While you napped in your sling on the third-base line in a wooden front-row box seat, I unbolted its neighbor, which undoubtedly had borne the weight of scores of joyous fans exultant with the pleasure of watching me play my can't-miss third.

"Can't miss?" I said to the empty field. I laughed, then banged the box seat's iron legs with a sledgehammer, splaying them open, then sliced them off with a hacksaw. The labor felt good. Now I needed a rope and a blanket. I searched the clubhouse with you on my chest. I was being a responsible father, I thought. You'd ride in the seat just fine. After I found what I needed, I tied the seat inside the truck backward so I could look at you, talk to you, as I drove. The blanket nicely cushioned the seat. Now all we needed was a strap of some sort to secure you so you wouldn't bounce when we hit bumps. We were rummaging around the clubhouse again when the team bus pulled up outside.

There was no avoiding them. The Dynos swaggered out of the bus like a victorious army. Comet Haley's red hair blazed in the late day sun. Bagman Jones was slapping rump. Tommy Chance was headed for the telephone, on his face a smile as big as his belly. It must have been a very successful road trip. I hid you in the sling and clutched you to my chest.

" 'Galupo!"

"Say hey! Dan!"

"Botchamagupa, welcome back!"

The team was as excited as boys at a birthday party, as a bottle of root beer shaken a hundred times.

Then Lefty Payne walked in and stopped and stared me down and said, "You, I want you in my office in ten seconds." I felt like the kid who'd got caught at the party doing something very wrong.

"There's absolutely no excuse for what you did," he said as I entered his office. "Talk about a bush play! You don't just walk out on a major-league team and then take nearly two weeks before you report!"

"What?" I said. "They reassigned me?"

"What do you think? They gave you a job in the front office? Of course they sent you back down." He shuffled some papers on his desk. "And in appreciation for this stunt the club's fining you—"

You didn't appreciate the threat to the fund that paid for your formula and diapers, because at that moment you began to cry.

"What in the world is *that*?"

As I brought you out of the sling, I watched Lefty's heart melt faster than a geriatric starter in a seventh-inning August sun.

Babies trigger something in adults. Babies make them bend at the waist, look silly, and say *ouuuuu!* Lefty followed the script.

"He's a pretty good kid," I said. "Cries mostly when he's hungry."

Babies also make grown-ups pucker their lips and talk funny.

Lefty puckered and talked funny until there was a knock at the door.

It was Leroy reporting the stolen box seat.

"Never mind," Lefty said. "What a beautiful baby! He likes me, Dan, I can tell." Leroy shrugged and left. "Look at this cute little guy, oh, you like your daddy's old coachie-woachie, don't you? Yeahhhh, sure you do! Dan, I didn't know you were a family man. Is your wife in town with you?"

"She's dead," I said.

That put the starch back into my old coachie-woachie. Clouds covered Payne's blue eyes. He stroked his cheek for a moment, looked at you, at me, then sat down behind his desk.

"Dead?"

"Yes," I said, "dead. As in grave in the Razor Bluff County Cemetery. We just came from there. She died in childbirth, and I needed to find—"

"Dear sweet God, Dan, I didn't know! I'm terribly sorry. Please." He shook his head, staring at me. "Please accept my deepest sympathies. You must be heartbroken. When did you say all this happened?"

I gave it a stab. "About the time I was up in Denver."

"No wonder." He swallowed. "Then this explains everything, Dan, though you might have informed the club. I'm so sorry. I—I just assumed—"

"It's OK. Things will work out for the best."

"That's a *very* impressive positive attitude, Dan." He exhaled loudly. "Good God, I feel like such a fool! I was so sure you just turned tail and ran away. I never thought—"

"Well," I said, remembering how I felt after I hit the ball that killed Adam Double, "when it happened it was a real shock, and I just couldn't—"

"Of course, Dan, of course the death of your wife was a real shock." He looked at his desk, then offered me a square of bubble gum. "These fines," he waved his hand, "I'll rip them up." He nodded as if to convince me. "And I'll give you as much time as you need."

The gum tasted good and sweet. It seemed like quite a while since I'd chewed some. "For what?"

"Why, to get back out on the field! We're in the last stretch of the greatest pennant race the league has ever seen! You didn't think you'd lose your spot in the lineup when you came back, did you?"

"I didn't even think about it. After what happened, well, I figured I was through with baseball."

"Nonsense," Lefty said. "Not with your new attitude, with all your tools. You were born for the game, Dan. I'll give you enough time to readjust."

Then he said that you and I should stay for the rest of the season at his house, that he had an extra room, that Wanda would be delighted to help me care for you, that he wouldn't take no for an answer. Then you fussed and I made you a fresh bottle. Lefty insisted on giving it to you himself. As soon as you were in his arms, he started to talk funny again. I paced the room.

I couldn't play again, I thought, not unless I intended to make killing first basemen a habit. But the game was all I knew, and we needed the money. But there was blood on my bat. Life's strikes come in threes, I thought. If I go back to the game it was bound, sooner or later, to happen again. I must have looked awfully sad, because Lefty tried to cheer me up.

"Come on, Dan. Shake off your doubts. Plenty of ballplayers go up and down in the beginning. That's no indication of your abilities. And you've still got a real solid chance at league MVP, and everybody here figures the batting crown's in your hip pocket. And you've heard, I'm sure, just how nicely that Double incident turned out."

"No. I haven't been near a newspaper or even heard a score since—"

He nodded, understanding. "You know that Denver's heart

went right out to the big guy. So the brass sat down and patched together a trade. A real shot in the arm for the gate, I might add. The organization couldn't be much happier. We had to give up some quality veteran pitching but we were able to keep Santos and at the same time protect the promising young players like Book Johnson and Comet Haley," he paused, "and you. The long and short of it is that Adam Double is a Dyno now."

The realization hit me like a punch to the stomach. "Of course," I said. I bent, then had to sit. "Mister Speed and Mister Bat. And Book will be named this season's Rookie of the Year, and later they'll win the World Series in seven and share MVP honors, and in twenty-some years, when they step down, Denver will retire their uniforms. Both will be inducted into the Hall of Fame. The guy who plays Book in the movie will win an Oscar. The fans will carve their faces in the Rockies—"

Lefty laughed and laughed. "Dan, we should put you in Promotions. That's a marvelous dream."

"It's not a dream."

"Sure," he laughed. "And you'll be part of it, at third."

I tried to remember if Mickey said I'd be a part of it. "Who's playing third now? Pellegrino?"

Lefty shook his head. "Patrick Hennessey, and he's doing really well. I don't know what he did to his ankle but lately he's playing like the Hennessey of old." Lefty put you on his shoulder and patted your back. "There'll be room on that club for you next year. Pellegrino announced that after this season he's going to retire." You liked the news so much you belched.

"I don't know," I said. "I was sure I was through, but all this sounds mighty tempting."

Tip, it was far easier said than done.

Because the liner off Double's Adam's apple must have sapped more than just the Mickey Meenan from me. Because the next morning at practice when I stepped out on the field I felt naked and vulnerable, and when balls whistled toward me I turned like a sissy and cringed. All of a sudden it seemed real dangerous to be out there on the diamond. Whenever I looked in at the plate, all I could see was the line drive that would crush my neck and kill me. When I looked at the stands all I saw was the missing seat.

Whose was it? I wondered. I feared I knew the answer. The empty space belonged to Mister Death.

Then Payne took the bat and sent me humiliating little grounders. Half trickled between my legs. Then he squatted behind the plate and rolled me bunts by hand, like a father trying to play ball with his baby. I stopped them with my glove like a baby. My throws to first sputtered dead in the dirt. My flame had turned to ash. I'd blown my fuses. I was a daddy in a dark house without a flashlight.

Lefty told me to relax, to take some cuts in the cage. My eyes squeezed themselves blind. The bat didn't leave my shoulder. He ordered me to open my eyes. Seeing was worse. Even pitches so far outside that they got past the scrambling catcher terrified me. I imagined every one cracking my eggshell of a head. So I ate dirt, so much I could have given demonstrations to vacuum cleaners. I swallowed Rhode Island. My teammates stood around the cage and laughed, thinking old Danny was horsing around, goofing off, once again up to his old antics.

Lefty walked me into the clubhouse, then slammed the door.

"All right," he said, "what the hell's the matter with you?"

I started to unbutton my uniform. "I don't know. Maybe you should put me on the DL or send me down."

"You'd send down a .352 hitter?"

"You saw me out there today. I can't play. I'm an embarrassment to the team. I can't stop a whiffle ball. I couldn't hit a cotton ball with a Q-tip if my baby's life depended on it."

"You know what's true," he said. "You know what's bullshit. You don't need me to remind you the difference."

I sat on the bench near my locker. He began to walk away.

"What happened to your wife was rough, Dan. Believe me, I'm the first guy to empathize. But you just looked absolutely ridiculous, so all I can figure is that you must really *want* to fail." He sat down alongside me. I don't know if he noticed the tears in my eyes. "You want me to tell you that there are guys out there with half your talent and twice your heart who'll play regardless of anything? You don't have a monopoly on suffering. It's your life, Dan. You decide. Three-quarters of this game *is* mental. You had your two weeks. Let it go."

Then he scratched me from the lineup. From the bench I watched us drop our next three games. Once the guys figured I wasn't pulling more antics, they stayed away from me like I had smallpox. Only Rodriguez came near me. He'd pulled a hamstring. "Is very tender," he'd say every other inning, then nod and rub the back of his thigh.

The losses dropped us a half-game out of first. Then we opened a series with the new league leader and fell behind a southpaw whom I usually hit so well they said I owned him. Down by two in the bottom of the eighth. One man on. Lefty paced the length of the dugout, then nodded to me. "Grab a stick, Dan. You're pinch-hitting."

"No," I said in a voice so low only he and Rodriguez could hear. "The game's too important. You got it wrong, Coach."

"*You've* got it wrong, damn it. Now get up there and get it right."

The phrase was clever enough to trick me out to the on-deck circle, where I knelt on one knee on the team emblem, spat on the dinosaur's eye, rubbed a little tar on my bat handle, doing the usual things batters do—though unlike usual batters I prayed that the man up at the plate would make the third out so I could go back to the bench again. Instead the goon lashed a gorgeous line-drive single, a clean, crystalline hit, the kind that managers love, that fans all too often don't appreciate. That sent the runner on first to third. The announcer trilled my name for the cheering fans. I strode to the plate with a lone thought in my head. *No matter what, I will not embarrass myself. No matter what, I will not eat dirt.*

"You looked like whale shit today in BP," the catcher said with a grin as I dug in. Then I heard him laugh.

I shut my eyes and didn't move until the umpire bellowed, "Stee-rike!"

The catcher snorted. The pitcher smiled and fingered the ball. He knew he had me. I knew he had me. The catcher knew he had me.

"Stee-rike two!"

I told myself to stop shaking, that there would be only one more pitch, a strike. But the sadist on the hill wanted to prolong my misery. He shook off the first sign. The third pitch was way outside.

"Baawl!"

You could see he was enjoying himself. He walked behind the mound, spat, picked up the rosin bag, and bounced it on his wrist. He stepped back onto the rubber. The next pitch came in high and tight, not that I saw it, since my eyes were shut with cowards' glue, but I felt it as it breezed past my head.

"Baawl!"

"You *are* whale shit!"

I was making sounds then, high nervous little *he-he-he-hes.* Then the fans started in on me. "Let's go, Butcheroopo!" "Are you sleeping out there or what?" "C'mon, get a hit, you bum!" I locked my knees so I wouldn't fall down. Normally I would've stepped out of the box, had a few words with Mickey, taken a couple of practice cuts, then stepped back in with aggression, energy, confidence. But instead I stood there like a broom.

The next pitch fiddled a little chin music. I fell back and away, folding in the dirt like an accordion. Anyone with eyes could see I looked terrible. Anyone with a nose could smell my fear.

"Baawl! Three and two!"

There are limits, son. Points beyond which men and women alike shatter like frozen Milky Ways. That fifth pitch came so close to my chin that I no longer cared if I killed the opposing first baseman or, for that matter, the entire population of Kansas. Because suddenly I realized how pitiful I must have looked to all the fans, my teammates, to Lefty Payne. And while there is some shit I'll gladly eat, some humiliation I'll willingly endure, some pain and degradation I'll heap on the stick I carry, *all because sometimes I'm so down on myself I think I deserve it*, there is also an edge to human pride that is keener than the sharpest razor, that snaps your spine and gels your blood and makes your mouth mutter a bottom-line, resolute *fuck you*. I mean, did they want me to wear daisies in my hair, a bell around my neck, and moo? How much of their spit milkshake did they expect me to swallow? For how long can a person wallow in guilt and not stand up and say, *I don't care anymore! I've got some vestige of worth and dignity too!*

I brushed the dirt from my pants, then dug in. The cocky chump laid it on the outside corner. I sat on the pitch. I jumped all over it, hey diddle diddle! The little dog laughed to see such sport! I creamed that cowhide so well it jumped over the moon, or at least Manitoba. I'm talking *straightaway center field!* Five hundred and sixty-four feet, and that's a conservative estimate, because I have a dozen eyewitnesses who'll swear they saw that ball light up the Canadian sky, circle the North Pole, come back around Siberia, China, Indonesia, Australia, the South Pole, Tierra del Fuego, Argentina, Bolivia, Colombia, Nicaragua, Honduras, Mexico, Texas, Oklahoma, and then have enough pop left to come back over the backstop and make it out over the park a second time. Tiparillo, the official scorer should have counted it twice!

I stood at home plate like an Oscar Mayer wiener and watched it, then strolled to first and touched my right big toe to the bag.

"Let me see your damn neck," I said to the first baseman.

"Say what?" the ninny mumbled.

"See, you're still alive!"

Then I jogged to second and came down on the base with both feet. "I'm back," I told the second-base umpire. I sprinted to third and slid into the bag. "Dan Bacigalupo is back!" I stood and dusted my uniform, then covered the last ninety feet pretending I was skipping rope. The home crowd ate it up. They gave me a standing O. At the plate I knelt, removed my helmet, spread my hands, then scored the go-ahead run with a headstand.

Lefty fined me fifty big ones for the theatrics, but the homer made that week's *Sporting News*:

TAPE MEASURE SHOT AT DEADWATER

As if it were a matter of *mere distance*. When what it meant was nothing less than how I'd be able to live the rest of my life, play the remaining innings of my game. Even if I'd barely squibbed it past the pitcher, it would have been cause to pop the cork from the bubbly. Because I'd picked myself up from the canvas and fought back.

That hit won the game, and the game vaulted us into first, and in the weeks remaining in the season we didn't look back. Though Triple-A, though minor-league, you still spell it with the same letters, and the letters read every bit as sweetly. Let no one take anything away.

Champions!

"Now we've got one hell of a task," Lefty told me over a rare T-bone in Deadwater's best steakhouse. "Now we've got to repeat. And it'll be difficult without you."

"Why?" I said. "You're kicking me and Tip out into the cold?"

"Not a chance." He smiled. "You're more than welcome to stay on this fall and winter, like Wanda said. Don't be coy with me, Dan. You know as well as I do that next season you won't be playing in Deadwater."

"I don't know, Lefty. Honest. You know I'm not playing winter ball this year because of Tip. Between you and me, I really think I could use at least another year here. I'm young and my game's still got a lot of weaknesses."

"That's exactly why you're ready to move up and stick." He gazed around. "I wish these places supplied every table with dental floss." We laughed. "But that's the element you were missing before, Dan. Besides, what more can you do at this level? You walked away with the batting crown, won league MVP, had only two errors the entire season, paced the championship team—"

"I can learn more from you," I said.

He rolled his eyes. "Yeah, you've figured how to play the game! You know those rumors are just rumors." He was referring to the talk that Denver might replace its manager. The *Deadwater Ledger* ran an article about it every day. If Denver made a move, the paper had it, Payne would be in the running to get the nod.

"No," I said, "I'm just starting to understand you. Like I used to think you left your starting pitchers in too long."

"You've got to in the minors, Dan. How else can anyone expect young arms to develop? Leaving a man in after he's been tagged some shows I still have confidence in him. Good things bring about more good things. If I believe he can do the job, maybe he'll believe he can too. A guy will let me know when he's been in too long. I've never believed in the quick hook."

"Bagman's really come along. Haley's super. Tommy Chance—"

"Chance is a year away. Haley will make the big club next year for sure. Jones has all the tools for a top-notch reliever." He wiped his mouth with his napkin. "You know, you scared the hell out of me the day after you came back. Not because you looked so bad before the game, but because I could see that you'd stopped believing in yourself." He sucked his teeth. "After I saw the tape of that play in Denver, I knew your next at-bat would be crucial. At first I considered putting you in when we needed only a bunt, but I didn't think coddling you would do you any favor. So the clutch situation presented itself, I believed in you, gambled, and like a winner you came through." He sipped his water. "If you'd just swung at a pitch in the strike zone, you'd have come through."

I took a breath. "I lied to you, Lefty. Or at least I let you believe in a lie. I was never married. I hardly even knew Tip's mother."

"I know," he said. "After you showed up, I called Denver to say we'd found you. They told me they'd heard from Wingert. He said you'd been down there to take custody of Tip, that he'd been abandoned. He sent them the letter they found in the basket."

"Why didn't you let on you knew?"

"I knew you'd tell me eventually, if you thought it was something I should know." His blue eyes smiled. "See, you just proved me right."

"I owe you a lot, Lefty."

"Good, then you can pick up this check." He pushed it toward me, then laughed. "Let's get home, see if I've had any phone calls."

I made a telephone of my hand. " 'Lefty Payne, this is Denver calling! We need a new skipper up here fast!' "

"Yeah. But even more important, I know where Wanda keeps the floss!"

Wanda. Small and energetic as a wren, she took us into her nest when I was still cuckoo and cared for me, for you, the cuckoo's egg, as if we were her own. Though you may not remember them, they were good days, the days of Wanda and her sewing room, your crib next to the loom and on the wall above your head a picture of baby Dumbo happily flapping his ears, a crow's feather in his trunk. "You're going to have to be both his father and mother," Wanda told me several times. So I paid close attention to her advice as we changed you, bathed you, held you.

She taught me the magic of Tempra Drops, Desitin, rectal thermometers. "Remember, Danny, fever is nature's way of making the body well." She came to love you, even at three in the morning when you woke everyone, your gums on fire as you teethed. She taught me to make the Singer sewing machine in our room hum its name. She filled our room with bolts of sturdy fabric and patterns for shirts, dresses, baby clothes. You played on the rug between us as she knitted in her maple rocker and I sewed. Sometimes she worked the loom and I did crewel embroidery. Sometimes both of us hooked rugs. You put everything in your mouth. Outside the window, Lefty raked and burned the falling leaves and tried not to think about Denver.

Her hair was curly and gray; her face, thin, intelligent, a face you'd notice at once in a room and be repeatedly drawn to. Her eyes seemed amused by a joke that only she knew. She'd turn them on you and you'd feel warm, interesting, even articulate. She'd turn them off and you'd wonder what you'd done wrong. She was a fine tennis player, breaking to the ball like a second baseman. She preferred to take long walks in the woods. She knew the names of plants, birds, insects. We'd push you in your stroller down paths in the woods and she'd point out a hundred things I'd never thought to notice. The life teeming in a fallen tree. A bush bearing edible berries. The way the late afternoon shadows of an old fence lay on a neighboring field, and she'd say, "Listen, that's a tanager," and the next moment you'd hear it, *"Pit-it-ick, pit-ick, pit-it-ick."*

I vacuumed, dusted. Washed dishes, pots, pans. Scrubbed floors, sinks, the bathtub, the floors again. I learned not to set the iron too high when pressing delicates. I learned when and when not to use bleach. I learned that the saying "A woman's work is never done" meant not that women should be more industrious but that no matter how hard you try, some work is never able to be completed. There was always something else to do, another dirty plate, glass, T-shirt, floor, sheet, window. With the coming of winter I fell in love with the smell of fabric softener. Each afternoon when you took a nap, Wanda and I watched a soap opera and shared a pot of tea.

"You never had any kids," I said to her one day after we'd watched the soap. We were making stew. I was chopping the carrots and onions.

"Didn't think I had time, living the life of a ballplayer's wife," Wanda said. She pursed her lips. "No. That's a lie. Truth is, I *was* busy, but I also had some trouble with my equipment. I never carried to full term." She stirred a pan simmering on the stove. "Then it seemed like just a waste and too much of a heartbreak every time for Lefty. So we stopped trying." Her eyes glistened. "That's when it's supposed to happen, as soon as you let it go." She shook her head. "Don't believe it for a minute."

I tried to smile at her.

"Don't feel sorry for me. I don't regret anything."

I nodded.

She stirred the pan for a long time and sighed. "Every time I failed—oh, I guess I felt all the guilt and inadequacy I was supposed to feel. But then I decided it just wasn't for me. Life's like that a lot, Danny."

"So you rationalize."

"No. That's too much head. You have to do more than just rationalize. I don't know how to explain. You have to accept."

She turned back to the stove. I felt sad and clumsy and almost chopped my thumb. "It nearly broke apart our marriage," she said, facing me again. "Not because I couldn't have babies, but because for the longest time I was so terribly displeased with myself." The onions were starting to get to her. "When someone's unhappy and frustrated, well, she's kind of hard to love." She sniffed. "Anyway, we got through it."

"Is it hard now, I mean, with me and Tip around?"

Wanda shook her head. Then she took a breath and wiped her eyes. "Yeah, I guess there are nights when I wake up because

I hear him crying, and you're in there with him fumbling for his bottle or a diaper or just talking to him like you do, and I listen for a moment and think he's my baby. Then I wonder why I'm so lazy that I'm still in bed. Then I remember, and it all snaps into place."

"I'm sorry. I shouldn't have asked."

"No. Don't think that. Your being here is good for all of us. I enjoy this time and know it's only for a time. And you don't know how Lefty gets during the off-season. He's like a little kid with nothing to do, no one to play with. He gets all bottled up. He really likes working out with you every morning at the gym, and how you'll go out sometimes at night and talk the game. And now with the possibility of him being named the Denver manager? Really, you and Tip being here's just what we need."

Then we talked about you, but I thought what a screwy, complicated thing life is: how here in Kansas a woman wanted something that in Arkansas brought pain and death, and in Chicago— Did my mother ever want a different life? Did she ever look up from her sewing machine in the sweatshop in New York and desire the two-flat on Olive, seven kids, one at her feet, one at her knees, one in her arms at her breast? Did she ever stare at us and want us out of her hair, out of her house, a nicer house, more things? Time to do what *she* wanted? She never did what she wanted. Did she ever feel the same longing to escape the city as I felt? Or had her days been too full of meals to cook, things to clean, kids to tend to, for her even to begin to think? I'll have to ask her, I thought. We heard you then, crying in your crib.

We went to you, sailing behind your bright cries, *Nina* and *Pinta* to your *Santa Maria*, as you discovered the new world.

Then Denver kicked its manager upstairs. Lefty flew up to interview. "Go with your pitch," I told him and raised my thumb. Wings had been invited to fly out too. I chopped three cords of wood while Lefty was gone. Wanda nearly scrubbed the enamel off the bathtub. You were becoming partial to sweet potatoes, broccoli, the dark meat of chicken, and by then had grown a six-toothed smile. I hoped and prayed there'd be cause to use it. The paper said every former major-league manager was under consideration for the job, but Payne and Wingert had the inside track. No matter how things went, I thought, I'd play my game, though I was sure that if Wings was named manager I'd grow old in the minors or be traded to Siberia or worse.

He said nothing when he got off the plane. He didn't know and wouldn't until the weekend.

"Good things bring about more good things," I said.

"We'll see," he said.

We did.

Popping so many bottles of champagne (for Lefty and Wanda) and carbonated grape juice (for abstinent me) that we dented the kitchen ceiling and woke you up. Rocking you back to sleep, I told myself that when I made it up it would be because I'd earned it, not because I was Lefty's friend.

Spring training camp. Triple Springs, Arizona.

Mickey was right, son. Have they got some fast arms in the majors! Talk about heat. You could light a Winston just standing near the box. I mean, I saw some change-ups that broke the sound barrier. And the way the big-league arms could move the ball! They could make those little Haitian horsehides do the fandango. Start in on you letter-high, then slide it below your knees. Be in the first-base dugout, then nibble the outside corner. I nearly turned into a Purvis, guessing and second-guessing. Then I stepped out of the box and told myself to play my game, watch the ball to the bat, allow my body to do the rest. Go with the pitch. I was too green to try to pull anything with power. So I hung in, hoping for contact, fouling off so many fastballs the cage looked like a popcorn machine. Then I worked on my timing and prayed my stroke was good enough. The fouls straightened out. The Arizona sun shone down on me. I came down with such a case of line-drive-itis that even the old graybeards in the

236

stands set aside their cups of prune juice and Gatorade and applauded.

"Way to hit, Lupo!"

Booker T., who I embraced with rib-cracking fervor.

We caught up on old times. Yeah, he was real happy being named Rookie of the Year, though he was tired of fielding questions about the sophomore jinx. No, he didn't take it personal that I walked out like I did. Yeah, your birth made a lot of sense, since me and Mickey were fertilizing so many gardens the odds were the seed would stick somewhere. But when I asked about Mickey, Book stepped back and balked.

"What do you mean, you haven't seen him?" I said. "You played with him for half a season! I tell you, Mickey's inside Adam Double!"

"Fruit Loops, I can't tell you how glad I am you're back."

"He came right out of my damn mouth, Book! Like a big round balloon in a cartoon. Don't shake your head. It was his *soul*, I tell you. Christ, you don't need me to tell you about soul! Double was dead, see? Mickey saw his chance for a big left-handed-hitting body. You remember. 'Short and first! Mister Speed and Mister Bat!' I can't believe he hasn't even said hello to you after all the two of you have been through."

"He's real quiet, Lupo, that's all I know. Likes his own company. Talks to reporters maybe five times a year, and then he only answers yes or no. He reads hardbacks at his locker, is real choosy when it comes to bats, and likes the throw chest-high so he can save his energy for hitting. And, Wolf, hitting's where the man excels. He's a machine. He checks his swing and the ball goes out to the warning track. You couldn't build a better man for the clean-up spot. And he makes the plays at first base."

"That's Mickey, I tell you. Jumping bodies until he found one that was ideal."

"You might be right, but I'd bet against it." His eyes grew dark. "Say, don't you think it's about time you dropped this psychosis stuff? I didn't have any trouble with the multiple personality, but this— You're bringing in other people. You're taking it outside the house. They could put you away for it, I mean *really*, you know what I mean?"

"There's one way to find out, Mr. Johnson."

He was sitting by himself in left field, running his fingertips over the fat part of a bat. His head down, probably studying the grain for some kind of secret message. Big, blond, his cheeks so rosy you'd think he used rouge.

"What are the names of Mickey Mouse's nephews?" I asked. "Come on, you must have had half their comics."

He stared at me as if I were speaking Swahili.

"I'm trying to settle a bet." I offered my hand. "Dan Bacigalupo, third base, originally from Chicago, North Side, Olive Street. Ever been there?"

He looked at my hand, then at me, then nodded and gave me a handshake.

"I really don't know much trivia, Dan." His voice stepped carefully across his words. "And the times we've played Chicago . . ." He shrugged. "Well, I really never went beyond the ball park or the hotel." His eyes narrowed. "Aren't you the ballplayer who struck me with the line drive?"

I stepped back and nodded. "I'm really sorry about that."

"No." He smiled real wide. "No apologies are necessary. In fact, it was a very nice turning point in my career. It changed my game somehow. I think up to then I'd been a bit lackadaisical, at least on defense. Now I'm playing ball with more aggression. And I've always had great admiration for the Denver organization. The Denver fans are the best in the game."

"Look at me. Tell me you never met me before."

"Of course we met, when you struck me in Denver. Though I blacked out momentarily, I guess." He swallowed. "You know, you really should've tagged the base. You earned the hit. You caught me sleeping, and that ball was very sharply hit."

238

"You don't remember me from the minors?" I wanted to shake him. "*Think!* Pirate's Hook? Razor Bluff? Deadwater?"

"I'm sorry, Dan. I came up through college ball. I was fortunate enough to bypass the minor leagues."

"You never met a ballplayer named Mickey Meenan?"

"Meenan," he said. "No. I'm sorry. It doesn't ring a bell. Why, is he here in camp?"

"I thought he was. But I guess not."

"There are so many faces, I have difficulty keeping them all straight."

"You've always been like this?"

"Like what, Dan?"

"Like you are. Like you are now. You can remember your childhood, your parents, your adolescence. Nothing weird happened to you when you were in third grade. Your father wasn't an ex-boxer, you don't remember big stacks of comics or the Alley League or Lucky Green or picking wax from your ears."

"That can be very dangerous, Dan, done outside a physician's office. The eardrum is very easily penetrated or infected."

"Yeah," I said. I began to walk away.

"Say, Dan?"

I turned.

"I like the throw chest-high."

I didn't know what to think, son. So I didn't. I put everything from my mind but the game. The bat was taking care of itself, so I concentrated on the glove. Scoop, dive, knock it down, set your feet. Make the throw or eat it if there's no play. Runner on, send it around the horn for two. I took the fielder's choice when it was there to take. I played for the sure out. Book knew my range and I knew Book's. My throws to Double were on the money. I didn't try more than I should.

Then Lefty told me I'd made it, so I flew back to Deadwater to get you. Wanda stayed behind to finish the packing. Everything was going wonderfully. The two of us would drive to

Denver, find a place to live. Wanda would care for you when I was at the field or on a road trip. Lucky you and lucky me! She kissed me as we said good-bye. I held her hands for the longest time. Then I strapped you safe and tight in the box seat. The pickup gasped like an asthmatic in a tobacco shop, then roared with life. We were off.

Up muddy back roads through the flat Kansas landscape until we came to Highway 70, and then it was a clean line drive. In the distance we could see the beautiful Rockies. "Tip," I said over and over, "Tip, we're on our way to Mile High!"

The mountains grew taller and more majestic as we drove. Then I pulled suddenly off the road.

Because I saw a lonely phone booth, and I had a dime. Because the past tugged at me, and I wanted to break free. This time, I hoped, I'd have the words. It was early evening. Before us, the sun was slipping its red sky behind the edge of mountains. I could picture the black telephone ringing in the house. He answered, said nothing, then accepted the charges.

"It's me," I said. "Danilo. No, I'm fine. I'm in Colorado, Dad. No, Col-o-rad-o. Out west. Look at a map later, after I hang up. Listen, I made the major leagues. In Denver, Dad. Let me talk. When I get there I'll send you my address. Because you should know where I live, that's why. I don't care about that. That's past. Leave it, Dad, it's over and done with. Can't we both start out new? Don't— Hey, I didn't call you to listen to a lecture about how much everyone's been worried, OK? I'm sorry. I'm not perfect. Listen to me, I have a baby. Yes! Yeah, a boy. No, she died. Yes, it was very sad. I know, Dad. Tip. Whatdya mean, what kind of name is that? I don't care what people think, that's his name, Dad. Nothing else, just Tip. Because that's what I wanted to name him, all right? Listen, you should know you're a *nonnu* now, and I love him. I love him more than anything—and I love you. And I'm sorry for everything. I just wanted to call to tell you that."

Then he put my ma on and I said everything again, and it was dark by the time I opened the door to the truck.

"Tip, I swear I'll never be like that with you."

"Da da," you said, and I kissed you, then changed you and fed you and held you as you relaxed, muscle by muscle, bone by precious bone, falling to sleep in my arms, your daddy's arms, with a trickle of milk on your chin. I slipped you gingerly back into your seat. Then I drove into the darkness of that long night. Feeling OK, glad I called, like it was a start.

The next day from Denver I called Charlie Grieves and Brother Gabriel. I gave them my news, told them thanks. Then I called Harold. I said the last time I saw him I just wasn't myself. He said no one was anymore.

"These are crazy times, Danny. All the marches, protests. Liberate this! Liberate that! Liberate Liberace is what I say, ha ha. You know that kind of baloney is right up my Grace's alley. We haven't heard from her in three years. What is it, Edna? Three years, seven months? Keep quiet, he's calling long-distance! You still there? Yeah, I'll bet Princess has turned into one of those Age of Aquarius hair-all-over-the-place hippies, so maybe you'd better look for her in San Francisco. You know, stick a flower in your ear and make love, not war and be a lousy liberal fifth columnist because this whole society has got everything turned upside down. I don't know, we try to keep up with things, but things're changing so fast. I think it's because we walked on the moon! Now we're in for it! You know, you spend your whole life trying to do right by God and country, and then your kids come along and tell you you did everything wrong. Tell me what that means! If you find her, tell her to give her mom a call. No matter what she's done, Danny. She'll always be our sweet little girl. Tell her we— Tell her we got supper waiting on the table."

If I find her? Where? How?

Opening day, Mile High Stadium.

And the field looked so magnificent, so green with promise,

so bright with summer's hopes, that I could hardly contain my fluids. Talk about a dry mouth and a wet faucet! I must have had to pee fifteen times. Lefty never seemed more on top of things as he told us in the clubhouse before the game that he needed and would use all twenty-five players, that we were equals in his eyes, that any problems or gripes had better come to his office and were welcome, and above all we should remember it was only a game—we were only boys with gloves on our hands, caps on our heads, green dinosaurs on our sleeves, playing a game with a ball and a stick. We should have fun, he said. We'd do as well as our abilities could carry us because we'd play for one another, and we'd play smart. That was his job, he said: being smart for the rest of us. Our job was to enjoy ourselves, play unselfishly, play our game. No single player was important, he told us. We were each part of something larger than ourselves. Collective effort would bring us victory. Selfish concerns and pettiness would bring defeat. You sat up with Wanda with all the brass. A coed from UD sang the national anthem. The governor threw out the first pitch. Then the stadium erupted as the Denver Dynos took the field.

From my spot on the bench I watched it all. Hennessey, the old veteran, standing with folded arms at third. Book, crouching at short, pounding his open glove. Fabio Ruiz, laughing, at second base. Double, conserving his energy, at first. Comet Haley, the surprise replacement for blistered Santos, firing his warm-ups to Riddle behind the plate. Al Wysocki in left. Puma in center. Big Dom DeVitto in right. What a sight, Tip! Major-league baseball!

Then Double ran in, something wrong with his sunglasses. The equipment manager brought him the tray. Double turned toward me with a grin.

"Ferdie and Morty Mouse," he said so clearly I thought I could see his freckles.

And later, in the seventh, after everyone stood and cheered and stretched, I saw the second of three old friends I'd see that week from Olive Street.

It was Purvis, warming the bench beside me, who nudged me and pointed. The disturbance in the first-base boxes had caught his eye. Three ushers were attempting to escort a fan with binoculars aimed at our dugout back up to the cheap seats. She was hacking at their legs with a suitcase-sized purse. Her hair was the color of straw strewn in an outdoor manger. No shepherd or wise man screamed more loudly than me.

"Grace!"

1 2 3 4 5 6 7 8 9

BASES LOADED

Because she was one of at least two people from my past who'd seen me on TV the previous summer line the ball off Adam Double's throat, and Hortense and Reason insisted that she get her feelings for me out in the open and deal with them once and for all. Besides, she said, New Mexico was getting kind of old. Hortense was beginning to pick up these negative vibes, especially after her boyfriend Speed got heavy in the local drug scene and then was nailed with three moving violations just outside Truth or Consequences. Free had wanted to split too because the same day I made my appearance on the morning news, *Le Bateleur* disappeared from her pack of tarot cards. *Le Bateleur?* I said. The Magician, Grace said, the smiley guy with the rod in his hand who juggles the horns and balls, and Free was more freaked than the night she went out to the desert and met Carlos Castaneda. Who's Carlos Castaneda? I said. Grace rolled her eyes at my ignorance. He writes books about magic, Indians, and drugs, and in them turns into birds, Grace said, and no one in the world has ever seen him or talked to him except Free. These people, I said, they're your frends? Better than that, Grace said, they're my family. We're a commune. You're on a baseball team. Different strokes for different folks. Everything's cool. Then she sat back and told me she really liked my new karma.

"I just can't get over seeing you again," I said.

We sat in the grandstands after the game, after I'd asked the trainer to tell Security to ask her to wait for me. The game had gone as splendidly as a Hollywood movie. Haley's fastball whistled through the lineup, and in the eighth Adam Double popped a solo home run. The Dynos won, 1-zip. I hadn't played, but there was always tomorrow. Wanda went to celebrate with Lefty and the brass. You napped in the sling on my chest. I couldn't believe it.

There she sat, as serenely as Buddha. And just as magnificently rotund. A purple-striped red dress draped her like heather on a rolling hillside. Around her neck were eight or nine necklaces, most of Native American design. Her face was tanned the color of a new penny. An open leather bag sat on her generous lap. More rings and bracelets bejeweled her fingers and wrists. Her toes protruded from her sandals like two rows of ever-smaller toads.

"I couldn't get over the size of your arms and shoulders when I saw you on TV," she said. "Come here, let me feel them. Hrrruh!"

You got squeezed between us. I gave her forehead a kiss. "Time's been good to you, Grace. Wow! You're even more lovely than I remember you."

She smiled. I stepped back, slipping you out of the sling to make sure you were still breathing. "I love your bod, Danny. What did you do, get a muscle transplant? The kid's cute too. But what a boring game!"

"Boring?" You were just fine. "A twenty-year-old rookie earning a complete-game shutout in his first big-league start before a capacity crowd of Dyno Maniacs on opening day and you thought it was boring?"

"Well"—she tried to push herself up in her seat—"none of those other batters even knew how to hit, and your side wasn't too hot either, except for that absolutely gorgeous hunk who smashed the home run."

"That's because both pitchers really knew how to pitch. Grace—"

Then I laughed, realizing what we were up to. Cat and dog, Punch and Judy. She looked at me and realized it too.

"You're right, Danny, it was the most exciting game I've ever seen."

"No, you're right, Grace. From a spectator's standpoint I can see that a pitching duel could get a little tedious, especially from way up here."

"What do you say we decide just how thrilling it was later, and you put down your baby and help me get out of this seat?"

At first I pulled on her shoulders, then tried to lift her from beneath her arms. I could have *used* a muscle transplant, son. For a moment I was afraid Grace might have to become Mile High Stadium's Perpetual Grandstander, but then I thought to hoist up her legs and twist them back and forth. Then we left.

Happily the pickup was engineered by Detroit to haul heavy loads. As long as I didn't inhale and more or less straddled Grace's left thigh, I was able to drive, though she had to shift gears for me. You trilled merrily from your box seat. I showed Grace a billboard advertising the team. In the foreground were two smiling archeologists at a dig. Looming behind them, the green shadow of a brontosaur enclosing the most popular players: Double, DeVitto, Santos, Wysocki, Hennessey, Puma, Book Johnson. At the feet of the archeologists was the campaign's slogan: DISCOVER DYNO MANIA! The billboards were up all over town.

"I can dig it," Grace said.

We drove without words. Strange, because I always thought that if I saw her again I'd have a hundred things to say, a thousand things to tell her. The silence wasn't uncomfortable, though I noticed it. She was aware of it too, I thought. Finally, to talk about something, I said, "Karma?"

"What about it, Danny?"

"You said you liked my new karma."

"Sure," Grace said after a moment. "Responsible every time."

"I don't think I understand."

"It's an Eastern concept." She shifted the pickup's gears. "Like everything you think and do puts out energy, like the vibes in your soul and your heart, and the ones you give are the ones you get back. Ask Hortense, she knows more than I do. But your karma is why I'm here, Danny."

"I gave out vibes that made you want to move to Denver?"

"Didn't you? Didn't you want to see me again?"

"Yeah. I even called your father."

"See?"

For a few blocks I wondered if it applied to baseball. I figured maybe a fielder's karma could affect the way he played the ball. But hitting? You could stand there and try to karma a base hit, and the pitcher's got his karma working on a strikeout, and all the fielders have their karmas going. What a mess! No wonder so many balls curve foul into the stands! They must feel all that karma and say forget it. Plus, they have little Haitian karmas of their own. What a jumble. I dropped the idea fast, figuring I'd be ruined as a hitter if I ever went to the plate trying to piece together all of that.

Then, as I followed her directions to Odie Street, some of the excitement over seeing her again returned. At a red light I faced her. She smiled. Her blond curls tumbled merrily to her shoulders, like they always did. Her eyes were a pair of deep tropical lagoons. "Grace," I said. I realized I didn't know quite how to act. What I felt: She was someone I loved, an old friend.

So I smiled, trying to say here I am again and we'd see what there is still between us. She laughed and pointed out the windshield. "Drive, Danny." The light had changed.

Though she didn't ask, I told her then all about how I found you, until the pickup rolled into the driveway beside her house.

The place was nothing out of *Better Homes and Gardens*, though it was just as meticulously designed. Mattresses and orange crates were the main elements in the front room. The former were covered by tie-dyed sheets and oversized pillows; the latter were filled with record albums and paperbacks, and held lamps, ashtrays, Zap comic books, candles. On the walls, posters of bearded revolutionaries and hairy rock 'n' roll stars raised fists or guitars toward the ceiling. Beneath the staircase there was a black-and-white poster of a woods and a clearing. In the clearing a young long-haired woman ran, chased by a helmeted policeman on horseback. At the top of the picture, in the trees: WE'RE THE PEOPLE OUR PARENTS WARNED US AGAINST. Below the girl and the charging hooves of the horse: "SEE JANE RUN." "RUN, JANE, RUN."

I turned away when I imagined what happened five seconds after the photo was taken. I took a breath. I liked the room. In my arms you pointed at Jimi Hendrix, then fidgeted, as if you wanted down.

In the middle room a lovely blond wood table and half a dozen different wooden chairs stretched beneath a sunny window. Five places were set on woven Indian mats. In the center of the table there was a gallon jar of honey, a dime bag of marijuana, a pepper grinder, an incense burner, a roach clip, a glass ashtray, a blue box of Morton's salt. Across from the table an altar of cinder blocks and hollow-core doors bore the stereo system, as complex a set of knobs, meters, buttons, and pulsing lights as I'd seen since I'd been to the Museum of Science and Industry. You reached immediately for what I assumed was the tuner's master control switch with a sharp *tshttshhhhh!* I moved your hands away. Then we heard a voice from the kitchen.

"Damn that Speed! He took the colander to strain the seeds out of his dope again!"

I gave you the truck's keys to play with and turned.

"Hortense," Grace was saying, "come meet an old friend."

"You found him, Grace?"

Though the apron tied around her T-shirt and patched jeans gave her the appearance of bulk, Hortense was undoubtedly the skinniest person I'd ever set my eyes on. A foul pole had more width. She was nearly all skeleton but clearly alive and actually pretty in her own Olive Oyl way; and I thought she jangled as she stepped toward us, until I realized I was hearing Grace's beads and many bracelets.

"Nice to meet you," I said, shaking her stick of a hand.

"Good-looking boy!" Hortense said, then jabbed Grace in the ribs. "And the baby ain't too ugly either!"

"Ay, noing doy doy," you said.

We then followed them into the kitchen, where vegetables steamed, where brown rice bubbled and rattled the lid of its pot, and where a hand-painted sign on the refrigerator door screamed with every color of the rainbow: YOU ARE WHAT YOU EAT! Beneath it, scrawled in pencil, were the words *and what you smoke, Little Mama!* Then the smell of burning marijuana overtook the scent of onions and green peppers in the room, and a very thin guy with stringy hair, a Grateful Dead T-shirt, and a billy goat's chinful of beard trucked in sucking on a number that was as fat as Grace's neck. The joint glowed orange as he inhaled, nodded, smiled.

"Danny," Grace said, "Speed. Speed, Danny."

He slapped my free hand and again nodded his head.

"You're cool, bro, so's the kid. Out of fuckin' sight! Whatdya say we listen to some tunes and get wrecked?"

"I certainly hope they're staying for dinner," Hortense said. "We have so much food! Grace, have you invited them?"

"Sure," Grace said. She looked at me. "You're not in a rush?"

"What, me worry?" Speed said, putting on an Alfred E. New-man face. You liked it enough to smile and chirp for him. "Me and the Dynos man and the papoose are going to adjourn to the smoking room and get mellow! Walk this way!" Then he did Groucho Marx.

"Thanks," I said to Grace and Hortense. "That's real nice. We'd be more than happy to stay."

"He's acting up because strangers make him nervous," Hortense said. She jerked her head to indicate Speed. "You know what I mean, how you guys always fall into that competitive insecure 'I'm real cool' chest-beating macho routine when you first meet?"

"Danny was never into a competitive insecure chest-beating macho routine, were you?" Grace said and then laughed so hard I had to laugh too.

"Tell you what," I said. "We'll arm-wrestle for superiority, then come back here and let you know who won."

Reason, or at least a guy I assumed was Reason, sat in the front room on one of the mattresses, his head buried in a book by the other Marx. "Oh yeah!" he said when he saw me. His wire-rims glistened. "Far out! You're the dude from Grace's past!" He stood, scratching a tuft of hair that poked out of the neck of his blue workshirt. "You know, the moment I saw you walk out of the kitchen with that baby in your arms, you made a statement to my head. Like I think I can really relate to a man into child care."

He offered me his palm, which I slapped.

I smiled. "What choice have I got? Tip's my baby."

"Oh no, Dan." He sat down again. I crouched, then sat down too. He, Speed, and I made a triangle. "You represent much more than just that."

"Turnabout of traditional sexual roles," Speed said, then hissed as he took a long hit off his joint. "I can relate to it too." He exhaled. "Say, this new weed is so excellent it's melting my

250

kneecaps!" He pulled himself up. "You or the kid want me to give you a shotgun?"

I put my hand over your nose and mouth. "No thanks. I feel like passing, and he's into formula and sweet potatoes. You know how it is, when you're still under a year old."

Reason took the number from Speed and conservatively sipped it.

"Waste of good dope, anyway," Reason said. "Kids are naturally stoned. That's a fact. Up to a certain age all they can see are color patches." He nodded. "That's why a lot of cultures use it in their religious services, why marijuana is thought by some to be holy. It lets us try to regain what we used to have naturally in our heads, what we lost." He stared at the joint, then smiled. "So Grace tells us you're a major-league ballplayer."

I shrugged. "Right now I'm just a rookie trying to crack the lineup." Then I shook my head when he offered me the joint.

"Sorry, man," Reason said. "I forgot. You must be in training."

"It's not training," I said. "I just don't want to get high."

That made them look away, made me aware that I seemed ungrateful for their hospitality. So I turned the subject back to them. "You say it really melts your kneecaps, huh?"

"Oozier than a handful of Jell-O," Speed said. Then he talked about some of the great lids he'd copped and scored. Nineteen sixty-nine, Albuquerque. 'Sixty-seven, Santa Cruz. Reason's best score was in 'seventy, Happy Jack, Arizona. We could have been three millionaire connoisseurs discussing the world's finest wines. I told Reason our training camp was at Triple Springs. He'd been there, remembered it was awful hot. You crawled over to Speed. He gently tickled your belly, then made you laugh as he hid his face behind his hands, playing peekaboo. These guys were all right, I thought. Hortense was pretty interesting. Grace's life was different but seemed really OK. I wanted to stretch so I stood and gathered you up. We walked out the screen door onto the front porch.

251

Then I saw him, running away down the street like a thief, a puff of his cigar smoke spreading in the dying light of evening.

It couldn't be him, I thought. My heart pounded beneath my ribs. Not after all these years. I felt like a baserunner who's taken too wide a lead off second. Suddenly he sees the pitcher whirl and throw. Pick-off City. There's no time in all of eternity to get back, slide under the tag. So you need to break for third and hope you're not dead in the rundown. Hope they fail to execute, make a mistake. Inside the house, someone was cranking up the stereo. I put you down on the front porch. Then I decided not to postpone the inevitable and raced across the lawn to see what he'd done to our truck.

It was taped to the top of the steering wheel, where only a blind man would miss it:

DON'T TURN AROUND!
THE CROSSHAIRS NARROW AT YOUR NECK!

It's one thing to think a horror awaits you; another to actually see it. The note gave me goosebumps. I did not turn around. Staring at you, I put it in my pocket and slowly walked back to the porch.

Perhaps you never seemed more helpless and needful, or maybe I just felt maudlin and awfully sorry for myself. I scooped you in my arms and covered you with a dozen kisses. "Hold me, Tip," I said. It was nearly dark. Two kids on bicycles coasted down the street. The music throbbed behind me. "Relax," I said. "It's just paper, just cutout newspaper letters, pasted together on paper to make words."

You drooled a dark spot onto my T-shirt. I wiped your mouth with my hand. "Hey, there are two ways to play something like this. The first is to be real scared. That's probably exactly what he wants. The second is to ignore it." I held you more tightly. "Are you thinking what I'm thinking?"

"Kee da doy," you said, then chewed your fist.

I nodded. "You bet."

Laid back on a pillow with his eyes shut, Speed looked gratefully dead. Reason was reading Karl Marx again. We swam upstream against the sound waves throbbing from the second room, and I was trying to figure which of the countless pulsing knobs and switches controlled the stereo's volume when from behind a hand came and stroked my belly and then a pair of hands ran down my back and then affectionately circled my waist. I lowered the volume and turned with a smile, expecting to see my grinning Grace.

"Like wow!" the woman I assumed was Free said, smiling, running her hands up my arms and then pausing to pat your head. Her honey-brown hair hung in two long braids. She wore skimpy cutoffs and a sleeveless tie-dyed T-shirt. Clearly braless, her nipples poked the thin cotton of her shirt. Her legs were shapely, very tanned. A single gold ring was on her left hand. Her eyes were green and sparkled, and her lips closed from her smile to a pout. She was easily the most attractive woman I'd ever met, and her eyes dreamily widened and stared at me as her hand left your head and touched the back of my neck and then pulled my head down toward hers. Then she kissed me at first with her lips and then with her lips and tongue and then with her lips and tongue and body pressed hard against my leg as her other hand lifted my T-shirt and fluttered for a moment over my stomach, then stroked the hair on my chest. Inside my boxers, the Prince of Blown Fuses stood at complete attention.

"You're friendly!" she said, then gave my jeans a playful slap.

I swallowed. Every drop of blood in the cosmos was rushing to my cock.

"Let me have your baby," she said, and reached for you as I blinked and once again swallowed, momentarily confused.

Then Grace walked into the room. "I see you've met Free."

"Oh, yeah."

Grace didn't look too happy that I had.

They didn't have a highchair, so you sat on my knee, and

inside of two minutes you ate more brown rice and veggies than Hortense did in the forty-five that we spent sitting around the table. Grace consumed more than the rest of us could in a week. Free sat on my left, now and then reaching over to touch you. Reason chewed steadily and read, occasionally lifting his glasses to his forehead and giving his eyes a squeeze. Speed picked his carrots out, ate the rest, then stared at things.

"You've got ideas," Hortense said suddenly to me. Her eyes grew large as saucers. They fell on everyone at the table, then shrunk and seemed to look inside herself. "Can't you just feel it? The excitement, the roiling, all the turmoil? Oh, he's got ideas, and he's worried, I can tell."

"I was just looking at everybody," I said.

Free's braids shook as she laughed. "Hortense, his aura's just fine."

"*I'm* roiling," Speed said, raising his hand like a shy second grader. "Squirrel's into being a hermit again. And like I try, I really try, but I can't understand him. You'd think I could maybe get into his head."

"Dan, he's really lovely," Free said and nodded at you.

"Ahem!" Hortense said. After she was satisfied that we all were looking at her, she lifted her fork, which held a single grain of rice, toward her mouth. "Danny, there are some things you should know." She dropped the grain of rice onto her tongue.

Grace lowered her head to her plate and for a moment shoveled furiously.

Hortense chewed, then swallowed and smiled. "Whatever you're into is cool, just as long as you don't hurt anybody. Now, I don't know what you're going to find here, but I can't shake this dark feeling, this dread."

"I'm *really* worried about him," Speed said. "Sometimes he gets so bummed out he doesn't even want to eat his seeds."

Grace slammed her fork to the table. Her blue eyes were so icy that I jumped. "She's engaged to be married to Carlos Castaneda! Tell him, Free!" Free smiled, then reached toward you again and stroked your arm. Grace turned to Hortense. "That's what you were leading up to, wasn't it?"

Hortense was chewing a pea. She raised a finger, shook her head, then pointed to her mouth.

"Not at all," Hortense said after she swallowed. "Something's bothering Danny, but it's not Free. Can't any of you *feel* it?" She looked at everyone, stopping with Grace. "And I thought that since he's going to stay with us for a while somebody should talk to him about the rules."

"You're going to stay?" Free said. "Great!"

Grace glared at her. Reason shut his book.

"People, if you're going to talk about rules again, I'm gonna split." He took a breath. "I think we waste far too much energy around here, I'm serious. Like we have to structure *everything*. Next you'll have us decide when we can take a crap. Once you let your head get into that—"

"I want to go upstairs," Speed told the Morton's salt girl. "My mind is like just sitting here telling my legs to go upstairs. Then how come I can't move?"

"Because you're wasted," Hortense said. She jutted her jaw at Reason. "And if you think structure is a waste, *you* try cooking dinner sometimes."

"Move," Speed said. "Come on, legs, move." The pep talk got him to his feet. Then Speed drifted from the room.

"May I hold him?" Free said.

I turned, then looked down at you. You reached for Free's open arms, then for a braid, then grabbed a breast.

"You're friendly too!" Free laughed.

"You're right," Reason said. "I'm, I'm just—" He took off his glasses and rubbed them on his workshirt. "I've been reading a lot of Kropotkin and my eyes hurt. Then I go back to Marx. Emma Goldman. Back to Marx. I don't know, I guess sometimes I must overreact to things."

"We should talk about it," Hortense said. She squeezed Reason's hand. "Where did Speed go?"

"Upstairs," Grace said. "Probably to relate to his filthy monkey."

Free was kissing the top of your head as you dug into her plate of rice and veggies.

"Look," I said, "if my being here's a problem—"

"He's no problem," Free said. "Dan, who said you were a problem?"

"No," Grace said, "like the hassle's mine." She shook her head. "I hate to admit it but I guess I'm into a kind of possessive thing with Danny." She turned to me and frowned. "You're free."

"No," Free said softly. "I'm Free."

"I'm the one who's been uptight," Reason said. "Like I snapped Hortense's head off after she slaved all afternoon over this outstanding meal." Reason spread his hands, then with vaudevillian exaggeration smacked his lips and rubbed his stomach and said, "Yum, yum!"

"Tshttshhhhh!" you chirped.

"No," Hortense said, "really, it's something else. I sense a darkness, a violence, a hovering terror."

Grace's fat curls were shaking. "It's just that I haven't seen him in—how many years has it been now, Danny?"

"I wish I could put my finger on it," Hortense said.

"Hey," Reason said, "like it really was my fault!"

Free smiled at everyone, then fed you a piece of cauliflower.

"Whoa!" Third-base coach, I put up my hands. "Hold it! Everybody shut up! Please. Look, I'm the stranger. If anybody's causing problems—"

"Dan," Reason said, "please try to be cool. Confrontation is an essential step toward synthesis."

I knew what dark violence Hortense was feeling. So I stood and threw the note onto the table. "Look at what I found taped to my steering wheel!"

"Far fucking out!" everyone said, including Speed and Squirrel, who was an actual little monkey, and who immediately leapt from Speed's arms onto the table, scampered toward the bowl of rice and vegetables, squatted beside it, then plunged in both tiny monkey hands. Chattering like static on a radio, he pulled out two monkey fistfuls of food, which he then commenced to rub on his chin and forehead. You pointed to him and gurgled with glee. Squirrel took one look at you and shrieked. Using Hortense as a vine, he swung past her and back into the safety of Speed's arms.

"Goddamn neo-Nazi anticulture John Birch right-wingers, if you ask me," Reason said. "This is a blatant attack against our commune!"

"But I found it in my truck."

"But your truck is parked in *our* driveway. You better believe it, man."

"It was probably the narcs," Speed said and shuddered.

"Narcs don't leave death threats," Reason said. "Narcs kick the front door down in the middle of the night."

"It wasn't the narcs," I said. "It wasn't the neo-Nazis." I knew who was responsible, and I looked at Hortense to see if she'd say anything. She stared at her plate, pressing her fingertips against her temples.

"Enough!" Grace shouted. She covered her ears. "I don't want to hear any more! It's only a piece of paper!"

Squirrel covered his ears too. You pulled on one of Free's braids, then looked at me and burped. Hortense ate a final grain of rice. Reason's specs sparkled as he stood.

"Clean-up time." He started stacking the dishes, then turned to Speed. "You wash tonight, *amigo.* I call dibs on wipes."

Then Free stood and gave me a smile and vanished with you, and Hortense swallowed and announced she not only had a headache but was stuffed. Reason and Speed began clattering things in the kitchen. Squirrel grabbed the dime bag and perched on top of the stereo with a pack of Zig Zag wheats and started to roll a joint. Grace took my hand so I could help her to stand, and said, "Let's go upstairs, Danny. We'd better talk."

Her room had a mattress and box springs on the floor, a poster of Mama Cass on the wall, the *Book of Dead Fatsoes* on the dresser, and candles everywhere else. Grace shut the door and lit a stick of jasmine incense and around twenty of the candles. I sat on the mattress and thumbed through the book. Then Grace kicked her shoes into the closet and turned.

"You really want to ball her, don't you?"

I didn't know what to say to that, son.

"Like it's not enough," she continued, "that you had to screw me over back in high school. But I came all the way up here to Denver and sat through a boring ball game just so I could maybe get a glimpse of you, and now tonight all through dinner I have to sit next to you and watch you drool."

"Watch me drool?"

"I'm not stupid, Danny."

"Grace, I don't know what you're talking about."

"I could cry right now. I really could."

"I never screwed that girl back in high school, Grace."

"Oh yeah? Well, do you want to hear something just as funny? When I told you I was a woman of experience, I lied."

"You lied?"

"Level with me, Danny. Right now you'd rather be with Free."

"No." I looked around. The candles flickered everywhere, as they did in my sickroom. "No," I said again. Though now I wasn't sick, and I'd never be sick again if I could help it. "If I could be anywhere in the world right now, I'd most like to be here, with you."

Then I made her sit on the bed with me, and I took her hands and told her I regretted every insensitive thing I ever did or said, and she should never feel jealous, because I loved her and always would, though I didn't know what form our love would take. Did she know? I asked. She said no. Did I find her attractive? Yes. I kissed her, then gave her the biggest hug. The women in the book are beautiful, I said. They're sensual and lovely because the artists who painted their pictures saw the beauty in them, and I was lucky enough in my life to have seen the beauty in her. You're my friend, I said. My very oldest, deepest, best-of-anyone friend.

Then she stroked my hand and told me her story.

Which began with the curse of conception, when the Almighty Double Helix gave her fat glands and genes that no diet could corset, stay, or stem, that expanded and prospered regardless of whether she ate or starved, that turned the very air she breathed into unending rolls of blubber. That was dandy if you were born a whale and had to endure the icy waters of the deep blue sea, but definitely not cool if you were a woman born into a country so blessed with autumn's harvest and overflowing cornucopia that not eating had become *de rigueur*. A pox on Twiggy's house, she said. A pox on every thigh thin enough to wear a miniskirt. Because their beauty mocked the truly portly and stout, who fashion all but tells, "You have only two choices, Miss Piggy, be jolly or be thin." Because society finds nothing so unlovable as an unhappy fat girl. The world defines women by the packaging about their cunts, and who wants one with so much extra wrapping paper? So they think it's your fault your body's fat and—in their eyes—ugly, and they conclude they're superior because they are thin. And if the smile of nonconcern doesn't dimple your apple-dumpling cheeks, you become the target of their phlegm, their cruelest insults. So of course she warmed to a nun who looked at the soul, not the body. Of course she fled from a culture that adored thinness, that seemed to be quite pleased with its war. We'll napalm them until they're dead or live in our image and likeness, the heads of state were saying. It was no accident hippies referred to themselves as *freaks*, because when normality is negative and evil, being different and trying to become an alternative become things to be proud of. So she became part of the counterculture, along with all the others who were cursed.

"That's what we are, Danny. Hortense, Speed, Reason, Free. In our own way we've each been cursed by something. We're fat, too skinny. Sensitive, intelligent, childish. We can't make it with the others, the plowhorses in gray flannel dragging their briefcases full of exploitive business behind them. Their profit comes from people's blood! What's the matter with them, can't they see? Or do they have blinders of denial on their eyes? That's why I dropped out, Danny, what it means to drop out. When you don't want to play at their game, or can't play."

"They're afraid," I said. "The plowhorses are human and afraid."

"That's no excuse. Freaks are human too. And we're going to start our own culture!" She smiled, then balled her hands into two fists. "Sometimes I get so angry. The more I see and learn. You know, the world's *real* devils don't wear red suits and have horns. They're the people who won't accept, who don't forgive, who are afraid to love. They hog the best land, the world's food, its energy, its resources. They take more than their fair share and hide the theft behind government and laws. They'll go to war and kill to protect those laws, Danny. And they're so taken with themselves they think people of color are their inferiors, and women are no more than their juicy slits. They're the ones who slaughtered the Indians. They tried to kill all the Jews. They're so twisted and unhappy that they deny others pleasure. That's the first sign of a pig, but we're not like them because we know what it's like to feel pain. And I'm not saying that we're perfect. No, not at all, because they get on my nerves a lot sometimes, and I know sometimes I get on their nerves. But like at least *we're trying*, you know? At least we're not consciously hurting anybody."

I nodded.

Grace relaxed. "Did I tell you that Hortense and I wait tables? Yeah, and someday we're going to have our own organic restaurant, Fat and Lean."

I smiled. "Then it isn't a curse at all, Grace. Being different's really more of a blessing."

"Maybe," she said. "I'll tell you the day after the revolution."

Some of the candles had burned down. I thought of you, then figured Free was smart enough to look in the truck for what you needed. I looked at Grace. She lay back against the wall. I could hear her rhythmic breathing.

"I really missed you," I said.

Her fingers touched my hand in the near-darkness.

"Friends?" she said.

"Through thick and thin. For ever and always."

Then we, as it's called, made love.

Part reunion, part discovery, the rest pleasure, sigh, and moan. She was a cherub. My kisses fell into each fold of her skin. Nail. Tooth. How we stretched, grew taut! Then there was only fingertip. Collapse. The gentle sound of our breathing.

I slipped on my jeans and covered her with a blanket and went for a walk through the silent house. Squirrel slept in a ball on one of the downstairs mattresses. My backpack with all your stuff leaned against the back door. In the garbage I saw a can of your formula and two paper diapers. Your two spare bottles stood upside down in the dish drainer, apparently boiled clean. The kitchen itself was immaculate. Though Wanda and I preferred Bon Ami, the odor of Ajax lingering in the air comforted me. I wanted to scrub the floor but the linoleum didn't feel as if it needed it.

The front door was securely locked. I went upstairs and looked for you. In one room Reason lay on his back, light on, sound asleep, Trotsky's *My Life* on his chest. I crept in and turned the light off. In the next, Hortense and Speed softly snored. I cracked open the third door.

"Who is it?" A child's whisper.

"Me," I whispered back. "Sorry to wake you. I wanted to check on Tip."

"He's right here, Dan. Come on in. It's OK, I couldn't get to sleep. Light a candle."

My fingers read the Braille of a dresser top until they found a pack of matches. The match flared in the small room. The candle's glow was warm and yellow. Free lay beneath a sky-blue sheet. Beside her, mouth open in a four-sided diamond, lay you.

"He's so beautiful," Free whispered. "His skin is so soft. I gave him a bath and found his formula. Do you ever just lie next to him and listen to him breathing?"

I sat on the bed, at your feet. "The first couple months I'd wake him up sometimes to make sure he was still alive."

"He breathes in little spurts," Free said. She sat up, holding the sheet across her breasts. "It's like his life is still flickering, you know, like he's not sure it'll burn."

"Oh, it'll burn. See his fists? He'll live to be a hundred and three."

Then she asked where your mother was. I told her the little I knew. For a while we watched you sleep. Then she asked how I could be a ballplayer and take care of you at the same time. I told her that was the sixty-four-thousand-dollar question, but Wanda had offered to help and I'd always try to do my best. Our whispering didn't seem to bother you. You slept like an angel, like a log.

"I love him, Dan." She touched my hand and smiled. "It's real strange. It's like I know him, like we recognize each other. Like there's a connection between us. It's not anything crazy like what I imagined when I was out in the desert."

I was staring at you and then noticed that her gold ring was tied with a piece of blue yarn around your neck.

"You mean when you met that guy who writes about turning into birds?"

She laughed. "Carlos Castaneda. Yeah. But if I tell you, it has to be a secret."

I nodded.

"It was just loneliness. It never happened."

"You mean it was a hallucination?"

"No, I didn't see anyone. It was never real. I made it all up."

"Why? Were you high or something?"

She touched my shoulder and frowned. "Yeah, something."

Then she stroked my arm and began to unravel her story about the desert. That she'd gone there searching for a sign because her life seemed empty, and she was unhappy. Because wherever she went she was judged by how she looked, and she was too conventionally pretty, and schoolboys were either cruel to or afraid of very pretty girls. Twice in high school she'd tried to kill herself. She didn't feel very pretty. She felt confused and lost.

But her parents' medicine cabinet didn't stock the right mix of pills, and twice the doctors woke her up and stuck tubes in her that dripped black charcoal. Then her parents sent her off to college. She tried to adjust. A teacher she thought was in love with her used her for a while. After she found out he was married, she changed her name to Free and split. Then she drifted, she said, until in New Mexico she met Hortense. She envied Hortense. Hortense was the skinniest, most together woman she'd ever seen.

"So I followed her home, like a stray puppy. Then I met Grace. They were so opposite and yet so similar, like a yin and yang. I knew they didn't like me much at first, but it felt right being with them, and I wanted so bad to become like either one of them, real fat or real skinny, you know? Even before my first period people flattered me for what I looked like. My looks have nothing to do with me, the *real* me. I've never done anything to deserve people's attention. Sometimes I think all I've done is fuck up two suicides."

You shifted in your sleep. We watched you.

"So like I guess I thought I should get crazy, you know, like Speed and Reason. Sometimes they're genuinely crazy, insane, so brilliant they blow my mind. So I was walking in the desert, and I found the ring in the sand. Then I made up the thing about Castaneda. I told people he appeared to me as a hawk, softly calling my name, saying he loved me. He was perfect because no one's ever seen him and could prove me wrong."

"Why? I don't understand."

"It gave me a front, see, a dodge. So people would leave me alone."

"If you want to be left alone, why do you come on so strong? I mean—"

"You mean why did I kiss you?" She smiled. "I'm embarrassed to admit it. I get into what the papers call a preemptive strike. You blow them away first, before they can get to you. If the guys hit on me later I say sorry and tell them about Carlos Castaneda. Guys either leave me alone then or end up making a play for Grace or Hortense."

"You get aggressive so they won't."

She nodded. "But I think that's all over now. This little baby touches something in me. . . ." Her voice trailed off.

"He's a real good kid."

"He's much more than that." Her eyes grew wide. "Look at him! He's so innocent. Just think, Dan, he hasn't been fucked up yet by all the bad things people learn to do. He doesn't hate. He doesn't fear. He's not part of the reality that at this very moment is firing napalm gel with a flame of over two thousand degrees on the flesh of Asian villagers." She drew her arms around herself. "He isn't beating all those who right now are being beaten. Raping the weak. Starving the hungry. Breaking the backs and wills of the world's poor. He could grow up to be ideal, perfect, someone who matters, who with others helps things to change."

I swallowed, then nodded.

"And Dan, there's something special about *you*."

I looked into her eyes. "I'm nothing, really. Just a grown kid lucky enough to still be playing baseball."

"You're more than that. You're Tip's father."

It made me smile. "I wish I'd just met you."

"You did just meet me, Dan."

"I mean—"

I didn't know what I meant, son. It was something like just meeting her, Free, not after again seeing and being with Grace. I felt confused, as if I were scattered in too many directions. Free was lying back on her pillows, the sheet still covering her breasts. You slept, head turned toward her, your breath as soft as moth wings.

"Maybe we can go out?" I heard myself saying. "I mean, out on a date? If that isn't too square."

Free laughed. "Do you realize it's the middle of the night and you're here in my bedroom and I'm naked beneath this sheet and all you're wearing is a pair of jeans. and—" Her hand brushed the hair on my chest.

"Preemptive strike again, Free?"

"Not this time, Dan."

"I must sound awfully silly to you."

"No. Don't be shy. Go with what you feel."

"Well, let's start at the beginning, with a date."

Then I leaned down and kissed her cheek. Her hands took my face and held me. I kissed her lips, then moved back, kissed you.

I remembered the two rules the game had taught me so far. *Go with the pitch. Leg it out.* But there are some balls you need to foul off, and this was one of them.

I blew out the candle, then stood in the dark hallway at the end of an amazing day that had brought three people from Olive Street back into my life. And now Free knelt in the on-deck circle. The bags were loaded, son. My mind buzzed. I made my way through the fuzz of darkness downstairs.

Where I slept and dreamed that a monkey dressed in your *dearest God* T-shirt curled in the crook of my arm and then sat on my stomach eating your zwiebacks and later peed against my leg, and when at last the morning light unglued my eyes I realized my dream was true.

Mornings on Odie Street were aquatic. Reason and Speed sipped juice and black coffee and moved as if underwater, then floated off to their construction jobs. Can't pass up time-and-a-half on Saturdays, they kept mumbling, as if to convince themselves they really wanted to go to work. I showered, then went out to inspect the truck.

No more messages hung from the steering wheel. Nothing resembled a bomb beneath the hood. I was sitting behind the wheel about to test my theory when Grace came out in a lavender muumuu, carrying a cup of tea.

"It's cool by me," she said.

"Grace, I really want to talk to you."

She smiled. Steam hovered over her cup. "Danny, there's no need. Don't look so glum, chum. I knew it yesterday, when I saw the two of you together. I knew it this morning when I woke up, when you weren't there."

"I slept downstairs, Grace. I didn't—"

"Danny, I know. I understand."

"What do you understand?"

"That we don't have to be together or share the same bed to love each other. That we can be real happy with exactly what we have."

"And what's that?"

"You tell me, Danny."

I stared out the truck's windshield. Grace stood next to me, resting an arm on the open door. I realized we had friendship, love, respect. All the big important emotions, and no daily demands to risk screwing things up.

"We've got each other. Like I said last night, for ever and always."

She smiled. "I'll say one thing for you. You were never dull."

"Grace, I was insane."

"All the good people are." There were tears in her eyes. "I loved every minute. Now, don't worry. I knew it would never be you and me, though ever since I was a little girl I was sure I'd end up marrying the boy next door." She looked back at the house, wiped her eyes, then sipped her tea. "By the way, your date will be ready tonight at eight."

"My date?"

"Never underestimate the sensibility and wisdom of women. Free and I had a long talk this morning. Then we woke up Hortense and told her all about it too. Everybody thinks it's real cool."

Like in a movie, I could hear birds trilling to one another in the trees. I tapped the steering wheel. "Go back in the house, Grace. I don't want you out here when I start this thing. I'm afraid it's going to explode."

"Nothing's going to explode, Danny. You're home now." Her eyes shimmered in the sun. "When you took your shower we all had a talk. Everybody wants you and Tip to move in with us."

I stepped down from the truck, then took her in my arms and kissed her.

"I'll be there in a minute for Tip. I'm supposed to take him over to Wanda's. But first I need to make sure the truck's safe."

"Slow down. Let us take care of him today. Free already called the co-op, she's taking the day off. Go do what you have to do."

What I had to do, after the pickup didn't explode and I phoned Wanda and explained, was to get out to the ball park. The second day of the new season, and I felt happier maybe than at any other time in my life. A few of the old bloods lay on tables, getting taped or rubdowns. Little schools of reporters wandered around the clubhouse, fishing for choice quotes. Motown popped from the tape deck. The juice was flowing, and some of the guys sat half dressed at their lockers and joked or sang with the music or did crosswords, and some sat off by themselves playing tonk. Book was checking the laces on his glove. Double was autographing a box of balls. I was pulling up my green stockings when Hennessey, the veteran third baseman, came up next to me.

In his day Hennessey had been as good as anybody, better than most. Then he played like a roller coaster, all peaks and valleys. No rookie yet had been able to knock him from the lineup. They'd get their chance and play like rookies, and Hennessey would get back in and play like an All-Star. Then slump. Rumor always had him on the trading block. His face looked made of stone, etched with veins too close to the surface of his skin. He said nothing after I nodded, and then he cleared his throat.

"He likes to take you up the belly with his heater, then he wastes one way outside, then nibbles the corners to death with his change of pace."

"Who?" I said. "Marco?" Marco was the day's opposing starting pitcher.

"No, Santee Claus. We go way back. He's a pattern pitcher. Fastball, waste one, junk. Most take the first and swing at the second. Then he's got you in the hole. You watch today."

"So you jump on his first pitch."

Hennessey smiled as he walked away. "If you're quick enough."

"Last year he fed me a diet of breaking balls," Book said when I told him. We didn't have time to talk about more than the game. We were taking BP, standing by the cage, watching Double at the plate provide souvenirs for the fans in the bleachers.

"Then you think he's giving me a line of bull?"

"Naw," Book said. "But he's got to know you're here to play."

My turn in the cage, and I looked at my feet, closed my stance, relaxed my hands, fouled back the first pitch, and then sprayed the field with crisp liners. Sure, I thought, he knows I'm here to play. I drilled one. Deposit it in the savings and loan. But Puma, who was taking live balls out in center, had other ideas, catching it over his left shoulder on the warning track. I dropped the next one five feet in front of him and smiled. I wouldn't let Book be the only Rookie of the Year on the team. I'd make Denver learn to spell my name. Once I cracked the lineup, I'd *stick*.

"Keep your hands back," Hennessey said when I finished. "You stepped into that change-up early. That's OK, but keep your hands back." He showed me what I'd done, then what would have been better.

The park was again at capacity. We had Tyrone Jackson on the hill. The visitors got to him for a pair in the sixth. Then we knotted it up and Ty's arm stiffened, so Lefty brought in Bagman Jones to relieve. His hummer had smoke on it, son. Eleven pitches later he'd struck out the side. You could feel everyone in the stadium beginning to really like the guy. They chanted his name as he trotted, sweat dripping from his ashy face, off the field.

"Bag-man! Bag-man!"

From the bench I watched everything. We laid a goose in the bottom of the seventh. Bagman set them down again, 1-2-3, in the eighth. Double led off the bottom of the frame, earning his name off the right-field wall. Marco still looked strong. Then DeVitto hit a soft bunt down the third-base line and was on first before it rolled foul. He bunted again, fouling it back. Marco nibbled. DeVitto battled, then hit one through the box. Double pulled up at third. The infield gathered at the hill. The opposing manager came out, spat at the dirt five or six times, then decided to leave Marco in.

The infield set up for the play at the plate. Hennessey stood outside the batter's box. I glanced at Lefty to see if he'd call on me to pinch-hit. So far in the season Hennessey had gone hitless. Lefty chewed his Bazooka for all he was worth. No hesitation. He was staying with his veteran.

Hennessey swung for the first pitch and missed by a mile, then took the second for a called strike. For a moment I found myself hoping he'd fan. Then I realized this guy was my teammate, and sooner or later I'd get my chance. Lefty would make sure I got my chance. Marco shook off a sign, nodded, then went into his stretch.

Hennessey slapped his old stick at the fastball, punching it over the drawn-in first baseman. Double leapt with both feet onto the plate.

I was the first in the dugout to congratulate Hennessey after the reliever got Riddle to pop up and Ruiz to ground into a double play.

"He shook off the junk pitch," Hennessey said to me, then reached past me for his glove. "Be patient, kid. You'll get your chance off him next time."

Then Jones held, and it was history.

Reverend James Cleveland sang from the tape deck as we showered. Lots of jokes, teasing, going over the game. Nothing like a come-from-behind win to get everyone loose. Hennessey held court at his locker stall, speaking slowly so the men with the pencils could get an exact quote. Bagman had another press of reporters around him. I got out of there as soon as I could and sped to the little apartment we'd rented. There I packed your clothes, shaved, looked for what to wear on my date. Fashion plate that I was, I didn't have a whole lot of choice. I pushed aside clean T-shirts and jeans and found a long-sleeved white shirt, stovepipes, a skinny black tie I still had from my days at Saint Paul's. I put a dab of Wildroot in my hair. On my way out I grabbed my black sports coat with iridescent sharkskin lining. I had errands to run. Presents in hand, I pulled open the commune's screen door at the stroke of eight.

"Will you get a load of him!" Reason said. "Talk about bourgeois!"

"Bro," Speed said, fingering my lapel, "like I really dig these threads! You look like something straight out of *West Side Story!*"

"*On the Waterfront* is more like it," Grace said and laughed.

"Da da!" you called from Hortense's twin railing of a lap.

I put the presents down and took you in my arms. Then Free descended the stairs, a pink blush on her face.

270

I stared at her with awe. Her dress was white, ornate, full-sleeved, ankle-length, and had at least a hundred yellow buttons. Her honey-brown hair fell past her shoulders, held back from her face by two tortoiseshell combs. I beamed at her, kissed you, then put you down. Then I turned to Grace, kissed her, and gave her a pound tin of Godiva chocolates. Then I kissed Hortense and gave her my other present, an immense bouquet of spring flowers.

"Nothing for me?" Free said.

"For you," I said, "for you, I saved the best for last." I walked up to her and offered my arm. "Shall we go? My chariot awaits."

"This scene makes me want to vomit," Reason said.

"Kick out the jams!" Speed shouted. "Stoke up the bong!"

"You two look so sweet!" Grace said, chocolate darkening her lips.

"I feel like a bridesmaid," Hortense laughed through her flowers.

"And for all of you," I said, "even Tip, I've got tickets for tomorrow's game." I took the tickets from my pocket and handed them to Reason. "They're not great seats, but they're in the sun. And it'll be Sunday, our first Sunday at home."

"Far out!" "Let's do it!" "I can get into that!" everyone said.

Then I hugged and kissed you until you squirmed. Hortense took you from me and buried your face in her flowers. Squirrel was chattering at everyone from the next room. Free took my arm. We walked together into the night.

"They're real happy for us, Dan," she said when we were outside. "Even Reason, though he doesn't want to show it."

I unloaded the box seat onto the front porch. "Where do you want to go?"

Free smiled, then shrugged. We got into the truck.

I started the engine. "What would you like to do?"

She shrugged again. "It's up to you."

I backed out of the driveway. "Well, more than anything, what do you want, what did you miss?"

271

"What did I miss?" She laughed. "Innocence."

"Then let's try to find some, Free."

So we drove and drove, son, through the bright streets of Denver, and I guess I realized that innocence was what my life missed too. If only we could step into a Disney cartoon and flicker away the rest of our lives, I thought. But old Uncle Walt didn't make any with ballplayers and hippies, Denver, a cool Saturday night. Free sat silently beside me. What he made, I thought, were very lovely dreams for children. What we were: two flesh-and-blood adults.

Then I saw some kids in tuxedos and formal dresses and corsages trying to hitch a ride. I knew what being on the side of the road was like, so I pulled over and shouted across the street to them. "Need a lift?"

"Right on!" All six spilled across the street.

Two squeezed next to us in the cab. Four had to hang on in the open back of the pickup. They said their car had broken down. I asked them where they wanted me to take them.

"Six miles the other way. Tonight's our formal."

I turned to Free. "Innocent enough for you?"

We had some trouble getting in. The Honor Society kids at the door said no embossed invitations, no in. "Not even if we pay?" I said. They said no. Then Free told them we were with the band. No in, no music. "Why didn't you say so right away?" They even held the door open for us. Once inside, we melted into the gymnasium.

At first, being in a high-school gym again depressed me. I kept thinking of sock hops, the days of the Lone Wolf. I was so quiet that Free asked if the cat had got my tongue.

"Not this time," I said, then tried to shake the gloomies off.

In a clear example of democratic compromise, the dance's theme was half Camelot, half Give Peace a Chance. We walked alongside bleachers camouflaged by gray castle walls covered with pictures of John Lennon and peace signs.

Make Love, Not War
Black is Beautiful
Off Our Backs!
Let me say, at the risk of seeming ridiculous, that the true
revolutionary is guided by great feelings of love. —Che

Kids with felt-tip markers scribbled faster than the chaperones could stop them. Maybe there was no innocence to be found anywhere, I told Free. Even the walls of the castle were covered with awareness. She told me to stop thinking, stop talking, to dance. So we got down and danced.

Now and then a pimply guy cut in on me. Free was very flattered. I grew tired of it after a while, so we got lots of the kids together and had them dance with us in a line. "Come on, everybody! Join us! Dance!"

Then the lights dropped a notch and the band began a long set of mellow slow songs. Free put her arms around my neck. My arms circled her waist. She rested her head on my shoulder. We tried to let the music carry us away.

"I don't know what's the matter with me," I said. "My mind— I can't stop thinking. I know what to do when I'm out on the field, but once I take off my uniform—"

"Don't think, Dan. Dance."

"I'm dancing, Free. See, look at my feet. I'm dancing."

"You're still thinking."

"I'm worried about Tip."

"I'm sure he's fine. Do you want to call to check?"

"No, but I'm still worried. And I wonder about you and me."

"We're fine." She laughed.

"The note on my steering wheel."

"Just paper, Dan, like Grace said. Stupid words on a piece of paper."

"The world—you can't say it's fine—and baseball. Like maybe baseball doesn't really matter one little bit."

"Sure it matters."

"How? It's just a game."

"It matters because it's what you're good at. It's what you are."

"And that's enough?"

"It better be. You don't have much choice."

"I don't know. Maybe I could quit and do something important."

"Like what? Save the whales?"

"Sure, and the whole world while I'm at it."

"You can't save the world. The world can't be saved. At least, not by any one person. The best we can do to help is by being what we are, by making good decisions. So be a good ballplayer and a good father."

"You mean, save my little piece of it?"

"Sure, and be responsible for everything you do. For even the things we do that we can't see."

I held her more tightly. "Part of me has always wanted to be just a kid."

"Maybe part of you still is. But being grown up can be a lot more fun."

Then she stood still in my arms and kissed me, so wonderfully that an indignant chaperone ran up to us and told us absolutely no making out was permitted. "We're not hurting you," I told the man. Free stared at him, then kissed me again. He stomped his foot and pointed to the door, demanding to know our names so he could have us put on detention.

"Lingus," Free said. The man took out a pad of paper. "L-i-n-g-u-s. First name, Connie. Get it, you uptight Yahoo? Connie Lingus?"

The chaperone didn't but I did.

Outside the city, Denver twinkling beyond the broad windshield of the truck like a string of sparkling jewels.

We made love so perfectly that we ached in each other's arms.

No ocean ever lapped a shore or pounded a reef or filled a cove or inlet as well as we. We became a wonder of the world. We flew past the blue moon, through the center of the sun. No Einstein would ever be able to calculate our physics.

Driving back, I saw a lonely playground. Teeter-totter as still as the end of the world. A streetlight's reflection in the silver curve of a slide. A green wooden swing only the wind was using.

"More innocence," I said and pointed. We parked. I put my jacket around her shoulders. Last one to the swing was a rotten egg and had to push.

I pushed her, firm and high, wanting her to be able to pluck the stars from the sky and put them in her pockets. "Be happy!" I shouted. "Please! You have to be happy!" Then I found myself shivering from the cold and something else—

A sudden terrible sense of misery racked me in dark waves and made me hold my stomach, bend over, fall to my knees. I think I cried, son. I must have sensed what would lie on the morrow. I know Free put my jacket over me and held me as she knelt, rocking me back and forth, forth and back. What Hortense felt: dread, violence, a hovering terror. Only magnified, amplified. Darker than a black hole. Deeper than the dark sky into which I'd just pushed Free.

She had to drive us back. Music boomed from the house.

The boys of summer were partying down with the counter-culture.

Because Book had remembered me mentioning the address, and he had nothing much going on, so he and Bagman and Comet and Adam and Leon figured they'd drop by to check me out. Reason and Speed found them all so cool and strange that they asked Squirrel to put in a little time-and-a-half with the Zig Zags. Then Comet met Hortense, and the sparks began to fly. Then something came over the Dynos first baseman. Adam Double made his play for Grace. The moment he saw her, he rushed up to her and swept her off her feet. Free and I found all this out two seconds after we walked in. In a happy circle in the front room were Reason, Book, Speed, Leon, and Bagman, tunes and weed in the air, everyone but Squirrel pretty much wiped out and smiling.

Then Book stood and we knocked hands. I introduced him to Free.

He touched her arm and smiled his widest grin. "Free, at last. Free at last! Great God Almighty, I'm free at last!"

Everyone: "Right on, brother!"

Free turned down the music. I went upstairs to check on you. Walking up the hallway, I could hear box springs squeaking in stereo. Hortense and Comet. Grace and Adam. I found you in Free's room inside an orange crate padded with blankets. I lit a candle, shut the door, and knelt.

"I love you, son."

Head turned, mouth open, little butt raised in the air, you slept the true sleep of innocence. So here it was, I thought. I'd rediscover it through you. Then I kissed you, so many times I feared I'd wake you up. But you were into some very serious Z's. You were sawing the Enchanted Forest. Then Free appeared in the doorway, holding two cups.

"Do you feel better now, Dan? You really scared me in the playground."

"I'm sorry," I whispered. "I didn't mean to make you afraid."

She handed me one of the cups, then turned and shut the door. "Drink it while it's hot." Tea. "I put in milk and honey."

I smiled. "Milk and honey."

She slipped off her shoes and sat on the bed. "Drink. Don't talk. Don't think. Just drink."

"I love you," I said.

She looked at her hands. The combs were gone from her hair.

You sighed, then continued breathing. I warmed my hands around the cup, then took a long sip. "Before you came here, what was that card you lost?"

"*Le Bateleur*. How did you know?"

"Grace told me." I drank some tea. "What does the card stand for?"

"The Juggler. Pair in one sense to the unnumbered card, The Fool. Most see *Le Bateleur* as representing skill, cunning, dexterity. Some say he's beginning of consciousness. You can read him many different ways. In some decks he's seated, unhappy, but in mine he stood and smiled. He's just a minstrel, a quick-handed artist, inviting you to play a shell game he's got spread out on a table in front of him. I don't know why I was so freaked out when I lost him. One morning I took out my deck to do a reading and he just wasn't there." She smiled. "Now you see him, now you don't. I don't know exactly what happened to him, I looked everywhere."

"I know what that's like," I said.

"You've lost cards from your tarot?"

"No, but I've lost things."

"It shouldn't have upset me. I can always buy a new deck."

"Or find a new juggler." I made like I was juggling balls.

She smiled again. "Drink your tea, Dan."

"I do love you, Free. You're—"

"Drink your tea. Then you can show me again how much you love me."

I did, until the sun broke from the Great Plains and shone on Denver.

When Adam heard they were all going to the day's game, he insisted they use his first-row third-base box, one of the perks he'd received when he signed with the Dynos. According to the breakfast table discussion of the previous night, he had also fallen head over heels for Grace, saying she was the sweetest girl he'd ever known. Grace's beaming face radiated the serious calm that follows a night of orgasmic bliss. "I'm in heaven," she sighed over a platter of bacon and eggs. Then she announced that Adam had popped the big question. "And, you know, even though it's impulsive and archaic and just too square for words, I'm actually thinking about accepting."

"Very far out," we all said. Then Grace asked me if it worked out would I give her away. I told her I'd be honored to be in the bridal party but only Harold could walk his lovely Princess down the aisle. She said I was right and that after breakfast she'd give them a call.

Hortense's thing with Comet Haley had burned itself out. "He was like a streaking star on the horizon of my cosmos," Hortense said nonchalantly, then chewed a single Cheerios wettened with a droplet of milk. "That's a fastball pitcher for you," Reason reasoned. Hortense squeezed Speed's hand, then cooed something in his ear that made him burst out laughing. Free caught the joke before I did.

"Fast ball, Hortense? Tsk tsk tsk."

I fed you oatmeal mixed with mashed bananas. An autographed baseball replaced Reason's usual reading matter. Bagman had taught him how to throw a slider. "It's just like a curve but with more on it, Dan, so it's faster but breaks less."

I nodded. "I know. You forget I'm a ballplayer too."

Then Hortense turned from Speed. "You'll play today, Danny, I can feel it." I started to ask her how I'd do, but then Reason begged me to get my glove so we could go outside and try the slider.

"Tomorrow," I said, "I promise. I've got a game to play in today."

"Sha la la la la la, live for today!" Speed sang, badly off-key.

Then Hortense tapped her spoon against her shotglass of orange juice and stood and began to sing "Take Me Out to the Ball Game" with a voice more lovely than a Christmas morning choir.

"I don't care if I ever get back!
For it's root, root, root for the Dynos!

If they don't win it's a shayyyme!
For it's one!
Two!
Three strikes you're out!
In the o-old ballllll game!"

On that high, happy note, the second-to-last inning ended.

1 2 3 4 5 6 7 8 **9**

DOUBLE PLAY

Any son of a ballplayer knows the ninth's not played when you're at home and you're leading.

The official scorer finishes his hot dog, glances at his watch, writes down the official time of the game, marks the bottom of the frame with an X. The happy fans spill out the turnstiles for the parking lots. The peanut and popcorn vendors count their unsold wares. In the clubhouse they break out the fried chicken and cold cuts. Everybody but the visitors is happy.

But when the game is tied or the home team is behind, the frame has to be played. Because it's winning or losing that gives the game its tension, its form, its fancy French reason-to-be. Without the contest's outcome dangling in the balance, you might as well be out on the diamond with Frisbees and hockey sticks.

The ninth can be over in a wink of an eye, a single flick of the bat. Sometimes all it takes is one pitch. It's the inning where you want your very best, your third, fourth, and fifth hitters—the heart of your order—to step up to the plate.

We were at home, son, and I thought we had the lead.

I thought I had it all. A spot on the team. Friends. You. A future. But had I taken a moment to check the scoreboard, I'd have seen that we were still a run behind. Had I looked down at the bullpen, I'd have realized that the opposing manager was saving his best cigar-smoking reliever to throw at me. That the ninth had to see me step one final time to the plate. And like a Greek tragedy, it was all inevitable from the game's first pitch.

I wasn't aware of any of that as I drove that Sunday morning to the ball park. The DISCOVER DYNO MANIA! billboards loomed over the road, and I thought how much better they'd look with my mug grinning from them. How my big number 13 would look really excellent alongside Book's skinny number 1, all the way to the right side of the picture. The VW van behind me honked. I let out the clutch. All I needed was time to ascend the billboards of Denver.

The fans outside the clubhouse door ignored me, knowing I was one of the rookies but figuring I wasn't worth their time. Inside, the veterans straddled the trainer's tables, getting their wrists or ankles taped. The whirlpools in the corner bubbled, eddied. Tyrone Jackson held his arm in one; his free hand fed his mouth an Eskimo Pie. Somebody had beaten the brothers to the tape deck and put on twangy Tammy Wynette. The same game of tonk was going on off in one corner.

The main thought on my mind was congratulating Adam. I also wanted to ask him if maybe it wasn't time we revealed the truth about our lives, though I was sane enough to realize the only newspapers that would buy the story were sold in checkout lanes of supermarkets. I could imagine the headlines.

REINCARNATED BALLPLAYER ADMITS
HE SHARED TEAMMATE'S BODY!
Boy Murderer Provides Haven for Slain Playmate!

I mean, reserve the padded cells.

But should we tell Grace, I wanted to know. After all, I thought, they were planning to marry, and though I was savvy enough to understand that buying the license and taking the blood test didn't also require a complete, detailed confession of every past sin, shouldn't he at least tell her they were once next-door neighbors?

He was sitting by his locker, head down, reading.

"Hey, I heard the good news! Congratulations!"

He looked up at me, startled, then smiled and shook my offered hand.

"Thanks, Dan. Coming from you, that means a lot. I understand you once carried quite a torch for Grace Marie yourself."

I nodded. "Yeah, at times it was even a bonfire. She's one of my oldest, dearest friends. Her and Mickey Meenan."

He shut his book. *Death in the Afternoon.* "Mickey Meenan. You know, I think I've heard that name somewhere but I can't for the life of me place it."

"Sure." I laughed. "You can't place it."

"No, really, I can't. Why? Is he someone I should know?"

"Someone you should know? Come on." I slapped his shoulder. "You don't have to play dumb with me."

"Dan, you're doing this to me again. I don't understand why—"

"Give me a break, Mickey, will ya? It's OK. I was there, remember, when you took over the big guy's body."

His face went blank. "I don't know what you're talking about."

"I'm talking about you, Mickey. Or Adam. Both of you." I pointed to his chest. "Whoever all is inside there. *I know.*"

"If this is a prank, Dan, I really don't appreciate it."

"Prank?" I shouted. "This isn't a prank! Hey, all I came by to ask is if maybe you think it's time we leveled with Grace."

He twitched his head several times, saying nothing.

"Don't you think it hurts me just a little to know you're in there and you say nothing about it? I mean, we lived together, Mickey! We've had our ups and downs. I know I wasn't nice to you all the time, but whatdya think, I'm perfect? Nobody is. Look at me! You always wanted to be a first baseman. You always wanted to hit the home run. When you were a kid you had the secret blood disease, so you ate my liner so you could hitch a ride with me through high-school ball to the minors. C'mon, Mickey, admit it! You'd have kept my body if you could've hit more than .241! But you weren't content with me. So you killed the big guy, the left-hander. You saw your chance and took it. I don't hold it against you anymore Last night you recognized Grace from when I introduced the two of you years ago. You're in love with her because I was in love with her. All right, so maybe now we've both grown up. We've got separate bodies again. But there's such a thing as common courtesy—like you don't see an old friend on the street somewhere and then snub the guy, walk right past. No, you go up, stick out your hand, say hello, how's it been—"

All at once he stood, next to me, over me, and he put his arms around me, then hugged me to his chest. He felt made of iron. He felt utterly calm. For a moment I could understand how Grace could so easily fall in love with him.

"Mickey," I said.

"Dan," he said, releasing me, then stepping back. I think I saw it in that instant, son. There was something about the way he said my name. "Dan, I don't understand a tenth of what you're saying, but I can tell this isn't a joke to you. Look at me. You've got it wrong. I wish it weren't so."

"But you knew the names of Mickey Mouse's nephews."

"It seemed important to you, so I asked one of the reporters."

"I'll never ask who you are again. If you're playing hide-and-seek on me, you can stay hidden till hell freezes. This is the last time."

He nodded. "We've never lived together. I hardly know you, though I'd like to someday. I'm Adam Double. No one more, or less."

Then it sunk in, Tip. The *Titanic* hitting the iceberg. The *Hindenburg* exploding in the air. That Mickey Meenan never really sat on my bench, shared my *cuccidatis* and crumb cake. That all of it had been in my mind. Nothing more. That in trying to make up for what I'd accidentally done in the alley, I tried too literally to bring life back to him. I didn't care if the truth had been obvious for so long to others. It hadn't been obvious to me.

You do what you think you're supposed to do. You're only a child. You trust them, you want to please them, you obey. So when your ma takes you with her each Sunday to church, you pray alongside her in the rear, side-aisle pew. So when the Sisters of Christian Charity teach you in kindergarten that a real guardian angel specifically assigned to you by God sits next to you, protects you from evil, listens to all of your thoughts, you don't raise your hand and debate realities. You're no doubting Thomas, too stupid to know what's what. You're a sinner, Mary Magdalene, kneeling at the grave. They tell you it takes strength to believe, and you want to be as strong as your big history book's picture of America. Like all the other kids, I'd always leave my guardian angel a little room beside me on my seat. I'd never eat the last bite of afternoon apple the nuns sometimes gave us. But after I killed Mickey Meenan, my angel disappeared. Had I simply replaced him, first by mocking Mickey and his death, then with guilt, then brazen audacity, then with Bernie the imaginary Saint Bernard, until my mind could perfect my dead playmate's voice, temperament, freckles? I believed what I was told to believe, son. My error was that I'd taken it all too literally. Stupid fish, I bought and fought

Christianity hook, line, sinker, and tackle box, not for the right reason—because I wished to praise the spirit of good that lives within us all—but because religion at face value increased my sense of helplessness, and after I killed Mickey I sure wanted to be helpless.

My thoughts were worse than a slow-motion game film of missed coverage, slipped tackles. My thoughts were as sobering as a slice of sun-forgotten Hell.

"Lupo," Book's voice behind me said. "Hey man, get it together!"

"I'm getting it together," I said and turned.

He pushed my head between my knees. "That's it, take deep breaths. In. Out. You look like you've just seen a ghost."

"No." I exhaled. "No ghost. Just a mouthful of reality."

"Well, just don't spill your mouthful on my shoes. They've seen only two games, and we've got a long season." Book laughed. He patted my back until I told him I was OK. "Say, I really like your friends. Not as much as Haley and Double liked them, mind you. But those two dudes and their monkey are really something else. And their smoke!"

"You got wasted, huh?" I stood, mechanically began dressing.

"You know those huge iron balls they knock into the sides of condemned buildings?" Book's fist curled like one of the balls. "I've got one of them playing skeeball inside my skull."

"All that from reefer? What'd you drink?"

"Wild Turkey. Hundred-and-one-proof Wild Turkey. After his relief victory yesterday, Bagman was thinking it was Thanksgiving."

I smiled. "Better shake it or those one-hoppers will gobble you up."

"Nothing I can't handle, Lupo. I think I may play even better with a bit of fuzz. Helps me to concentrate. But you— Are you sure you're not coming down with something? You still look mighty queasy."

"I'm fine," I said, then stared at him, thinking he'd known I was nuts all along and still he'd been my friend, joked with me, cared for me. "Did I ever tell you thanks?"

"You never needed to, Wolf." He grinned, then touched my arm. "See you on the field."

I finished dressing then, trying to shake the empty feeling. So I'd been a real fool. Well, better to know it and try to get past it than walk around for the rest of your life with it all over your face.

I tried to look forward to the game. Despite Hortense's prediction, I felt Hennessey would play the entire time since he'd delivered the game winner the day before. My stroke in BP had some snap, was alive. I'd be ready if called on. I dug down at the plate and looked for more. Then I stepped into a juicy pitch, held back my hands until it was time to pull the string, and hammered it into the left-field bleachers. Scramble for that, sports fans. They'd swarm me soon enough in the parking lot, I thought as I slapped the next pitch down the alley in left-center. Two bases, easy. Maybe three. I'd make a contribution to this team, I thought. Just give me time. You were probably leaving the house about then. Even though I got under the next ball and popped to shallow right, it looked like a perfect afternoon for baseball.

Most of Denver agreed, for the stadium was standing-room-only. Lefty told us to enjoy ourselves, be loose, play our game. He was starting Miguel Santos, one of the few veteran arms we had left after the previous summer's trade for Double. Santos had been slated to pitch opening day but developed a blister. He was a real favorite with the fans. A tough-luck story when he first came up, Book had told me. He was the pitcher the team hardly scored for, so he lost a lot of 2-to-1s. Plus his favorite saying back then was "I'd rather have a bottle in front of me than a prefrontal lobotomy." In his locker he kept a cigar box full of white chips, the ones you pick up from AA the first day you decide to stop drinking. Now he'd ɔeen on the wagon for years and was our stopper, the ace of our staff.

Lefty took the lineup card to home plate. Book would play shortstop and lead off. Leon Puma, in center, would bat second. Al Wysocki, in left field, would hit third. Then Double at first in the clean-up position. Hennessey, Saturday's hero, would bat fifth. Dom DeVitto, right field, mcved down to the sixth spot. Fabio Ruiz, our second baseman and still hitless, batting seventh. Luther Purvis would replace Riddle behind the plate. Santos would bring up the caboose.

Santos looked absolutely brilliant in the first. He was one of those big right-handed journeymen who came up on his fastball and now lived and died by his cortrol. He pitched better the more he weighed. From the stands he appeared ungraceful, even sloppy, with his broad belly hanging over his belt. But from the batter's box he was a prima ballerina. His motion was pure corkscrew. Whirl his right shoulder back around so that it pointed toward first, come up with the hands, unwind and swing that big pinstriped gut back at the plate, and that's what the batter saw, that greenish belly, not the arm or the hand or the ball flirting with the plate's edges, teasing the outside corner, nipping the inside strike.

From where I sat on the bench, amidst the leisurely splashes of brown spit from the team's many chewers and dippers, I thought Purvis handled him real well. Santos didn't shake a sign. Inside, outside, mix-'em-up, medium-hard sliders. Grounder to Ruiz for one. Two-bouncer to Booker T. for two. Chopper back to Santos on the mound, and the top of the first was history.

Lefty blew bubbles on the first dugout step, smiling at it all.

Then Book lined the first pitch to center for a single. The fans began to clap. The opposing pitcher was a snappy young southpaw named Eddie Slade. Slade was as slight as a coat hanger and had a delivery so exaggerated that after he released the ball he ended down on the third-base side of the mound, looking like an iguana, all eyes, no chin, dumb grin. Book worried the bag, darting back and forth, so Slade and his first baseman played catch for a while. Universal baseball law: If a pitcher throws three times or more to first, chances are his next offering to the plate will be a ball.

Book led off the base, dropped his hands, counted. The pitch to Puma was outside. The catcher came up, arm cocked, ready to throw. Book was timing, measuring. Lefty gave him the green light. Now Book's lead was all the way to the edge of the grass. Slade and his first baseman played catch again. Slade looked in at his catcher. Went into the stretch. Mister Speed was off.

The catcher's throw disappeared in the cloud of dust around second.

Safe.

Puma hit behind the runner, advancing Book to third. The fans shouted, "Go! Go! Go!" as Wysocki stepped to the plate. Book took a wide lead off third. Now he was behind Slade's back. He fell so far off the mound he and Book could nearly shake hands. Wysocki drilled the next pitch to left. Book returned to the bag. The ball fell in the outfielder's glove. The throw from the cutoff man to the plate wasn't even close.

A run on a single, son. That's what speed and teamwork can do for a ball club.

Though Double hoped to remind everyone there was also something else. Power. Sheer and simple strength. He tripled down the gap in left-center. The stadium rose and cheered. The infield played back, for the third out. Hennessey strolled to the plate.

Lefty put his hand in his back pocket, took off his cap, brushed the *Dynos* on his chest twice, then twice clapped his hands. The third-base coach conveyed the play. *Suicide squeeze.*

The boldness of the play so surprised the bench that we stared in disbelief. Then I understood Lefty's gamble. With Slade's exaggerated delivery depositing him on the far left side of the mound, and with their first baseman standing deep, flat-footed, behind the bag, all Hennessey would have to do was drop a bunt toward first. Hennessey was one of the team's ablest bunters.

Slade checked the runner, licked his iguana lips, then stretched.

Double sprinted to the plate as Hennessey stood there like a scarecrow in a cornfield, as still as the Statue of Liberty, the bat never moving from his shoulder.

"Shit on a stick," Santos said from the bench, and picked up his belly and headed for the mound.

"Didn't you see the sign, Pat?" Lefty asked Hennessey as he came in for his glove. You could hear the fans grumbling, misunderstanding, wondering why Double was so dumb as to try a straight steal of home. Missing signs happen, son, to everyone who plays the game. From the stands the game appears to be serene, superficial, a man with a ball on a hill, another man at the plate holding a stick. But there's a vast and complex world to see once you learn where to look. The wiser fans were telling the others there was probably a play on, the rookie manager's way of announcing to the big leagues he was there to play gutsy, unpredictable ball.

You have to take advantage of any weakness, keep track of which way the wind is blowing, who is playing where. Is the catcher back on his heels or set up over the outside corner? What does the pitcher's face reveal? His hand, even though he tries to hide it in his glove? Where are the umps positioned? What's the situation, the strategy, the count?

There are dozens of things to consider as you stand at the plate, each of which could decide the ball game. Hennessey shook his head, told Lefty no, then said nobody puts on a squeeze play in the first inning. "You're dead wrong about that," Lefty said. "See the sign the next time."

The gamble coupled with the mental error let them back into the game. Santos was still sharp, but their cleanup hitter singled to left and took second base when Wysocki let the ball bad-hop him. Mistakes have a way of compounding themselves, tripping you down, one after another, like dominoes. Their next batter popped to Hennessey, who squeezed the ball with both hands, but then Santos gave up another single and the score was tied, the success of the past erased. Brand-new ball game. Start from scratch, though with fewer remaining innings, less space, a step closer to the tolling of the ninth.

Pat Hennessey led off the second and fanned. Big Dom DeVitto singled sharply over second base, and the fans clapped and cheered until Fabio Ruiz grounded into a double play. They went down without a murmur in the third. Then Purvis thought too hard, or not hard enough, and inspected three fastballs without lifting the lumber from his shoulder. Santos popped to short. Book flew out to shallow right.

In the fourth, Santos blanked them. Then Puma golfed a shot to left, where the fielder made a shoestring catch. Wysocki lined to third, and Double got one in on the fists and made everyone in the park say *awww!* as the drive fell a foot short on the warning track.

The fifth is both luxury and burden to a starter. Luxury because the man is happy to still be in there. Burden because he needs the pesky inning and a lead to have a chance for the win. I could see that Santos was tiring—now and then he'd walk off the mound and look at his blisters—but the man wasn't letting up. He was thinking out there, not throwing but *pitching*. His ball moved everywhere around the plate except across the middle. They were taking what he offered, fouling the strikes off, not willing to give him an easy out. There are no easy outs, I thought from my spot on the bench, unless you make yourself one. Unless you lunge for something beyond your reach. Swing for a ball up around your eyes. *This* was learning to win, I realized. The key was waiting, watching, *control*.

There was the balance, the soup's missing spice. Sure, you go with the pitch. Sure, you leg it out after you connect. But above all you need to play like this veteran Santos was pitching: You throw *your* game, no one else's, and you work on your control. To place something, anything, exactly where you choose it to be—ah, son, that's what it's all about! Do that and they'll applaud you, remember you, give you a place in the sun. And, more important, do that and you can make some peace with the wolves who howl inside your soul.

Santos was working inside, outside, keeping the ball low, where he wanted it. They were taking him to the full count, but he didn't let himself become untracked. If they were going to hit him, they'd have to hit *his* pitch. He took his time, nodded at Purvis, and delivered, never overpowering, always precise and true.

Son, I *was* learning. I felt clear and bright. I know it took me a long time to find it out, to take what Grieves and Gabriel had to teach me, to learn from my parents, Grace, Book, Lefty, Wanda, you, Free. To pull it all together, place it in the palm of my hand, then close down upon it with my fist. To be Dan Bacigalupo. No more. And not a jot less.

Santos finally retired the side, then came to the dugout breathing like a freight train. I told him he was the way to be. Then Hennessey at the plate tapped a little marshmallow to Slade. One away. DeVitto singled off the lizard, and Ruiz advanced him with a bunt he nearly beat out. Then Purvis dropped a Texas leaguer into shallow left, and after DeVitto scored and Santos looked back from the on-deck circle, Lefty stared at the blue sky, as if looking for the answer, then nodded to Santos. Purvis on first looked more pleased than a kid waking up in the middle of his first wet dream. Santos took his time sweet time going up to the plate. Someone got up in their bullpen. Though Santos killed the inning by striking out, we had the lead.

Lefty started Bagman and a left-hander in our pen. Santos was facing the top of their order, and Lefty didn't want to give him an opportunity to lose. Their lead-off hitter ran the count to 3-and-2, then grounded to Double, who charged the ball, turned, scooped the throw to Santos as he covered. One out. Santos blew on his fingers, then stepped behind the mound, taking deep breaths and wiping the sweat from his forehead. He didn't look sharp to me anymore. His first two offerings to the next man were a whisker low. Then he laid one down the middle of the plate.

Puma and Wysocki raced for it as it bounded in the gap to the wall. A run behind, three and four hitters behind me, I'd have held up at second base. It's a mortal sin in baseball to make the first or second out at third or the plate. But that afternoon they were greedy. The play was in front of the runner, and he ran on. Book had gone out to make the cutoff. With his arm, I thought, the man didn't have a prayer.

The throw looked good to me. The third-base ump got behind the play and crouched. Hennessey stood to the outside of the bag, came up with it, slapped the tag on the man's head. The ump's arms flew to his sides. Safe.

Lefty sprang from the dugout. Some kick dirt, some spit and scream, some gesture wildly as if they're covered with a swarm of killer bees. Lefty's style was to point to the exact square inch of dirt where the tag had taken place, then stand and fold his arms across his chest, jut his jaw, and get as close to the ump as is humanly and heterosexually possible. He always started out by calling the umps by their first and last names and saying he just could not believe they'd missed the call. This ump was having none of it. He pointed to the inside corner of the bag. Lefty's head bobbed back and forth. The ump scooted his way toward second. Jumping sideways on his toes, Lefty held his hands at his sides and trailed the man like too much after-shave. Now he was discussing insanity, hallucination, and cornea transplants with the back of the ump's head. The other umpires jogged toward them, hoping that strength of numbers would break the rhubarb up. Our third-base coach was waving his hands at the crew chief, who stood calmly with folded arms. The fans hooted and howled. Lefty was up to bleeding mothers and sons of bee-hives, and then he spun and shouted to the crew chief, and you could tell some of the steam was cut of his radiator. The fans rained down a long *boooo!* Lefty got down on his knees and pointed to the dirt with the home-plate ump. His hand banged the earth again and again. Bagman and the other relievers were working all the while in the bullpen. Hennessey had stayed out of it, coming into the dugout for water and a cigarette. Santos relaxed with Purvis and the other infielders on the hill.

Then Lefty put his hands in his back pockets and ran back to the dugout, as if he didn't want to hold the game up any longer, and the fans gave him a hearty cheer. They knew he'd given our bullpen time to get warm. Plus, you pay to see something when you go to a ball game, and now they'd seen it. Though the run came in on a deep fly to DeVitto, the bad call seemed to give Santos new strength. Maybe he needed only to catch his breath, collect himself, get back his rhythm. He got the next man, their clean-up hitter, on a swinging strike. Then he raced back to the bench like a rookie. Tip, we were pumped. We laid off the ump but gave the field plenty of chatter. Book started us off with a line-drive single to left.

Lefty was playing it safe. No steal. No run-and-hit. He put on the bunt, which Puma executed. Mister Speed danced off second, one away. Slade, his manager, and infielders gathered on the mound. Now they'd have to look at the heart of our order.

Should they keep their southpaw in to face the right-handed Wysocki? Double knelt on deck. Sure, then when the big lefty came up they could go to their right-hander ready in the pen.

The logic proved to be a mistake, because Wysocki promptly scratched out an infield single. Dynos on first and third. Mister Bat strolling to the plate.

"Dan," Lefty said, "get out there. Hit for Hennessey."

Hennessey shoved his bat back in the rack. Could he see my

trembling hands? A Niagara Falls of adrenaline spilled onto my thudding heart. *This was it!* And I'd come through this time, no doubt about it. The right-handed reliever was strutting in from the bullpen. Double was saying something to the home-plate ump and the catcher that made them laugh. Oh, I thought, he's a pro! Joking at a time like this! I went out to the on-deck circle with my bat. I reached for the pine tar. The third-base coach flashed the series of signs to Double. Swing away.

"Danny!" they called behind me. I turned and looked at you, the motley group in the front-row box. It would be real bush to go up and say something, I thought. But I grinned nevertheless. Free held you in the aisle seat. To her left sat Hortense in a bright flowered blouse, laughing with Speed in his Grateful Dead T-shirt, which showed a skull wearing a ring of roses. Grace, in bullfighter's red, waved at me and blew me a big kiss. Reason had his head down; more than likely he was keeping score. Free's green top kept moving, making your little hands pretend to grasp a bat and swing. She had you slicing up severely. I'll have to correct that later, I thought. You were wearing a little Dynos cap and green Dynos shirt they'd probably bought from a souvenir vendor on their way into the park. The reliever was tossing his warm-ups. Grace shouted Adam's name. I tended to my pine tar, stretched out, took my thirteen lucky practice swings. Double dug in the box and waited.

Beneath the crowd noise I could hear them behind me. Hortense humming "Take Me Out to the Ball Game." Grace urging Adam to knock the ball out of the park. Reason asking if anyone knew what my last name meant. Free telling you the story of the Three Little Pigs, then segueing it into "Little Red Riding Hood," and Free said, "Oh my, what big *teeth* you have!" and for some reason I turned around.

Son, there are moments in the game when you get the sense that something is wrong, that some kind of play is on. It was good and smart of me to turn, because then I saw him, one hand hidden in his red hunting jacket, coming down the aisle of the box seats. Why? I thought. I stood, stared. Behind me at the plate the ump called the first pitch a ball. He was maybe thirty yards away. Between us sat Free, holding you.

The crowd was chanting, "Double! Double!" In the side of his mouth was the stub of his cigar. A puff of smoke flew behind his head. Why would he be coming down to see you? *Don't turn around. Crosshairs.* Hand in his jacket. I dropped my bat and walked toward him, toward you. Free looked at me then, bewildered. You said, "Da da!" and reached out your arms.

His hand slid a pistol from inside his jacket pocket. Surely, I thought, it was some kind of toy! A present for you. Surely the gun's silly barrel would pop out a red flag that said BANG!, and everybody would laugh.

"Mr. Meenan?" I said.

His eyes seemed focused on nothing. At the wall there was a gate. I swung it open. He pointed the pistol at me as I stepped up through the gate. Now I stood in the lower third-base boxes, at the base of the aisle. Free, with you in her arms, looked up at me and asked what in the world was wrong.

"Hey, you don't need that gun," I said to him, trying to smile. My mouth was pretty dry. My tongue felt like sandpaper. Mr. Meenan stood two or three rows above me, with the gun pointed at you and Free.

"Sure I do, maggot," he said. Then he looked from me to Free and you and laughed. His laugh was wooden, creaking like an old garage door. It made me think of Lucky Green. "How do you like them apples? Now the shoe's on the other foot, you lousy scum."

"Is this a joke?" Free asked. The others in the row now were asking what was up. Other fans shouted for us to sit down so they could see.

He stood so close I could smell him. Then he stuck the pistol in Free's back and said, "Let's go, sweetie pie. On your feet."

"Leave them out of it," I said.

"What? And spoil all the fun?"

"Please. Go back up to your seat."

"You mean you don't want your little boy to die?"

He laughed again as Free stood, all color having fled her face. You reached for me but he pushed down your arms. To everyone the four of us must have looked like we were one big happy family embracing.

"Come on," I said, "this is just between you and me."

"Not any more. I'm a walking bomb." He pulled open the flap of his jacket. Inside he had what looked like several road flares and sticks of dynamite taped to what I guessed was a bulletproof vest. He puffed on his cigar. "See this string?" He fingered the string on one of the flares. "One tug and a few seconds later you'll go *poof*." A cloud of smoke surrounded his face. He laughed again, like splintering boards.

Two ushers stood several rows above us, looking confused. Mr. Meenan took my batting helmet and tossed it to Free's seat, then pushed us through the gate in the wall and down onto the field.

As we stepped onto the field, the home-plate ump immediately threw up his hands and called time. Adam squinted at us from the box, bat resting on his shoulder. The catcher stood, hands on his hips, mask on top of his helmet. The ump strolled toward us, thumb jerking us back into the stands. Then he saw Mr. Meenan's pistol pressed into the back of Free's head. The sight stopped him dead.

"It's real," I said. "He says he's a walking bomb. You'd better clear the field."

The ump stared at me, flabbergasted. By now the other umpires were gathered behind him. He turned and said a few words to them, and they turned and shouted to the players and both benches, which now were on their feet, trying to see what the commotion was all about. The players threw down their mitts

296

and jogged back to their dugouts. The fans began to boo. Adam picked up the ball and stayed at the plate. The ump sighed.

"All right, gentlemen. What's the beef?"

I shrugged. "It's a long story."

"The son of a bitch killed my son," Mr. Meenan said. We crossed the foul line, then stopped. "Hit a line drive right off his throat." Meenan eased his grip on Free and gestured. "He wasn't sorry, ask him yourself." The ump listened like he'd heard it all before.

"I was sorry," I said. "I was plenty sorry."

The ump rolled his eyes at me, then nodded to Meenan. "Mister, I know exactly what you're describing. It took place right here." He pointed over to first base. His voice was tinted with the sarcastic patience of someone used to speaking to numskulls. "When was it?" He turned to me. "Last June, July? Irregardless, it was one of those flukey plays that only happens once in a lifetime. And your boy didn't die. See, he's right there." He pointed to home plate, where Double stood twirling the baseball.

"That's not my boy," Mr. Meenan said.

"Sure he is," I said. "See how nice he turned out?"

"Don't confuse me." He scratched his chest with his gun hand. "My boy's dead. He died in the stinking alley behind Leona Misiak's garage."

I nodded to the ump. All the while I was trying to wedge myself between Free and Mr. Meenan. She'd regained some color, but now and then she squeezed you so hard you grunted. By now the umps had cleared both dugouts. We stood on the pitcher's mound, the fans' gibes and jeers falling down on us. You watched everything from beneath your little Dynos cap. Mr. Meenan took puff after puff off his cigar.

"I saw the game myself," the ump was saying. He pointed to third base. "I stood right there. I remember it like it was yesterday. It was the kid's first big-league game."

I nodded. "You wished me luck when I first came out."

He raised his eyebrows. "I wished you a long career. Every rookie's first game, I wish him a long career. See, to get anywhere in this business, you gotta stay away from injuries." He shook his head. "They're a curse, know what I mean?"

"He's the curse," Mr. Meenan said. He pressed the pistol into my chest. I stepped closer to him and pushed you and Free further away. "He killed my son. With a fucking baseball."

"You mean it happened before?" the ump said. "It happened twice?"

Before Mr. Meenan and I could nod, we heard the crack of a bat. It was Adam at home plate, playing fungo, hitting a mile-high pop-up over the infield of Mile High Stadium. As Mr. Meenan jerked his head to see it, I slammed my arm across his face. *Pop* went his nose. The ump went for the gun. It fired twice into the ground. I tried to grab Mr. Meenan's other hand, diving to my right. His cigar fell from his mouth. I got the hand, but then with his gun hand he tripped the flare.

At first his chest began to smoke, and then the sharp red flame of the flare blazed a hole through his red hunting jacket. Some of the fans in the bleachers and upper boxes began to cheer. Spinning, I pushed you and Free away and then like a linebacker dove into him. We fell, wrestling, to the ground. "Run!" I was screaming. I straddled him, embracing his back.

Then all time stopped. The pop-up fell, uncaught, at third. I lay on him so closely that I could smell the burning flare, his sweat. Into his ear I whispered, "Why?" He tried to roll over, to press the death against me, and growled, "Why do you think, you stupid shit, because you're guilty. Because you murdered my only son, because you were never sorry." I said, "No, no, I *was* sorry, I *am* sorry, believe me." Tip, we were so close I could have kissed his cheek. Then all at once the earth beneath us exploded.

My neck and shoulders jerked violently back. We flew upward, backward, into the air. The mound was nearly level with the infield. My face and arms felt on fire. Even with his body cushioning mine, the blast kicked my chest so hard it took away my breath.

I stared down at him. Mickey's father. Mr. Meenan. Whose first name I didn't even know! What a strange thought to be thinking, I thought. I didn't even know the man's first name. I watched my body fly from the cloud of dust and bounce on my ass. Why wasn't I wearing my helmet? I still have to bat, I thought. I have to get back to the on-deck circle and find my helmet! Then I saw that the front of my uniform was a real mess. I opened my mouth to ask for a new uniform. An ugly sound came out. Free crouched inside our dugout. Your face was set to cry. Then a roar of undeniable panic rippled through Mile High Stadium.

In the falling dust Free turned to the field and screamed, "My God! Oh my God! Oh my God!" Sobs racked her chest. Her hand tried desperately to cover your eyes.

I looked down then at my miserable body. To all appearances number 13 was dead. Powder burns covered my forehead. Parts of my arms were singed black. I stood outside myself, along the third-base line. The home-plate ump was sitting mutely in short right field, unhurt but in shock. Adam was running toward Mr. Meenan. Behind him, in the stands, Grace's face was twisted in a wretched scream. Speed was openly weeping, his thin arms circling Hortense. No one comforted Free. *Someone go to her!* I tried to shout. *Someone hold her! Please!* But I wasn't inside my pinstripes any longer, and they and my broken bag of guts held the equipment I needed for screaming. The coaches and players were running from their dugouts in underwater motion. In the distance there was the wail of sirens. I tried to reach out for you and Free then, but other things were pulling me away. Away from the foul line, out of the light, into the dark dugout, and then I saw Adam reach Mr. Meenan and kneel and hold him lengthwise in his arms. They were waiting for the ambulance. Next to him on the grass was a fallen glove.

Then I stood in a long, dark runway, like the runway from the dugout to the clubhouse, and I thought, What am I doing here? I'm supposed to be out on the field. Not back in the dugout. I'm supposed to be in the on-deck circle, ready to swing away. But didn't I just hurt a first baseman? I thought. Then I realized no, I'd just been part of a twin killing, a classic game-ending double play. And I wanted to say *Adam*, and I wanted to hold you and Free, but they and everything else were starting to fade. There was someplace else I had to go, I thought. The locker room. At the end of the runway, where I could see the light.

Because that's where you go when the game's over.

It seemed suddenly simple, suddenly crystal-clear. I no longer knew why I wanted to get back out on the field. It made no sense to me any longer. I wasn't a dummy, I thought. Not me. No way.

Because even a rookie knows that when the ball game's over you walk up the runway to the light.

EXTRA INNINGS

It's not real easy to put what happened next into words.

Words slip from the mouth all too easily, like the fish man's knot of squirming eels. Believe what you want to believe, son. The mind can be a very powerful creator, seeing in times of shock and stress whatever it most desires or fears. Think of all the people who swear they've spoken with angels, wrestled with demons. Think of lost travelers dying of thirst on broiling deserts who conjure up shimmering seas and the cool shade of swaying palm trees. Think of Carlos Castaneda, who claims he ate peyote and with the help of a shaman named Don Juan flew like a bird. Fiction or fact? Where does one lay down the foul line?

It's not easy to ask you to believe me, son. And I'm real aware that what follows comes from a witness who at one time would've sworn on a Library of Congress of Bibles that he played the bag with an actual dead earwax-eating first baseman in his dugout. So maybe you'd better swallow this plate of *pasta cu sugo* with a grain of salt. I'll ladle it out pure, no embellishment, no sprinkle of romano cheese, no neckbone, no *calamari*, no meatball.

I wish I could testify that I stood inside a room, but it wasn't a room exactly. Nor can I say I really stood. I *was*. Simply *was*. In a space that wasn't quite a space, but was more like just being next to or a part of a very strong and peculiar light that had begun as a soft yellow glow, like the flame of a candle seen through a translucent sliver of yellow wax, then progressed through dawn, through noon, through TV camera light, then became too much for me to endure as it shone more brilliantly than a star going nova and seemed not only to be outside me but inside me as well. Then the light tripped past blinding white into some other spectrum. It filled the space more wholly than water fills a glass. It was thicker than water, though not entirely solid. I think I breathed it, though *breathed* isn't right. I had no body, no gills, no lungs. I was *in* it, and it was in me. At first I tried to shut the eyes I didn't have, to deny it. And, all the while, the light was beginning to warm me, though *warm* isn't the right word. It wasn't really heat I was feeling. It was more as if I were being *absorbed*.

The sensation wasn't all that pleasant. It made me feel like a buttered heel of Gonnella bread inside a nuclear-powered toaster oven. Like an atom of gas in a burner on the stove. Worse, as if I were becoming part of the flaming light itself. I figured sure as anything I'd ended down in Hell. The idea that I was dead was just starting to sink in.

"That hurts!" I tried to shout, though I had no voice. "Hey, go easy on the thermostat!"

Then the air that wasn't air around me began to thin. Or perhaps I was getting used to it. It grew thinner than ether, thinner than a vapor, though increasingly more burning and intense. It pushed past heat into cold, beyond temperature into sound, beyond sound into light as solid as concrete. I was trying to turn around so I could see if anybody else was there when the light began to throb like a strobe in a disco, and then a door that wasn't really a door started to open though it really didn't open. I heard trumpets and violins that weren't really trumpets or violins. Then I felt better than I could ever imagine feeling. Take the sense of being so pleased with something that your eyes well with tears, and multiply the feeling by a hundred times the number that, written on a strip of paper, would wrap the world a thousand times. I felt better than that, son. Filled beyond limit, dream, ambition.

"Yes!" I hissed like a snake. "Yes, yes, yes, yes, yesssss!"

I shed any dignity I had and turned into a hungry mouth. An exposed retina. An arched back of a housecat wanting to be petted for all of eternity. If I had to grovel for the feeling, I thought, I'd grovel with the best. If I was capable of wriggling, I wriggled. I felt as if my entire being lay on the edge of an immense grin. Then flakes of plasterlike heaviness fell away from my eyes, which really weren't eyes. Then a wall that wasn't exactly a wall disappeared, and for a few throbs of light I could see a magnificent stadium. The stadium was bigger than the heart of Texas, more crowded and decorated than Marshall Field's on Christmas Eve. Higher and more majestic than New York City in May at sunrise. More than anything I wanted to run there and roll my body on the ground, though *run* and *there* and *body* and *ground* are all wrong words, cousins to the sister my tongue desires to marry.

But I couldn't budge a single inch. Something else held me, son. I felt as if I were strapped to something inside a nervously speeding metal can; then I saw the gray ceiling of the ambulance, a bottle of some clear liquid running into the tube stuck in my arm. I want none of that! I thought. No thank you! Just looking at those pitiful objects made my sides grow heavy with weariness and want to cave in. I knew there was a ball game going on somewhere inside that grand stadium. What I wanted was a time at bat.

Then something appeared next to me, though it wasn't a thing and it didn't really appear. It just—*was*. All at once I could feel it there. Woman, man, child—I can't say. If memory serves me it was wearing blue jeans, sandals, a T-shirt that pictured Diana Ross and the Supremes. Perhaps someone in these clothes crouched beside me in the ambulance.

I couldn't make out the face. The face was in the light that hung over the wonderful stadium just on the edge of the other side of the wall. The person and I talked for a while, though to say we used words or even radio or light waves isn't what happened. We just kind of nudged each other and sort of exchanged essence for a second or two, though there was no time there: all simply was.

Think of those old movies in which the mad scientist discovers a genius ray. He tries it out on animals who get as smart as Mister Ed. Then he drags in the village idiot and tests it on him. The guy's head glows for a month of Tuesdays. This is more or less what happened to me. Though I had no brain, no courage, not even an empty Tin Man's heart, I learned a couple of things in the timelessness of that other space.

I learned that the light was inside me and had always been inside of me. There is light inside you too. There is light inside everyone you see. Thus, where I'd gone was *inside* myself. Not inside my body, which I could feel was being lifted from the ambulance. And not to Heaven, Hell, Purgatory, Nirvana, or a Beatles concert. The dead go inside their spirits, then sort of juice up like plug-in-the-wall flashlights, then go outside again. All the time. All at once. Real real fast. Like those time-lapse movies you see of flowers opening and closing. Speed the projector up until it's all a blur. Then make it go even faster. That's existence, Tip. Expansion and collapse. Diastole. Systole. The person next to me told me.

I learned that it seems slow to us because we're stupid.

I learned that if you work on your stupidity for a couple thousand blurs, if you really try you get smart.

Then, when you're so smart that your blur seems so rapid

that it appears not to be able to move at all, you become eligible to make the jump to the big club. There you ooze into what was crystal-clear to me then but by now my limited vocabulary can compare only to a giant amoeba. You swim in its protoplasm stew for a couple millenniums. You eat as much as you can. Then you break off and start the whole process from scratch. The person next to me was sort of a public-relations director, assigned to sit around the reception room and shoot the breeze with souls like me who'd slipped inside themselves before they were ready.

Then I realized that the person was also the Great Amoeba Itself, as well as the water, the slide, the lens, the mirror, eye, hand, microscope. Light. Part, as well as whole. The Amoeba was speaking its name. I didn't hear all of them, son. They were uttered in a single syllable all at once. The ones I remember are Proton, Lord, Confucius, Yahweh, Jesus, Allah, Cell, Buddha, Holy Ghost, Brahma, Nucleus, Great Spirit, Vishnu, Shiva, Ra, Masau'u, Woden, Baal, Energy, Mass, Marduk, Zeus, Hera, Jupiter, Ahura Mazda, Mitochondrion, Africa, T'ien, Sun, Rain, and Womb. If I had knees, I fell to them pronto.

The light around the Amoeba's face grew dark.

"Don't bow before Me, unless you bow before Yourself. For I am You, and We are It, and It is You, and It is for All Others."

I saw what It said. "Circle," I said, furiously beating my chest.

"That which flows eternally into Itself," It said. "The Round. The Ring. Inscribe it before you. Now you know the first letter of our alphabet."

I had a million and one questions. I struggled to raise my hand. But my eyes were growing heavy, and the light was starting to fade. The wall between me and the stadium was beginning to materalize. I paused, understanding that the petals of my life flower weren't ready to close all the way just yet. I had no power to stay there, to resist. I realized I'd return in another trillionth of a second, though I was so stupid, so near square one, that it would seem to me as slow as another forty, fifty, or sixty years.

Before I felt the jolt of the gurney's wheels on the miserable ground, I tried to say thank you. But then there was ordinary sunlight on my face. It depressed me deeply and felt like a shroud. Then I was pushed down a terrible dark corridor. My arms and face felt made of fire. The misery and tension in the air around me was as thick as smoke and so fetid that I gagged and started to choke. The hand of a man and another of a woman pushed down on my chest. I cried out when I realized I could feel them.

I don't know how much of the rest you remember.

Grandma and Grandpa flew out from Chicago, made a big fuss over both of us, then went back. For about a week I got a lot of press. Wanda saved the clippings. Free pasted everything in a book.

DOUBLE SAVES DAY AT MILE HIGH
Murder Attempt Foiled, Man Kills Self
Revenge Plot Became Dead Man's Obsession

One newspaper even ran a graphic that detailed my injuries and treatment. Outline of a man from the waist up, little Dick Tracy arrows. I had third-degree burns on both arms, and powder burns on my neck and forehead. Beneath POWDER BURNS the paper put *No Scars* in smaller type, and beneath 3RD DEGREE BURNS they printed *Skin Grafting Successful*.

I thought I'd made it. But then a few days later I began getting spasms in my neck and upper back. The doctors said I had a hyperextension injury of the neck. Something like whiplash, from when the explosion jerked my head and shoulders back.

The Dynos still needed a third baseman to back up Hennessey, so they patched together another trade. They sent Gonzalo Rodriguez and Tommy Chance to the other league for Ralph Devine, who you know from following the Dynos wasn't nearly as good as his name, though he was dependable, there when you needed him. Rodriguez went on to be a truly excellent defensive shortstop. It was a good trade, one that helped both clubs. Chance, you never heard about anymore. I think he got a start or two in the majors but didn't do much and then just vanished.

The game?

Well, it wasn't over like I'd thought. One out, runners on the corners, bottom of the sixth, no mound to speak of, play was stopped that Sunday in a 2-2 tie. The league office postponed it until the middle of July. Free took me to see it. I was still wearing a neck brace then. Nobody warned me that before play resumed the brass would come to my seat with a wheelchair, then push me to home plate, where the club owner would give a speech, then introduce me. Everyone meant well, I guess—Free said later she honestly thought I'd be thrilled—but had I known their plans, I don't think I'd have gone. I didn't want people to cheer me just because I'd lived. I mean, garden slugs live if you don't step on them all the way.

I sat in the damn wheelchair wearing my neck brace, watching everyone in the park rise, hearing the stands roar with cheers that were like slaps to my head, when all I wanted was to go back inside myself.

"Don't," I said when the owner stuck the microphone in my face.

"Say something," he said in my ear, then smiled and waved at the fans.

"You shouldn't do this," I said. They sat, grew real quiet. "I didn't do anything to deserve this. What I am is a ballplayer—just trying to make the team." I could feel them leaning forward, straining to understand. So I took a breath, then gave them what they wanted. I slowly said *thank you* and *God bless*, then raised my arms and waved.

Nobody could score through nine, so it went into extra innings. Then they picked up a run in the eleventh. Then the Dynos knotted it back up. It went scoreless for another seventeen full, until the umpires called play because the other team had a plane to catch. I stayed awake through all of it. After twenty-eight innings it stood at 3-3. The papers called it The Game That Wouldn't Quit.

The league office postponed it again until the final week of the season. By then its outcome didn't really matter because, two days before, the Dynos had clinched their first pennant in club history.

Haley took the mound and held them through another seven, then gave up a two-run triple in the top of the thirty-sixth. Both teams were nearly down to nine players each. The Dynos seemed out of it but then Puma clawed his way on base and then Wysocki socked a two-run homer. Then for six more it was all seesaw. Just when the other team had it sewed up, the Dynos came back, rallied.

Payne got down to nine players, none pitchers. You could tell then that the game's survivors decided just to have themselves some fun. Book tossed two fine shutout innings, displaying a surprisingly zippy fastball. 8-8 after forty-four. Adam took the hill and promptly surrendered a run, then got it back again with a right-field shot when he led off the bottom of the forty-fifth. Riddle didn't fool anyone during his turn in the forty-ninth, but the Dynos put on their hitting shoes and came back and tied it. Stars twinkled above everyone's head. Beer vendors hawked hot cups of coffee. Dew descended on the outfield grass. The ump at second fell to his knees, sound asleep. Neither team could hit the floor with their bat. Finally, around five in the morning, after fifty-seven complete, with the score stuck at 13-all, the loud-speakers yawned word that the league president had just tele-phoned. "Drive home safely, ladies and gentlemen, and on behalf of the Denver Dynos, thanks for attending this evening's, er, morning's game."

Mickey wasn't right about everything, son. Denver didn't win that year's World Series in seven games.

The Dynos won it in six.

I got back on my feet. Two years of Double-A ball in Razor Bluff. A year up at Deadwater. Free left, not because she didn't love us but because living in Arkansas with a ballplayer who's on the road half the time isn't a life you'd wish on anyone, and she wanted to finish school, get a degree, do things, important things. Now she works with kids. She said that's where the world had better start directing its consciousness.

Now everyone has kids. Wanda and Lefty adopted a pair, orphans of boat people. Grace and Adam have a houseful—nine, their own complete team. My folks, still living on Olive Street, at last count had sixteen grandchildren.

I saw your mother's daddy in Razor Bluff back when Free was still with us. I walked out of the clubhouse after a night game we had in our pocket but let slip, and he was there, smoking a hand-rolled cigarette, standing by my truck. He said he'd been reading about me in the newspaper, thought he'd see a game, seen it, didn't think too much of it. Then he asked about you. I showed him the pictures of you I carry in my wallet. I let him take his pick. He got in his truck then, nodded at me, then headed on down the highway.

You know, sometimes when I'm driving from one town to the next I think a piece of Mickey really did fill me all those years. Not Mickey Meenan himself, but a little piece of his spirit, maybe nothing bigger than a pea. I think the Alley League *was* blessed by having a future big leaguer playing in it, but the brilliance was stuck in a body doomed with leukemia. I just did my part, carried the piece around the track, like a runner in a relay race taking the baton, passing it on. I know the blood on my bat made me a better, hungrier ballplayer. My life intersected his, and that led me to Grace and made her rule of the ruler apply to me too. It set everything in my game into motion. It prepared me for the day I found you. I passed the piece on to Adam; then it changed him as a ballplayer and led him to Grace too.

The papers said Mr. Meenan had buried his wife the summer before he tried to blow us up, just about the same time replays of me hitting the ball off Adam Double's neck appeared on all the news shows. They said investigators found newspaper and magazine articles about the incident all over his hotel room. He'd stabbed my name with a knife wherever it appeared, doodled bull's-eyes or a rifle's crosshairs over every one of my pictures. In the deluxe Dynos souvenir player book he drew tears dripping from my eyes and a bubble coming from my mouth. Inside the bubble he'd printed something about how sad I was now that you were dead. The police figured he thought wearing the bulletproof vest would save his life. One of the Chicago papers speculated he'd trailed me all along and struck out when I received a lot of publicity. They dug up the bleacher fires and death threats at Saint Paul's and linked him to them. I guess once a guy is dead you can blame him for every weird thing under the sun. I feel agony for his pain, for the sorrow I unintentionally brought him, but I'm also grateful to him in a way. Because if he hadn't tried to blow me up I wouldn't have nudged the edge of my existence and seen the light I saw that Sunday.

I'm trying. Life goes by pretty fast sometimes. One season blurs into the next. I'm a vegetarian now, a suckermouth algae eater, not a piranha or an oscar or a Jack Dempsey. Ideally I'd like my life to be completely free of eating death, even the benign death of carrot, onion, pepper, okra.

I always pick up hitchhikers, and I like meeting people after a game. They shake my hand, say they've never met a big-league scout before. Buy you a beer? I say no, but I'll take a cold 7-Up. Then they ask me what I think of the local talent, tell me this kid or that kid just can't miss, and did I see that girl they got playing over in the next county? Yeah, they say, one of these days women'll be trying to crack the majors too.

"Sure," I say. "We'll see it. And wouldn't it be something if her name was Jacqueline Robinson?"

It gets a laugh every time.

312

"What's the best thing about being a scout?" they ask.

I tell them it's that all the games I see are free.

"And the worst?"

"The time I have to spend away from my son."

Then they talk about their sons. I say I'll try to see them play. Then they ask me if I want to coach or manage someday, as if being a scout isn't enough by itself. I tell them I have enough trouble managing myself.

Some tell me they remember my story. "Yeah, you know I have a cousin who got himself blown up. That really must have been something."

"Yeah," I say, "it was something."

They nod, disappointed that I don't elaborate, give them a story they can take home. Then some get to what they're really curious about and ask me if it was as hard as they think for me to work my way back into baseball. I tell them it was and it wasn't, that I was lucky, that a lot of people helped me on the way. They nod their heads at that, though they don't believe the lucky part, and say I sure could have been a good one, if only—

I pick them off right there. I *was* a good one, I say. I had more than any ballplayer has the right to expect. I've traveled the country, played on three championship teams, won a batting title, once was league MVP, for a total of fourteen years with five different organizations, and the people I've met, the sights I've seen, the fans I've heard cheer me!

"But after your accident," they say, "you were a full step slower, always a fraction of a second behind with the bat. Don't you regret—"

"I played with what I had," I say.

Some are content with that, tell me they're glad to have met me. Others, mainly reporters looking to verify a whatever-happened-to human-interest piece they've already written in their heads, frown at me and press. They want a sob story, tragedy, bitterness. Something that will jerk their readers' tears.

"But Dan, let's get serious here a moment. You were once a

first-round draft pick, best in the Midwest. You had can't-miss written all over you. Except for the accident and your one plate appearance in Mile High when you struck Adam Double, everything you did was in backwater towns. You spent nine of your fourteen years playing no higher than Double-A. You never got the opportunity to prove yourself against the best. Everything you ever did was in the minors."

Tip, I shake my head, smile, then tell them that even though I never made it back up to the Bigs, every inning I ever played, from the alley in Chicago to Triple-A, was still baseball.

Any *real* fan understands that.